CW01011347

The Quest for Shambhala

The Stone of Destiny
Part 1

BOOK ONE IN THE SHAMBHALA TRILOGY

D. T. Angell

Limited Edition
13/20
June 2014

Published by D. T. Angell

Copyright © 2014 D. T. Angell

Illustrations by Tom Keeldan

ISBN: 978-0-9929422-1-2

Printed by CreateSpace, an Amazon.com Company

www.dtangell.com

In loving memory of Tom Keeling

Forward by Author

Some time ago an unusual journal was given to me by an old acquaintance. It was delivered to me unannounced along with a letter in which he did not make it clear how the item had come to be in his possession.

After reading it, I understood its significance. After I read it, I understood that he meant for me to share its contents.

What follows is the largely unaltered content of that journal.

I ask you to read it for yourself.

D A

(below is a copy of the letter I received along with the journal – make of it what you will)

David,

It is my fondest hope that this letter find you well. Too long has it been since we last spoke, but often I find myself reminiscing about that day you offered me a lift home from the hospital. Never shall I forget how in that time of sorrow you saw fit to offer help to a stranger.

Your counsel and friendship in the weeks that followed helped set me on the path I walk today; a path that has led to this very moment.

It is my recollection that you once told me of your dreams to become an author. Dreams that were made unobtainable by the absence of a story you felt passionate about. I pray that in the time since we last spoke success has come to you in a bolt of inspiration. If it has not then I believe I may now finally be able to return the help you once gave me.

Enclosed is a journal most curious in both its writing and origin – given to me as unexpectedly as it has now been to you. Its story does not yet have an ending, few stories in journals ever do, but I expect you will forgive the author this omission upon reading it.

There is inspiration here for the taking, a story that should be told. It is the beginning of a quest that is yet to fully unfold.

Read it my friend and read it well. What you do with it after that is a choice I leave to you.

Warmest Regards

A

Table of Contents

To You, the Finder of my Journal

If you are reading this, know that what you hold in your hands maybe all that is left of me. I have carried this story, this adventure for as long as I could. My faith has been tested, my beliefs shattered, my life changed forever. These pages tell of a quest through the past and into the present, taken by those who sort the truth. The ripples of whose footsteps could still prove to affect the destiny of mankind.

My part in this story has been that of a bumbling observer, swept along on the tide of a man who dedicated his life to following a legend. It is a part that has unwittingly left me as chronicler, the one person who can pass on the knowledge and discoveries we found along the way. But my time ran out. Betrayed and taken from the light of the world, my part in this tale has now come to an end. All I can do is put my memories to paper in the hope that my story will not be lost.

If you are reading this, friend, the weight of this story must pass to you. You are my successor. You are the person upon whose shoulders I must place the great responsibility of picking up a trail that will have long gone cold.

At best guess it has been about twelve days since I was unjustly incarcerated and thrown into the dark cell I now call home. What I know of my captors and place of detainment will be revealed, but not yet. You must live this journey through my eyes and learn all you need to know the way I did.

In truth I am hoping that the writing of this journal will also help focus my mind. The abject loneliness of imprisonment is, I fear, beginning to take its toll on my sanity. The secrets contained within my memories cannot be lost to madness should I fail to escape.

The ending of my tale will no doubt contain my final words and as such I humbly request that, once you have read and used it however you feel best, you would see it brought to my family who will be, as yet, unaware of my fate. I do not wish to divulge my true identity here however. It is possible that my family and friends may already be in danger from those who imprison me. I do not wish to add to that chance should this journal fall into the hands of others who would seek to possess that which I hide. Therefore I must trust that, from the detail I do give within these pages, you will be able to figure out how best to complete this task.

I realise now that to you my words must sound somewhat incredulous and farfetched, but please, allow me the chance to enthral you the way I was so many years ago.

Now, where to start...

Day 2
A Night of Destiny

They've found me!

This single thought, this nerve shredding moment of realisation, was where my quest truly began. On a road between two castles, I fled a persistent enemy I had unknowingly attracted the day I offered help to a stranger. They came for a secret I carried, that much I knew. What they intended to do should they catch me however, was a mystery I had so far managed to postpone finding the answer to.

Fear pounded in my chest as I imagined all the terrible outcomes that might await me, each one becoming more and more horrifying and farfetched, all the while thinking how foolish I had been. With a desperate longing for excitement and adventure, I'd jumped blindly into something I had no business with.

I had left home barely two days previous to deliver a package to a friend of a friend I had but known only briefly. It had been a foolish thing to do. On this day I should have been heading home. Destiny it seemed had other plans for me though.

Under the murky veil of a stormy summer night, the road before me seemed endless. The cone of light projected ahead by the vehicles lamps penetrated but a short distance, leaving the dark to close in around me like a prison cell.

So dark and oppressive was this shroud that I almost didn't see the sign. With a sudden sharp turn that threw me hard against the door, I found myself heading toward an inevitable dead end. It was an action beyond my control, and the lights behind had been too close to have not seen the change in direction. The fear pounded harder.

The twists and turns of the serpentine road were hard to follow. I could feel my heart beating behind my eyes, pulsing like a timer counting down to my doom.

The end to this futile escape attempt was now before me. To the reach the causeway crossing that stood between me and the island, only to find that it had already been claimed by dark tidal waters, was to literally find myself caught between the devil and the deep blue sea.

I asked myself then....how had it come to this?

This is where my quest really began as I said. A traumatic wake up from the quite life I had led before. However, it is not where my story must start. For that I need to go back two years ago to a night that was to change everything.

'Through the stars I come. I bring the chalice covered with shield. Within it I bring a treasure, the gift of Orion'

Two Years Ago – Penrith, UK
An Unexpected Friendship

It all began with a single twist of fate. I was 25, barely a man in the eyes of society, and yet my life seemed to have hit an immovable road block. In the years since leaving school at 18, I'd twice attempted to further my studies at university, tried just about every job available to someone of average qualifications and partaken in numerous volunteer projects out in South Africa. Out of a desire to find my way in the world I'd gone from shelf stacker to student to conservationist, and for the briefest of moments I was content and happy. Yet somehow, despite all this, I had ended up back home, working in a petrol station for little more than minimum wage, tied down by financial commitments to my family and constantly trying to avoid bankruptcy. Indecisive and easily bored with a tendency to quit anything that ever became too much like hard work; that was me in a nutshell.

Truthfully, I don't think I ever really knew what I wanted to do. I'd juggled so many grand ideas of how to achieve a life of worth, ignoring all sensible options in the process, that in the end I'd left myself with a worthless life. Instead of playing it safe I'd gone all in to find a job that would make me happy, only to find that I didn't have the cards to back up the gamble. Time was passing me by and I felt powerless to do anything but watch motionless; spiralling into depression with seemingly no way out. That was until the day I met a stranger with an incredible story.

It was late February and though spring was racing toward us on the calendar, winter had yet to release its icy grip on the country. Every day seemed to be cold, wet and devoid of any colour. I lived in a part of the country that was surrounded by mountains, lakes, forests and fields, and yet, whether due to the time of the year or simply my own hollow state of mind, all I could see were different shades of grey. To make matters worse I had found myself foolishly agreeing to work night shifts for a while, desperately needing the extra money it paid. It wasn't a hard job, far from it in fact, but it was a very lonely one. The night crew consisted of just me rattling around the site with only the customers for company and, during the winter months, there weren't even many of those. Every night became the exact same bitterly cold and repetitively boring experience.

Occasionally though, someone would pull in for fuel or snacks and would stop and talk a while. They probably felt much the same as me in those early hours of the morning; grateful for a little bit of company. Some were travelling home, others to work, and some just seemed to be travelling for the hell of it. It was on just such a night that I met a man by the name of Archer.

Weathered would probably be the best way to describe his appearance, looking every inch the typical windswept traveller. Long scraggy hair framed a face impossible to age, he could have been 30 or 60 for all I knew, but his eyes suggested the experience and wisdom of advanced years. In seconds I had invented a whole back story for him based on how he looked. I imagined him to be an eternal nomad, never stopping long in one place, beholding to nothing and no one. Before ever having spoken to him I had made myself envious of the person I believed him to be. A side effect of working alone for so long I suppose; you start to make up stories for people just to give your brain something to do. As it turned out however, this time I wasn't far off the mark.

What first caught my eye about him was the fact that, unlike most customers I saw, he had walked into the forecourt, with bags hanging off every available part of his body. This admittedly may not seem such a strange thing for someone to do, except we were pretty much in the middle of nowhere sitting just off a duel carriageway on the edge of the Lake District National Park. Usually if a person came walking in it would be because they had run out of fuel somewhere along the road and they'd be carrying only a jerry can. This guy was carrying his whole life on his back, everything he owned, everything he needed looked to be packed inside those bags. He seemed to be the opposite of everything I was and yet everything I longed to be. This man was free.

During nightshifts at the petrol station the shop doors where always meant to be locked and customers served through the night hatch for safety and security reasons. Hence when he first tapped on the window and asked if it was possible to come inside out of the cold, my first reaction was to say no. But then, for some reason, I found myself feeling that perhaps just this once I could make an exception. At the time I rationalised that this decision was due to the temperature outside having dipped below freezing (yet again), along with the fact that there was an almost visible layer of frost clinging to the poor man like an icy blanket.

However, upon opening the doors, I immediately chastised myself for doing so; fearing I had, out of pure stupidity, just let some kind of psycho killer inside who was going to murder me and rob the store. But, before I had chance to convince myself that this was true, the man gave me a warm smile that radiated kindness and somehow managed to put my mind at ease. A mere facial twitch gave me that familiar comfortable feeling you get upon meeting an old friend. In an attempt to convince myself that I wasn't being gullible, I decided to give him the benefit of the doubt for now whilst remaining wary and vigilant until he left.

'Give him a coffee,' I thought, *'let him warm up and he will be gone in no time at which point I can pretend that this odd situation had never happened.'* That's what I told myself anyway.

As he untangled his body from his bags I brought him out a chair from behind the counter and pulled the portable heater around as far as it would reach, making sure he would stay somewhere I could easily see him. Again I was trying to prove to myself that I was too savvy to be caught off guard should the man turn out to be insincere in his intentions.

As he savoured the warming effect of his coffee and stretched out on the chair with a sigh of relief, we exchanged the usual pleasantries and idle chatter of a civilised introduction before engaging in that greatest of British traditions; moaning about the weather. Truth be told it gave us plenty to talk about as already the country had experienced crippling blizzards, gale force winds, devastating floods and temperatures that dropped as low as minus twelve degrees. It didn't bode well for the rest of the year, but it did make for a very effective ice breaking conversation, if you pardon the pun.

As we talked I couldn't help noticing the strange manner in which he spoke. His tone was very relaxed and calming yet authoritative and charismatic at the same time, enriched by a vocabulary of words rarely used by ordinary people. The combined effect made you feel that if he said the moon was made of cheese you would readily believe him, even if it was but for a few seconds until common sense kicked back in.

Eventually, I asked him where he had come from, to which he replied;

'That is a question whose answer begins a long time ago!'

I can't say why but the obscure way in which he had answered plucked at my curiosity and left me encouraging him to explain more.

He told of being born and raised in the area (although he never did say exactly where) and of how he'd grown up in a very dysfunctional family. His father was an abusive drunk at whose hands he and his mother had suffered greatly for many years.

'By the time I had reached my teens,' he went on to explain, *'I was an extremely angry and hot headed young man with no respect for authority and a complete lack of discipline. I hated my father so completely that I would rebel against him at every opportunity.'*

This was something I could quite relate to, drawing certain parallels with my own childhood which dragged me deeper into his tale.

'I was forever in and out of trouble with the police, which always gave my old man a convenient excuse to beat me, not that he ever really needed one. But it was on one such occasion that my life took a turn that would lead me to the path I now walk. I suddenly realised, in an odd moment of clarity that came as but the calm before a great storm, that I was a man, bigger and stronger than he, and that I no longer had to take the abuse he gave. In a rush of emotion and painful memories, I snapped.'

He described how this confrontation had turned into such a vicious fight between father and son that there could have only ever been one outcome.

'Eventually my mother threw herself bravely between me and my victim begging me to stop. The fear and pain written across her face broke my heart, extinguishing the flame that had burned so fiercely within. In the lull that followed, my father, realising he could no longer control me, called the police and had me arrested for assault. He cast me out and told me never to darken his doorstep again. I ended up spending the night in police lock up before being released without charge on the condition that I found somewhere else to live. What hurt the most in the following days was just how little my mother had seemed to fight

for me. If not for my defiant nature, and the pure hatred I held towards my father, I do believe this moment in my life could have ruined me. Instead it served only to force me away from the place I had called home and out into the world.'

He paused at this point and a strange look came across his face, suggesting both acceptance and regret of time lost that could never be returned. What surprised me though was the fact that, despite having expressed the hate and anger he had felt for his father, there wasn't a single trace of it in his voice or on his face as he talked about the man who had failed so completely in his parental duties. This I struggled to understand as the scars left by my own father ran deep. Hating him is something I doubt I could ever give up.

When he continued he described how he had travelled the world over, stopping wherever and whenever he felt like, taking on casual work as needed to sustain himself, never staying in one place long enough to take root or form any lasting attachments.

'I was having the time of my life,' he exclaimed, *'experiencing every kind of emotion from unbridled joy to debilitating loneliness in some of the most amazing places on the planet.'*

Slightly puzzled, I asked him how he could class loneliness amongst his fondest memories, to which he replied;

'Times of hardship may not seem as great as those of happiness, yet it is through them that a man builds strength of both heart and mind.'

Curious about how he perceived such life events I asked him what was the worst experience he had endured during his aimless wanderings. He paused briefly, as if unsure what his reply should be, then somewhat cautiously said;

'What an unusual question to ask. Most people only ever want to know of a person's best experiences?'

There was a look in his eyes that unsettled me as, for the first time that evening, this seemingly all-knowing figure of calmness appeared to be ever so slightly rattled. The moment passed quickly as a look of understanding washed over him returning his previous state of composure. Ironically this actually unnerved me more as I felt like he had just looked right through me and seen something I could not.

'Well, in answer to your question,' he began, *'I suppose my worst experience would have come during my time in Asia. You see back then I was neither a considerate nor courteous*

10

traveller, holding a complete disregard and disrespect for the cultures and religions of the countries I visited. Being English I believed that everyone else should speak my language and accommodate my behaviour, a belief that generated some very interesting situations.' In the back of my mind I felt a twinge of conscience for having once also held similar intolerances during my travels. *'The more I travelled, the worse my attitude seemed to become, laughing at people's beliefs and touting their laws. I thought myself superior to all and untouchable for my sins. But that was all to change as I found myself travelling the border between China and Tibet. There it was that I set myself on a collision course with destiny.'*

He explained how when visiting a small monastery with a girl he'd met, he decided it would be fun to steal one of their treasured statues of the Buddha, finding it rather pathetic how men would forego life's pleasures to spend their days praying to a piece of metal.

'I believe at the time it was a state of boredom that convinced me to do it, desiring the challenge of such a task. I didn't want it to be a dash in and grab scenario either; that would have been too easy. No, I knew it would take planning and finesse to pull it off without being caught.'

As he described how over a couple of days he'd infiltrated the monastery as a man desperately in need of food and shelter, allowing him to scope out the place and wait for his chance, there was a genuine look of remorse on his face. If it hadn't been for his eyes I would have been convinced that he truly regretted such an act, but there was an ever so slight twinkle of satisfaction and pride. It was something I could relate to.

'Yet for all my planning and preparation,' he continued, *'the outcome of this childish prank was beyond my control; I was betrayed by the most unfortunate of timings. With the little statue, that I believe may actually have been made from solid gold judging by its weight, stuffed safely in my bag I took my leave and headed for the exit. I successfully escaped only to be confronted by a small Chinese army patrol that just happened to be passing by at that exact moment.'*

There was an inference that fate had somehow orchestrated this, a concept I had to refrain from balking at.

'Barrelling into the column of men at some speed, I found myself engulfed by a lot of shouting and pushing which resulted in me being thrown to the floor. Frantically I scrambled to retreat from the line of riffles aiming at my head; never before

11

had I been so afraid. Hearing the commotion, a few of the monks came rushing to my aid, able to communicate with the patrol where I could not. The rifles began to lower and I allowed myself a small sigh of relief, grateful for the timely intervention of these gracious monks. I had almost forgotten about that which I had been doing only moments earlier until one monk decided to kindly pick up my bag and pass it back to me. In a flash of panic I could see in my mind's eye what was about to happen. Not expecting the weight of the statue, the monk would be unbalanced by it and drop the bag, the flap would open, the statue would roll out, and all hell would break loose. With rifles back in my face I would be dragged away kicking and screaming by the patrol and thrown into some horrific foreign prison to await my fate...'

He left the story hanging on a pause, the strange anticipation of which had me involuntarily holding my breath. He painted such a vivid picture with his words that I found it hard not to get so caught up the story.

'...and that is exactly what did happen,' he eventually continued. *'For two weeks I was beaten and humiliated, cast into a cell without any kind of explanation of what was to become of me. Frightened and alone, grief began to set in. I was in denial, believing what I had done did not warrant such punishment. I became angry and bitter toward the guards for my treatment, the monks for betraying me, and myself for having been so stupid. I tried bargaining with my captors for freedom. I would have done anything, given anything to be let out, but they took no notice of me. Eventually my futile efforts faded into a state of depression for knowing they probably couldn't even understand me or wouldn't have cared if they could. Finally an acceptance of my fate washed over me. I knew I was going to be either executed or left to rot. The Chinese have a very low tolerance for any crime, save those committed by their own government. My act of thievery no longer held the amusement I had anticipated and I knew my childish ignorance had this time cost me my life,'* he paused, *'but that was not to be my fate...'*

'FIVE, FIVE, FIVE!'

I was suddenly shocked back to reality, unceremoniously torn away from his story. It took me a few moments to realise that the voice shouting at me was that of my till indicating that someone had picked up a pump nozzle outside. Impatiently I set about serving this most inconvenient of customers, retrieving the snacks they kept indecisively requesting from around the shop, wishing venomously that they would just go and bother someone else.

When eventually I turned away from the night hatch, I was caught by a blast of icy wind that cut straight through to my bones. Somehow it seemed to be getting colder outside and in response I decided to move my own chair around from behind the counter to join Archer by the heater. After taking a moment to absorb some warmth back into my body, I asked him to continue on, eager to hear the outcome of his story and learn how he had escaped.

'I didn't,' he stated quite simply.

A smile crept in at the edge of his mouth giving away the amusement he felt at seeing my face contort, trying to contemplate how his statement could be true.

'I was saved,' he laughed.

He went on to explain that, without warning one day, his jailors returned and dragged him out of his cell. Fearing his time had come, he was bewildered to find that he was instead being handed over to a monk. A monk he instantly recognised as being the same one that had tried to hand him back his bag.

'My mind was filled with a chaotic confusion. Why was this man here? Why were the Chinese letting me go? And why did I still feel resentment towards he who had just saved my life? The monk led me away from the prison, which for the first time I could now see was half built into the side of a mountain making it almost impossible to see by anyone who did not know it was there. As we walked he explained that, despite my betrayal of their trust, they could not have knowingly left me to die at the hands of the Chinese. His name was Ling and as we walked he told me of how he was relatively new to the monastery and to the Buddhist way of life. His family had been forced from their home by the Chinese during their initial invasion of the country. Left homeless and starving, they were eventually taken in by the very monastery he now devoted his life to in gratitude. It was only then that I realised just how badly I had abused their generosity with my story of being in need of shelter. Consumed by such guilt, I almost missed the well-disguised resentment and hatred he still held toward the Chinese for what they had done. Of course this was entirely understandable, but it surprised me none the less. Through what little I knew of Buddhism, I imagined them all to be a naturally peaceful and forgiving people who could rise above the common emotions that weigh

13

heavy in the hearts of others. It is sometimes all too easy to forget that you cannot judge the quality of a painting simply because it was painted with the same brush as many others,' I couldn't quite decide if his words were an eloquent insight or an ill-conceived attempt at one. *'Eventually I asked how he had managed to secure my release from that horrible place and, with a trace of smugness, he explained that he had simply told the commander of the patrol that they had been mistaken in their assumption of my thievery and that the statue had been a gift to me. Furthermore, he explained how I was to aid them in the renovation and up keep of the monastery, which needed expanding due to the increase of homeless people arriving there. I realised then that, although they would never ask it of me, it was expected that I would now fulfil this role in thanks for my freedom,'* he looked mournfully distant as he talked of this moment. *Despite feeling that there was more that Ling was not telling me about my release, I asked no more questions and happily offered to work for them as implied. It was, after all, the least I could do considering they had gifted me a second chance at life.'*

That whole experience had changed him forever. He had been a broken man in the prison and a re-born one in the monastery. He told of how being truly humbled by the pure generosity and un-questioning selflessness of the monks had eventually lead him to learn their ways and become a Buddhist himself. Six years he lived there, feeling a sense of peace and belonging that had until then been missing from his life.

Eventually I asked him what had made him leave such a place and he answered thusly;

'In my last year there I had begun to have strange dreams. Dreams of people and places I had never seen nor been to before. I discussed these visions with the head of the monastery on a number of occasions. He was a great man, both wise and compassionate, and together we agreed that these dreams were a sign that the time had come for me to leave the monastery and find their meaning. He believed that through doing so I would begin to heal the wounds of my earlier life and eventually bring peace to my soul. And so, for the second time in my life, I left my home and the people I called family to travel the world once more. This time however, I was no longer filled with anger and hatred. This time I was setting off with a tranquil mind and a determination to do good in the world whilst ever expanding my

knowledge and understanding of Buddhism and the spirit of man.'

And that is exactly what he did. From aid work in Africa to conservation work in South America, he travelled the world on a shoe string helping people in any way he could and only taking money for it when the time had come to move again. Occasionally he would meet other travelling Buddhists on their own journeys of discovery and join them for a while to learn from their knowledge. It was during these times that he began to discover many of the old legends of Tibet and the Buddhist religion. He repeatedly heard talk of a fabled place called Shambhala and a great power that resided there, along with an ancient prophecy that seemed to describe the world as it currently was.

'When the earth seems lost to greed and materialism, terrible battles will engulf the nations of the world. The age of man will reach its climax of bloodshed and the people of Shambhala will rise up to cleanse mankind's corruption,' he recounted it to me.

'Wow!' I said, feeling it was an appropriate response, despite my scepticism of such things, *'So, when is this "climax of bloodshed" supposed to come about?'*

'Many dates have been suggested for the time of the great rising,' he replied, *'but all seem to agree that the countdown will begin with the ending of the ancient Mayan calendar in 2012.'*

'2012?' I said with modicum of genuine surprise, *'That's next year. When was the prediction made?'* I asked curiously, *'It's quite eerie really if you think about it, the prediction for the state of the world is already sounding alarmingly accurate.'*

'I am inclined to agree with you there my friend, its words do seem to ring ominously true,' he replied. *'As for when they were first spoken, I have not been able to clarify. Do not give this cause for doubting its authenticity mind, in Tibet such foresights are seen only by the wisest of the Lamas; men who do not waste words frivolously.'*

It was an interesting idea and there was an intriguing accuracy to the prediction, but believing that people could see the future was too farfetched for me. Not because I cynically believe that people who claim to see the future are just peddlers of cheap parlour tricks designed to con the gullible (even though I do by the way) but rather because I cannot stomach the idea of there being a future to see. To believe that there was a future meant believing that my life had already happened and that there was nothing I could do to change my "destiny". If I believed this

15

then what point would there be in ever trying to make my life better? If it did get better in the future then I might as well sit back and just wait for it happen, if it didn't then there was nothing I could do to change it so why bother trying?

Anyway, all that is beginning to make my head hurt so I think I should just get back to my story. You can at least understand now why I was so sceptical of what Archer was saying.

'This is but one of many prophecies regarding the rise of Shambhala as I said,' he continued on. *'Some give different dates, and some seem to differ on their opinions of just what such a time will bring, but all are in agreement that it will happen this century and that it will herald in a new age of man. Of course, the coincidence with the ending of the Mayan calendar has led some to believe it is in fact a prophecy of Armageddon.'*

'I don't usually go in for that whole "End of the World" stuff if I'm really honest,' I said, trying to hide a returning scepticism. *'I mean, in my time alone there have been umpteen predictions that have come and gone without even so much as a change in the weather.'*

'Initially I too was somewhat sceptical as to the substance of such predictions, but the stories of Shambhala piqued my interest regardless and I found myself wanting to know more; intrigued by the idea of an undiscovered civilisation lost in time. Thus I began my own research into it.'

Curiously I asked him why this legend was not known in the West; we knew of others such as the lost city of Atlantis so why not this one? He fixed me with a look of one about to drop a bombshell....and then did.

'But my friend you almost certainly have heard of it. You just know it as Shangri-La.'

My mind raced! I had heard of it, most people have, Shangri-La, Heaven on earth, a place where all is good. It couldn't really exist could it?

A feeling came over me that I can't quite describe. It was almost as if a piece of my life had fallen into place, like I was meant to be here on this night. Long had I dreamed of having been born back in the days when there was still uncharted places in the world. When blank areas on the map cried out to those willing to set off into the unknown in search of great treasures and perilous adventure. And now there I was, standing on the edge of those dreams made real. Excitedly I wanted to know

16

more but, before I could ask him about his research, a look of sadness drifted across his face.

'*Unfortunately,*' he began, '*my journey was prematurely cut short. During my time at the monastery, finding a degree of inner peace, I forced myself to write a letter home. Much to my surprise, about a month later, I received a reply from my mother. After much apologising and bridge mending we began to keep a regular correspondence going which was a real comfort, especially during some of the more difficult times of my travels.*'

There was warmth in his voice as he talked about his mother that warned me of what was to come. It was the warmth of remembering a loved one passed.

'*Then one day I received a strange letter. At that time I was living and working in an Ethiopian aid camp that, rather fortunately, had quite a regular mail supply all things considered. The letter was addressed in a hand writing I did not recognise. As I held it in my hand I could feel the weight of news I did not wish to receive. Somehow I knew something bad had happened and the opening of the letter proved this to be true. It was from a friend of my mother apologising for telling me what she was about to tell me in a letter and not in person but that she had found no other contact details for me in my mother's things. My heart sank. As I read on she described of how my parents had been in a serious car accident and were both critically ill in hospital. Without a second thought I gathered my few possessions, made my apologies for such a sudden departure and set off on a long journey to the home of my youth. I hoped and prayed to any gods that would listen I could make it back in time to stand at my mother's side.*'

His eyes were glazed with tears and a catch in his voice told me that his emotions where still quite raw. I knew before he continued he had not been granted his wish.

It had taken roughly a week for the letter to get to him and, due to his lack of money, it had then taken him nearly two weeks to get home. In the end he was just too late. They told him his mother had been a fighter, as if she was holding on for something, but her injuries were just too severe.

'*I was inconsolable; filled with both sadness and rage. She had held on knowing I would be coming but I had taken far too long. I had failed her. Through my faith I would eventually find solace. In the teachings and mantras of Buddha I would find the strength to pull through. But there in that terrible moment, I simply wished I could have seen her one last time.'*

There fell an uncomfortable silence between us as he seemed to reflect on the memory and I sat not knowing if I was meant to offer condolences, try to lighten the mood or just keep my mouth shut. Social etiquette in such situations has never been my strongest trait.

'It was then that I was told of how my father still lived,' he at last continued, bringing an welcome end to my indecisive battle. *'A million and one emotions and thoughts raced through my mind, twisting my soul into two halves. One side still held all the resentment of old joined now by blame for the death of my mother, yet on the other side came the monk I had become pushing me to make things right with this man to heal the wound in my heart that had been the greatest of all. The doctor told me that, whilst he had survived his surgery and was now conscious, they had not been able to repair all the damage and it was only a matter of time until he too passed on. I think it was this knowledge that made me realise, should I not attempt to right things with him, my only chance of true redemption would soon be gone. In her letters to me, my mother had tried to explain that he was no longer the tyrant I had known. For all his spilt anger at the time, my disappearance and complete lack of contact had broken him. He realised too late the error of all he had done,'* a pained smile crossed his face as he talked of this.

'She said he had been delighted at the sight of my first letter. His relief at knowing I was alive and well had apparently given him a new lease of life. I had never responded to anything about him though, and sitting here now I cannot think why.'

Archer told me of how he eventually plucked up the courage to go and see him and of how his mother had been right; he was not the man he remembered. They talked for hours, convincing the nursing staff to let him stay well after visiting hours were over, but he wouldn't go into any detail about what they talked about. He simply said;

'After some painful tears, difficult apologies, hard truths and time catching up on each other's lives, we finally embraced as a father and son at peace. Later that evening he drifted off into a sleep from which he never woke.'

He said it had been a liberating feeling, unloading the baggage he had carried all his life Despite the sadness of losing both parents, and of never having the chance to speak to his

18

mother in person again, he felt truly happy in himself for the first time in as long as he could remember.

For many years he went back to live in his parents' house. He spent much of his time initially sorting out all the things that need sorting after someone dies. But eventually he returned his concentration to the furthering of his research into Shambhala and his studies of Buddhism. He said he had ended up staying far longer than he originally wanted, but there had been something keeping him. Almost a need to make peace with the home he had once hated as he had done with his parents.

'And that basically leads us up to date my young friend, sat here as we are on this night,' he said with an endearing smile.

I sat back in my chair, mentally exhausted by the intensity of my engrossment in his story, and looked at Archer in amazement. It was only then that my eye was caught by a necklace he wore around his neck.

'Where did you get your necklace from?' I asked him.

I realise now that it was an odd question to hit him with, one that had nothing to do with our previous conversation, but I couldn't help my curiosity. It would latter prove to be an important observation.

In response to my query, he looked down to where the necklaces pendent rested upon his chest.

'This here?' he said lifting it up against the back of his hand, *'I made it myself many years ago'*

'The pendant looks like a claw. What's it made out of?' I inquired further.

'Well, that is an interesting story all of its own,' he replied enticingly, *'Alas I fear we have not the time to talk of it. The time has come for me to be back on my way, I have kept you from your work for too long already.'*

I sat for a moment in stunned silence as he started to get up, feeling as if someone had just ripped the next page out of a good book before I could read it. I had to think fast; think of a way to make him stay a while longer.

'Wait, it's still below freezing outside,' I enthusiastically pointed out. *'I don't know where it is you are heading, but nowhere is going to be open at this time of the morning. You might as well stay here a little longer and keep warm.'*

'Are you sure? What about your work?' he asked considerately.

'Hell, all I have left to do really is clean the floor and, to be honest, at this time of year it's like pissing into the wind anyway.

Come five o'clock when I open the doors it'll take all of ten minutes for the farmers and workmen to muck it up again with their dirty boots. Seriously, sit yourself back down and let me fetch us some more coffee.'

'Thank you my young friend,' he said whilst making himself comfortable again, *'I will not turn down such hospitality.'*

With warm cups in hand and the quietness of the night falling around us once more, I subtly suggested he continue with his story about the necklace.

'So, you were about to tell me about your necklace?' I prompted. It had sounded subtle in my head at least.

'Ah yes,' he replied with a knowing grin, *'Well, during my travels I spent some time in Southern Africa,'* he paused briefly, *' a part of the world I would say you too have visited by the way your eyes just light up.'*

His assumption was correct. I had travelled there a few times after leaving University on various conservation projects, mostly in South Africa. From the very first time I set foot there, I'd felt an affinity with the place that has stayed with me ever since. When I told him this he simply smiled and nodded, allowing me to reminisce about my own adventures there. It had been a long time since I'd had someone to talk to that wasn't already bored of my stories, so I revelled in the chance to do so. Eventually I realised that I had rudely interrupted his own story and apologetically urged him to continue.

'It is in Zimbabwe where the roots of this tale lie,' he started, *'must have been late 1984 I think it was. Time for me past very differently then, a day's length was judged by how long the sun stayed above the horizon and not by the hands on a clock. I had no use for modern time measurements, no need to record the days of the week or even the months of the year.'*

I knew the pace of life he talked of, I had experienced it myself. It is pace at which you can actually enjoy time as it passes rather than spend your time chasing after it.

'I was working as a missionary of sorts, much as I had been everywhere else I travelled, offering aid and assistance to whomever could find use for it,' he paused briefly, *'actually, that's not entirely true. My time in Zimbabwe had a more deliberate purpose. Early on in 84 food supplies to Matabeleland were disrupted by President Mugabe's Army and much of the Ndebele population who lived there suffered food shortages. Upon hearing of this I decided to cut short my travels in neighbouring Botswana and join an aid caravan trying to get*

over the border with food packages and in an attempt to scout out a safe supply route into the area. It turned out to be a very gruelling trip that tested my faith and my will to their limits. The things I saw became nightmares burned forever into my waking mind,' at distant look of pain appeared briefly on his face before he continued, *'For the most part our mission was successful in that we managed to establish a sustainable aid supply into the Lupane District, a rural area of Matabeleland, which at that time was reasonably peaceful. I spent my day's travelling between the small villages and providing the aid caravans with "shopping lists" of what was needed and where. It was upon one such day that the finding of this pendant occurred. I was walking a road between two villages that had become quite familiar to me with a family whose hospitality I had recently been enjoying. Counting many of the locals within the number of my friends I had come to learn of many useful shortcuts along those roads, one of which I intended to use that day. Arriving at the start of the shortcut I had to part ways with the family to take it. You see, although convenient, travelling that path was a risk a father would not make with his children for it involved leaving the relative safety of the well-used road for the wildness of the untamed bush. I respected his reasons and likely would have been just as cautious had I been in his position. However, I had already used the trail a number of times before and felt confident that the respectful traveller could walk it with relative safety. Needless to say I was somewhat startled that day to then find myself happening upon the freshly killed remains of an antelope lying at a turn in the trail. Judging by the size of the animal, and the size of its wounds, I deduced that the owner of this hardly touched meal was probably quite large and almost certainly still close by. Realising the potential danger this find had put me in I quickly made the decision to about face, return to the road and take the long way round to my destination. Rather stomach the extra distance, I thought, than find myself being stomached by a wild animal.'*

I'd had experiences like this myself and therefore knew exactly how dangerous the situation would have been. You never want to disturb a wild animal on a kill.

'Before I left the gruesome scene however, I noticed something imbedded in the hind quarters of the poor creature. An admittedly ill-advised closer inspection revealed it to be a rather large claw that must have snapped off during the hunt. Yet another reason to make a hasty retreat one might say, the

predator in question likely to already be of a foul disposition as a result of its injury. But for all the warnings in my head, I felt an inexplicable desire to retrieve the claw and take it with me. It was a task however that proved to be quite difficult, so deeply hooked into the hardened hide was it. When finally I managed to dislodge the claw, I stood looking at the fruits of my labour. The foolishness of this action was revealed by a low rumbling growl vibrating through the ground behind. I had lingered too long. Slowly turning, I found myself locking eyes with the cold, unyielding stare of a young male lion. As a primal fear of the savage beast awoke inside me I stood unmoving, terrified by the sight of the sheer untamed force of nature staring me dead in the eye. As clichéd as it may sound, in the moments that passed I felt my life pass before my eyes as I waited for the inevitable attack and the sinking razor sharp fangs into my soft flesh. I closed my eyes in acceptance of my terrible fate.......but it never came. With time seeming to have stalled before me, I opened my eyes believing for a moment that I may have now been but a disembodied spirit about to look upon the ending of my mortal life. Instead what I saw was the regal beast eying me with a complete disinterest having judged me no threat to its meal. With a dismissive snort it proceeded to simply walk past me with an air of indifference and returned to his kill. Whether by luck or fate, I had been spared a horrific death. Maybe it wasn't my time to go or perhaps it was simply the fact that the lion had no reason to attack me with an already caught and killed meal waiting behind me, who knows? What I do know though is that it wasn't the only lucky escape I had that day,' he paused for a moment staring off into the distance as he rubbed the pendant with his thumb. *When at last I unfroze enough to cautiously back away from the scene, knowing that it is never wise to turn your back on a predator, I suddenly heard a series of rapid gun shots off in the distance. It came from the direction of the road! I ran back along the trail and arrived at the road side with just enough time to duck down behind a bush as a truck full of machine gun wielding troops drove past. Praying they wouldn't see me, a sickening feeling rose up from the pit of my stomach upon catching a glimpse of the red berets the men were wearing. The most distinguishable feature of the Fifth Brigade, Mugabe's personal death squad, is not something you easily forget. Watching them pass, praying that I wouldn't be spotted, I broke from cover as soon as it felt safe and I ran in the direction they had come from. Though I desperately wished it was not so I was*

22

now unable to deny the truth...Mugabe's dark hand had finally reached Lupane,' the paling of his face as he prepared to continue came as a warning of what was to come. *I ran like you would through treacle, a part of me knowing I would not want to see what lay before me, yet on I plunged preparing myself for the worst. Never could I have been ready enough though for what I found. Lying at the side of the road where the bullet riddled bodies of my former host and his family, murdered in cold blood. Ever shall the image of a father lifelessly slumped over his wife and young children, in a futile attempt to shield them from the searing force of the bullets that pierced their bodies, be burned into my soul. Dropping to my knees I was without words or cries that could express my pain. Death is a sight you cannot un-see.'*

His eyes stared off into a memory so vividly painted by raw emotion that it felt like I too had looked upon that harrowing scene.

'Had I not stopped to retrieve the Lions claw,' he continued, whilst noticeably trying to re-bury the sorrow that had come flooding back to him, *'and subsequently had the run in with the Lion itself, chances are that I would have been out on the road as those bastards drove by. After that day my time in Zimbabwe was short. The presence of the Fifth Brigade made it too dangerous for aid workers to stay in the region and so we had little choice to pull out. I left Southern Africa within the week never to return, for a part of me died there in the blood soaked sands of Zimbabwe. A part of me I have long since tried to forget,'* with that he fell silent, and out of respect I made no attempt to push him any further.

'So!' he said eventually with a deep intake of breath that startled me, *'I shaved the lion claw down like this and have worn it ever since as a symbol of luck and as a reminder that things always happen for a reason.'*

The sudden abruptness to the end of his story left me feeling a bit disorientated. As reality slowly fell back into place around me, I found myself staring upon the necklace with wistful eyes. I had become fascinated by lions ever since having had my own encounters with them out in the African Bush and would have given anything to have a necklace like that. Where it not for the strong emotional attachment I now knew that he had for it, I think I'd have tried to buy it from him. It was one piece of jewellery that I would never forget.

Archer's Necklace[i]

A glance out the window revealed a now more visible layer of frost upon the ground suggesting that the temperature was only getting colder. This prompted me to ask Archer what could possibly have persuaded him to abandon a warm bed on such a night, sensing that there was still much more to his story that he had yet to impart. To this he simply replied;

'My young friend, you would not believe me if I told you.'

Once again he had me intrigued. I considered myself to be quite an open minded person and so, by this simple act of assuming my disbelief, he left me questioning exactly what it was I would not believe?

I all but begged him to explain causing him to smile in a way that suggested it had been just the response he intended to illicit. He told of how his research into Shambhala had lead him to a tale of a mythical stone that had travelled throughout the ages of human existence. According to legend it held a great power that entwined its fate with the future of humanity. For reasons he did not explain at that time, he had decided to take upon himself the challenge of finding its final resting place. After years of preparation and research he had finally reached a point where there was nothing left to do but set out on this quest. Having sold just about everything his parents had bequeathed to him, freeing himself of anything that could have tied him down or held him back, he'd set off this night to do just that. His plan was to gain passage on a boat headed to Europe, by any means possible, from where he would then trek and hitch-hike his way to every point marked as a place of interest on his map. He had been heading to the nearest bus station to catch a ride over to the east coast when an inexplicable pull had brought him down to my door.

Recovering from my initial burst of excitement over the prospect of such an adventure, my overly suspicious mind picked up on something slightly odd. Why, having just sold all of his possessions, was he willingly making his journey harder by foregoing the use of a plane to get to his destinations? Upon voicing this query as politely as I could, he just smiled in way that made me feel transparent. It was as if my suspiciousness was written all over my face.

'A man must first find himself before he can discover real truth,' he began in answer. *'My destination is said to hold both a physical and a spiritual existence and so this must be as much a spiritual journey as a physical one. Such a path cannot be one of ease. Only through adversity and dedication can one ever hope*

25

to achieve such goals. To that end I have donated most of my money to charities for its use to me would be of no help in the long run.'

A feeling of doubt clouded my mind as despite our earlier conversations, and knowing he was a Buddhist, I had little time for all that philosophical, feng-shui, spiritual nonsense and found it abrasive to my interest in his story. Archer must have been able to read me like a book.

'Do not feel that you have to suppress your cynicism for the sake of being polite my friend, much of what I say can sound conceited and full of self-importance, believe me I know.' I was quite surprised by his perceptiveness which lifted some of my doubt. *'However,'* he continued, *'I challenge anyone to spend time living amongst devout Buddhists monks, or experience the emotional pain of watching children suffer and starve to death simply because they were born into poverty, and not be effected both spiritually and mentally.'*

Shamed by his words, I felt guilty for having been so ready to write this man off purely because of his beliefs and how he spoke. Once again he read my feelings correctly.

'There is nothing wrong with doubting someone's sincerity, or even their mental state, because they seem weird or different to you. Always be suspicious, always question that which you do not understand and ask yourself what motivates the person before you. Doing so will protect you from those that are false and would lie to you in order to conceal their true intentions. But what you must not do is close your mind to a person just because they are different. You have to give people a chance otherwise suspicion will turn to paranoia.'

His strange manner and compelling personality made everything he said sound so convincing. I was left urging him once more to explain further whilst I listened with avid intent. The research he had done and the knowledge he had was staggering. But it wasn't until he produced an impressive leather bound journal, from one of his numerous bags, that I started to really believe how serious he was about it all. He invited me to read its opening page, and I did so with great relish. It read like the preface to an epic adventure yet to be written. In just a few short paragraphs I found myself so completely captivated that I felt a surge of excitement welling up inside.

'Through the stars I come. I bring the chalice covered with shield. Within it I bring a treasure, the gift of Orion'

26

The Chintamani Stone, an artefact of ancient power and myth from time immemorial. Its story is one that spans the length and breadth of human history, and yet it ends quite abruptly in the 1920's with a Russian explorer called Nicholas Roerich.

It is said that Roerich had been entrusted with a shard of the stone by a high abbot of the secretive Tashilhunpo Monastery in Tibet. Its purpose was to aid the establishment of the League of Nations in Europe. However, when the League began to fail, Roerich took back the shard and set off to return it home.

This is where the story ends and the stone vanishes from history...Until Now.

Did Roerich make it back? Was the shard returned?

It is with these questions that I start my quest. One that my initial research suggests will span the globe piecing together clues from Buddhism to Christianity, Native Americans to African Tribes, the Third Reich to the Illuminati and even links to the legend of the Holy Grail.

This is my story. This is my adventure. This is my Quest for Shambhala!

I was hooked! Questions bounced round my head, exploding like fireworks, making it difficult to hold on to any one long enough to ask. But before I had chance to bring order to this chaos, a warm glow had started to creep through the darkness of the night heralding the arrival of the morning sun and the inevitable departure of Archer. I realised that having spent most of the night talking to this man I had forgotten about the jobs I was supposed to have done. But in that moment I could feel how little I cared; work seemed such a trivial matter now compared to what had transpired on that night. All I could think about was how much I wanted to accompany him and learn more of what he knew.

Daybreak however, brought with it the rattling chains of my life, a suffocating bond of commitments and debts, reminding me of a reality I could not escape so easily. Desperate to be involved with his adventure in any small way, I asked Archer to take my contact details and keep in touch to inform me of any discoveries he made. Furthermore I told him of my desire to help and that if ever he needed any assistance he need only ask.

'Truly that is a kind offer my friend, but are you sure you wish to make it to a man you have known only for a few hours? Could I really count on your help if the time ever came?' he solemnly asked in return.

'I know this may sound strange, but for some reason I feel connected to this story now,' I replied quiet naively. *'Man, I'd give anything to be going with you on your quest. But, that being impossible, I would love to just be a part of it in any way I can. If the time ever comes when I can be of use, I promise that you can count on my help.'*

He looked at me with smile that suggested he was pleased by my response. For the second time that night I had the feeling that somehow this was the outcome he hoped to achieve the whole time. As he stood and prepared to leave, rearranging the trappings of his life, he stopped and said;

'Life is like a road, some people are content to sit at its side and just watch it go by never knowing or caring about the experiences they will never have. Others yearn to know where the road leads to and stride out upon it with determination and adventure in their hearts. You, my young friend, are neither. Instead you are stuck in a limbo between the two. Never will you be content with a life on the side-line, you have too strong a spirit and a longing to explore, yet you lack the courage to take that first step out to find the life you desperately wish for.'

A wave of depression and hopelessness washed over me as the truth in his words hit me like an oncoming bus. But then, as I reeled from this stranger's ability to so accurately analyse my existence, he handed me a large book from one of his bags.

'Take this,' he said, *'it was given to me for luck by a great friend. I pass it now to you with equal intent. The work inside is my own and I believe it may help you in the times ahead. Do not wait for life to find you. You must go out and find It. Give in to relentless routine and forced acceptance and before long your spirit will die and the adventure in your heart will diminish, leaving you but another wasted empty shell of the modern world. Take the first step and live without regret,'* he paused to offer his hand. *'Until we meet again, farewell my young friend,'* then he left.

I felt oddly saddened by this parting. During the course of the night I had gotten to know this man quite well and, though I had actually told him little of myself, he had somehow managed to understand me more clearly than anyone else ever had.

Looking down at the book he had given me, bound in leather and worn of age, it seemed to have a weight that was not completely physical. Flicking through its pages I saw it contained all of Archer's initial research into the Chintamani

28

Stone and the legend of Shambhala. Right then I understood. He had given me the greatest gift anyone could have bestowed. A reason to take that first step.

Standing in the doorway, watching him walk out of sight, I felt the sun bathe me in the first rays of a new morning. It seemed stronger, warmer and purer than I had ever noticed before. It was the dawn not only of a new day but of a new period in my life as I made a silent promise to myself to follow in Archer's footsteps, learn what he had learned and somehow find a way to join him on his great quest. I held destiny in my hands and knew that from that moment, my life would be changed forever.

Penrith, UK
The Letter Arrives

Two winters passed, two hard years that saw much change in the world, some good but most bad. Though I was still resistant to the "end of the world" prediction Archer had talked off, what with the whole Mayan calendar thing having come and gone without even a noticeable hiccup, I couldn't deny that things were getting noticeable worse the world over.

Yet despite all this my life had hardly changed. I still lived in the same small market town in Cumbria and still went to the same job at the petrol station. The only difference seemed to be that I was two years older. I repeatedly attacked myself with a single question that grew more poisonous with every blow;

'Where had it all gone wrong?'

For weeks after that meeting with Archer I had poured over the research book he had given me, hungry for the secrets held within. I can remember how captivated I was at just the binding alone. For the longest time I just sat starring at it, lost in how beautifully it had been crafted. A single smooth piece of dark leather bound it, longer round the back than the front producing a flap that folded back on itself to create an overlapping cover. Decorative patterns had been carved all over, lightly round the edges forming a subtle border and then more heavily towards the centre. The most startling thing about it was the fact that there were three stones on the cover placed diagonally from right to left. Each was held in place by a circular piece of rough leather with a hole cut in the middle which was then attached onto the cover with leather stitches creating yet another decorative pattern. The centre stone was much smaller than the other two but, at the same time, was the most captivating for its colour. I can only describe it in words as being an incredible blend of perfect sky blue and pure emerald green, but that doesn't even do it a shred of justice. It gave me the feeling that if I stared at it

30

for long enough its strange smokiness would begin to clear and allow me to see glimpses of the future.

Eventually though I was able to tear myself away from admiring the cover and began to untie the black cord that was wrapped around it. Then I began to read the pages within.

Hours passed, days could have without my noticing, so engrossed had I become in the information that unravelled before my eyes. It was amazing. The detail and depth of what he had researched must have taken him years to compile. It formed a kind of A-Z guide to the people, places, religions and events that were in some way connected to his quest. There were brief histories of everyone from King Solomon to the Dalai Lama, maps and descriptions of temples and ancient ruins in places like Tibet and South America. Analysis's and comparisons of the world's religions, some of which I hadn't even heard of. He'd even uncovered evidence to suggest that the expeditions Hitler sent to Tibet during World War II, reportedly to measure the skulls of its people for his Aryan race research, were really sent to find the hidden land of Shambhala in order to harness it's great power. It was like reading a history of the human race filled with prophecies and secrets that were not meant for my eyes to see. A thrilling, yet all too believable, read.

I remember coming across the other versions of the old Tibetan prophecy Archer had told me about, one which told of how;

'When the world declines into war and greed and all is lost, the twenty fifth Kalika King will emerge from Shambhala with a huge army to vanquish the corrupt world rulers and usher in a worldwide Golden Age.'

Another one predicted;

'Materialism will devastate the earth, terrible battles will engulf the nations of the world and at the climax of the bloodshed in 2020, the people of Agartha (just another name for Shambhala from what I could tell) will rise out of their cavern world.'

All of them seemed to fairly accurately describe the world as it currently was; the way it was falling into chaos. Though the sensible, and devoutly practical, side of me knew they were nothing more than vague predictions that could have just as easily been accepted as true at many points in our history, I

31

couldn't completely stop myself from thinking that there might just be something to them all the same.

As I delved further I found details of Nicholas Roerich, the man Archer had mentioned in the opening page of his journal. According to his research, Roerich had spent much of his life studying the history and legends of Tibet and was well known and well respected in his time. He was even reported to be quite influential in the Roosevelt administration. This made me think. If someone as prominent as this man believed that Shambhala had a physical location here on Earth, then maybe there really was some truth to it all. His wife, Helena Roerich, wrote of the time during her husband's possession of the Chintamani Stone fragment. She described it as having "possessed a dark lustre, like a dark heart". To this point Archer had added some of his own thoughts saying that he believed this could be relevant to stories of the stones ability to corrupt those who possess it.

The more I read the more I began to understand how strong a belief Shambhala was in Buddhism. Many of the great Lamas are believed to have either been there or to at least know of its location. There was one thing though that really caught my attention. It was about the 13th Dalai Lama who, at some point during his reign, apparently declared that all the fragments of the Chintamani Stone where to be kept in separate places for safe keeping. Why would this be? What could be so dangerous about this stone that its fragments needed to be kept apart; what kind of power did it hold? Could it be linked to what Helena Roerich had said about it?

Reading on I discovered that these fragments had all, at one time or another, been in the possession of such acclaimed conquerors and empire builders as King Solomon, Genghis Khan and Akbar the Great. There was even some indication that one piece could actually have been the sacred stone of *the Kaaba*, the one brought by Mohammed that has united millions of Moslems around the globe. A smile cracked across my face as I thought on this and wished Archer a lot of luck if he ever planned to go after that piece. Rather him than me.

Each page seemed to reveal a plethora of revelations and theories that seemed so believable I could easily see why Archer had become so intent on discovering the truth. By the time I had finished absorbing all that the book had to offer I felt I was ready. Filled with all the knowledge it had provided, I knew I could help Archer - I wanted to help Archer. It was then just a matter of waiting.

At first I waited excitedly and then I waited patiently. After that though, I just waited. All too soon my dreams of being a part of this great story eroded into nothingness. A week went by, then a month, then a year and nothing changed; it was as if that night had never happened. I found myself falling back into the routine of my normal life were work and the struggle for money took over once more. I waited a long time for Archer to keep his promise, but with every day that faded away without hearing from him, so too did my memory of that strange night and of the research I'd read. In the end I had to resign myself to the fact that he was never going to keep in touch. Eventually the whole thing just dissolved into a distant dream; a small flicker of light in the darkest corner of my mind. But then the letter came.

Spring had arrived a bit late that year, as was becoming usual, but with it came the warmth of a new sun waking from its winter slumber. Thankfully I was no longer working the night shifts and was back to mornings and evenings. My days off seemed to change every week making it harder to form any kind of stable routine than it had been on nights, but at least I had company on my shifts.

I remember the day that changed my life like it was yesterday, though I did not realise it was so at the time. I'd set off for work one afternoon just as I had a thousand times before, coasting along on auto pilot resigned to the routine monotony of the life of a nobody. Little did I realise though just how different that day would turn out to be.

The sun shone brightly without a single cloud in the sky to obstruct its view and only the hint of cool breeze clinging to the air as a reminder that winter had not long left us. It filled me with a sense of peace and happiness that had become almost foreign to my life. But that feeling was not to last long.

Arriving into work I could feel something was wrong. Normally the crossover of shifts would be met with light hearted conversation and friendly banter. That day, however, there was an air of seriousness and a look of concern on my friends faces. When I asked what was wrong the reply I got unsettled me. They explained how, not long before I'd arrived, two men had come in asking about me; whether I worked there and if so when would I be working again. As they described the appearance of these men the image that formed in my head was one of your clichéd secret service types. Tall stocky build, black identikit suits and sunglasses, no personality and faces devoid of any emotion what

33

so ever. I felt a subtle strike of panic as I thought about what they could want with me. The same irrational feeling you get when confronted by the police even though you know you've done nothing wrong.

I voiced the unnerving question aloud to my colleagues, but apparently they had not said, just that it was important they find me. Fortunately the guys hadn't been daft enough to give out any information, other than the fact that I did work there, for which I was very grateful. I couldn't for the life of me think what they could have wanted. I knew I hadn't done anything that could have landed me in trouble with the authorities, but this did not give me much comfort. Eventually I just thought to myself that, if they did want to talk to me, they would come back and everything could be straightened out. Still, it spooked me enough to ask that everyone keep an eye out for the men and let me know if they turned up again.

The rest of the afternoon passed without incident and I began to forget about what had happened. It was my last shift of the week and, having done a run of evenings, I was really looking forward to my days off.

That night I remember having a dream about my meeting with Archer. It was strange, I very rarely had dreams that I could remember yet that night I dreamt one so vividly that it was as if our meeting had happened only the day before.

I woke to the light of the new morning sun caressing my face through a gap in my curtains. A glance at my phone said it was 8am; typical considering I wasn't going to work and I had no need to be up at such an early hour. Knowing I would not be able to get back to sleep I just lay in bed enjoying the peace of an empty house, pondering the events of the dream that still floated in my memory waiting to fade away. A stiff metallic creek followed by a wooden thud indicated the arrival of the morning post. Dragging myself from the comfort of my covers, I threw on some clothes and, with sleep still clinging to my eyes, made my way down the stairs. From the amount of mail we had I imagined that the poor postman must have had an extra bag just for us. Sadly though, as is normally the way, it was mostly bills. Throwing them one by one into the bin, where all bills went unless they were a final reminder, I came across a padded envelope that was unusually addressed by hand and had a foreign postage stamp attached to it. Curiously I opened it and discovered the following letter;

My Friend

I hope this letter finds you well. Must be quite a while now since we last spoke. Ask me not how but this brain of mine did manage to lose something very important. Your address. Help arrived to me soon though. You put your address on your last letter my mind managed to recall.

Are you having any luck finding a new job? In this poor economic climate we all are feeling the noose tighten. Great is the struggle for many people living all over the world. Danger awaits those who do not plan for hardship and learn how to ride it out. Time was you could just walk out of a job and straight into another in the same day, such a shame those days are long gone. Is your work still affecting your mood?

Short is the temper of a man unhappy with his life. A man once said to me 'Friend, listen well to my words. Waiting for your life to change is a waste. For only through seeking it can change ever come.' You may find this confusing but read this letter a few times and you will understand its capital meaning. Where my recent travels across the world have taken me, the local people have been wonderful in making me feel like royalty. The King himself gets no grander a welcome, simply for a few wisdoms shared with them, feelings of passing a ship inn the night fill me with a desire to stop and rest.

Of all the places my eyes have seen on this great earth the sun sets here are the most astounding. Our lives are so short when put in terms of the existence of the world. Meeting you was a highlight of mine and our conversation will never fade from my memory. Once long ago, a belief of invincibility had filled me but not anymore. Besieged now by demons biting at my ankles hounding my steps, a longing for this feeling fills me again. Angles will aid those on holy ground a priest once told me. Take from life all that you can while you can. That is the only way to fulfilment. Step out on to the road of life and you never know where you will end up.

Now the time has come for me to go. My journey must continue. Young are the days but long are the hours. Friend, this may be my last letter for some time for my path leads now to dark places where communication will be difficult, so until next time my soul bids you good luck and good will.

See The Rise Of The Sun
archer

Archer's Letter[ii]

My Friend

I hope this letter finds you well. Must be quite a while now since we last spoke. Ask me not how but this brain of mine did manage to lose something very important. Your address. Help arrived to me soon though. You put your address on your last letter my mind managed to recall.

Are you having any luck finding a new job? In this poor economic climate we all are feeling the noose tighten. Great is the struggle for many people living all over the world. Danger awaits those who do not plan for hardship and learn how to ride it out. Time was you could just walk out of a job and straight into another in the same day such a shame those days are long gone. Is your work still affecting your mood?

Short is the temper of a man unhappy with his life. A man once said to me 'Friend, listen well to my words. Waiting for your life to change is a waste. For only through seeking it can change ever come.' You may find this confusing but read this letter a few times and you will understand its capital meaning. Where my recent travels across the world have taken me, the local people have been wonderful in making me feel like royalty. The King himself gets no grander a welcome, simply for a few wisdoms shared with them, feelings of passing a ship in the night fill me with a desire to stop and rest.

Of all the places my eyes have seen on this great earth the sun sets here are the most astounding. Our lives are so short when put in terms of the existence of the world.

Meeting you was a highlight of mine and our conversation will never fade from my memory. Once, long ago, a belief of invincibility had filled me but not anymore. Besieged now by demons biting at my ankles hounding my steps, a longing for this feeling fills me again.

Angles will aid those on holy ground a priest once told me. Take from life all that you can while you can. That is the only way to fulfilment. Step out on to the road of life and you never know where you will end up.

Now the time has come for me to go. My journey must continue. Young are the days but long are the hours. Friend, this may be my last letter for some time for my path leads now to dark places where communication will be difficult, so until next time my soul bids you, good luck and good will.

See The Rise Of The Sun

archer

Upon reading it I felt both delighted at having finally received some correspondence from him and yet equally confused as to its meaning. I well remembered his strange way of talking but this just made no sense at all. What last letter? How could I have sent him one when I did not know where he was? Why did he not say where he was? Demons? Angels (which he even spelt wrong)? What the hell was he talking about? He said this may be his last letter....it was the *only* letter I had received. What dark places was he going to and why end a letter with 'See The Rise Of The Sun'?

All these questions crowded my mind as I could not understand why he would send me such nonsense. I finally concluded that this man I had met was, in fact, crazy and I chastised myself for having been taken in by his ramblings.

This final thought completely deflated me. For two years I'd held on to the thought that he was out there forging a trail on his grand quest for truth and that one day he might return to tell me all about it. But now I knew there was no magic or mystery left in the world, just crazy men with vivid delusions.

The next week passed by me in a haze. I had lost all hope of life ever getting any better, convinced that this pitiful existence was all I could ever achieve. Once again I felt like I was trapped in a maze, depression drawing me ever closer to the darkness at its centre. I remember going away for a few days up to see my sister who was studying at Glasgow University. It was something I used to do quite often; a break away where I could forget my troubles and live the student life I so envied her, even if it was only for a short time.

Upon returning home I was confronted by my mum with a look on her face that instantly told me I had done something wrong and should probably dive for cover. Sure enough she proceeded to inform me, in a way that made me feel about 8 years old again, that whilst I had been away two very official looking men had shown up at the door looking for me and asking questions about any strange mail I might have received. Shocked by this, I told her that this wasn't the first time they had appeared and that I truly had no idea why they were after me. She must have been able to read the honesty in my face as her expression began to soften and became more a look of concern.

I asked what she had told them and she described how, when they would not tell her what this was all about or even who they were, she promptly ejected them from our property. I could picture the scene in my head and was unable to stifle the need to laugh which seemed to break the mood slightly. But this was no laughing matter. What did these men want and why where they asking about my mail?

All of a sudden it clicked in my mind...Archer's letter! I remembered that, in angry disappointment at the contents of Archer's cryptic letter, I had shoved it back into the envelope and cast it into a draw. With this in mind I rushed to retrieve it in the hope that the answer to all my questions still lay hidden inside. I carefully removed the letter, this time feeling a weight to the envelope that I had not noticed before. I gently up ended it over my palm and into my hand dropped a large, yet deceptively light weight, pendant attached to a leather thong. It was a round metal disc comprised of two circles one inside the other. The inner circle contained what looked to be some sort of fire symbol surrounded by the outer ring containing eight strange images. On the very edge was a kind of writing I had never seen before followed by the words; *"Om Mani Padme Hum."*

The Amulet[iii]

My excitement at this discovery soon ebbed when I realised that it made no more sense to me than the letter had. I read the letter again; something still bothered me about the way it had been written.

'Okay,' I thought to myself, *'just assuming for a minute Archer isn't crazy, what could the letter mean?'*

As I re-read, it one thing that stood out to me was the fact that, apart from the very beginning, at no point did he refer to himself as I. If he wasn't crazy when he wrote it then he must have known what he was doing. What if he was trying to tell me something?

'Maybe there is a code buried amongst the words,' I thought, before realising how stupid it sounded.

This wasn't some spy novel; people in real life didn't write coded letters. But just then, something caught my eye. I kept being drawn to the line 'read this letter a few times and you will understand its capital meaning'. It didn't make any sense. How can something have a "capital meaning" Then, in a strange moment, like my eyes were adjusting to a new level of light I saw it, I saw the connection. Why had Archer only once referred to himself as I? Because he was using capital lettered words to send me a message.

Using this cipher I excitedly read through the letter again and picked out all the words that started with a capital letter, writing them down in sequence on a piece of paper. I couldn't believe what was happening; the words where forming a message. When I finished I sat back, took a few deep breaths to calm my anticipation and then began to read;

My Friend I Must Ask Your Help You Are In Great Danger Time Is Short A Friend Is Waiting For You Where The King Of Our Meeting Once Besieged Angels Take That Step Now My Young Friend See The Rise Of The Sun

I was hit by a wave of ambivalence; uncontrollable excitement and undeniable confusion. Whilst this proved Archer was not crazy, I still had no clue as to what he was saying. The man definitely had a passion for being cryptic and vague. What I did know now however, was that whatever information this message held had to be important. If he felt that I would be in danger and that time was short then I needed to unlock this cryptic clue as quickly as I could. My mind soon grew tired though of staring at words which seemed reluctant to give up their secrets. I knew I needed to take a break and clear my head, so I got up and walked away. This message was beyond my ability to decipher alone, so I decided to round up some help and arranged to meet some friends at a pub in town. The only problem was that until this time I had told no one about meeting Archer or about receiving this letter. This made me apprehensive about how they were going to react to the story I was about to tell them. I remember the feeling as I walked through the doorway of the pub; it was a feeling of dread.

I found myself constantly looking over my shoulder. The thought of those two suits trying to find me now seemed all the more sinister after discovering Archer's warning. Moving up to the bar, I ordered myself a drink in an attempt to settle my nerves before making my way to a table away from the main activity of the pub. I was the first one to arrive and, as I waited anxiously for my friends, I eased my mind by convincing myself that of all the places I could be this was probably the safest. It was too public a place full of people I knew for anyone to try anything.

One by one my friends began to appear, blissfully unaware of the incredulous story I was about to tell. Catching up with each of them, I waited till all had arrived before divulging the meaning behind our gathering. Over the next hour I recited the whole story from meeting Archer right up to being sat there in the pub with them, watching their faces turn from expressions of amusement to disbelief as I did. Some seemed to have a hard time believing the truth in my words whilst others must have at first thought this was another one of my sarcastic satires, which in all fairness I was well known for. But when no punch line came, no daft joke at the end of it all, I got the feeling that almost unanimously my friends became concerned for my mental health.

The more I thought about it though, the more I understood their position. This was an insane tale that I myself still struggled to believe. Thankfully they soon began trying to rationalise the things I had said to convince each other that it all made sense, especially the stuff about the two strange men whom many of them had actually seen. The fact that they were doing this, despite the doubts I knew they must still of had, made me feel very humble and very grateful at being surrounded by such an incredible group of people.

'So! Now that you have convinced us that you've finally gone nuts, why don't you tell us the real reason we're all down here

41

on a school night?' came the voice of my old boss Andy being his usual diplomatic self.

Thankful of both the humour and the acceptance in his statement, I reached into my pocket and pulled out the letter. Giving them all a chance to read it, finding much amusement in the confused looks appearing across their faces, I eventually explained the cipher and showed them the message I had discovered. This seemed to validate my story for most of them as they all went quiet seemingly stunned by what they had read.

'I think I need to deliver the necklace to whoever this "Friend" is,' I said eventually, noticing as I did a slight, but ever so noticeable degree of condescension on their faces.

'Look, all I know is that whatever this is it must be important for this guy to have gone through all the trouble of sending it to me along with this cryptic message,' I added, waving the piece of paper it was written on. *'I've got a funny feeling that those two men that keep showing up looking for me are involved in this to somehow.'*

'What? You mean those two brick walls dressed in suits that came to work the other day? You think those guys are after you because of this letter?' the tone in Mel's voice suggested that there was still some doubt in her mind.

'Yes I do,' I replied. *'It's too much of a coincidence, the fact that they show up looking for me around the same time it arrived. Unless they were coming round wanting to pay my water bill that was delivered at the same time, what else would they be after?'*

'Why don't you just let them have it then, eh bud?' this came from Martin who had until then remained unusually quiet. *'Why are you getting so involved? It's not your problem is it?'*

'It is my problem though,' I stated defensively, *'Archer sent it to me and I told him that if he ever needed any help he had only to ask. Well now he's asked. Am I supposed to just let him down and back out of my promise, is that what you're saying?'*

Anger began to creep into my words, annoyed by the inability of my best mate to be supportive and understand how important this was to me.

'I have been a useless failure all my life and I'm sick of it. I'm sick of being a quitter, giving up at the first sign of things getting difficult. This is my chance to do something worthwhile, to keep a promise and make a difference. I'm not going to let it just pass by!'

'Jesus Christ mate! You spend one night talking to some nut job, receive some stupid letter from him two years later and all of a sudden you think your bloody Indiana Jones or something. So what, you gonna pack up now and go off in search of this "Friend" who is supposedly waiting for you, is that it?'

'Yes, that's exactly what I'm going to do, why is that so hard for you to believe? You're supposed to be my best friend.'

I wish I could say it was the alcohol that was causing the somewhat petulant and self-pitying tone in my words, but at that point I was still nursing my first pint.

'That's it! I've had enough of this shit, I'm outa here,' Martin said as he stood up and started to walk away, clearly frustrated with the situation, then stopped, turned around and added, *'Oh by the way, how do think you're gonna find this guy when all you have to go on is some stupid clue about a King, eh?'*

I desperately wished that I had an answer to this question, I always hated not being able to have the last say in an argument, but in truth he had a point. I had absolutely no idea how I was going to find this man and it must have shown on my face as, before he left, he said, obviously quite pleased with himself;

'Yeah, that's what I thought. Let me know when you've come to your senses. I'll see you later.'

Quick to anger and offended by his attitude, I wanted to follow him out and continue the argument.

'Oh, just ignore him hun, he's being a right moody sod. He probably just doesn't want to see his best mate leave that's all. I'll talk to him later'

As Mel said this, the realisation that he had been going through some really rough times made her words ring true. I suddenly felt bad for not having considered it before and my anger dissolved into a reluctant understanding. I told myself I would talk to him later and sort it out but, for now, I needed to concentrate on finding an answer to the question he had raised. Where did I need to go?

Day 1 - Penrith, UK
My Journey Begins

I didn't have to wait long for the answer to my question. Having shaken off Martin's heated exit, the rest of us returned to working on Archer's clues. At first the whole thing might as well have been written in Japanese for all the sense it made; the more I stared at the words the less they began to seem like words at all. Then out of the blue Andy piped up with a tone of revelation.

'Hang on! Look at this bit here,' he pointed to a part of the message, *'A friend is waiting for you where the King of our meeting once besieged angels.'*

'Yeah! What about it?' I asked, confused at the reason for his emphasis.

'This bit about the "King of our meeting", he's talking about Rheged.'

'Bloody hell guys, when did Sherlock Holmes get here?' I said with an excessive amount of sarcasm, *'That much Boss, I had managed to figure out myself. But, unless there's something you're not telling us about one of the directors, I'm pretty sure Rheged does not have a King. Therefore that revelation is about as useful as a chocolate fire guard isn't it?'*

'Oh ye of little faith,' he replied with a grin that suggested I was about to regret my tone, *'Obviously you never went to watch the History of Rheged movie down in the visitors centre did you? You see if you had you too would know, as I do, that back in the early Middle Ages this whole area belonged to the Kingdom of Rheged, hence the name. And what do Kingdoms have.....Kings.'*

He sat there with such a smug look on his face, enjoying the fact that he had been able to get one over on me. I couldn't help but laugh and grant him fair play for, whilst he had just made me look a fool, he had also given me the answer to the riddle. I couldn't believe that in all my time working there I had not realised the origin of the name. Forgetting about the rest of the riddle, excited by the breakthrough, I sat back in the chair and said;

'Well guys, you didn't let me down. Maybe now I can find out where it is I'm supposed to go.'

I turned to Liz and asked if it would be alright taking some last minute holidays if things worked out; as she was my supervisor I figured she would be able to swing it for me. The place did owe me some lieu days for all the extra shifts I'd been doing, and I would only be gone for a few days after all.

'Of course,' she replied enthusiastically, *'I know this is important to you. I'll just say that you've had a family emergency or something. Ooo! This is so exciting, it's like being part of a film or something'* she then said turning to Mel.

'I know, it is isn't it!' Mel replied, *'We'll make sure your shifts are covered, you just make sure you keep us informed of what's happening and let us know if there is anything else we can do to help.'*

Promising to do so, I thanked them for the understanding they had shown and the help they had given in solving part of the riddle. Bidding them a fond farewell I left the pub; desperate to get home, look up the King of Rheged and discover the destination behind the clue.

Fuelled by this new revelation, I practically sprinted home as question after question stampeded through my mind like a herd of wild horses. On stepping into the kitchen I was greeted by the open arms of my nan who had decided to come up and visit for a few days. Surprised and delighted, I realised that the clue was going to have to wait. She was there to spend some time with me and my mum and I couldn't let her down.

When eventually the two of them had gone to bed later that night, I allowed myself to once again focus on solving the riddle. Attempting to check the internet for the information I needed, I was eternally frustrated to find that the connection was down. I tried again and again to reboot it but nothing happened. With frustration rising, it got to the point where smacking the hell out of the computer seemed like a good idea....it really wasn't. Sat in the study, alone in the dark with what was now a broken computer, I started to think about what I was doing. Perhaps Martin was right. Maybe I really was being stupid in trying to pursue this thing. All too easily I accepted defeat once again and slunk off to bed.

45

The following morning my nan woke me up early, wanting us to go out for a walk up Barton Fell being that it was a nice day (albeit a little cloudy). Sitting just inside the Lake District, not far from Pooley Bridge, it was a favourite walk of hers and one that held great significance for the whole family. It was the place where my grandad's ashes had been released.

Up on top of the fell, where it flattens out into a bit of plateau, stand many small clusters of limestone; one of which bears the name "Tom" carved in remembrance. This may all seem irrelevant to my tale, but that walk actually played a significant part in its beginning.

I had always admired my grandad for his attitude towards life, his patience and kindness, wisdom and generosity. But most of all I was forever grateful for the way he'd always been there for me when my own father had not. One of my only real goals in life was to make him proud. Until that moment, however, I felt that I had never been able to achieve it. Of all my failures, this was the one that haunted me the most. Staring at his name that day, I could not hold back the tears that began to burn painful tracks down my face. Trying to hide it from my nan, I turned away and looked out over the majestic view right down Lake Ullswater. In that moment the sun broke free of the morning clouds behind me lighting up the whole valley. I turned back and saw my Granddad's stone shining a brilliant white, reflecting the sunlight that had fallen upon it. I remember feeling at the time that somehow my grandad had just sent me a message, for with that most convenient of cloud movements I suddenly saw part of Archer's riddle in a new light......Rise with the Sun. The Sun rises in the East. My destination was a place in the East where the King of Rheged had besieged Angels. My tears of sadness and regret dried up as a feeling of hope stirred within my chest. I knew how I could make my Granddad proud. I would find this place, journey there and maybe, just maybe, in doing so I would have the chance to write my name alongside those of Roerich and Archer in the story of the Chintamani Stone.

That afternoon I stopped by the visitors centre at work before heading in for my next shift. I figured I could catch the History of Rheged film before starting and just maybe unravel a little more of the riddle. I was dismayed however, to find that the film was no longer being shown and hadn't been for some time. Once again I felt like a door had been slammed shut in my face, but I

46

wasn't going to let it get me down this time. I knew, one way or another, I would find out the answers; even if I had to camp out in the public library for a week and read every book they had on the local history. I would no longer admit defeat without putting up a fight.

My shift that day passed far too slowly and I couldn't seem to focus on anything but the riddle; getting quite angry every time a customer came to be served breaking my concentration. Eventually 11 o'clock came and I got to go home to a sleeping household, sit in my chair and ponder the events of the last few days.

I woke up the next morning to the sound of my mum and nan talking in the kitchen, which confused me at first until I realised that I had fallen asleep in my chair. Stumbling through to them, feeling half dead, I was still too dazed to comprehend the things they were saying to me. This seemed to offer them no end of amusement.

'Hello! Is anyone in there? Wakey wakey,' came the sound of my mum's voice before she began to ever so kindly poke me, feeling the need to accompany each jab of her finger with the word, *'Poke.'*

'Aww, leave him alone he's only just woke up you cruel thing,' my nan said jokingly, coming to my rescue and batting my mum's hand away.

No matter what was going on in my life I could always rely on them to make me laugh. Just being around either of them made me feel safe; something I really miss now. I wish I'd made the most of it back when I had the chance.

When I eventually came too properly, they asked why I hadn't gone to bed. Not wanting to explain to them the truth of all that was happening, I said that I had been trying to figure out the answer to a quiz in work about Rheged's history and must have just fallen asleep.

'That's funny!' exclaimed my nan.

'What is?' I asked in reply.

'Well, talk about coincidence but last night on the T.V we watched a documentary on the history of Rheged. Didn't we Karen?'

'Yeah, there was bugger all else on so we thought we may as well see what it was like. It turned out to be quite interesting actually.'

I could have wasted time pondering the strangeness of such a coincidence, but I had more important things on my mind.

With a degree of caution, not wanting to give myself too eagerly to hope, nor risk giving away the real reason behind the question, I asked them if it had mentioned anything about a King of Rheged who had besieged Angels.

'*Angels?*' said mum with a laugh '*Son, don't you mean Angles?*'

Not being able to see what was so funny, I quite snappily replied '*No! Angels! Why would someone attack bloody angles for Christ's sake? Pissed off with a load of protractors was he?*' my voice filled with an unnecessary level of condescendence which I was soon to regret.

'*Not those kind of angles you wolly. Angles as in the people who settled here from Germany after the time of the Romans.*'

What a fool I had been. The letter hadn't said Angels, it had said Angles. Archer had not misspelt it, I had just been too historically ignorant to understand his meaning. The fact that I had "corrected" it to Angels in my translation of his secret message meant that it was no wonder nobody else had been able to understand it.

After they were both able to stop themselves from laughing, my nan continued with, '*King Urien of Rheged subjected Theodric of Bernicia and his army of 'ANGLES' to a three day siege on the island of Lindisfarne where they had been forced to retreat after a long battle.*'

'*Lindisfarne?*' I asked her, '*Where the hell is that then?*'

The tone in my voice easily gave away the embarrassment I felt at my earlier stupidity.

'*It's over on the east coast just up from Bamburgh, your grandad and I took you and your cousin there when you were kids. It's also known as Holy Island and is famous for the Lindisfarne Gospels which is a beautifully illustrated Latin copy of the Gospels of Matthew, Mark, Luke and John made sometime in the early 700's. During the second half of the 10th Century a monk named Aldred...*'

Her voice trailed off into the distance as my mind focused on one thing; the answer I had been searching for.

'*The East Coast,*' I said in a sigh of relief.

'*Yes, the East coast, that's what I said,*' my nan stated, obviously quite disgruntled that I had interrupted her history lesson.

I quickly saved myself by explaining that, thanks to the both of them, I now had the answer to the quiz and I was just really excited. They both seemed to buy this, saying they were glad they could help. Satisfied that I hadn't upset anyone, or gotten myself in trouble, I made the excuse of going to claim my victory and left.

In truth I really was excited. It all made sense now. The letter, the riddle, all of it pointed to Lindisfarne Island. I now knew my destination and set off into town to find out the cheapest way to get there. I was on my way.

Arriving at my local train station, I took my time studying the timetable on the wall outside the ticket office, trying to figure out which train I would need. There had been two options of travel to choose from, but in truth one wasn't really an option at all. Though more expensive, I had settled to go by train as the journey time was considerably shorter than if I had chosen the other option which was to go by bus.

It took some organising to ensure I picked the right train however. My nan had informed me that access to the island was only achievable at certain times of the day, due to having to cross a causeway that spent large portions of the day under the sea. Seeing as how I needed to make this trip on a budget, which meant relying on the fairly sparse bus service that ran from Berwick-upon-Tweed to Lindisfarne Island, I hadn't wanted to leave things to chance and possibly end up needing to spend an extra day waiting to make the crossing if I timed it wrong.

To cut a long, and fairly boring story short, it worked out that I would need to catch the 7:30am train from Penrith the following morning or wait another week. I knew the longer I waited the more chance it gave the two suits of catching up to me. I couldn't risk the letter or the necklace falling into their hands. My little adventure was about to begin.

On returning home, I was just in time to say farewell to my mum and nan as they had decided to treat themselves to a weekend away at a spa resort. This was great as it would mean I could get away and back before they returned and so avoid having to tell them where I was going.

After they'd left though, I thought it probably best that I leave them a note to say that I'd decided to go and visit a friend over in Newcastle, just in case my trip took longer than expected.

That evening I set about packing some things so that I wouldn't have to rush in the morning. Rooting out my old canvas duffle bag, and throwing in a couple changes of clothes, I then grabbed my leather satchel and filled it with the things I might need close at hand.

This included a mini First Aid kit, torch, notepad, pocket knife, binoculars, drinks and snacks along with a few other bits and bobs. Most important of all was a book for me to read on the way; I hated travelling on trains and reading would help keep me occupied.

With all that done, I spent the rest of the evening watching T.V. before turning in. With a busy day ahead of me, I knew I was going to need an early night.

Though I hadn't really done much that day, the stress of the last few had finally taken their toll and it wasn't long before I'd fallen into a deep sleep.

I don't often recall the dreams I have, but that night I did. I dreamt of many things, strange places and strange people that I had neither seen nor met before. They all seemed important in the dream, but I had no idea why.

At some point I awoke, disturbed by a noise. My room was still shrouded in darkness suggesting it was either very late or very early. Standing up to try and pin point where the noise was coming from, I remember feeling like someone was trying to talk to me. There was a voice somewhere in the distance, but I couldn't work out who it was or what they were saying. I just knew it was calling out to me. When I tried to concentrate on hearing it though, the sound just seemed to disappear. It was like trying to grab a wisp of smoke with your bare hands. Soon the noise disappeared altogether and was replaced by a ringing that built and built and built until it was like wailing siren in my head. It seemed to come from outside my window.

Wincing against the now painful sound, I threw my curtains open to see what was causing it. It was like looking into a dark wall of smoke. There was nothing out there at all. I leaned closer to the window, straining my eyes to see through the mist. There was nothing, no movement. Closer I leaned my face towards the glass, grabbing the torch from my bedside table as I did. Shining it out into the darkness seemed only to make things worse as the glare of the light reflecting off the window blinded me further.

The sound started to disappear. I lowered the torch and decided to just get back into bed. Something made me turn back and look out again though. Everything went quiet. Everything was still...then a crow flew into the window!

I woke with a start to the sound of my alarm telling me it was time to get up. Frantically fumbling for the off switch, desperate for the annoying noise to go away, I eventually managed to make it stop and slumped back onto my pillows, breathing a sigh of relief at the sudden peace that filled the room. It had just been a dream, but one so vivid I had not had in as long as I could remember. Unfortunately, it was to be the first of many.

I closed my eyes again hoping to drift back off, but I felt as if the bad dream was waiting in the dark to drag me back in. With my pulse only just starting to calm and my body still feeling quite clammy, I had to open my eyes so as not to let it.

Realising the futility of trying to get back to sleep, despite that only being the first of four alarms I'd set at 15 minute intervals to ensure I got up at 6am, I eventually managed to drag myself out of bed and headed for the shower. It had not been the best start to my day.

Twenty minutes later, feeling a little more refreshed and alert, I set about getting dressed and double checking that I'd packed everything I needed. There was still about two hours before my train would be arriving but, now that I was properly awake, I felt a nervous excitement building for the day ahead that would not let me rest.

Looking down at my bulging bags and the wide brimmed leather hat laying on top of them, I suddenly realised that Martin had been right; I really did think I was Indiana Jones setting off on some grand adventure. This brought a smile to my face, amused by the irony, but I began to regret having left things the way we had.

Almost on cue my phone rang and, without looking to see who it was, I answered.

'Hello?'

'Mate, you need to get out of the house now!' a familiar voice cracked through the earpiece.

'Martin? What the hell are you on about?' I asked, surprised to hear from him.

I knew he had been working the night shift, but it was a strange time to call when, were it any other day, I'd have still been asleep.

'No time to explain,' he insisted with a tone of distress, *'Let's just say that I'm sorry for how I acted the other day and I understand now how serious this all is. Now just trust me and get out!'*

'Oh really, so you believe me now, what's changed your mind all of a sudden ay? Thought I was just being stupid?' I don't really know why, but I was more interested in chewing to

death his miraculous change of heart than listening to what he was trying to tell me.

'For Christ's sake mate will you just shut up and do as I say for once?' there was an urgency in his voice that made me pay attention this time.

'Okay bud, just calm down and tell me what's going on,'

'Those two guys you were on about just showed up at work again and asked if you would be in today.'

'What!' I cried out, letting a stunned pause hang momentarily in the air, *'what did you tell them?'*

'Look mate I'm sorry, I was still a bit pissed off with you from the other day and,' he hesitated ominously, *'I told them that you weren't and that you wouldn't be in for a few days as you were going away.'*

'You WHAT?'

'I'm really sorry mate, I wasn't thinking. When I saw how the two of them looked at each other and then raced back to their car, I realised just how stupid I'd been. I think they might be heading your way as we speak.'

'Well that's bloody great! Thanks a lot mate! You should have asked them to give the knife a fucking twist for you when they got here while you were at it?' I hissed at him.

Dropping the phone away from my face as I darted to the side window to scan the road outside in case they'd already arrived, I heard Martin's voice growing ever louder and more desperate as he tried to get back my attention.

'What do you want?' I barked at him.

'Look, I've locked the place up and I'm on my way to your house as fast as I can. Get out of there and take the cut through round the back of the school. I'll meet you where it comes out onto the road just down from the North Lakes Hotel alright?'

My pulse began to race; beating through my ears like an executioners drum roll. This had all suddenly become far too real. Why did they want to find me so badly?

Hanging up the phone, I quickly finished packing; throwing Archer's research book, letter and necklace into my satchel before slinging both my bags over my shoulder and dashing downstairs.

As I slid into the kitchen to get my jacket and shoes, my heart stopped as I saw the lights of a car pull up outside. Peeking out of the front window into the gloom of the early morning, I saw it was a silver Mercedes with tinted windows. There was an ominous feeling about it; I knew it could only be them.

My phone rang again.

'Where the hell are you?' Martin's voice erupted in my ear, *'Please don't tell me you're still in the house?'*

'It's too late mate, it's too late! They're already here... I'm trapped!' I said with alarm, as one of the men got out of the car and began to walk down my drive.

Ducking down beneath the window to avoid being seen, I grieved at the realisation my journey was moments from failure before it had even the chance to begin.

'Can't you get out the back and go through your neighbour's garden?'

'I can't,' I answered through a breathless whisper, *'they're right outside, I'd never make it without being seen.'*

This fear was confirmed as the sound of footsteps at the side of the house was accompanied by a knocking on the front door suggesting that both of them were out there now.

'Shit!' he cursed before falling silent for a moment, *'Ah Sod it! You still with me Bud? On my signal you're gonna have to make a run for it.'*

'What signal?' I asked him.

He did not answer.

'Mate, what signal, what are you doing?' I repeated desperately.

'I'm making a diversion, you just be ready to move.'

'What kind of a diversion...Martin, what are you doing?'

The screeching of tyres and the high pitched whine of a turbo charged engine soon answered my question. Martin's car came racing down the road ... on a collision course with the Mercedes. In a moment where time seemed to slow to a crawl, I could feel the scene as if I was directing it for a big budget movie. Metal crumpled, twisting together in the heat and anger of the impact, as shattered glass was sent tinkling to the floor like musical rain; a symphony of destruction ignited in my imagination.

The reality of it all actually passed by in a blur though, as I peeked out of a window to see what had happened. Whilst Martin couldn't have reached more than forty miles an hour down our street, he'd hit the Mercedes with enough force to shunt it out into the middle of the road. For a time the whole world seemed to fall silent in shock and disbelief at the sudden violence that had erupted. The silence didn't last long though. Voices soon rose in anger all around as the two men went running back to their car. Shaken from my daze by this, I wasted little time in making the most of the diversion.

Gathering up my things again, I cautiously poked my head out of the side door and darted round into the back yard when I saw that no one was looking. Hopping into the neighbour's garden I ran around the side of his house and made a break for the alleyway Martin had mentioned. I looked back briefly at the scene, unsure as to what I should do next. There I saw my friend standing up to the two suits and arguing fault; like a Yorkshire Terrier before two Rottweiler's. If I didn't leave then all he'd done would have been for nothing. I knew this but felt terrible all the same. I didn't have to worry about him being outnumbered by these secretive men, in truth they were probably in more danger than he was should he have really lost his temper, but it just felt wrong to run away. What would happen to him when the men recognised him from the forecourt? What if they were with the police?

At that moment my ears caught the sound of approaching sirens off in the distance; likely someone on the street had seen the crash and called the police. Concerns for Martin then faded into concerns for myself; I had a job to do and could not risk being delayed. I realised then that I couldn't go back. The point of no return had passed and I had no choice now but to see this though to the end. The problem was...where did I go?

The suits knew where I lived, where I worked and probably even knew where all my friends lived too. Where could I go where they would not find me? My train didn't leave for another couple of hours and I couldn't risk just waiting at the station. Then it dawned on me. I did know of one place I could go where I would be safe; somewhere I knew they wouldn't look. The reasons why I knew this though filled me with guilt, but it was my only option. With that in mind I set off towards the edge of town, to the house of an old friend.

Staying hidden was the key. Being out in the open was too much of a risk in case the men had gotten away and were back on my trail. Every lurking shadow was an enemy and every corner hid a potential threat as I navigated my way around the outskirts of the town. Through gardens and over fences I went, utilising every back alley I could find to stay off the main pathways and roads.

Reaching the edge of town I was faced with prospect of having to cross quite an open expanse of land, devoid of the cover I had been using up until that point. Though feeling greatly exposed, I had no choice but to quickly make a run for it. My destination was not far now.

The house I was finally approaching belonged to one of my oldest and dearest friends from back in my (all too brief) university days. Where I had dropped out, amidst excuses of the course being too poorly run, she had stuck it out and was now studying at a P.H.D level. If I'm being completely honest with myself it was probably a degree of jealousy towards her over that which had prevented me from keeping in touch as much as I should have. A feeling made all the more poignant as I stood there about to knock on her door and ask for help.

When the door opened, a warm light from within poured out into the coldness of the morning and I was greeted by the happy, albeit somewhat tired and confused, face of my friend Donna. Surprised to see me, she spoke my name as if to make sure she wasn't seeing things.

'My God, what are you doing here?' she said with a yawn as she rubbed sleep from her eyes, *'It's so good to see you,'* she then said whilst giving me the warm hug of old friends reunited. After the morning I'd had it was a most welcome embrace.

Stepping through the doorway and following her into the living room, I procrastinated over telling her the reason for my visit as we began to catch up on each other's lives; highlights of the highs and lows that had occurred since we last spoke. Relaxing in the comfort of her company, I almost forgot about the events that had led me there until she asked;

'So, what brings you here at such an ungodly hour of the day?' it was then that I suddenly, and somewhat guiltily, realised that I'd likely woke her up.

'Not that I mind of course,' she quickly added to ease my conscience, *'though it just isn't like you to drop by unannounced?'*

I debated for a while just how much to tell her, not knowing if she would even believe me, nor wanting to risk getting her involved any more than I already had. In the end I just decided to tell her everything.

'Donna, I'm here because I need your help.'

Once again I found myself having to recount all that had befallen me since that fateful meeting with Archer, and once again I found myself being looked upon with scepticism and concern. But just as before I was soon left realising how valuable true friends really are.

'Only you could get into this kind of trouble from a simple conversation with someone,' she said eventually, with a light

hearted tone of acceptance, *'I mean how the chuffin hell do you manage it?'*

We looked at each other and then began to laugh.

'Does this mean you'll help me then?' I asked, hoping that she might give me a lift back into town to the train station.

'Of course, I will,' she replied with a warm smile, *'Isn't that what friends do?'*

The time to go came around all too soon and I found myself lacking the enthusiasm I had originally felt. It was supposed to be just a simple delivery job, but what could I be delivering that was worth this much fuss?

Reluctantly I dragged myself off the comfortable sofa and grabbed my things before heading out to her car. Donna had indeed agreed to drive me to the station, and for this I was very grateful. Having lingered a little too long in recounting my tale to her, I doubt I would have actually made it in time if she hadn't.

Neither of us talked for a while as we made our way down the winding country road back towards town. The calmness of a world still stirring in to life acted as a stark contrast to the chaos of little more than an hour earlier. There was a crispness to the morning air, as the sun sleepily dragged itself up over the mountains to a chorus of birds happy to see a new day. Perhaps it was because I knew I was leaving, or perhaps because a part of me now feared I may not come back, but for the first time in many years I truly appreciated just how beautiful the scenery was.

'So what are you going to do when you get there?' asked Donna breaking the silence.

'To be honest, I haven't really thought that far ahead,' I admitted, *'I have absolutely no idea how I'm going to find this guy without even a name or a description to go on. I guess I'll just have to play it by ear.'*

We drove into the town, passing through residential areas and on up to the station, when Donna suddenly told me to, *'Get Down!'*

'What? Why...?' I asked in confusion.

'Just do it will you,' she said pushing my head forward towards the floor, *'Shit! What kind of car did you say those guys where driving?'*

'A silver Mercedes with blacked out windows, why?' I asked quite stupidly.

'Well, I don't want to panic you ...'

'It's a bit bloody late for that,' I cut her off, *'if my head was any lower to the ground my arse would have to do all the talking ... Don't say anything!'* I quickly added seeing the glint in her eye as she was about to pounce on the obvious opening I'd just created.

'As I was saying, I don't want to panic you but a car exactly like that has just pulled out behind us and is following quite close.'

'Shit!! How the hell could they have found me so quickly? Who are these guys?' I said as panic did start to set in.

'What the hell am I going to do now?' I said more to myself than anyone else.

'Hold on I'm going to try something,' she said speeding up a bit.

Instantly, panic turned into fear for my life as I thought about what happened the last time someone "tried something" to get me away from these guys.

'What are you doing?' I asked as I felt the car slow down again and turn off the road, *'Where are we going? If they see us stop at the train station it will be the first place they look for me.'*

'Shhh! Just stay down and be quiet will you,' she replied sternly.

'What are you doing?' I repeated in a strained whisper as she pulled to a stop and got out of the car.

Completely ignoring me, she closed the door and started to walk in the direction of the DIY store whose car park I realised we were in. Desperate to see what was happening I started to look up but quickly ducked down again as I saw she was heading back.

'Ok, here's the plan,' she said getting back into the car, *'I've parked near to the front wall of the car park, made it look like I wanted to go into Wickes, which is of course shut, and have just seen the car go past. If you quickly bail out here, keep low and make your way along the wall you should be able to jump over into the train station car park without being seen.'*

'What about you? What are you going to do? I don't want you putting yourself in harm's way,' I said trying to quietly open the door and squeeze out as small a gap as possible.

'I'll be fine' she replied, trying not to laugh at the contorted mess I was getting myself into, *'I'm going to carry on the way they've just gone and go back home to try and throw them off. It*

will give you chance to get on that train, which will be arriving any minute now so you best get moving.'

I tried to think of something meaningful to say, to thank her for helping me, but in the end all I could muster was a simple, *'Thank You.'*

'Don't' mention it. You just take care of yourself and get back here soon and in one piece if possible,' she said with a warm smile before untangling my foot which had somehow gotten caught up in the seat belt. *'Now go on, get out of here and remember to stay low.'*

I closed the door and quickly pressed up against the small wall staying crouched down to conceal myself.

Waiting behind the wall until I could hear the train arriving at the platform, I took one last look around before jumping over and racing towards the station. Dashing down the steps and through the tunnel that lead to the north bound platform, I heard the beeping sound warning of the imminent closure of the train doors. Jumping up the last few steps, I hurtled out on the platform and launched myself through the doorway seconds before it slid shut behind me. I'd made it.

Catching my breath I let out a short laugh knowing that, unless they'd somehow gotten here first, I was about to leave my pursuers far behind.

Finding my seat and tucking in next to the window, I dropped my bag down next to me and I breathed a long sigh of relief. I had no idea of what lay ahead of me, or what obstacles I would face in finding this friend of Archers. All I knew, sat there on the speeding train watching the world merge into a blur out of the window, was that I was on my way.

Exploring the Darkness

And so began my part in this story. A long road lay before me upon which my beliefs would be shaken and my nerve tested many times. It would begin with my arrival on the island of Lindisfarne. Little did I know at the time of how my world would be turned upside down.

I must take a break. The emotions that have flooded my mind from remembering how I left my family and friends have drained me. Too painful are the thoughts of home when I know that I will likely never again return there.

I miss my friends. I miss my family. I wonder now if they can even imagine the things that have befallen me. Do they even miss me? I left never telling them the whole story. How long will it be before they realise I won't be coming back? I see their faces as clearly as if they were here with me, but the sound of their voices has begun to fade. I want to remember all the good times, but for now it is too hard.

It has dawned on me that, in all the time I have been in this cell, I have not yet explored beyond the circle of light provided by the single bulb that hangs above me. The echo of dripping water falling into a distant puddle with torturous repetition has convinced me that this room, hewn from natural rock, may extend greatly beyond the size of a mere prison cell. Covered with dust and grime the bulb casts a dull illumination, beyond which is a seemingly impenetrable blackness.

I have a bucket for a toilet that gets replaced once a day, as long as I leave it by the hatch at the bottom of the door. So far as I can tell that door is the only way in or out; solid and sturdy with no handle or visible hinges on this side. Along with the bulb these are the only features to my cell, all else is just cold bare rock. I do have a few personal items however. Either by some happy chance, or the incompetence of the men that threw

59

me down here, I still have my satchel containing a few small reminders of life before this hell. This journal and a hand full of pencils comprise the most useful items left to me.

I do not know what lies beyond the edge of the light and I feel this is something I must now rectify.

It will probably be a pointless exercise, as I doubt very much that I will find a hidden door leading out of this place, but I think it may help settle my mind. The shadows have begun to take on a sinister presence, watching me with sleepless eyes. The sheer loneliness of my days causes my imagination to play tricks on me. I go now to dispel these fears and to know my surroundings better. I pray that it will comfort my thoughts and allow me to once again focus on my task. I will not fear the dark. My story will continue...I must keep hope alive.

Well I'm back, and what a colossal waste of time that was. I strode out with purpose to prove to myself that the dark held nothing to fear, but I regret to say that I did not get very far.

Stupidly, I walked straight out into the void when sense should have told me to follow the wall. After only a few strides, I found myself engulfed by a suffocating blackness. Not just the mere absence of light, out there it is like the darkness has taken on an almost physical form that no light could penetrate.

Despite feeling a slight uncomfortable shiver I pushed on into the void with determination, swallowing back the frightened child within, resolute in my mission to find the boundaries of my cell. Alas, I foolishly negated to adjust my speed to suit the loss of sight as a usable sense. Either on an uneven stone or a large crack in the floor, I lost my footing and fell over, landing hard on my knees and elbows. Cursing the floor, the cell and just about everything else I could think of, I tried to get up only to be struck by a searing pain in one leg. Strenuously I tried to peer through the shadows to see what damage I'd done, but my eyes could see nothing more than a very murky silhouette.

With building frustration, feeding off the throbbing in my leg, I had to cut my little expedition short and quickly limp back towards the light. Initially I was frightened by the amount of blood that I found myself covered in, but thankfully a lot of it was from the superficial grazes sustained to my elbows and left leg. My right leg however, was a bit more serious. It seems I must have landed on a sharp edge as that knee was split almost to the bone. Perhaps that is an over-exaggeration, but either way it bloody hurt. Thankfully, of the few things left to me by my captors, one of them was my first aid kit which has enabled me to adequately treat my wounds that may have otherwise become infected.

I wish I could say that I did at least manage to dispel my fears of the surrounding dark. But somehow, that which lies out beyond the light still holds an oppressive presence towards me. I must attempt to break that fear again, but not now. Now I must allow time for my leg to heal before tackling anymore walking. After all what else do I have if not the time to wait? For now, I will return to my story and attempt to pick up where I left off.

Day 1 - Lindisfarne, UK
To the Holy Isle

The journey passed by surprisingly quickly. From Penrith I had to change at Carlisle for a train to Newcastle. The wait had been a little nerve-wracking, knowing that the suits could be only moments behind me if they'd discovered where I was going. The change at Newcastle was easier though and the closer I got to Berwick, the further the thought of my pursuers drifted away.

Arriving at my destination I stepped from the train onto an open aired platform with a thankful stretch of my aching limbs. A helpful ticket officer pointed me in the direction of the bus stop where I would need to wait for my journey onward to Lindisfarne. And wait there I did, happy enough in the certainty that I could not have been followed this far.

When the bus finally arrived, I boarded and found a seat on the back row, still determined to keep alert and on guard just in case. Staring out of the window as the vehicle set off, my mind drifted away taking in the scenery as we passed through Berwick to join the main road heading south. Time seemed to drag as endless fields of sheep fell away either side of me into the rolling hills off in the distance. The sky above was an incredible blend of white and blue ascending in ever deeper shades up unto the ceiling of the world, broken only by a small smattering of clouds. The further south we travelled, the more the hills began to flatten out. I felt like I could actually see the curvature of the Earth as the edge of the sea just became visible on the horizon.

Eventually, after travelling for what seemed like an age, I spotted a sign directing us to leave the main road in order to reach the Island of Lindisfarne. The road we turned on to was akin to the small country roads of back home, twisting and turning like the spine of a serpent through the fields.

Looking around I could see that the land had now become very flat, pointing to the fact that we were quickly approaching the coast. Away in the distance I could just make out a stretch of land that looked to be floating in thin air above the horizon. Obviously, as we got closer, the "thin air" became the sea and the land upon which my eyes now fell was finally that of Holy Island.

As the road slopped down towards the sea, we passed a sign that read:

DANGER
HOLY ISLAND CAUSEWAY
CONSULT TIDE TABLES FOR SAFE CROSSING TIMES
150 YARDS AHEAD

I noticed that the area around us seemed very wet; as if it had not long ago rained. The road was in quite a poor condition, looking as if it had been eroded away. Tall poles stuck out of the ground every couple of metres and grass quickly gave way to sand where small pools of trapped water lay. I soon realised that I was not witnessing the effects of a heavy rain, it was the sea. That whole area became swallowed by water every time the tide came in. In that moment I understood the importance of that "Danger" sign as I looked ahead and saw just how long the road to the island was.

The truth of this became apparent at the sight of what looked to be a life guard's tower sitting above the road about halfway across. Raised up a good ten or twelve feet high on four concrete pillars, it gave a chilling indication of just how deep the sea would become. Deep enough to drown a man? Deep enough to wash away a car? Deep enough maybe to even overturn a bus?

The sand eventually gave way to marsh grass and soon after we reached dry land once more. The road continued on around the edge of the island towards the outline of a small settlement looming up ahead. There in a large car park on its outskirts came the end of my travels. Alighting from the bus I shouldered my bags and, taking in a lung full of fresh salty air, I set off for the village of Lindisfarne to find Archers friend. Thoughts of how I was going to accomplish this, having no clue as to the identity of this person, were put to the back of my mind. For in that instant, brief as it may have been, I was swelled by a feeling of triumph. Despite the obstacles I had faced, I had finally made it to the place where Prince Urien of Rheged had besieged ANGLES.

Having arrived on the island at around 1pm, I spent the afternoon acquainting myself with the area. Following nothing but my feet I investigated the local shops, explored the impressive castle and walked among the ruins of the priory that still stood proud. I even went into the visitors centre and took the tour which told of the islands history, from the monks that lived there to the arrival of the invading Vikings. But as the sun began to fall from the sky, taking with it the warmth of the day, I was still no closer to finding Archer's friend. The ridiculous futility of this errand was beginning to beat upon me.

As I wandered back through the village, a glance at my watch told me it was just after 7pm. Six hours I had spent searching yet found nothing. It wasn't really surprising, seeing as I'd had no clue as to this person's name, address, occupation or even their bloody shoe size, but it was deeply depressing. If I had not been able to find him in all that time, chances are I never would. I knew, for that day at least, there was little more I could do. It was time to find somewhere to eat, according to the rather grumpy noises my stomach was making. I also knew that I was going to have to find a place to sleep for the night. Being a popular tourist spot I just had to hope that all the B&B's where not already full.

No sooner had the thought crossed my mind than my eyes were drawn to the rather welcoming door of a pub called "The Ship Inn". I couldn't quite put my finger on it but somehow the place seemed familiar. I was quite positive that I had never been, seen it or even heard of it before, but there was definitely something about the place that pulled me in. Walking into the bar area, I was soothed by the warm atmosphere the room seemed to generate. With wood panelled walls adorned with artefacts of a seafarer's life, it gave the impression of a traditional sailing ship's interior; obviously befitting given its name. There were also a variety of photographs and paintings dotted about that seemed to portray a history of life on the island throughout the ages. One picture in particular caught my attention. It was a beautiful oil painting of a scene looking along a sandy beach towards the great castle. In the foreground was a weatherworn fishing boat complete with an old ships wheel propped up against it. Despite its immediate beauty, created by the arrangement of colours and the sense of a masterful hand guiding each brush stroke, there was something else in the picture itself; something about it that puzzled me.

Eventually I managed to pull myself away, the pain of hunger and need of a shower being more powerful than my desire to analyse the picture. I asked a lady behind the bar if they had any rooms available for the night. To my great relief it turned out that they'd just had a cancelation from some fool who had not checked the tide times and missed his chance to cross the causeway. His loss was most certainly my gain as I was given a key and shown to a cosy en-suite bedroom with a view looking out over a peaceful street. A hot shower, and a clean change of clothes later and I began to feel human once more; the grime of the long day having earlier seemed baked into my very pours. The next item on my list was the need to hunt down some food, for which I happily headed down to the dining area.

Later that evening I decided to retire to the bar and sample some of the local beers before turning in for the night. Without consciously realising, I sat down at a table facing the painting I'd been admiring earlier. Something still bugged me about it and I stared fixatedly for some time trying to put my finger on what it was. Then it clicked. The old ship's wheel!

I stood up and walked closer, suddenly noticing the extra detail contained within that one object. It was slightly sharper in contrast to the rest of the painting. Raising a finger to touch it, positive I could see a difference in the texture, I was startled by a voice from the corner of the room.

'Something wrong with the painting there lad?' it said in the unmistakable lilt of a Southern Irish accent.

Turning to face the owner of the voice, my eyes fell upon an older gentleman sat alone reading a newspaper.

'Erm...No. I mean Yes....Well I'm not really sure,' I stumbled in response, thrown briefly by the question, *'the wheel here just seems a bit odd. Out of place almost, if that makes sense? It looks like a ship's wheel and yet at the same time..doesn't...so....much.'*

I knew how daft it sounded as soon as the words had left my mouth but didn't know how else to describe it. Without looking up from his paper the old man just smiled and said;

'Tis a Dharma Wheel lad. That's why it looks different.'

'A Dharma Wheel?' I asked in confusion.

'Yes lad, it's an old Tibetan symbol full of hidden meaning. Well actually to be more precise that one there is the artists own take on the ancient symbol, with a few extra hidden meanings thrown in for good measure.'

The way he sat there talking to me, without physically acknowledging my presence, made him seem like the clichéd "wise old man". At least it would have were it not for the fact that ever since having a wise cracking geography teacher from

65

Southern Ireland, I found it hard to take anyone with that accent completely seriously.

'You see the way it's painted slightly different?' he continued, *'A finer brush stroke and a softer paint, giving the feeling that it exists both within the picture and yet separate from it at the same time?'*

I could see it. Now that he'd mentioned it, I could see how it stood out simply because it was painted differently. I was astonished by how easily my perception of it had changed just from being told what it was exactly that I could see. Turning back towards the old man, I asked him how it was he knew so much about the painting. For the first time since our conversation began, he actually looked up at me.

'Simple my lad,' he said as he folded up his paper, stood up from his chair and then moved towards me with an outstretched hand, *'I just happen to be the artist of this particular painting. Aidan Quinn's the name, friends call me Paddy, a pleasure to meet you'.*

It was a statement I hadn't at all been expecting. Able now to get a better look at him, with a tall gangly frame, mop of wild white hair and long shaggy beard, he seemed more like a weathered old seadog than a soft handed artist. Not that I had ever really met an artist before, or an old seadog for that matter, but I guess we all have preconceptions of how we expect certain people to look.

I quickly realised that an impolite amount of time had passed without me giving my name in return. This I immediately remedied whilst shaking his hand.

'You know, you're only the second person to ever notice that wheel in the two years since I painted it,' he said with an air of approval before asking where I was from and what had brought me to Lindisfarne.

I was about to reply to this when something the old man had said earlier twitched in my mind.

'I'm from...erm...I'm sorry, but what did you mean before when you said the wheel contained "hidden meanings"?' I asked in a slightly perplexed tone.

He looked at me with an amused interest before nodding his head towards the painting.

'Have another look at it and tell me what you see.'

Sceptically, feeling that I'd already seen all there was to see, I did as he asked and returned my focus once more to old wheel in the picture.

66

'Okay I see a wheel, from an old galleon or something, leant up against a small worn out fishing boat,' I answered quite matter-of-factly.

'Good. We've established you've got a pair of eyes and a sarcastic tongue,' he replied in the tone of a cantankerous old school teacher unimpressed by wit or cockiness, 'Now, look closer and tell me what you can really see. Don't just think of what the object is, think of what it's made up of.'

Confused slightly as to why I was in turn acting like a chastised student, I began to study the picture more sincerely; getting as close as possible without going cross-eyed. To my surprise I began to see clearly the finer details that formed the wheel.

'Whoa!' I exclaimed admiringly, 'how did you manage to paint in such minute detail?'

'Tell me what you see lad,' he repeated patiently.

'I can see four handles around the outside of the wheel each with a different pattern of three lines. It looks like...is that W...and an E...are they compass directions?' I said in disbelief.

'Very good lad, I'm impressed. They do indeed represent the four main points of the compass along with the four elements Wind, Earth, Water and Fire. They are depicted clockwise around the wheel by the arrangement of the three lines, two of which you correctly identified as looking like the letters E and W for east and west. What else can you see?'

Enthused by his praise I continued to look, spotting that there were eight spokes to the wheel each of which looked like a pawn from a chess board. He explained that these where representative of the eight teachings of Buddha. Then I saw what looked to me like a three bladed throwing star in the centre of the wheel. Paddy explained that it was called a Tomoe.

'A spiral of comma-like shapes emblematic of flames representing the Earth, Heavens and Humankind. It can also be linked to the image of the Chintamani Stone.'

I froze on the spot as a shiver shot down my spine.

'Did you just say the Chintamani Stone?' I asked cautiously to which he gave me a nod, 'How do you know of it?' I enquired quite petulantly.

'The same way you do lad. A mutual friend of ours once told its story to me.'

I was speechless. A million questions flew around my head like a swarm of butterflies, and my catching net seemed to have a hole in it. Eventually I managed to stutter out;

'Y-you mean...?'

'That's right lad, I'm talking about Archer. I'm the man you have been sent here to find,' he said gently, obviously able to see the state of shock I was in.

'How...Who...Where...What...?' the words just would not articulate themselves in my mouth.

'Oh come now lad, you think you were the only one he sent a letter to?' every sentence he spoke crashed against me like waves against a beach, 'He told me that a young friend of his would be coming to see me, someone who, if he had made it this far, would see things that others did not without even being fully aware of it. Remember I told you that you were only the second person to ever notice the wheel? Take a guess as to who was the first.'

After the shock subsided, Paddy invited me to join him at his table, promising to explain everything, and asked the bar tender for two cups of "Lindisfarne Mead".

'You have your own mead here?' I asked incredulously.

'The best in the world my boy,' he joyously proclaimed, 'favoured drink of the God's don't cha know. It is said that along with its sweet honey taste and intoxicating effect, this drink once carried the gift of immortality. Sadly this one here has only the power to give you an immortal head ache should you drink too much of it,' he said, winking at the waiter as he placed the drinks down onto the table.

Taking a tentative swig from my cup, made wary of its content by the pungent smell that seemed to stick to the back of my throat, I found myself pleasantly surprised by the smooth taste that washed over my tongue. Savouring his own drink, Paddy then brought us to the crux of the matter.

'Right then,' he began, 'I'm sure you have many questions, the most pressing of which will be "why exactly have you been sent to see me", am I right?'

'Well, I thought I was here to give you this necklace,' I said whilst producing said item from my pocket.

'Gosh now, ain't that a pretty thing,' he replied admiringly, donning a pair of wiry spectacles from his shirt pocket as he did. 'Best be popping it back into that bag of yours for now though ay,' he then added, 'you never know when unfriendly eyes might be about. Got to keep it safe my lad.'

'It's just a necklace,' I protested my confusion whilst doing as he asked, 'why would anyone else be interested in it?'

68

Of course I already suspected that there were people interested in it, I doubted the suits had chased me simply for the letter alone, but I didn't know why they were. From the look the man gave in response to this question, a quizzical eyebrow lifting his eyes up to peer at me from over the rim of his glasses, I was pretty sure that he did.

'First of all, that be no mere necklace lad, that there is an Amulet, and secondly it's only part of the reason for why you are here today.'

I didn't like the sound of that last part; it gave me a terrible sense of foreboding.

'You're here today to learn about the Stone and to discover what Archer came here to find,' he continued.

'But why, what has that got to do with me bringing you this necklace?' I interrupted.

'I told you it's an Amulet, and if you put a sock in your mouth for five minutes and give me a chance to talk I might actually be able to answer your bloody question,' he expressed in a mildly irritated tone before re-composing himself. *'Look, you can't get off the island till the morning so why not sit back in that comfy chair, enjoy your mead and listen to me as I tell you a tale the likes of which you will have never heard before?'*

Resigning myself to the truth in his words, and to the fact that if I didn't let him talk he would probably beat me to death with his mead cup, I relaxed into my chair and let him begin.

'This story dates right back to the ancient time of Babylon,' he said in a tone that suggested I should be amazed, *'and to the building of the Tower of Babel by King Nimrod somewhere around 2300BC.'*

'King Nimrod?' I chortled, unable to help myself, *'You can't be serious? There was actually somebody called "Nimrod"?'*

'Tis as true as I stand here today,' I decided against commenting on the fact that he was actually sat down at that point, *'where do you think they got the bloody insult from? Now are you going to let me tell this story or not?'*

I apologised for my attitude, realising that I was being rather disrespectful, and asked him to continue. I was genuinely quite intrigued as to where he was going to go with all this.

As the heat of the open fire seeped through my clothes and warmed me from the outside, and every cup of mead warmed me more and more from the inside, I felt myself slowly begin to unwind. For the first time since I had received that letter, I felt a comfort and safety that gave my mind freedom to wander off; visualizing the pictures Paddy painted as he returned to his story.

'According to the biblical account, the generations that survived the Great Flood came together as a united humanity, speaking a single language, and created the ancient city of Babylon. In time these people wanted for their city a tower so immense that it would have "its top in the heavens". Thus the Tower of Babel was created.'

'Why was it called the Tower of Babel?' I asked, *'surely it should have been the Tower of Babylon.'*

'That is actually a good question,' he said, seemingly quite impressed, *'but let's not get ahead of ourselves. Cause and affect my lad. The story will reveal all.'*

I found it slightly irritating that he couldn't just simply answer my question, but as long as he kept the mead flowing I resolved to allow him his theatrics.

'You see, the tower was not built for the worship and praise of Yahweh as you might expect, instead it was erected as a monument to the glory of man. "And they said, Go to, let us build us a city and a tower, whose top may reach unto heaven; and let us make us a name, lest we be scattered abroad upon the face of the whole earth." *Genesis 11:4.'*

'I'm sorry, can we just go back a sec, who is Yahweh?' I asked slightly confused.

'You must be joking, right?' he asked with genuine shock, *'Yahweh is the name of God. You know, the almighty, creator of Heaven and Earth, our lord and saviour. Did you fall asleep in Bible class or something?'*

'I'm sorry but I've never read the bible and I don't believe in the presence of an all-powerful "being in the sky",' I admitted, feeling quite affronted by his assumption that I should automatically know any of that religious rubbish. *'I've just never been able to wrap my head around the whole concept I'm afraid'*

'Oh I see, too good for God are we? You heathen little pup! This is exactly what's wrong with the world today. You young'uns have no respect for God or religion. You're just like King Nimrod,' he began to rant.

Seeing that I had obviously upset the old man, and knowing that regardless of his beliefs I was still going to need his help, I quickly tried to diffuse his growing anger.

'Whoa! Whoa! Calm down, I didn't mean to offend you,' I apologised. *'Look I'm sorry okay, I just have a hard time understanding that if God does exist why does he allow innocent*

people to suffer all over the world? Young children starving to death, people dying horrible deaths every day. If he's "all powerful" why does he not help them?'

Not much of an apology I know, if anything I realise that I had probably just made things worse, but he wasn't the only one with strong feelings on the subject.

'Hmm,' he looked at me ponderously, *'Alright then. While I don't agree with your lack of faith, I can see that you have at least thought about why you don't believe. This bodes well,'* he said as a large smile broke across his face, *'You haven't simply accepted that which you've been told by others, you have questioned the reasons. Blind faith can be just as dangerous as no faith at all. Anyway, let's get back to the story.'*

He motioned for the bar tender to bring over another round of drinks and I sat there feeling a slight sensation of déjà vu. Had he just been testing me the way Archer had when we met?

After the barman had refilled our cups, this time leaving the mead bottle with us at Paddy's request, we both took another drink before the story continued.

'It was Nimrod you see, a descendant of Noah himself he was, who made the people act in such an affront and contempt of God. He persuaded them that it was through their own strength and courage that they had been able to create a tower so magnificent, not their belief in God. He gradually changed the government into a tyranny, foreseeing no other way of breaking men from the fear of God than to make them dependent on his power. Angered by their blasphemy, God knew they must be punished. But seeing as the destruction of the sinners in the Flood had taught mankind nothing, he resolved instead to cause turmoil among them. He did this by muddling their common tongue and creating amongst them a diversity of languages in order that they should no longer be able to understand one another. Confusion and chaos followed with the formation of language groups, suspicious of what the others were saying, causing the united to become divided and humanity to become scattered throughout the Earth. We fear that which we do not understand.'

Though I doubted its truth, I thought this was a rather interesting explanation for the diversity of languages in the world.

'Do you know what the Hebrew word for confusion is my boy?' he asked, though I could tell it was a rhetorical question,

71

'Babel. That is the reason for the Towers name. Its building was the cause of the great confusion of mankind.'

'I always thought that the Bible was more a collection of moral lessons presented as stories to teach people, rather than historical accounts of ancient times,' I said trying to be as diplomatic as possible.

'Well yes and no. The bible does teach many moral lessons but, while its stories may have been slightly exaggerated over time, it still details true events. This is always the biggest problem we have when looking for truths in this kind of history. History is written by the victorious and the wealthy. Many stories become twisted over time. Especially when it comes to ancient histories because the languages they were written in no longer exist and, despite what the archaeologists tell you, we can never fully comprehend what is truth and what is fiction. This is something you need to bear in mind as you delve deeper into the story of the Chintamani Stone. Not all history is truth and not all myths are fiction. Often it is easy to become swept up in the more fanciful tales or just dismiss them out right depending on the openness of your mind. Just remember that to every story there is always a degree of truth.'

My head began to swim. Was I meant to believe what he was telling me or question it, analyse it or accept it? One thing I did know was that I was going to need a lot more alcohol in order to wrap my head around all of this.

The bottle of mead was already half empty; I should have realised that was a bad sign. I excused myself to go the toilet, in need of the break more than anything else, but upon returning I noticed that Paddy was smiling to himself.

'I see that I'm beginning to confuse you lad so I will move on. I just want you to understand that the story I'm about to tell you, that brings us from the Tower of Babel to this very island, is based on historic facts tied together by historic myths and theories. You must not simply accept it because it seems to fit into reason. Always question and always seek to know more. This is simply a very quick summary of what you need to know to proceed.'

'This pub isn't going to contain enough alcohol,' I thought to myself.

'Okay. Sometime after the dispersal of the confused languages, a Scythian King called Fenius Farsaid came to Nimrod's Tower to study them. Scythia was a kingdom spanning from the 8th Century BC to the 2nd Century AD covering what is

now Kazakhstan, Southern Russia, Ukraine, Belarus...basically just a big-arse chunk of Eurasia. After 10 years of study Farsaid, along with his son Nel, apparently created a perfect language by taking the best pieces of all the confused tongues. There he created Goidelic, the forerunner to the Irish Gaelic language.'

I had some reservations about the idea of the Gaelic language being perfect, but I thought it best to stay quiet.

'Now here's where we have to fill in some gaps and use a bit of imagination,' he said with a glint in his eye. *'If you have studied Archer's research thoroughly then you will know that it is said the Chintamani Stone, or at least pieces of it, has been given to humanity at various points throughout our history to aid evolution and advancement,'* I nodded in acceptance of this statement as I took another swig of mead. *'That being so it's reasonably safe to believe that it was probably floating around somewhere in Babylonian times yes?'* Again to this I simply nodded, vaguely recalling having read something about it, *'Right! Now, what if it was present in the Tower? What if by its presence it somehow aided Fenius in his work? And, in perceiving this, what if he stole it?'*

A gentle chill danced down my spine, not so much because of what he said but more because of the way he said it. That and I think the mead was beginning to work its alcoholic magic making everything seem more radical.

'It is said that Fenius left Babylon and returned home around the time when the great tower fell...perhaps it fell because the stone was taken from it,' he continued, *'Sometime after this Farsaid's son Nel was invited to Egypt by the Pharaoh Nectanebo II; the last King of the 30th Egyptian Dynasty. There he was given the hand of Scota, the Pharaoh's daughter, in marriage. This was possibly an attempt to gain Scythian alliance against the Persians that threatened the Pharaoh's kingdom. Alas though, no alliance could prevent Egypt from falling to the Persian King Artaxerxes III. Nectanebo fled and disappeared into history as the last true Egyptian Pharaoh. Although there is an interesting theory about his fate involving Alexander the Great, but that is a tale for another time.'*

The wink he shot me was actually quite unsettling and I wasn't sure I really wanted to know what that theory was.

'Nel, Scota and their son Goídel Glas, who by the way is credited with perfecting Fenius's language into Gaelic, also fled in exile along with members of the Egyptian nobility. Their

73

decedents wandered the world for four hundred and forty years before eventually settling on the Iberian Peninsula.'

'This may seem a stupid question,' I asked, anticipating another attack on the level of my intelligence, with a slightly elongated pause suggesting that the alcohol was beginning to inhibit certain functions, *'but where exactly is the Iberian Peninsula? I have never heard of it.'*

'Not stupid at all lad,' he replied quite calmly, *'it encompasses what is now modern day Portugal, Spain, Andorra and Gibraltar,'* I found it quite strange that he chastised me for my lack of religious knowledge but not my geographical knowledge. *'There, Goídel's descendant Breogán founded a city called Brigantia, in the land of Galicia. At the edge of the land he had a tower built of such a grand height that his sons Ith and Bile could see a distant green shore from its top. The Isle of Destiny.'*

He paused, seemingly for dramatic effect, while taking a swig of his drink as if his last statement should mean something to me. Noticing the blank look on my face, he wiped a sleeve across his mouth to catch the drops of mead making a bid for freedom down the corridors of his bushy beard, and leaned towards me.

'Ireland lad. They were looking at Ireland.'

Feeling as if I should probably make some kind of input at that point I asked, *'Oh right...where exactly..is Brigantia meant to have been then? You know..in relation to modern day countries I mean?'*

I could feel my head becoming a little bit fuzzy and noticed that my speech was starting to slur. Looking down at the table I saw that we were already into our second large bottle of the mead. Yet despite this, I couldn't stop myself from finishing what was left in my cup with one gulp and pouring myself another. It really was addictive stuff.

'That's a bloody good question, I like the way you're thinking. "Was it in a place from where you would actually be able to see Ireland?" *that's what you're thinking ay?'* he said in a way that made me feel I had just done something clever. Although, with an alcohol induced haze starting to weaken the walls of concentration, I wasn't quite sure what that was. Still, I took a victory sip of my mead anyway as a reward for not pissing him off.

'Brigantia can most probably be identified with the city of A Coruña on the north-west tip of Spain,' he continued, *'A Roman*

lighthouse there known as the Tower of Hercules has been claimed to either be or be built on the site of Breogán's tower. As it is thought to be modelled after the Pharos Lighthouse of Alexandria, it's not too difficult to imagine that they are actually one and the same seeing as Breogán's ancestors were of Egyptian origin. I don't actually know though if it is at all possible to see Ireland from that tower, but a map will show you that, providing you were up high enough, the southern coast of Ireland would potentially be in you direct line of sight,' I made a mental note to dig out my pocket atlas later and see for myself if this was true. *'Anyway, the glimpse of that distant green land lured them to sail north to Ireland where they were ambushed by the Tuatha Dé Danann tribe and lost one of Breogán's sons in the ensuing battle. Decades later, Míl Espáine, Breogán's grandson, sought to take vengeance upon the Tuatha Dé Danann and invaded Ireland. According to legend he died in battle but his wife Scota, named after the founding mother, and his sons went on to conquer Ireland and settle there. Incidentally, it is believed that, as Scota became queen of the Gaels, it explains the origin of name Scoti. This name, applied by the Romans to Irish raiders, was later also given to the Irish invaders of Argyll and Caledonia which became known as Scotia and then Scotland, Land of the Gaels.'*

The more he revealed the more I sat forward in my chair, hanging off his every word. I was fascinated by how his story played out, like a giant dot-to-dot throughout history, linking people and places in ways I couldn't have imagined.

'And invade Scotland they did' he said whilst thumping a clenched hand down onto the table, making me and my mead jump out of our respective places.

'Nno!?' I gasped with drunken surprise, eyes wide and mouth agape, ignoring the liquid running off my arm.

'Yes! Upon the western coast of Scotland they formed the kingdom of Dál Riata with some territory on the northern coasts of Ireland, and with them they brought.........the Stone of Destiny.'

If we had been in a movie this would have been the moment when lightening would have cracked loudly outside and the pub doors would have been thrown open by a strong wind. Sadly this was no movie so nothing actually happened, yet in my mind I was flung through time and space almost picturing the story that had been relayed to me. Giant towers, great journeys and epic battles all played out in my mind's eye. Then again I suppose that's what nine large cups of, rather potent, mead finally going to your head can do to you.

I felt exhausted, as if I had taken this incredible journey myself, and slouching back into my chair I let out an exhalant *'Wow!'*

'Hold on a ssecond' I then added, my booze addled brain managing to just about grasp onto a metaphorical hand rail, *'What hexactely ish the Shtone hof Deshtiny?'*

'Please tell me that you're pulling my leg?' said Paddy in disbelief, *'Surely you must have heard of the Stone of Destiny before?'*

'Nope!' I replied dopily, looking into my cup searching for any remaining dregs.

'Well Mary bloody mother of da holy Christ! What the feck de they teach in the schools these days?' I can vaguely recall him saying as the drink began to reach my ears; muffling all sound into a hazy drone.

I remember then trying to stand up quickly with a sudden urge to go the toilet. As I did everything started to spin. My stomach began to churn. Legs went rubbery. I closed my eyes in an attempt to make it all stop and then...THUD!!

It all went quiet.

Day 2 - Lindisfarne, UK
Long Way from Home

I woke to a world in darkness; my eyes struggling to adjust feeling hazy and out of focus. I could see nothing of my surroundings save for a brilliant golden light shining through an archway away in the distance. As the featureless black gave way to the vague silhouettes of dark grey, I looked down and noticed that I was wearing strange clothes yet did not seem to care where they had come from. They were comfortable and warm and that was all that mattered. I began to walk forward towards the light, feeling that I would find safety there from a threat I could somehow sense but not yet see. An oppressive atmosphere surrounded me. There was not a wisp of wind I could perceive, yet a chill at the nape of my neck suggested that something was causing movement in the air behind me. Eyes were watching me. From where I could not say, but they were definitely there, watching, waiting. I dared not look behind me. There was no sound apart from what my own quickening breath made. It was the same silence you find in the wild when a predator is near. I was being hunted.

The walk quickly became a jog. I was desperate to reach the light, but no matter how fast I moved the archway never seemed to get any nearer. Panicked by this torturous illusion I soon found myself breaking into a wild sprint. I ran and I ran, my feet barely touching the ground as my body cut through the air like an arrow. Eventually the light started to grow in front of me, as if I was coming to the end of a dark tunnel. Closer and closer it came as my lungs screamed in agony for respite. I could almost feel the breath of my pursuer upon my skin keeping up with me. I knew it was close. I had to look back, had to see just who or what was behind me. It was a mistake.

As I turned my head, a nightmare on giant wings swooped out of the dark with a hideous screech and flash of talons. In that moment I stumbled and fell through the archway, instantly transported into a world of healing light.

Feeling a strange sense of euphoria, I found myself stood on soft ground enjoying the feeling of warm sunlight on my face; as if I had not done so for such a long time. My eyes began to adjust and I was just able to see the outline of a great city enveloped in the light with a grand tower reaching into the sky. Something was before me, something that I could sense was important. Squinting my eyes, trying to see beyond the brightness, I could almost see it.

Suddenly the earth shook. Caught off balance, I fell forward and struck my head against an invisible object. Strange images began appearing around me as out of the sky came a sound that attacked my ears and vibrated through my brain;

'Wake up my young friend! It is not yet time! You Must Wake UP!'

The words had echoed all around me in a voice that seemed somehow familiar. On its final command, I was ejected from the dream with that sudden abruptness of waking from a sensation of falling. It had just been another strange dream.

Slowly I opened heavy eyelids only to snap them quickly shut again in protest of the bright light that assaulted them. Shooting pains sent causing through my head caused me to let out an extremely pathetic groan.

'Well, well! Finally decided to return to the land of the living there did we lad?' I heard Paddy say in a tone far too happy for the way I was feeling.

'What the hell happened to me? I feel like I've been hit by a bus,' I said trying once again to open my eyes, much more carefully this time, and focus on my surroundings.

'What happened was you drank too freely of the Gods nectar. The Meads relaxing effect on the mind that accords you the ability to think clearly, comes at a great price should you overindulge in its intoxicating flavour,' he replied whilst trying to sound wise and mystical.

Leaning up onto my elbows and risking no more than a squint, I looked over in the direction of his voice and could just make out the shape of his body through blurry eyes. He was sat by a window, silhouetted by the bright light filtering into the room, and seemed to be arranging something onto a small table. It was only then that I realised where I was; my hotel room.

'What the bloody hell are you talking about?' I replied in the irritable tone of one who is suffering from a horrendous hangover and can't fully recall the last 8hrs of his life.

'For fecks sake lad, do I have to explain everything to you?' he snapped back, *'Unable to handle your drink, you passed out in the middle of the pub whilst trying to go for a piss. At that point the barman and I picked you up by your arms and legs and carried you up here to your room.'*

A wave of embarrassment washed over me at the thought of being in such a state.

'No sooner had we gotten you through the door,' he continued, *'you started to throw up on yourself so we quickly got you into the toilet where you spent an hour vomiting everything from the mead to what looked like the partially digested remains of a fish and chips supper. By the way, on that note I would just like to say that you really need to learn how to chew your food. Swallowing whole pieces is not good for your digestion lad,'* I cringed slightly at that last remark having been berated with the same advice by my sister on many occasions previous. *'Eventually when you stopped, I pulled you away from the toilet, which you seemed hell bent on hugging for the rest of the night, washed off your face and then put you to bed where ever since you have lain like the dead.'*

As I tried to take all this information in, the horror of having gotten into such a state that a stranger had to look after me all night made me want to just hide back under the covers. That feeling must have been evident on my face.

'Don't worry about it lad,' said Paddy with a short laugh, *'I've been in far worse states myself in my younger days. I remember one time in particular, my friends thought it would be funny to get me pissed and then tie me butt naked to the front of my girlfriend's car like a hood ornament. Worst of it was, when I woke up the next morning there was a crowd of Chinese tourists stood around me taking pictures, and it was a very cold morning if you catch my drift,'* laughing to himself he walked towards me offering a cup he had filled with, what I assumed was, water. *'Here drink this, it'll have ye feeling better in no time.'*

I dragged myself to a seated position, leaning my back against the headboard of the bed, and took the cup with both hands. My head was throbbing, my eyes pulsing and my whole body was shaking as I raised it to my lips and gulped at the liquid inside; desperate to quench the desert-like thirst burning in my mouth. Too late did the smell of it send warning signals to my brain indicating that it was not water contained within.

'Jesus Christ!' I exclaimed in shock after spraying out what little of the liquid I hadn't already swallowed, *'Are you trying to kill me? It's bloody Mead that. Why would you give me more of that evil stuff?'*

'Hair of the dog lad. Tis the best cure for a hangover,' he stated quite casually. *'Now stop your whining and just drink up.'*

Reluctantly I drank the rest of the Mead, feeling sick at first before my body seemed to remember how easy and pleasant it was to drink. A sweet spirit flavour with the smooth sensation of warm honey sliding down your throat combined with just the right amount of kick. I have to admit that there was truth to his words. Whilst it didn't quite cure my hangover, having another drink of it did make me feel surprisingly better. Less than half an hour after waking up and wanting to die, I found myself able to sit up in bed without the room spinning or feeling the need to throw up again. A slight headache and a stiff body where the only reminders of a rough night.

'Did you watch over me all night?' I asked him, knowing he must have and actually quite grateful of the fact.

'Well I couldn't really just leave you could I? You hadn't let me finish the story,' he replied with a cheeky grin. *'Besides, I didn't think it wise for you to be by yourself considering who is after you.'*

The weight of this last statement hit me like a brick wall.

'What did you just say?' I asked, almost choking on a mouth full of water.

'You heard me lad,' he replied.

I racked my brain trying to recall if I had ever mentioned my pursuers to him in our conversations; despite being positive I had not. How did he know there were people after me? More importantly though, how the hell could he know who they were when I didn't?

Rendered speechless by the questions colliding in my head, I just sat there in shock, somewhat fearful of a situation I couldn't really comprehend.

'Don't look so surprised lad. Do you really think I would have sat here all night simply twiddling my thumbs? I went through your things, looking for the letter I knew Archer must have sent you. I was curious as to what he would have told you.'

Shock turned quickly into aggrieved disbelief at the knowledge he'd felt it acceptable to go riffling through my bags whilst I lay unconscious.

'Now you can wipe that look off your face lad, before I do it for you,' he said sternly, 'I am no thief, nor do I appreciate the insinuation.'

'I didn't say anything,' I protested guiltily.

'Aye, but you were thinking it lad, just try telling me otherwise,' I sat for a moment feeling quite sheepish, not sure how to respond to his apparent ability to read minds. 'Would I have not already left if robbing you had been my intent?'

'That maybe so, but it still doesn't give you the right to go through my things,' I said in a rather sulky tone.

The logic of his words had eased my affront a little. But I still wasn't happy about it. His features softened and he regarded me with an understanding smile.

'How's your head feeling now?' he asked.

'It's fine thank you,' I replied in a supercilious manner, still wanting him to know that I was unhappy with his actions.

'Well then, why don't you come and join me over here, there's something I'd like to show you,' he said cheerfully, obviously ignoring my indignant attitude.

Able now to properly focus my eyes again, I noticed that the thing he had been arranging on the table was in fact a chess board. Intrigued I reached for my clothes, quickly dressed and made my way over to a seat opposite him that he pushed out with his foot.

'Do you play?' he asked gesturing towards the board.

Sitting myself down, I nodded in response. In truth it had been many years since I had last played properly. It seemed that the older I got, and the more tactically minded I became, the harder it was to find willing opponents. Many people find the game too boring and slow paced, completely missing the concept of having to out think your adversary and always be three or four moves ahead. Needless to say I was excited to finally have the chance to play again.

As we began I found that the familiar feel of the pieces in my hand recalled my memory to happier times. It was both relaxing and comforting to be able to focus my mind on a complex yet immediately solvable problem. There I could face my opponent, study him and watch for patterns in his movements. It becomes easy to predict and counter them when you know who they are.

'Why couldn't real life be more like chess?' I thought to myself.

Such thinking eventually brought me back to Paddy's earlier statement.

'What did you mean when you said it wasn't wise to leave me alone knowing who was after me,' I asked after we'd been playing for a while, 'and how did you find out who it was from Archer's letter? I've read that thing like twenty times or something and seen nothing like that.'

'What do you know about Chess lad?' he asked as if he had not heard my question.

'What? What the hell's that got to do with the price of fish?' I replied impatiently, 'You can't answer a question with another question, it's ridiculous.'

'And yet you have just done so yourself have you not?' he said, taking the wind out of my sails. 'You answer my question and in turn I will be able to answer yours.'

'For God's sake! Did you and Archer go to the same "Yoda's School of Talking in Riddles" or something? Why can't you people just talk normally and answer simple bloody questions?' I was exasperated, knowing that whilst I could out play him and stay one step ahead in Chess, the same could not be said of our conversations.

He responded to this by simply folding his arms and staring at me with grin that basically said "Your Move".

'Fine!' I expressed flippantly with flamboyant arm gestures, 'What do I know about Chess? Well I know how the pieces move, I know how to sacrifice a piece to gain the upper hand, and I know how to play my opponent to win the game.'

'That's not what I asked lad. I know you know how to play the game, that is evident in the fact that you've played me into defeating myself in less than half an hour,' he said whilst laying down his king to give me the win.

I took great pleasure in that moment; prematurely allowing myself to gain an air of smugness as I took a victory sip of my water.

'What I asked you,' he continued, 'was what do you Know about Chess?'

At this point I mentally gave up. Perhaps it was the ghost of my hangover still lingering, but talking to Paddy felt like banging my head against a wall.

'Once again, I have absolutely no idea what the hell you're talking about,' I expressed, far too tired to play this game any

82

longer, *'so why don't you please just tell me and put us both out of our misery.'*

'I'm talking about secret signs lad, symbols and meanings hidden all around us, often in unassuming everyday objects such as this here game of Chess. Take the board for example. You see just a simple black and white checkerboard when in fact the pattern itself is symbolic of the world we live in. Opposing forces, male and female, light and dark, positive and negative, good and evil,' the enthusiasm he expressed here was a little annoying, but it did pique my interest. *'Then there's the number of squares that make up the board. Eight rows of eight squares. Eight is the number of infinity and of completion, hence the sign for infinity being a figure of eight turned on its side, and what are eight eights?'*

'Sixty Four!' I practically shouted at him, unable to stop myself from butting in.

A fit of the giggles took hold of me, tickled by the memory of a private joke, as the startled look on Paddy's face turned into a quizzical one.

'Am I missing something lad? Something funny about the number is there?' he probed, struggling to hide the annoyance in his voice.

He had every right to be annoyed really as it looked for all intent and purpose like I was laughing at him. That, however, was not the case. Realising that I should explain the origin of my amusement I managed to re-compose myself.

'I'm sorry Paddy, I'm not laughing at you,' I said as he looked at me like I belonged in a lunatic asylum, *'it was just the way you said* "what are eight eights", *it reminded me of my grandad. You see when my cousin and I where boys he used to try and help us learn our times tables. Every week he would ask us a random multiplication, and every week we would get it wrong. Then one day he asked us* "What are eight eights?" *As we were stood there trying to work it out with our fingers and toes, my younger sister came walking past. She would have only been about four or five at the time and yet, without even breaking her stride, she answered* "Sixty Four Grandad" *in the most nonchalant manner you've ever seen,'* I couldn't help chuckling away to myself as I relived that moment. *'We were gobsmacked. There was no way she could have known the answer at her age, but my grandad never let us live it down after that. It wasn't until we got older that the truth of the matter came out. See, the* "random" *question he had been asking us hadn't been random*

83

at all. Every week he asked us the same one, "What are eight eights?", *but neither of us had been clever enough to realise it. My sister hadn't worked out the answer, she had simply remembered it parrot fashion from weeks of hearing it repeated. Even now the family still jokes about it. Anytime we do or say something clever all we get is* "Ah yes, but what are eight eights?" *The way you said it just then, it was just like he used to. I guess the memory just tickled me is all.'*

Paddy's expression softened once again upon hearing my reasoning, and he gave me a warm smile.

'Well lad, I'd say your grandad was a very wise man,' he said having sensed the tone of loss in my voice. *'Of all the numbers to teach you, Sixty Four is a great one for it is the number of cosmic unity. It's the magical number that was used in sacred geometry as the basis of ancient temple construction. Do you see now how all things are connected lad? Your grandad taught you this seemingly insignificant number and, if for no other reason, the seed he planted has come to fruition helping you to understand and open your mind to the possibility that you are destined to be here.'*

I thought he was taking a bit of a leap with that idea as there didn't seem to be that great a connection. However, I couldn't help being struck by the amazing coincidence of the matter. I mean, what are the chances really that my grandad would choose the same multiplication to repeatedly ask us that Paddy would use nearly twenty years later?

He went on to describe how the Chess board also represented the stability of the earth and its four corners, the directions of the compass and the four basic elements all symbolised by its square shape. Then to the idea that the pawn piece, arguably one of the most important pieces on the board when used properly, symbolises how even the most insignificant person can affect the outcome of the "greater game".

As if to further prove whatever point he was making, he then proudly called attention to how all these things where present in his painting. Eight spokes in the wheel and eight pawns from the chess board making sixty four, the number of cosmic unity. The directions and elements unified on a wheel of eternity. It all fitted and made a strange kind of sense. I was beginning to see what he meant. If you but widen your gaze, even a little, and truly open your eyes to what is around you, there are connections everywhere. Whether these connections are intentional clues to some grand cosmic plan or simply the misinterpretations of amazing, yet not all that hard to believe, coincidences was another matter entirely.

When he finished his lesson Paddy sat back in his chair. With elbows leaning on the arm rests and the index finger and thumb of each hand forming a cradle for his chin, he stared at me waiting for a reaction. For some reason I felt like he already knew what I was going to ask next, but that he wanted me to do so anyway. So ask I did.

'Okay, I sort of get the meaning behind all this, but what does it have to do with you knowing who is after me?'

'I told you that if you answered my question I would in turn be able to answer yours, yes? Well there is one more thing I have to tell you about the secrets of the Chess board. The checker design is copied upon the temple floors of a certain secret society, as a constant reminder of both the harmony and tension between opposites. A society whose name has, throughout history, been synonymous with the keeping and fierce protecting of many great secrets,' he paused to let his words sink in before leaning forward, *'I'm talking about the Freemasons lad!'*

If I had been a punch bag my stuffing would have been starting to burst out of the seams, so numerously had I been hit by unexpected revelations of late. This last one though, more so than any other, hit me like a Mike Tyson haymaker.

'What?' I cried out after a moment of stunned silence; an odd combination of fear and awe having rose up inside me.

'It's true lad, them be the men who've been chasing your tail. All the way to this very island no doubt.'

'Holly Shit! They're here? Where, Where? Please you've got to hide me,' I pleaded desperately as a fit of panic caused me to jump up and back myself into the corner of the room away from the window.

The more I thought about it the more frightened I became as, from what I knew of them, the Masons where a well organised and well-funded global network of people willing to do anything to protect their secrets. Their members ranged from world leaders to school teachers, able to operate outside of the law should they need to. Not the type of people you want to be on the wrong side of.

'It's alright lad, calm down! They're not here now,' said Paddy in a soothing tone, picking up my over tuned chair as he did, *'Come and sit yourself back down.'*

'How do you know that? You can't be sure! They could be anywhere! Why is this happening? What do they want from me? I can't do this! I knew they'd find me! I want to go home! I'm.. Not.. Meant to.. Be.. Here...'

Blind panic is probably the best way to describe my reaction. An attack of fear that forced all manner of rational thought from my mind and caused me to start hyperventilating.

'Whoa, whoa lad! Take it easy. Sit yourself down. You're OKAY, just breath. In...and out...In...and out, that's it now, you're alright.'

Moving surprisingly quickly for an old man he had grabbed my shoulders and sat me down on the bed, the calmness in his voice helping me to control my breathing again.

'I apologise, didn't mean to frighten you like that lad! I'm guessing from your reaction you've already had some kind of contact with them, yes? I think it's time you told me Your story.'

I nodded in agreement and, slowly regaining my composure, told him everything that had happened since opening Archer's letter.

'Then it is as Archer feared,' Paddy said once I'd finished my recounting, *'He told me in his last letter that he felt he was being watched and that things had become too dangerous. He planned to hide his work to prevent it from falling into the wrong hands. At the time he wasn't sure exactly who was after him but must have later discovered their identity as he encoded it into your letter.'*

Walking back over to the table, he returned holding out Archer's letter towards me.

'Hold On! What do you mean he encoded it into my letter? Where exactly did you see that? There is no mention of the Masons! Not even a hint in the code I deciphered!' I said whilst snatching it from him in disbelief.

'That is because the clue was not in the code you deciphered. Archer is a very clever man, he had many messages to give you. You found the first by yourself, were unknowingly influenced by the second and now know the last. He knew that should the time come when he had to send you the amulet, you would be in need of my help.'

'Wait! What second message? How was I "unknowingly influenced" by something I did not see?' I said, becoming ever more irritated.

'How is it, do you think, that you ended up coming to the exact pub where I drink?'

'Simple, I was tired and hungry and this place looked inviting.'

'Come now lad, we both know there was more to it than that. Did you not feel somehow drawn to the place? Did you not feel a sense of familiarity that you couldn't place?'

There was no use in trying to lie to him, the look of consternation on my face betrayed the truth of what he already seemed to know.

'Have another read of that letter now and see if you can't find the hidden message that led you here,' he said with a compassionate nod.

I did so apprehensively, feeling under pressure to succeed least I disappoint the faith he seemed to have in me. As I read the letter once more, I did get the feeling that there was something obvious staring me in the face.

'What is it?' I thought to myself.

Reading it though again more carefully I finally saw it, sat as clear as day about half way down the page hidden in the following passage;

~made me feel like royalty. The King himself gets no grander a welcome, simply for a few wisdoms shared with them, **feelings** of <u>passing a ship inn</u> the night fill me with a desire to <u>stop and rest</u>. *Of all the places my eyes have seen, the sun sets here are the most astounding. Our lives are so~*

Highlighted ever so slightly, in a bolder pen stroke, where the words I have here underlined.

"Passing a Ship Inn stop and rest", that was the second secret message. I guess it must have acted as some kind of subliminal message when I read it all that time ago and only triggered when at last I saw the Inn.

When I revealed my discovery, Paddy looked to be very pleased and commended me for my observation. I can't help but admit that this made me feel good. With each new discovery, I found myself astounded by the depth of the letter I had once believed to be nothing more than the ramblings of lunatic.

'What of the last message though?' I asked after a while, agitated by my inability to find it, *'Where is that one, I still can't see it?'*

'In many ways lad, this one is probably the simplest of the three to find, though the fact that it's buried within the first

message makes it also the most elusive. Run your eyes down the left hand side of the letter and tell me what you see.'

I did so excitedly, revelling in the feeling of "knowing things other people don't know" that came from cracking these codes.

'M','A','S','O','N','S'.

There, using capital letters from the first message, was a warning to whom it was that had pursued Archer and so now in turn did pursue me.

I stood up and walked back to the window, staring out into space as I tried to make sense of it all.

A few small drops of water trickled down before my eyes, in a series of invisible pathways, indicating that the weather outside was on the turn. Black clouds stretched menacingly above the rooftops opposite me, confirming that a heavy downpour was imminent.

'So what now?' I asked, eventually turning back towards Paddy, *'What do we do now and what does this "Amulet" have to do with it all........actually,* I paused, *'I have to ask. Just what is the difference between a necklace and an amulet? You seemed slightly peeved last night when I kept referring to it being the former.'*

'I was wondering if you were ever going to ask me that,' he replied with an intense look, *'Quite fortuitously though you have asked the question at a time when the answer will help explain that which you need to know,'* I looked at him with a great deal of puzzlement, not entirely sure that I'd understood what he'd just said. *'But first. We need some coffee,'* he added with his expression instantly shifting to a more jovial one.

He asked me to go down to the bar and retrieve the refreshments which I agreed to do; albeit rather reluctantly. I did not look forward to coming face to face with people who may have seen me in my intoxicated state the night before. Fortunately though, I encountered no one I recognised, nor did anyone mention anything about my passing out, to which I took great relief in.

The morning staff graciously provided me a tray with a pot of coffee and two cups asking if there was anything else they could get for me. Gratefully assuring them that there was not, I thanked them and made my way back to the room.

'Here we go,' I said placing the tray down onto the table, *'Now, what of the Amulet?'*

'All in good time lad, all in good time,' he said as I suppressed the desire to grind my teeth and roll my eyes, *'First I*

must finish the story we started last night in order for everything else to make sense.'

Sitting down, I readied myself for what I could tell would be another bum numbing history lesson. With that thought in mind, my eyes looked longingly for the bottle of mead Paddy must have had stashed away somewhere. Though a part of me would have screamed in protest of another hangover from hell, the thought of having to sit through the rest of Paddy's fact heavy story without any alcohol made the hangover seem the lesser of two evils. Alas, my eyes did not find the bottle and so I had simply to accept my fate.

'Okay, so where were we?' he began after a sip of his coffee, *'Ah yes, The Stone of Destiny. Known to many as the Coronation Stone, it has been used in the crowning ceremonies of Scottish and English monarchs for centuries. The earliest tales of its appearance into Scotland are found in the stories of St Columba. He was an Irish monk who introduced Christianity to the Picts of Scotland [liv] through his missionary activities during the latter half of the 6th Century AD. In 563 he was granted land on the island of Iona, off the west coast of Scotland, which became the centre of his evangelising mission. It was an area that the Irish Gaels had been colonizing for the previous couple of centuries. He soon took on the role of a diplomat amongst the native tribes, based on his reputation as a holy man, and is believed to have performed many miracles in his time there. Now you see, while it is not clear as to whether the Stone of Destiny was brought to Scotland by St Columba, or if it had been brought earlier with the invading Gaels, it is said that during his missionary work Columba carried the Stone with him using it as a travelling altar...What's wrong lad?'* he paused asking me about the uncertainty written across my face.

'Nothing really, it's just well... from all that I have learned about the Chintamani Stone, I had pictured in my head that it would be the size and shape of a large egg or small rugby ball perhaps. The idea of it being an altar just doesn't fit within my preconception of it,' I answered disappointedly.

'Well now, what's to say you are wrong? You are assuming that an altar must be a table like structure,' he said, taking pleasure in the confusion he caused me.

'I'm guessing that would be wrong then,' I said flippantly, *'and I suppose you are now going to tell me why?'*

'Not if you're going to take that attitude with me boy I won't' he replied disgruntled. *'I don't have to tell you anything if you're*

89

finding it all too boring. I just thought I'd be nice and explain it to you seeing as "surprisingly" you seem to know feck all about altars.'

His tone suggested that he was rapidly losing patience with me. Realising I couldn't risk him deciding to get up and leave, I apologised and blamed tiredness for my misplaced lack of interest.

Annoyingly vague (yet ridiculously detailed) our conversations may have been, but I dared not think of what I'd do without this new friend. Placated by this he, somewhat begrudgingly, returned to his explanation.

'An altar can be any structure used as a focal point for religious ceremonies or upon which offerings are made. While it is true that now days the term refers more to some kind of table, back in the times of travelling missionaries and monks it became customary to have an 'altaria portatilia' or portable altar. These where more commonly known in English as "altar stones". When travelling, a priest for example could take one of these stones with him and place it on an ordinary table converting it into a temporary altar for saying Mass. In fact, many Roman Catholic schools, unable to afford proper stone altars, would have a full-sized, decoratively carved wooden table that could be taken out and prepared for Mass by placing an altar stone in the "Mensa[v]" space. In those situations, it was actually the altar stone that was considered liturgically to be the altar,' he paused for breath and almost seemed to be relaxing having received no further interruptions from me. *'So you see, technically, an "Altar Stone" can be of any shape or size and therefore there is no reason for you to feel disillusioned by the idea.'*

This explanation did actually make me feel better about the idea of the Stone of Destiny and the Chintamani Stone being one and the same. Ironically though, it also made me feel like an idiot for having not wanted to originally hear it. I told myself that from that moment on I would have to keep a more open mind about everything and try to truly listen to the knowledge that Paddy was imparting upon me. I was beginning to get the feeling that if I didn't do this, I might just end up missing something important.

Day 2 - Lindisfarne, UK
Of Saints and Kings

Getting back to the main thread of his story, Paddy continued by first admitting the following.

'Now, here is where my knowledge gets a bit patchy. You see, the Stone of Destiny has also been known as the Lia Fáil. A stone that stood at the Inauguration mound on the Hill of Tara in Ireland and served as the Coronation Stone for its High Kings. The thing is, that stone still stands there to this day but it is a huge pillar of a thing. It is actually said to have been brought to Ireland by the Tuatha Dé Danann whom, you may remember from last night's part of the story, were the native people of Ireland conquered by Scota and the invading Gaels. Now, at some point in their history, the Tuatha Dé Danann apparently travelled to the Northern Isles, which is believed to probably be modern-day Norway. There they learned many skills and magic in the four cities of Fáilias, Gorias, Murias and Findias. Upon returning home, they brought with them a treasure from each; the four legendary treasures of Ireland. From the later three cities came the Claíomh Solais[lvi], the Spear of Lugh [lvii]and The Dagda's Cauldron[lviii], but they have no relevance in this story so I won't go in to any detail about them. It is the treasure from Fáilias that is the important one, the Lia Fáil (Stone of Fáil). The problem then is, how can we link the Stone of Destiny, brought by the Gaels, to the Lia Fáil of the Danann and then to the Altar Stone of St Columba?' he stopped to take a refreshing sip of coffee and for a horrible moment I thought he was actually expecting me to answer the question.

'So!' he began again to my relief, returning his cup the table, *'Here's where we have to use some more "What Ifs". What if, after the Gaels defeated the Danann, they kept some of the Danann traditions alive in order to aid an easier transition of power and change of religion for the remaining populous? Perhaps this would have included the revering of the Lia Fáil, turning it into an even greater symbol of power by somehow*

attaching to it the Stone of Destiny; using it from then on as a Coronation Stone. It would explain why the Lia Fáil became known as the Stone of Destiny and the idea has merit in that this type of thing has been done many times throughout history. Whenever an invader has wanted to gain the support of the people they are to rule, or convert them to a new religion, they often look to keeping that peoples beliefs and traditions alive. In doing so, they can then begin slowly integrating their own over time. Another bit of information to support my theory is that the Lia Fáil was thought to be magical. It is said that when the rightful High King of Ireland put his feet upon it, the stone would roar in joy, telling him of the years he would reign and the names of those who would succeed him. More importantly though, the stone was also credited with the power to rejuvenate the king and bless him with a long reign.'

'Why is that important?' I asked sheepishly, trying to avoid any more upsets.

'Patience lad, patience. All will be revealed soon,' he replied.

I think he enjoyed the fact that having to wait for the answer would irritate me. I guess he somehow knew that this time I would not challenge it.

'Now the last time the Stone was used to coronate a High King of Ireland was with Muirchertach mac Ercae who died in 534 AD. After that, it somehow ended up in the hands of St Columba who used it as his travelling altar. Its next use in a coronation was in 574 AD when St Columba used it to anoint and crown King Aedan of Dalriada. From that day on it became the coronation stone of all future Kings of Scotland. How it came to be in St Columba's possession, and why it was no longer used to coronate the Irish Kings, I do not know. But, what if for some reason the Stone of Destiny was separated from the Lia Fáil? What if it was decided that the stone was needed in Dalriada to help bring Christianity to the Picts and so given to St Columba to aid in his missionary work? It would then make sense why Columba eventually used it to coronate the Dalriada King would it not?'

I was beginning to enjoy these "What if" moments, despite all the other irritations his form of storytelling brought. I found it incredible the way he could thread, what was potentially, make believe into history in such a way that it was hard to imagine it not being the truth. The ideas he used to support his theories had me lapping them up.

'Thereafter,' he continued, 'the stone was then kept by St Columba and his monks on Iona, which became the traditional headquarters of the Scottish Celtic church. It was there mostly until sometime during the 9th Century when Viking raids caused them to move to the mainland. First to Dunkeld the stone went, then to Atholl, and finally to Scone. There the stone continued to be used in coronations, as a symbol of Scottish Kingship and became known as the Stone of Scone.'

I couldn't help laughing at the rhythmic nature of the name and, to my surprise, rather than tell me off for it, Paddy actually joined me.

'I know, I know. Tis a ridiculous name for sure. You couldn't make this stuff up.'

As we both took mouthfuls of coffee, refilling the rather small cups once again, I took a moment to look out of the window; distracted by the sound of a heavy tapping. The rain had finally managed to escape from its captive clouds and was making itself known to all. Each single drop came down with such force that they literally bounced back up a good few inches from whatever surface it hit, making it almost seem as though it were raining up.

'The seas will be rough today,' Paddy said following my line of sight. 'You can't tell so much from here but, out there in the open, that wind will be strong enough to stop you dead in your tracks. I hope my brother hasn't been daft enough to try and make a run in this.'

The last bit he stated with an almost absent mind; staring out the window as if trying to see the person he was talking about.

'What does your brother do?' I asked.

'He's a smuggler,' he stated, as if it was something quite normal.

'I beg your pardon?' I responded in delayed realisation after nodding for a couple of seconds before it sank in.

'He's a smuggler. Well technically he's a fisherman that does a bit of smuggling on the side. Only stuff like alcohol and tobacco in defiance of the ridiculous taxes this country puts on the things. Him and his crew bring it over from Europe through Denmark, which means he makes regular crossing over the North Sea. She can be a cruel stretch of water in a storm so she can. Whilst the fisherman in him knows not to risk the crossing on such days, the smuggler in him sometimes wins out seeing it as the perfect time to avoid unwanted attention. He's always been the black sheep of the family, but what can I say, he's still *my brother. Besides, he saves me a fortune in beer so I can't complain.'*

I wasn't quite sure what to say to this. I suppose I didn't really disagree with what the man did, the bastard taxman had always bled me dry enough so I had no problem with idea of him being diddled by anyone brave enough to risk it, but it just wasn't the type of thing one generally hears in polite conversation.

Paddy gave me little time however, to really ponder over his family revelation before jumping right back into the story.

'Now, an interesting tale comes if we briefly jump forward in the storyline to 1296 AD and the attempts to conquer Scotland by King Edward I of England. Invading at the head of his army, King Edward sacked Berwick, beat the Scots at Dunbar, and laid siege to Edinburgh Castle from where he stole the Scottish regalia. From there he moved onto Scone, intent on stealing the Stone of Destiny kept at Scone Abbey. So precious an object was it to the Scots, symbolic of their independence, that he knew it would be the final humiliation. What he found when he got there was a great lump of sandstone which, thinking it was the real thing, he removed and took back to Westminster Abbey. There he placed it under the throne of England as a Coronation Stone for the English monarchy and a potent symbol of his claim to lordship over Scotland. However, the stone Edward stole was not the real Stone of Destiny. It was a fake.'

'What do you mean "a fake"?' I prompted, feeling that little buzz of excitement you get when someone tells you of a compelling conspiracy story.

'I mean that the sandstone slab he left with was not the real Stone of Destiny,' Paddy replied simplistically.

'No, I get that part. What I mean is, how could Edward have been fobbed off with a fake? Did he not know what the real one looked like?'

'That is a very good question lad,' Paddy said, looking at me with a warm smile. *'You know, I've never actually looked at it like that before. I suppose he mustn't have. Perhaps he had simply been told of the sacred stone kept at the abbey, saw the sandstone slab being guarded when he got there and just accepted that it was the real thing? He was probably too arrogant to even consider the idea of being tricked.'*

'So you don't really know any of this for sure then?' I cautiously pried.

'Of course not lad,' he stated with an affronted matter-of-factness, *'we are talking about the hidden truths behind the versions of history people accept simply because that is what they are told happened. There is no definitive proof to any of this. There is only speculation. Speculation that fails to simply accept the gaping "plot holes", if you will, that pepper historical stories such as this one.'*

'What do you mean by "plot holes"?' I asked without really thinking.

'Alright, let's think shall we,' he began in a tone of rising irritation, *'how about the fact that if the coronation stone of the Scottish kings is the same one as brought by St Columba, it couldn't possibly be a large sandstone slab? Or the apparent disregard by historians as to the time it took Edward to reach Scone from Edinburgh?'*

'What do you mean?'

'His army crossed the Scottish border in mid-March 1296, but didn't reach Scone until June. Three months the guardians of the Stone had to anticipate Edward's arrival. Ample time for a switch to be made in order to protect the original relic, wouldn't you say?'

'Well, when you put it like that, I guess it does seem daft that they wouldn't have tried to protect it,' I admitted.

There fell a short silence between us. I believe Paddy was trying to regain his calm after having to, once again, justify his reasoning to me. I, on the other hand, was simply wondering how it could be that such versions of history had never been more widely accredited. Either it was conveniently ignored by those who wanted certain secrets kept, or there was strong evidence to discredit such theories. As I was neither a secret keeper nor a history scholar, I could not argue with the things that Paddy told me. It was intriguing though. I'd have probably paid more attention to my history lessons at school if they had offered up these alternative theories for us to ponder.

'Can you imagine,' Paddy eventually continued, trying to bring us back on track, *'the Great King Edward fobbed off with a large piece of heavy worthless sandstone. It would have been the ultimate "Up Yours" to the English, the Scots laughing as they watched em hump the thing all the way back home.'*

'What happened after that though,' I queried, *'what became of the real Stone?'*

'Well, once the English had left, it is said that the real stone was retrieved from its hiding place in the River Tay and secreted

95

away. Many rumours abound as to its fate. Some say it was given to Angus Og MacDonald, Lord of the Isles, by Sir Robert the Bruce. Others have suggested that the Bruce gave guardianship of the stone over to the Knights Templar and charged them with keeping its secret safe. Unsurprisingly though, no evidence has ever been brought forth to prove either of them. That is where the story of the real stone ends, replaced in history by that of the fake. After centuries of being sat on in London by many a fat royal English arse, the Stone of Scone finally found its way home to Scotland where it has resided safely in Edinburgh Castle since 1996.'

He sat back in his chair with an air of completion as I sat back in mine with a feeling of mental exhaustion.

'So there you have it, a basic line of history for the origin of the Stone of Destiny. There are of course other versions and other tales that can be told about it, but this is the most complete and believable version I have found.'

'Hold on! That can't be it,' I said as something jarred in my mind. *'You said, just before the bit about King Edward, that we had to "briefly jump forward in the storyline". What exactly did we jump over?'*

I asked this question feeling cheated out of a piece of the tale. It's funny though, I've only just realised the irony of trying to perpetuate the story I'd earlier groaned about listening too.

'Good lad, very good,' he replied with that cheeky grin, *'I was hoping you would ask that. I was simply testing to see whether or not you have paying attention. Okay so, what have we learnt thus far? We know that the Stone of Destiny was given to Nel by his father Fenius all those centuries ago, at least in our version of the tale anyway. We know that it was passed down through the generations until it eventually arrived in Scotland, and we know that it became the coronation stone onwards from the time of the early Dál Riata Gaels, right? Good,'* he said, all without any input from me. *'Now, what you want to know is what happened to the stone between it being used as a Coronation Stone by St Columba, in 574 AD, and it leaving Iona for Scone in eight hundred and something AD? That question can be answered with a story that brings us closer to home with the life and death of King Oswald of Northumbria, and it begins around 604 AD.'*

He paused for effect and I shifted my weight in the chair to keep my backside from going numb. I could tell there was much more to come.

'Oswald was both a king and a saint who united the kingdom of Northumbria and brought Christianity to its people; one credited with many posthumous miracles. But that's getting ahead of myself. Let us first go back and start with Oswald's father Æthelfrith. As a successful war-leader, Æthelfrith became the first to unite both the kingdoms of Bernicia and Deira; the area that is now Northumbria to you and me. Oswald's mother, Acha, was a member of the Deiran royal line who Æthelfrith apparently married as part of his consolidation of power. The boy who would be king was born soon after in or around the year 604. In 616, Æthelfrith was killed in battle by Raedwald of East Anglia at the River Idle. After this Acha's brother Edwin became king of Northumbria while Oswald and his brothers fled to the north in exile. The boy spent the remainder of his youth in the Scottish kingdom of Dál Riata, eventually reaching the island of Iona. There he and his brothers were kindly taken in by the Irish monks residing in the Christian monastery founded by St. Columba. These monks guarded them, taught them and eventually baptised them; washing away the wrongs of their pagan faith and cleansing them with the light of Christianity,' I bit my tongue. *'They taught young Oswald, the most serious of the princes, about the ways of Christianity as opposed to the dark heathenism of his father's kingdom and converted him to their faith. It was there on Iona that the young Oswald would fatedly meet, and befriend, a young Irish man studying to become a monk. His name was Aidan and that meeting was a moment of destiny. Through it was to come the conversion of the greater part of England to Christianity,'*

I had to choke back my opinion that this hadn't necessarily been a good thing. I feel I should explain that my prejudice against religion was not from a blindness to all the good that it can do, but more from a keen awareness of the evil that is all too often done in its name.

'Years later the brothers returned south to reclaim their home from their uncle. However, before they arrived, Cadwallon, the king of Gwynedd in alliance with the pagan Penda of Mercia, killed Edwin of Deira in battle at Hatfield Chase. As a result, Northumbria was split back into its constituent kingdoms of Bernicia and Deira.'

Sometimes, listening to Paddy really was like listening to an Audio history book. It baffled me how he could remember all the names and dates. Then again, I suppose I must be just as strange to be able to recount it all word for bloody word in this journal. I guess the mind can do marvellous things when it is being tasked with nothing else but remembering.

'Oswald's elder brother Eanfrith became king of Bernicia, but he too was killed a year later by Cadwallon after attempting to negotiate a peace. This provoked Oswald to take up arms, avenge his brother and reclaim his father's kingdom once and for all. Now, how's this for strange, the night before battle he apparently had a vision of St. Columba in which he was told:
"Be strong and act manfully. Behold, I will be with thee. This coming night go out from your camp into battle, for the Lord has granted me that at this time your foes shall be put to flight and Cadwallon your enemy shall be delivered into your hands and you shall return victorious after battle and reign happily."'

'It was probably just a piece of bad beef repeating on him,' a part of me really wanted to say sarcastically. To me, visions are just vivid dreams that the beholder puts too much relevance on. Fortunately I was able to suppress that desire and allowed Paddy to continue on uninterrupted.

'Oswald described his vision to his council and all agreed that they would be baptised and accept Christianity after the battle if it came true. The following morning at the head of a small army Oswald met Cadwallon in battle at Heavenfield, which is over near Hexham if you wanted to know. Before the battle, Oswald had a wooden cross erected to show that he fought as a Christian against a non-Christian foe. It is told of how he knelt down, holding the cross in position until enough earth had been thrown in the hole to make it stand firm. There he then prayed and asked his army to join him. In the battle that followed, the British were routed despite their superior numbers and Cadwallon was killed by Oswald, just as his vision had foretold.'

'Okay, so it was a very strong piece of beef,' I thought to myself.

'Following his victory, Oswald reunited Northumbria and is said to have held imperium for the eight years of his rule as the most powerful king in Britain, ordained by God as Emperor. On becoming king, Oswald chose Bamburgh, just away over there on the main land, as his main fortress. One of his most ardent wishes was to then convert all the people of his land to the ways of Christianity, just as he had been. And so he turned naturally to Iona beseeching them for a missionary to aid him. Thus the monks sent to him his old friend Aidan.'

He paused as if considering another train of thought.

'I find this quite amusing really,' he then said.

'Why?' I asked.

'Well the Britons had actually been Christian before the Irish ever were. Britain was part of the Roman Empire you see were Ireland was not. Some of the missionaries who first took the faith to Ireland were actually British; St Patrick the patron saint of Ireland for example. But, when the power of Rome declined, the English (who originally came from North Germany in case you didn't know) began to infiltrate into Britain and gradually turned it into England. These incoming settlers were pagans and the British accepted their heathen ways, to spite their former rulers. Renouncing all that the Romans had taught, you daft buggers voluntarily cast yourselves back into the dark ages,' he said with a scoff. *'And you say we Irish are idjets.'*

I had to agree with him there. Throwing away skills and technologies just because they were taught by people you didn't like can only be described as pig headed stupidity.

'Anyway, when Aidan arrived, along with 12 other monks, Oswald gave to him the island of Lindisfarne as his Episcopal see, the official seat of a bishop. Upon Lindisfarne, Aidan established an Irish-type monastery of wooden buildings where the monks lived a life of prayer and study and from where they would go out on mission. First they needed to learn the English language, a task in which Oswald helped them. They went out, using Aidan's only method as a missionary which was to walk the lanes, talk to all the people he met and interest them in the faith if he could. His monks visited and revisited the villages sowing the seeds which in time came to form many Christian communities. That period of the first monastery is referred to as the 'Golden Age' of Lindisfarne. In time the island became known for its skill in Christian art, of which the Lindisfarne Gospels are the most beautiful surviving example.'

I remembered these from the tour I took in the visitors centre and, while I was not a religious man and didn't care for the content of such books, I couldn't deny the incredible beauty of the pages so skilfully decorated.

'Many stories are told of King Oswald and Saint Aidan. The most famous of which recounts Oswald's generosity to the poor. One Easter, as the story goes, the pair where dining together when the King was informed that a crowd of poor people had gathered in the street outside begging alms. Upon hearing this, Oswald immediately had all the food from his table given to them, along with the wealth he carried and all the silver table

99

settings which he ordered broken up and distributed. Saint Aidan was so moved by the king's generosity that he grasped Oswald's right hand and exclaimed, "May this hand never perish" and it never did.'

'Yeah right, as if him just saying those words could have that effect,' I scoffed.

'Do not doubt so readily something that you do not know for sure,' Paddy warned me, *'Just because something is improbable in your understanding of the world, doesn't mean it is impossible.'*

I sat quietly and gave no further interruption as I thought over the possibilities of what he'd just said.

'That hand, which was severed in Oswald's last battle,' he continued, *'has indeed survived uncorrupted, and was enshrined as a relic in the Bamburgh church.*

I wanted to argue the impossible "improbability" of what he was suggesting, but I knew it wouldn't do any good. Either Paddy believed that what he said was actually true, or there was something he wasn't yet telling me.

'Alas,' then said with a sincere tone of sadness, *'as is the way of the world, the strong light that burns brightest burns all too briefly. In 642 AD the great king died at the age of 38, killed by the pagan king Penda of Mercia at the Battle of Maserfield. Oswald's body was hacked to pieces on the ground where he fell; his head and arms impaled on stakes in triumph. It is said that he ended his life in prayer, praying for the souls of his soldiers when he saw that he was about to die. "God have mercy on their souls" he said. Like all Anglo-Saxon kings Oswald was a warrior and, like other kings, he expected to die on the battlefield. And so indeed in the end he did. However, unlike other kings, Oswald had won for himself the reputation of being a saint and his death in battle was seen as a martyr's death. In the wake of this Oswald's younger brother Oswiu succeeded him in Bernicia and retrieved his remains in the year after, ordering them to be distributed throughout the land.'*

Rather a grim thing for your own brother to do, I thought.

'The spot where he died came to be associated with many miracles. So much so in fact that people took dirt from the site which led to a hole being dug as deep as a man's height. One story recalls that his right arm was taken by a bird, perhaps a raven which he was believed to have kept as a pet, to an ash tree giving it an ageless vigour. When the bird dropped the arm to the ground, a spring of fresh water emerged from that very spot.

Both the tree and the spring were subsequently associated with healing miracles. Tales of him even gained prominence in parts of continental Europe,' he said this in a way that suggested it was to hold some future relevance.

'Other notable tales told are that of a horseman who was riding near Heavenfield. His horse developed a medical problem and, as he rode it across the old battle field, it fell to the ground rolling around in pain. At one point it happened to roll over the spot where Oswald had died and was immediately cured. The horseman told his story at a nearby inn and, upon hearing it, the people there took a paralysed girl to the same spot where she too was cured. Another tale tells of a little boy who was cured of a fever simply by sitting at Oswald's tomb in Bardney.'

It felt like these stories could have gone on and on. I was very glad that they didn't.

'These are but a few of the miracle stories told of Oswald and the healing power of his relics,' Paddy said with an element of conclusion that suggested he'd seen the glaze of boredom slowly taking over my face. *'His head was interred along with the remains of St. Cuthbert of Lindisfarne, in 875AD, and shared the wanderings of his body until 1827. Cuthbert was a saint with whom Oswald became posthumously associated, though the two were not associated in life; Cuthbert becoming bishop of Lindisfarne more than forty years after Oswald's death. The arms of St. Oswald were enshrined in silver at the Northumbrian Royal Seat of Bamburgh, traditionally in the Church of St. Oswald. This no longer exists sadly, but appears to have stood on the site of the present Castle Chapel. His uncorrupted arm is said to have been stolen and taken to Peterborough Abbey later in the Middle Ages. There it was preserved as one of the monastery's most prized possessions. It's still there to this day,'* he paused, watching my face for the expression of disbelief he knew it would illicit, before adding, *'the chapel that is, nobody knows where the arm is now, probably destroyed when they realised it was a fake. But we'll come back to that later.'*

It registered too late what he'd just said. Before I could enquire what he had meant, the story had already moved on.

'Many other churches up and down the country, and all over the continent for that matter, have claimed to have some of his relics, and told of the miracles accomplished by them. The term "relics" included fragments of his wooden cross and earth taken from his grave, as well as parts of his limbs, his banner, ivory horn, ivory sceptre and parts of his mail-shirt. Seventy churches

101

were dedicated to him in England, including Hexham, Carlisle, Oswestry, Bardney, Paddlesworth, and Winwick. Archbishop Willibrord recounted tales of miracles worked in Germany by Oswald's relics and was recorded as having taken a number of them to Frisia himself. His foundation of Epternach in Luxemburg is even said to have once possessed a supposed head of St. Oswald. Similarly, a splendid octagonal German casket, dated around 1180 AD, survives at Hildesheim cathedral treasury which they claim encloses the head of St. Oswald.'

'Christ how many heads did this guy have?' I mused to myself. To me this just proved the reliability of such stories.

'He was remembered as one of England's national heroes. His bravery and military skill, his generosity and piety, together with a sacrificial death in battle for country and faith, combined an Anglo-Saxon hero with Christian saint. You know, it was commonly said that whoever fasted on his vigil, the 4th of August, would have foreknowledge of his own death.'

As sceptical as I was about such a thing, I made a mental note to try it out for myself.

'*What happened to Aidan?*' I asked, feeling that the poor man had been looked over in favour of his more famous friend.

'Well, after 16 years as bishop, Aidan died at Bamburgh in 651 AD. We do not know his age, but what we do know is that, whilst what he had achieved may not have been clear to him at death, subsequent history has shown the strong foundations and lasting success of his mission. He is celebrated right here on this very island in its history, with a statue in the ruins of the Priory and, in the greatest dedication of all, with this,' he reached down to his bag and pulled out a bottle of the Lindisfarne Mead and handed it to me to look at, '*his very own winery named after him that creates this heavenly drink.'* he finished in a jovial tone.

After straining my eyes to read the information printed on the back of the label, through the magnifying effect of the glass and the liquid, I handed him back the bottle; my stomach churning slightly at the mere sight of it.

'*Hang on a minute though? What does King Oswald have to do with the Stone of Destiny?*' I asked in a moment of realisation.

'*You know I'd clout you round the head if I thought you had any brains to shake up in there,*' was his immediate response, '*I guess I'm going to have to spell it out for you...Again. Right, the Stone came to Scotland with the Dál Riata Gaels yes? King Oswald sought refuge amongst the Dál Riata Gaels as a boy*

102

yes? Then the monks of Iona sent Aidan to him to help convert the English to Christianity did they not?' I nodded cautiously in agreement, expecting any minute for steam to come out of his ears in frustration, *'Yes, so now is it that difficult to imagine that they also sent to him the Stone, or at least a piece of it, as a gift?'*

I gave him a blank "rabbit-caught-in the-headlights" kind of look, not really sure what to say.

'Okay, you want another link then do you? Right, you remember Fenius Farsaid's son Nel, who married Scota the Pharaohs daughter yes?' I nodded, *'He had a **Vision** that his descendants would reach an island of emerald green and it is that vision that set them eventually on course for Ireland. In the Book of Genesis the stone is believed to be the very one used as a pillow by the Israelite patriarch Jacob, who subsequently had a **Vision** of god telling of his **destiny**. King Oswald had a **Vision** of St. Columba the night before the battle of Heavenfield, predicting his victory. St. Cuthbert, who I told you briefly about, began his life as a monk after having a **Vision** of the soul of St. Aidan being taken to heaven,'* he paused as if to let it all sink in. *'Can you not see the common factor here? **Visions**. They all had **Visions**. Visions of their **destiny**. The stone of **Destiny**, get it now?'*

I didn't know what he expected me to say, it all seemed a bit thin to me. A lot of if's, but's and maybe's. In all honesty, his tirades where beginning to wear at me to.

I bowed my head, rolled it round my neck to free up the stiffness that had begun to settle in and rubbed the ball of my palm into the centre of my forehead.

'This is all giving me a head ache. Why am I here Paddy, what does all this have to do with me?' I asked in exasperated annoyance, masked somewhat by the whiny tone in which the words came out.

Breathing a long sigh, like a jet of steam releasing the heat of his building anger, Paddy stood up, walked to the window and propped himself up against its ledge.

'Alright lad look, Archer came here researching all that I have just told you. He was searching for links to pieces of the Stone. Now, I'm not sure why but, he seemed certain that the answers he was looking for lay in Germany.'

'Germany? Why Germany?' I asked incredulously.

103

'It was something to do with King Oswald's head. Of all the stories told, he was fixated by that of Oswald's head being placed in the coffin of St. Cuthbert.'

'Why?'

'St. Cuthbert died on the Inner Farne Island and was buried here on Lindisfarne. People came to pray at the grave where more miracles of healing were claimed. To the monks this was a clear sign that Cuthbert was a saint in heaven and that they, as the saint's community, should declare this to the world. To Archer this just suggested that Cuthbert too had obtained a piece of the Stone, believing it to have healing properties hence all the miracles associated with those who possessed it. Perhaps Oswald had given it as a gift to Aiden as Bishop and then perhaps it was passed on respectively to Cuthbert when he eventually took on the same role? This is something I can only speculate on though, as I have seen no evidence to support it. However, there is an interesting story that surrounds Cuthbert's death; the same one that intrigued Archer. You see, back in those days, people felt it important when they prayed for help or healing to be as close as possible to a saint's relics. And so, if a community made relics available, that was equivalent to a declaration of sainthood. The monks of Lindisfarne determined to do this for Cuthbert. They decided to allow 11 years for his body to become a skeleton and then "elevate" his remains on the anniversary of this death on the 20th March 698. It is believed that it was during these years that the beautiful Lindisfarne Gospels where made, to be used for the first time at the great ceremony of the Elevation. The declaration of Cuthbert's sainthood was to be a day of joy and thanksgiving. It turned out also to be a day of surprise, for when they opened the coffin what they found was no skeleton but rather a complete and un-decayed body. To them, that was a sign of very great sainthood indeed.'

I'm not sure that "great sainthood" would have been the first thing that came to my mind upon witnessing such a scene.

'So the cult of St. Cuthbert began,' Paddy continued with a sigh. *'Pilgrims began to flock to the shrine and the ordinary life of the monastery continued for almost another century. Then, on the 8th June 793, the Vikings came and the monks were totally unprepared. Some were killed and some were taken away to be sold as slaves. Gold and silver was stolen and the monastery partly burned down. After that, they lived under constant threat*

104

and, gradually, the people began to leave this exposed little island.'

He said this with a degree of personal sadness that I couldn't quite understand. Why did he care so much about something that happened hundreds of years ago?

'The traditional date for the final abandonment of Lindisfarne is 875 AD. The body of St. Cuthbert, together with other relics and treasures that had survived the Viking attack, were carried by the monks and villagers onto the mainland. For over 100 years the coffin was transported from place to place for safety until finally it was settled at Durham. After the Norman Conquest in 1066, a Benedictine community replaced that of St Cuthbert's people and began to build the great Norman cathedral there. They proposed to honour the body of the saint with a new shrine immediately east of the new High Alter which was completed in 1104. At this point it seems, spurred on by doubts expressed by others over the truth of the un-decayed body, the Durham monks opened up the coffin and found that the body was indeed still uncorrupted. Throughout the Middle Ages, the coffin was placed in a beautiful shrine and visited by great numbers of pilgrims. But at the reformation, brought by King Henry VIII, the monastery was dissolved, the shrine dismantled and the coffin opened. Once again it seems that the body was still complete. It was then buried in a plain grave where it remained undisturbed until 1827 when the coffin was opened for the last time. Only that time, all that they found was a skeleton and the head of King Oswald was missing. Now, let's look at this timeline.'

At this point, Paddy reached for a pen and a piece of paper to scribble down the following;

687 AD - Cuthbert dies.

698 AD - Cuthbert's coffin is opened to find that his body has not decayed.

1104 AD - Cuthbert's Coffin was opened in Durham to find that his body was still un-decayed.

1180 AD - a German casket, which survives now at Hildesheim Cathedral treasury, is claimed to enclose the head of St. Oswald.

1827 AD - Cuthbert's coffin is opened for the last time and the body is found to have decayed leaving only a skeleton.

'So then,' he continued, *'somewhere in the time between 1104 and 1827 AD, Oswald's head must have been removed from Cuthbert's coffin. I'd say that it is no mere coincidence that*

105

the saint's body was found to be suddenly decayed after having been preserved for 417 years. The only thing noted to be missing from the coffin was the head...but where did it go? Odd, is it not, that a supposed head of Oswald appeared in Germany 76 years after the coffin of Cuthbert was last seen to contain it?'

Here came the "What If's" again.

'What if the stone, or at least a piece of it, lay within the coffin preserving the body? What if say it was inlayed into the crown worn by Oswald or some other piece of jewellery? And what if it was stolen? These where the questions that Archer asked and what he went to Germany in order to find out. Thus my lad, Germany must also be your next destination'.

'WHAT! Oh Shit!!'..."Thud".

It was rather unfortunate that at that precise moment I had been leaning back on my chair, rocking it onto its back legs to try and regain some life into my butt cheeks. The shock of his statement caused me to roll right over backwards and smack my head on the floor...again.

Indignantly picking myself back up, pushing away the hand he offered in aid, I stood up and looked at him.

'You can't be bloody serious?' I cried, *'I can't go to Germany, I have a life, a job, a family to get back to. I've only come away for a few days to bring this bloody necklace to you so that whoever the bastards are that are following me will stop and leave me alone. There is no way in hell I'm going to Germany. Why should I? This is not my problem. It's not my quest!'*

The words flew out of me in a rage, powered by the pain of the growing bump on my head.

'For the last bloody time, it's an AMULET,' he said, his own anger growing, *'and this IS your quest. What, did you just think that Archer had gone through all this trouble to send you the amulet along with a cryptic letter, that would be easy enough for a pea brain like you to decipher, simply so you could come all this was to deliver it to me? If he wanted Me to have it, wanted Me to follow his trail, he would have sent it to Me along with the half he already did. Why do you think I have exhausted my patience and given freely of my time to teach you the history of the Stone? Believe me it was not for the benefit of my own health lad. No, it was because Archer requested me to, for he saw something special in you that made him think you, of all bloody people, would have the balls to help him finish his work.'*

106

He left the statement to hang in the air as he regained some composure, his shoulders relaxing back into his chair as the granite look on his craggy face began to soften.

'He believed all of this was of great importance, and I believe he is right,' he continued after a deep breath, *'but I'm beginning to fear that he may have backed the wrong horse.....I dare you to prove me wrong.'*

The ferocious bonfire of passion in his words had thrown me off balance and put a damp cloth over my equivalent matchstick temper. I stood there feeling quite belittled but still defiant. I'd never accepted male authority very well, having growing up without a father; the bastard bailed on my mother before I was born. Growing up too fast, full of resentment for him, I felt duty bound to become the man of the house and look after my mum and my sister. This left me with no respect for men, especially those who tried to come into my life and tell me or my family what to do. This attitude intensified after my grandad died and I lost the only father figure I'd ever had. It got to a point where I would use any little excuse to pick an argument with a "dominant" male figure to prove that no teacher, no boss, no policeman and definitely no rivals to my territory would ever, could ever have control over me. I was no pack animal, I was a lone wolf and proud of it. Too proud in fact and too stubborn to realise that, whilst it was a good stance to take to a certain degree, the power of the hate that fuelled me in later years was doing so to a dangerous level. A hate that stemmed from one simple question... *'Why didn't my father want me?'*

Fortunately, there had been a few select men who had the wisdom to see how my pride could be used against me in order to get a desired reaction. My grandad had known, my old boss Andy had often seemed to know, and Paddy knew. In that provocation to "prove him wrong", he had thrown down a challenge that my pride would not easily allow me to back away from.

'Well, what's the point anyway?' I said, as forcefully as I could, in an attempt to regain a foot hold of dominance in this conversation, *'We don't know where Archer went, so how the hell could I follow him? He was following a trail he'd laid out in his journal. Without it, there is no way of knowing where he went.'*

With an almost imperceptible curl at the side of his mouth, Paddy reached once more into his bag. This time he pulled from it something that left me speechless.

'You mean this journal?'

There it was. The very same journal Archer had shown me all that time ago.

'How did you get this?' I asked insistently, snatching it from him and opening it to the first page to check it was real.

This is my story. This is my adventure. This is my Quest for Shambhala!

That flood of excitement I'd felt the first time I had read it returned again only stronger now as I saw, flicking through the pages, that he had added so much more. Details of places he had been, people he had met, histories, legends and rumours he had found. It was incredible, the trail was there from here to Denmark, Denmark to Germany, Germany to...it stopped.

'Hey!' I exclaimed, *'Where is the rest of the journal?'*

It had been torn right down the spine into at least two pieces ending where he was about to find some big revelation in Germany.

'Did You do this?' I said accusingly.

'Don't be stupid lad, this is how I received it. Archer felt like someone was after his work and so he separated his journal and sent each piece to a different person he had met upon his travels.

'What? Who?'

'Guardians intended to keep safe the secrets he discovered until you arrive to reunite them and solve the ultimate riddle. He sent me the first piece and gave me the wonderful job of trying to prepare you for what you might face along the way. He also sent me the other half of your Amulet and a small stash of money to keep you going. Know that it is likely, with each journal guardian, there will be a similar stash to help you fulfil his work.'

I looked at him searching for some clue as to when the cameras were going to appear and it be revealed that this was all just some stunt for a T.V. show about gullibility. To my dismay, there was nothing. The more I looked at him, the more I saw how serious he was. That didn't make it any easier to believe though.

'This is all some big joke right?' I said trying to convince myself more than anyone else, *'Things like this don't just happen to regular people. They just don't!'*

'No lad, it doesn't happen to regular people,' he let hang a dramatic pause, *'but it is happening to you. This is your chance*

to rise above the mediocrity of a "regular" life that you feel in your heart you weren't meant for; your chance to be a part of something great. This lad, this is your Destiny.'

He grabbed my hand at this point and thrust into it something that felt like my Amulet in size and shape. When I looked down I saw that, whilst it was *a* Amulet, it was not the one I remembered.

The Complete Amulet[ix]

This one was chunkier with only four symbols showing, compared to the eight on mine, through a bevelled face plate shaped something like a four pronged throwing star. It also had a blue stone set at its centre, through which I could see a familiar symbol.

'That's the sign of the Chintamani Stone there isn't it?' I said with a swell of excitement, recognising it from Archer's research.

'Indeed lad it is.'

'But what's happened to my Amulet? Where did this one come from?'

'You really don't listen do you?' he said more as a statement, *'Did I not just say that Archer had sent me the "Other Half" of the Amulet? This is the whole thing combined. Your piece is an Ashtamangala, my piece is a four flamed Tomoe, and the gemstone in the middle is a Topaz, your birthstone I believe'.*

So many questions buzzed round my head fighting for prominence that I had to take a second to order my thoughts and present them in order of least to most important.

'Okay. Firstly, what the hell is an Ashtamandala–'

'–Ashtamangala!' Paddy instantly corrected.

'Fine, "manGala", whatever! Secondly, where the hell did the gemstone come from, and lastly, but possibly most importantly, how the hell do you know what my birthstone is?' I said with my hands and arms becoming quite animated and a voice straining to remain calm.

'Good questions lad, analytical of everything, that's how you need to be,' the pseudo-patronising praise in his voice that appeared every now-and-again made me feel like a puppy that had just learned not to pee on the carpet.

'Translating from Ancient Sanskrit, Ashta-Mangala means literally "Eight-Auspicious" and refers to the eight auspicious symbols of Himalayan Buddhism. Each symbol represents an important Buddhist idea; the meanings of which are hidden within them.'

At this point he took the Amulet off me, twisted the back and the front in opposite directions and separated his piece from mine. He then proceeded to point to each of the eight symbols shown on my half and explain their meaning thusly;

The Symbols of the Amulet

The Lotus Flower

The Endless Knot

The Dharma Wheel

The Treasure Vase

The Two Golden Fish

The Victory Banner

The Conch Shell

The Parasol

The Parasol – Represents the sky, is a symbol of protection and a sign of expansion and learning.

The Two Golden Fish – A symbol of the eyes of the Buddha acting as a reminder to be fearless regardless of what life throws your way.

The Treasure Vase – Contains the spiritual treasures of good health, long life, good luck, wisdom and prosperity.

The Lotus Flower – Symbolises purity of mind, body, action and speech. Rising above the failings of attachment and desire as the flower rises above muddy water.

The Conch Shell – A reminder that you need to be open to the sound of Buddha's teachings and to always stay alert and aware.

The Endless Knot – Symbolises compassion and wisdom combined along with the need to unite spiritual and material matters.

The Victory Banner – Represents the triumph of the positive mind over negative obstacles.

The Dharma Wheel – Represents the teachings of the Buddha.

He then went on to point to the edge of the Amulet and say;

'The words round the edge here, written first in Sanskrit and then Tibetan, mean "Aum, to the Jewel in the Lotus, hum". *It's what's known as a mantra, a sacred phrase that when repeated over and over effects your spiritual vibration and unifies you with the greater cosmos. This particular one is THE most important and profound mantra in Tibetan Buddhism. It has many transliterations and meanings but is generally regarded as containing* "all the teachings of Buddha". *These six simple syllables have a deeper meaning that lies at the very heart of the faith, one known only to the worthy.'*

He sat back in his chair, shifting his weight restlessly from one side to the other before continuing on to answer my second question.

'Now, as for where the stone came from, that one's simple. Last night, when I was going over Archer's letters and the two half's of the Amulet, I noticed this pretty turquoise stone laid into the front of the research book he gave you. A grand little thing it is too, you can lose track of time just staring at it,' he said raising the stone up to his eye and then seeming to drift off.

'Erm, Paddy? You were saying?' I prompted him.

'Yes, right, anyway...where was I?' he said as if he had been lost in his own world, *'Ah Yes, the stone. Well you see, what*

113

makes an Amulet different from "normal" jewellery is that it holds magical significance that is particular to its wearer. This usually comes in the form of bringing good luck or averting evil. Now I have to admit that, as it was, the significance of this Amulet was beyond my grasp; I couldn't figure what importance it held, if indeed any. But then something dawned on me. Checking through your personal belongings,' he said with a sheepish look which I took to mean that he'd checked through my wallet, *'I discovered that your star sign must be Sagittarius. Am I correct?'*

'Yes it is, where is my wallet by the way?' I replied sarcastically.

'Don't worry, its back in your jacket pocket. I had to pick it up anyway as it had fallen out during our struggle to remove said jacket from you in your inebriated state.'

'Touché,' I thought to myself for him having turned the shame back on me.

'Anyway, I don't know if you know but, as a Sagittarius, your birthstone is Topaz, turquoise topaz. The very same kind of stone I gather this one to be,' he said offering it up to me in the palm of his hand, *'Granted, I'm no expert on these things but it's the only stone I know of that resembles that colour there. As I was looking at it, somehow it managed to become dislodged and fell from its mount. Picking it back up I noticed that, it seemed almost perfect in size and shape to sit in the inner circle of the Amulet.'*

'It just "fell" out then did it?' I said feigning suspicion, *'No "accidental persuasion" on your part perhaps?'*

'Alright, Alright! So I prised the damn thing out Okay. Are you happy now?' he replied, with equally feigned affront, *'I did it as a favour for you though. An Amulet needs a significant symbol, identifying the wearer to it, and birthstones are one of the best. The way it all fits together seems fated don't you think? I mean look,'* he said as he put all the pieces back together, *'damn near perfect. And how about this?'* he said pointing to the stone as it sat in its new home, *'Look what it does to the strange symbol in the centre of your piece.'*

Despite having noticed it before, it wasn't until then that I realised what had happened. What I originally thought to be a sort of fire symbol, had been somehow distorted or refracted by the presence of the clear gemstone. This came to form what I knew to be a symbol of the Chintamani Stone.

114

'But why does your piece cover up so much of mine leaving only these four symbols?' I asked eventually.

'Honestly lad, I couldn't tell you,' he replied quite dejectedly which surprised me, 'I've been racking my brain this whole time trying to figure that one out. Alas, this time, whatever clue or message Archer intended this to show, is far too clever for even I to figure out.'

I sat back down at the table staring intently at the Amulet, resetting my chair without even once taking my eyes of the stone. There was something there, something behind why those specific symbols where highlighted.

'I've Got It!!' I practically shouted after being lost in thought for a good ten minutes, 'It's you!'

'What the hell are you talking about lad?' Paddy replied, seemingly oblivious to the irony of the role reversal.

'It's you!' I repeated, 'Look, the Dharma Wheel! It's how I found you, staring at the wheel in your painting. Don't you see? This Amulet is the key to finding the other journal pieces.'

'What?' he responded, speechless for the first time since I'd met him.

As he came round to look over my shoulder, I revelled in the moment; the feeling of knowing something he didn't.

'Come on, it's so obvious. Didn't you say that Archer was the only other person besides me that had ever noticed something strange about the wheel in your painting? That's the symbol he has used for you. The Dharma Wheel. He must have known that it would be how I would find you. It's the key to the puzzle. The other three symbols must therefore also, somehow, identify the people who Archer has given the remaining journal pieces to.'

I could hardly contain my excitement at having been able to figure it out. It was like getting a sudden rush of adrenalin.

'Well bugger me! You've done it! You've gone and done what I could not. You found the secret meaning behind it,' he roared with a jovial laugh as he slapped me on the back hard enough to make my teeth rattle.

'Four symbols must mean that there are four pieces of his journal to find,' I said, half to myself as I pondered the possible meanings behind them.

'Now do you see lad,' he exclaimed, 'You are destined to do this. You have the ability to follow the clues left by Archer, clues that could even fox me. It's up to you to go and find him, finish his work and solve whatever Ancient puzzle he has discovered.'

115

He stood there staring at me with eyes full of pride and encouragement. I could feel him almost willing me to accept the challenge.

'*What say you lad? Will you do it?*'
'*No!*'

Day 2 - Bamburgh, UK
The King of the Castle

I felt changed by my time on Lindisfarne. Since my arrival, I had experienced many things. I'd walked round the impressive castle perched on its rocky crag, staring out across the water like a vigilant watchman. I had explored the serenity of the ruined Priory and been awestruck by the incredible craftsmanship of bygone years; the tall and decorative arches and walls, standing in defiance against the raw destructive force of the coastal winds. I had tasted mead for the first time; drank from the nectar of the gods and suffered a devils hangover in the morning. But most importantly of all, I had found the answers to my most pressing questions. Why Archer had sent me the letter and the Amulet? Why had those men been chasing me, and why I had come to Holy Island?

The answer to all of these was simply that one man had believed a magical stone made it through history, from the ancient city of Babylon down to that small island on the coast of England and then somehow vanished across the sea to Germany. The hours of history lessons from Paddy had all been in aid of convincing me that Archer was right. He pieced together the old legends and stories, with historical dates and facts thrown in to give them weight, all to try and make me see what Archer had seen. Admittedly it had made for an entertaining, if somewhat fanciful, story, just as all the secret messages, hidden symbols and concealed codes had been exciting and engaging.

However, none of it was enough to convince me that I too must go to Germany. It was ridiculous, real life doesn't allow you to just go off on some grand adventure at the drop of a hat. I had responsibilities to take care of and a job I couldn't afford to lose. It wasn't feasible for me to forget all that and go treasure hunting, regardless of whether I would have liked to or not.

I had done what I set out to do; travel to Lindisfarne, find Archers friend and deliver to him the Amulet. Now it was time for me to go home.

The flat refusal to do what he expected had not sat well with Paddy at all. We argued for a while over my decision, each of us believing our reasons to disregard the others to be sound. At one point I actually thought that he was going to explode and lash out at me, so red had his face turned with frustration. But then, all of a sudden, a look of calmness washed over him; relaxing his shoulders and soothing the contorted scowl of anger on his face.

'Okay lad, you win,' he submitted, *'I guess it wasn't fair of us to expect so much from you. You have a life to get back too and responsibilities you don't want to run out on. That I can respect.'*

He had the look of a sales man who had just put a lot of time and effort into giving the best sales pitch of his career, only for the customer to turn around at the end and say *'Na, I think I'll leave it for now'*. I did feel quite bad for letting him and Archer down, but what could I do?

'I guess you'll be going home now then ay?' he added with a sigh of disappointment.

'Afraid so,' I replied as a touch of guilt began to set in. *'Look, you know it's not that I don't want to help, I did...I do. It's just, when I offered my help to Archer, I expected it would entail things like looking up information for him or something. Not jetting off around the world....I mean yeah sure, a part of me would love to do it. Just not the realistic part.'*

'It's alright lad, I understand,' he said, *'It was a fools hope we had that you would even make it this far. But make it you did, despite the obstacles, and for that I am grateful. I can't condemn you for wanting to go no further.'*

'What will you do now then?' I asked, handing him back the Amulet.

'Well, I suppose it's up to me now to follow Archer's trail and find out what kind of trouble he's got himself into. Just hope these old bones can take it,' he replied with a clichéd old man's hand-on-lower-back gesture, *'but don't you worry about it, you've done your bit. You got this to me and I thank you for it.'*

The sudden change in his attitude made me a little uneasy. What was he up to?

'Tell you what lad,' he said in a happier tone, as he gave his knees a slap, *'how about you let me drive you back to the train station ay? I've got to make a trip up to Berwick for a bit of shopping anyway and it'll save you having to wait for the bus.'*

'Thanks...That's very kind of you,' I answered cautiously, expecting for some reason that the old git had at least one more card up his sleeve.

'That's settled then,' he said with a big smile, *'You get yourself sorted, maybe have something to eat if you're hungry, and I will meet you outside in about...oh let's see, what time is it? Ah good, in about an hour's time.'*

With that he picked up his things and was gone.

It was very strange suddenly being all alone. The events of the past two days swirled around inside my head as I began going over all the things I had learned and all the questions I had forgot to ask. I soon decided that it didn't matter anymore now though; my job was done and I was going home.

Feeling quite lank and bedraggled from the previous day's walking under the beating sun, followed by the unfortunate reappearance of my stomach contents during the night, I felt that above all else I needed a nice warm shower and a clean change of clothes.

I remember well the sensation of the water blasting down onto my skin, so hard that it stung a little, pounding out the troubles from my mind as well as the dirt from my body, leaving me feeling completely revitalised and invigorated.

Drying off I found myself in front of the bathroom mirror, its surface dulled by the steam in the air. Using my towel I created a window through to its reflective surface only to be confronted by judgmental eyes from the person staring back; judging me for the decision I had made.

I quickly dressed and packed up my bags before having one last look around the room to check I hadn't left anything. My eyes passed over, then immediately shot back to, the little table we had been playing chess on.

'The crafty old sod,' I said aloud to myself.

There, sitting pride of place in the centre of the table, was that bloody Amulet. I approached it tentatively like it was some kind of trap, and gently picked it up. Staring at its beautiful craftsmanship, the robust yet delicately detailed design, I felt compelled to put it on. Despite its reasonable size and slight weight in your hand, when I put it around my neck it felt almost weightless. The length of the strap left it dangling in the centre of my chest and I decided to leave it there for now rather than stuff it into a pocket where I might forget about it. I was going to make Paddy take it back whether he liked it or not.

Still not feeling one hundred percent fit and able, I thought better of assaulting my recovering stomach with any food and instead settled for just another cup of coffee while I waited down in the bar; watching the last ten minutes drain from the hour Paddy had allotted me.

Time ticked by. Ten minutes came and ten minutes went. No sign of Paddy. I waited patiently believing that he must just be running late. But as I stared fixatedly at the clock on the wall, I became hypnotised by the sound of seconds passing by, louder and louder with each 'tock' coming as the clash of a hammer pounding against the hourglass of my life. I watched as the hands ticked by at a painfully slow speed until the clock read 1:30pm, nearly an hour passed our original meeting time. My patience began to wear thin.

It really annoyed me sitting around waiting for people who couldn't be on time; to me it was highly insulting. Fuelled by this annoyance I resolved to wait no longer. I picked up my things, settled my bill and headed for the door with the intent of waiting defiantly for the bus instead......even though that wait could have been all day with the way the busses ran on the island. But that wasn't the point, there was a principle involved.

It's typical isn't it, one of those things in life that can only be explained by "Sods Law", like waiting in for a parcel all day only for it to arrive when you decide to risk going to the toilet. Typical, for no sooner had I walked out of the pub than Paddy did pull up in a rather large Toyota Land Cruiser and sauntered out as if nothing was wrong.

'You going somewhere lad?' he asked jovially.

I thought about tearing into him for having been so late but, as I stood there in the rain, which had soaked through my clothes in seconds, I thought better of it. The principle involved would not have kept me dry at the shelter-less bus stop.

'Na, I just needed some fresh air,' I answered with the pained sigh of reluctantly letting a sore point go.

'Well then, if you're all sorted, we should probably get out of this dreadful rain and make tracks.'

Chucking my things into the back of the vehicle, I can remember thinking to myself how out of place this great tank of

120

a thing looked. It was what I'd have classed as an expedition 4x4; the kind of vehicle you'd see explorers going off into vast deserts in. It was a rusty red colour, beneath the mud splatters, and had high wheel arches that housed thick set durable looking tyres. At its front sat a large bulbar and tow cable, and upon its roof lay a huge metal cage/rack; a thing that could have quite happily held a double mattress in it. It was a beast of a machine with enough extra lights on it to light up the darkest depths of hell. The most peculiar thing about it however, was the long black pipe sticking up out the side of the bonnet. As I stepped up into my seat, I asked Paddy what the hell it was for.

'That there? It's an engine snorkel lad. What did you think it was a bloody periscope or something?' he laughed to himself, obviously finding the fact that I didn't know what it was quite amusing.

In truth though, to me the idea of an engine having a snorkel was just as ridiculous as it having a periscope.

'Alright, alright, how was I supposed to know? I've never seen one before,' I paused not wanting to ask my next question, knowing that it would get a similar response. However, curiosity soon got the better of me. *'What's it for?'*

'Well it's a snorkel for the engine funnily enough,' he said with excessive sarcasm, to which I just shot him a very unimpressed look. *'Okay lad, fair enough it's a legitimate question, no more jokes. The engine snorkel was invented originally for military vehicles, to allow them to wade through relatively deep water without flooding the engine.'*

I remember thinking to myself as he spoke, could this man ever answer a question without giving an associated history lesson?

'Now-a-days you can get them on most four-wheel drive vehicles, allowing the driver to do some serious off-roading with their engine protected from the hazards of dust and water. It's all to do with the air intake dependability of the vehicle. You see, in order for any combustion engine to run it must be fed air. If the air intake becomes submerged in water, or blocked by dust, the engine can no longer breathe and will stop running; much the same as you or I would. However, this problem can be solved by the vehicle being made waterproof, which basically entails all electrical devices being sealed up and a snorkel being fitted to let the engine breath. Of course, it's a little more complicated than that, but you get the general gist of it.'

'I honestly didn't realise that you could do that,' I said, quite enamoured by the thought of being sat in a submersible car. *'So how deep are we talking here? I mean a large puddle spraying up under a regular car can flood the engine. What depth can this thing handle?'*

'Well, they say it can tackle anything up to five foot deep. But basically, if it's been done right the only limit is the height of the snorkel and the drivers head. No good your car being able to drive under water if you can't breathe ay?' he said with a wink and a nudge, *'We could be swimming around up to our necks in here and this baby would still take us through.'*

I realised that it actually made a lot of sense to have one of these things equipped if you lived on the island. I thought back to the previous day and could remember seeing the warnings signs about the dangers of crossing the causeway outside of the safe times. They all showed pictures of cars getting stuck when the sea water rose high enough to flood the engine, but with one of these snorkels you would have no such trouble. Clever!

Upon finally setting off we spent the first couple of minutes in silence, the sound of the harsh rain bouncing off the roof and windows making it hard enough to hear yourself think. As we reached the start of the causeway though, a burning question popped into my head. One I had meant to ask him earlier but it had completely slipped my mind.

'What happened to the arm?'

'What's that lad?'

'The arm of St. Oswald that was stolen by the priests from Peterborough?'

'Oh that. It most likely was lost or destroyed during the Protestant Reformation that began in 1517; the movement that established Protestantism as a constituent branch of contemporary Christianity in Europe. A hundred and thirty one years of religious wars. So many people dead, so many holy relics lost. A sad waste to be sure,' there was a very real inflection of sadness in his words that made the following few moments of silence seem all the more poignant.

'That's not what you believe though is it?' I pried upon breaking the mournful atmosphere, *'When you mentioned it this morning you said, and I quote,* "Nobody knows where the arm is now, probably destroyed when they realised it was a fake. But we'll come back to that later". *We never did though.'*

If I'd have blinked at the wrong moment I'd have missed the very brief smile that began to lift at the corner of his mouth. Had

I been a more suspicious man I might have foreseen a trap being laid out that I was blindly heading straight towards.

'What time is your train home lad?' he asked in an enquiring tone.

I looked at my watch and let out a short groan as I realised Paddy's lateness would cause me to miss the train I had planned to catch.

'Well the next one now is going to be at around four o'clock if I remember right,' I replied, reaching into my jacket pocket for the list of train times I had made.

'You might want to phone up the ticket line and double check that. In weather like this the trains often get delayed due to trees being blown over onto the tracks etcetera.'

As he said this, a great gust of wind slammed into the side of the car as if just to add dramatic effect to his words. Being in the relative shelter of the village, and then the sand dunes, I hadn't really noticed how strong the wind had become until we were out in the open straight of the causeway. On days like that it's not hard to see how ancient man would have believed it a sign that the gods where angry. The wail and whine of the wind, frustrated in its attempts to pierce our flesh with icy fingers, thwarted by but glass and metal as it whipped and thrashed the stinging rain around the vehicle in anger. Raw fury unleashed.

'I fecking hate this weather,' he added after having to noticeably fight against the elements to stay in control whilst visibility was down to a couple of meters as the wiper blades struggled to keep up with speed of the rain, *'Not only is it a nightmare to drive in but its screws with the safe crossing times for the tide. If this is on fer the day the tide will be back early. It's at times like this lad you'd be glad of that there snorkel. You best be checking them trains, mark my words.'*

'I don't have the number for the ticket line though,' I replied, *'and I ain't paying for one of them sodding "enquiry" numbers to put me through at a bloody pound a minute or whatever the hell it is. I think I'd rather just take my chances at the station.'*

The thought of wasting money on something like that always got my back up a bit.

'Here then!' he said as he flipped his own phone into my lap, *'Use mine. The numbers stored in there somewhere for when my niece comes to visit.'*

Not wanting to question his generosity, I began searching through his phonebook for the number. As I did my mind succumbed to constructs of polite conversation and, almost absent mindedly, asked;

'How olds your niece?'

'Too old,' he said in the tone of a guardian charged with the care of a young woman. *'She's 17 and thinks she knows it all; my brother's daughter and no mistake. Just as reckless and hot headed as he ever was. Her poor mother sends her out here for a weekend once a month to get a bit of peace and quiet while her father's out at sea. For sure she's a diamond though. Wants to be an artist like me, fascinated with painting castles so she is. Loves going round Bamburgh Castle taking sketches and seeing the old masters works hanging from every wall. Which reminds me,'* he then added as if he were making a mental note for himself, *'I've got to run by there today to ask if she'd be allowed to stay after closing time one weekend for a few hours to paint undisturbed.'*

He' said this more to himself and, having switched off a bit, I just offered a simple *'That's nice'* in response as I finally found the number I wanted and raised the phone to my ear.

It's funny how fate can play tricks on you. Allowing you to feel like you're in complete control of your own destiny, and can chose what road to take in life, when in fact all you're doing is following a path already laid out for you. At least that's how it feels sometimes.

'A man often meets his destiny on the road to avoid it,' someone once said, I wish I could argue.

'Great, just great that is!' I groaned, hanging up the phone and thrusting it back at Paddy, *'You were right. This stupid weather has blown a load of trees across the line that have to be cleared before anything can move this side of Newcastle. It could be three, four, five hours before the next train out. What the hell am I going to do now?'*

I leant against the window with my face smushed against my fist and sat like a sulky little school boy who couldn't get his own way.

'Tell you what lad, why don't you come with me down to Bamburgh?' offered Paddy, *'We can have a wander round the Castle and grab some lunch. Then hopefully by that time the lines will be clear and we can get you on a train home. It'd be far better than you just sitting by yourself at the station all day don't you think?'*

A suspicious man might have looked to this offer with caution. But staring out at the truly miserable day before my eyes, there was only one thought in my head. How could what he offered be any worse than being sat at that tiny station waiting for a train that might never come?

'Why not,' I replied in submission, *'It's not like I've got anything better to do.'*

'Excellent!' he said in jovial tone, *'It's always nicer to have company when driving on a day like this. There's something at the Castle I'd like to show you anyway.'*

Not really paying attention anymore, disheartened by my current predicament, it didn't fully click on to what he had just said.

For the next 10 minutes I zoned out, losing myself in the intricate dance of the rain and wind together in a kind of twisted unison, as Paddy's voice became a hollow drone in the background.

'Why do they call you Paddy?' I said quite out of the blue, interrupting whatever story he had been wasting to deaf ears.

'Who...What?' he stumbled, thrown by such a random question.

'When we first met you said that your name was Aidan Quinn but that your friends called you Paddy. Why?'

'You know lad, it's amazing how your brain works. Remembering every unfinished train of thought in a conversation to ask at a later date. I can barely remember what I said 10 minutes ago let alone last night,' he said letting out an impressed chuckle. *'But to answer your question, the people on the island call me Paddy, one because they don't like the idea of someone having the same name as their St Aidan, and two because apparently my own name isn't Irish enough,'* he must have seen the look of disgust on my face as if to say *'how backwards are these people'* for he quickly added, *'No, No, it's nothing like that. It's all good natured and meant as a joke. To be honest, it suits me fine; never did really like my birth name anyway.'*

The expression on his face suggested that there was an interesting story there, but I decided not to pry. Instead I asked another question that had been itching away in the back of my mind for some time.

'How did you end up on Lindisfarne?'

'Well, as unthinkable as this may seem for an Irishman to be saying, I never really liked living in Ireland. No, it's true,' he

125

said as if I had offered up some kind of shocked reaction, *'I never felt like I belonged there and always wanted to break away to see the world. So when I was old enough I left and came to England to study history at university...No need to look so surprised lad. Yes I went to University, and came away with a degree in History if you must know. How else did you think I knew so much?'*

I have to admit that, despite his obvious wealth of knowledge, I had never pictured him as a university man. Regretfully I think it was more down to my own unfair stereotyping of his Southern Irish accent than anything else. As awful as it is to say, I think most people do this to some extent. Whether it's thinking that anyone with a Liverpudlian accent is a jobless criminal living on the dole, or that a girl with an Essex accent is a brainless airhead, stereotypes are as hard to ignore as they are to rise above. It doesn't mean it is ever justified though.

There I was, surprised by an Irishman who'd been to University; a million and one old jokes about the Irish flooding into my mind. Yet in the end the joke was on me for here was an Irish man who had not only been to University but who'd finished with a degree. I myself could claim no such thing.

'Anyway,' he continued, *'to cut a long story short, in my later years I became fascinated by ancestral history and started to research into my own. What I found was that I could trace my lineage back to a monk on Holy Island; one of the first that arrived with St Aidan and settled there. You see, apparently, he had a hard time keeping his vows in his robes and ended up planting his seed in the garden of and English Rose, if you get my meaning,'* I did get his meaning, a deaf, celibate, Buddhist monk would have gotten his meaning by the gestures alone. *'Okay, so she was a local farm girl, but that still makes me a descendent of the first island inhabitants and therefore, technically, that makes Lindisfarne My Island!'* a smirk crept across his face, *'Sadly though, nobody else saw it that way so in the end I decided to just retire here instead, and spend my days painting the landscape of my ancestral home.'*

Many more questions bloomed in my mind. How had his family ended up in Ireland? What had he done in the time between University and retirement? Why did he not like his own name? But before I could voice any such question, my train of thought was interrupted by Paddy announcing;

'Ah! There she is!'

Bamburgh Castle

As we came in to the village of Bamburgh, passing a serenely set church that I noted with interest was called St. Aidan's, we followed a road heading towards the coast. The driving rain was so harsh that it formed a misty veil all around us, cutting visibility to within only a couple of meters. Until, that was, we rounded a corner and it all seemed to just ease away; as if having been poured from a watering can that suddenly ran dry. The sky began to clear and, in response to Paddy's announcement, my eyes fell upon a scene that was like a window into the past. Towering above the village came the outline of a great wall and grand turrets, appearing before me like something out of the mists of time.

'There she is indeed,' I thought to myself.

Sitting proudly upon a rocky outcrop, as if having risen violently out of the earth itself, was Bamburgh Castle in all its monumental glory. Standing as a majestic guardian, it seemed to stare out over both land and sea with a watchful eye against an unseen enemy.

'Whoa!' was all I could manage to articulate, awestruck by what I had just seen.

'Aye, it's an impressive sight to be sure,' replied Paddy as we followed the road passing right in front of it. *'But you ain't seen nothin yet lad!'*

He wasn't wrong. The road turned off up a short hill, leading to the castles car park, from where I could see out over the grassy sand dunes rolling down onto the beach and disappearing into the sea. Stepping out of vehicle I was quickly reminded that, whilst the rain may have died off for now, the wind had lost none of its temper. Still enjoying its boisterous games, catching me off guard and off balance, the strong current blowing through the air nearly sent me crashing down to the gravel floor on more than one occasion. As I battled to stay upright, my eyes followed each gust as they played through the tall grass, making it ripple like a dance of green water, swirling around until it broke with a whine against the unmoving stone of the castle walls.

Buffeting our way up towards the entrance, the great gateway seemed to grow taller the closer we got; watching us with suspicion as we passed through. Inside the unyielding walls, I thought we would be shielded from the force of the wind. Yet the corridor of stone seemed only to act as a funnel to focus its might against us. Upon reaching a little gatehouse, guarding another set of heavy gates, we paid the small entrance fee and proceeded into the castle proper.

Magnificent is the only word I can use to describe it. Built up on many levels with turrets, guard towers and stables, all protected by rows of cannons worn now beyond use but still standing proud and defiantly battle ready. At the centre of it all was an imposing, and impenetrable looking, Keep towering high above; large enough almost to be considered a castle by itself. I stood there surrounded by hundreds of years of history, filling the air full of echoes from a more violent time of great battles and heroic deeds. It took me back to my childhood and the feeling of wanting to dash off and explore everything, running along the battlements with a plastic sword and shield that the obligatory gift shop would no doubt sell. Fortunately, I managed to refrain from doing so and instead just followed Paddy around as he gave me a very detailed guided tour.

I'd always had an enduring love of castles from the days of touring Scotland with my grandparents, insisting we had to stop off every time I saw one of the brown tourist signs indicating one. My granddad had even built me a wooden one that came apart and was like a jigsaw to put back together which I would then fill with plastic soldiers of varying historical periods and stage epic battles. I used to wish that I had been born back in the days of knights, kings and grand quests. But then I suppose that's not an unusual thing for children to do, especially when they don't feel like they fit in anywhere. I've always been a bit of an outsider, often thinking that maybe I was born out of my time.

As we walked around, Paddy told me about all the archaeological works that had been done there over the years which had unearthed traces of previous settlements.

'They've found evidence dating from as early as the Neolithic Period, back in 3,500BC, right up to the Roman occupation and the coming of the Anglo-Saxons,' he said.

'Wow, that's a lot of settlement,' I thought to myself.

He then went on to tell me the sad history of 1464 and The War of The Roses.

'The civil wars between supporters of the House of Lancaster and the House of York brought about an end to the age of castles,' he began, *'It was a time when gunpowder and shot proved stronger than stone and mortar, blasting to shit the strategic advantage of such fortifications. The siege of Bamburgh by Yorkist forces, under the Earl of Warwick, brought the castle to its knees with heavy artillery. The first castle in*

England to be destroyed by gunfire; a sad accolade for sure. Left abandoned to ruin and decay for centuries, the castle was eventually bought by Lord William George Armstrong in the 1890's. Extensive restorations where started by him, and then continued by his descendants, leading to the structure that stands here today; the appropriately labelled Finest Castle In England.'

Presumptuous as that label was, having seen more than my fair share of castles, it was one I couldn't really argue with.

Gazing over the ramparts out to sea, I could feel the salty air wearing at my skin as the unrelenting wind tried its hardest to blow me down. Away in the distance, through the haze left by the receding mist and rain, I could just make out the silhouette of another castle off to the north.

'What's that castle over there?' I asked rather stupidly, showing a complete lack of geographical awareness.

Understandably, Paddy looked at me with an expression of mild disbelief as he replied;

'Lindisfarne Castle lad. You know, the one we just bloody came from.'

'Cool!' I said, ignoring his sarcasm, *'I didn't realise we'd be able to see it from here.'*

'Aye lad you can. Tis better on a nice clear day though. To be sure you can only just about see the bloody Farne Islands today.'

'The what islands?' I asked quickly.

'The Farne Islands lad, out over that way,' he answered sweeping his arm around to point in a sort of south-easterly direction. *'They're a collection of small islands about two to three miles off the coast and happen to be one of the most famous bird sanctuaries in the British isles and –'*

'– I know what they are,' I said cutting him off, *'I've been there when I was younger,'* I added as I racked the archives of my memory. *'We stayed at a place called...sea...Seahouses, that was it. I didn't think we were anywhere near there though?'*

'Sure be Jaysus, tis only about five minutes down the road from here.'

That revelation did surprise me. Knowing how I was as a kid, I couldn't fathom why if we had been so close to Bamburgh had we not gone to see the castle.... or had we?

So many things become fuzzy in your mind over time; like old toys in the attic that get covered with dust and forgotten about. I can remember there being quite a few of us there on that holiday. My Nan and Grandad taking me, my cousin Thomas and both our mums away as they often did; treating us to things we could not have otherwise afforded. I remember going across on a small boat over to one of the islands. A trip that took us past a colony of grey seals lazing about on the rocks whilst a myriad of various seabirds flew all around, nesting in the cliffs where their young where beginning to hatch. The noise of so many tiny voices echoing over the water was quite amazing. Landing on the island we were able to walk the pathways and see hundreds of nests full of chicks crying out for food. At the time though, those cries fell upon deaf ears as their parents where otherwise engaged. One of my most lasting memories from childhood is from that day. It is of my cousin and me clinging to our grandad to get away from the angry birds pecking his head in an attempt to protect their young. We were told that it was quite a funny sight from afar, the two of us hiding under our guardians coat as he danced around trying to avoid the flock of dive bombing birds. He suffered a lot for us did that man.

As I told Paddy this story he laughed and nodded his head in acknowledgement before informing me that they now supply visitors with hard hats for that very reason.

'Was there a church and a lighthouse there?' he asked me to which I nodded pretty sure that I could remember seeing them. *'Aye, it'll have been Inner Farne you went to, the largest of the islands. Interestingly, that island was home to St. Cuthbert before he became Bishop. It's also one he returned to before he died. In fact, that church was built as a dedication to him in 1370 so it was.'*

Odd it may be, but I can remember feeling comforted at being so close to a place that held such precious memories.

'Would you be interested in going back to Seahouses then?' Paddy asked, catching me off guard.

'What, really?' I replied with an almost childlike anticipation.

'Sure,' he continued, *'I know a great little place that does amazing food. If we go now we can be back here just after closing time and I can show you the answer to your question.'*

'What question?' I asked confusedly.

'What happened to Oswald's arm?'

My mind raced as I realised that, through clever conversation, Paddy had once again made me forget he had not answered one of my questions. More to the point, it raced with many new questions. What could he show me that would provide an answer to the whereabouts of Oswald's arm, and why did we need to come back after closing time? For that matter, how where we going to get back in?

I knew that it would be a futile waste of time to ask him any of this, for he would not give up the answers until he was good and ready.

Leaving Bamburgh, we travelled down the coast for five or so minutes and arrived at the St. Aidan Hotel & Restaurant in Seahouses. Upon seeing the name I turned and gave him an unimpressed look.

'What?' he said with a defensive crack to his voice, *'They do good food.'*

The statement in itself at least was not a lie, the food there was fantastic as once again I found myself drawn to fish and chips. It must just be something about being by the sea, as anywhere else I can take or leave fish and chips. But whenever I get near the sights, sounds and smells of the coast, there's nothing else I would rather have. The place itself was nice too, set on the sea front with magnificent panoramic views of the Farne Islands to the east and the castles to the north, all made somewhat mystical by the faint mist that still refused to fully disperse.

We sat there for some time enjoying our meals and talking about everything and nothing. It was the first time since I had met Paddy that he came across as more of a friend than a teacher. I enjoyed it.

Soon it was though that five o'clock came and went, signalling the closing of the castle and with it the time for our secretive return.

Arriving back at the castle, after leaving enough time for both visitors and staff to have cleared off, Paddy told me to wait in the car as he went up to the, now closed, main gates and gave a short sharp whistle. Seconds later a man appeared from a little side door, gave him a nod and then proceeded to open the gates for us. Words past between the two of them as the gatekeeper glanced around Paddy back towards me before, reluctantly, returning through his little door. As Paddy got back into the vehicle, driving up through the gates and into the main courtyard of the castle, I asked him what their conversation had been about, curious as to how it was we were allowed in after closing time.

'Simple really,' he stated, *'as well as being a painter for the Armstrong family, I'm also an amateur archaeologist. Instead of taking payment for my paintings in money, I am granted free rein to come and explore the castle and its grounds away from the crowds of tourists. Old Bobby there was just asking who you were, as normally I come here alone. I told him you were my assistant and that if he had any problems he could take it up with Lord Armstrong....Prey to the holy mother that he ain't that clever.'*

I restrained from asking why, realising he probably didn't have permission to show me what he was about to, and thought it maybe best not to bring it up.

As Paddy parked up by the imposing keep, I made to exit the vehicle and grabbed my satchel from the back seat.

'Arrh, you won't be needing that with you,' Paddy informed me.

'I rarely ever do need it, but I always take with me just the same,' I said passively, not taking much notice.

'What do you have in there?'

'Nothing much, just a first aid kit, torch, note pad, compass and a pocket atlas. You know, just the essentials,' I answered as I stepped out of the vehicle.

'Let me guess, you weren't a boy scout by any chance were you?'

'Always be prepared,' I replied with a smirk as I slung the bag over my shoulder and shut the door.

'A wise sentiment lad,' he said coming round the vehicle to meet me, *'but seriously though, it's a bit of a squeeze where we're going and that bag will just get in the way.'*

'Well where are we going Paddy?' I pressed him, growing a little tired of not really knowing what was going on, *'I like the idea of leaving my bag behind even less than being taken somewhere I don't know.'*

It was a bit of a pissy attitude, but I really didn't like being told to leave my kit behind. I think Paddy could see this and rather than push me further, he simply said;

'Trust me lad.'

Walking over to the ruined chapel of St. Peter, where a sign post indicated that it was once the resting place of King Oswald's relics, I couldn't help but feel a bit naked without my bag. From the remaining foundations and few standing walls, you could roughly make out the size and shape of the original structure. It was a long rectangular building with a semi-circular

133

bay at the far end. There a large bell now hung from a wooden frame, sat slightly raised upon a stone platform.

'What you see here lad are the remains of a Norman Chapel. Over there at the east end, the semi-circular apse dates from the 12th century,' he said pointing to where the bell was, *'These walls running around here to the west are the much more recent remains of a 19th century reconstruction that was never finished. More importantly though, it's what's underneath all of this that we are here to see. For, as the sign over there says, these ruins stand upon the foundations of the Church of St. Peter. The church founded by King Oswald.'*

Remembering that it was here where King Oswald's arm was meant to have been kept before the alleged theft, I found myself wondering where Paddy was going with all this.

'In 1999 a team of archaeologists conducted an investigation of these ruins using modern geophysical survey equipment,' he continued in full "History Lecture" mode. *'From the data collected they were able to construct a 3-D interpretation of the results. This revealed that down there in the south west end of the chapel is a rectangular structure, stretching along the back wall some five meters by four meters with a probable depth of about two meters. They believed that they had found an underground vaulted room or crypt, indicated by a short passage leading off the north-east corner. It should have been an important discovery, one that would give the site international significance were it proved to be Anglo-Saxon in date. With that in mind, you must ask yourself this....why has it still not been excavated?'*

It amazed me how he could make anything sound like a conspiracy. But I did have to admit, something didn't quite add up there.

'More than ten years have passed since that discovery, so why has no one been allowed to dig down and see what is in there?' he asked rhetorically, like a showman trying to stir up the crowds curiosity, *'The answer to that is what I have brought you here to see.'*

The Bell in the Ruins of St Peter's Chapel

He walked over to the large bell, stepping over the low chain that cordoned off the apse, and placed his foot upon one of the stones.

'Be ready lad' he turned and said to me, before pressing down with his foot.

To my amazement, the stone depressed easily under his weight. No sooner had it done so than I heard the grinding of stone as the top section of the platform began sliding heavily to the side revealing a dark hole beneath it.

'Quickly now lad, get yourself down there. It doesn't stay open for long.'

With that, he half pushed me down the hole before following soon after himself. Dropping easily about 8 or 9 foot down into the dark, I was surprised by the sudden arrival of the ground beneath me. Landing awkwardly, my legs buckled under the weight of own my body and I fell backwards, my head just missing Paddy's feet as he landed behind. The sound of grinding stone again indicated that the trap door was closing itself as Paddy had said it would. The little bit of light we did have from above slowly disappeared until, with a settling thud, we were left in complete darkness.

'You okay lad?' he asked as he lit an old wooden torch with a match.

The explosion of light from its flame hurt my eyes which had been straining, trying to adjust to the dark.

'Yeah, yeah, I'm fine,' I answered through gritted teeth whilst rubbing my aching legs, *'Just didn't expect it to be so long a drop that's all.'*

As the dark spots dissipated from my vision, I fought the urge to comment on the fact that a proper torch, like the one I had back up in my satchel, would have been really useful right now. Following the direction Paddy began to walk in with my eyes, I could just about see a narrow passage exposed by the flickering fire light. It seemed to lead off to the right, heading back towards the west end of the chapel and the location of the crypt.

I felt like a tomb raider, having suddenly dropped from reality into a dark, damp and dusty underworld filled with ancient cob webs and ghostly shadows that danced along the walls in tune with the torches flame. Despite my reservations I couldn't deny that is was rather exciting.

I followed Paddy into the passage way, having to turn slightly side on in order to get through. After around 25-30 feet, the passage ended abruptly and Paddy disappeared through an opening to the left. Following him through, I stepped into a rectangular room where he was stood lighting candles at the far end in front of a stone altar built into a recess. The altar was draped in a deep red velvet cloth edged in gold and upon which were set many things. At its centre lay a silver platter containing fragments of wood around which stood a sceptre to one side and a horn the other, each supported by a thin but decorative metal frame. Both items looked to be made of ivory, although with only the flickering candle light to see by, it was hard to tell. Jars filled with earth and pieces of chain-mail added to this eclectic collection, lovingly arranged as a shrine to the main focal piece; a beautifully carved cabinet which sat raised up at the back, ominous and yet alluring at the same time. Behind it, the wall was adorned with a shield barring a coat of arms, through which crossed two antique swords framed by a banner suspended above.

'Beautiful isn't it,' said Paddy softly. *'The True relics of King Oswald, crafted into a shrine around the most important one of all. Are you ready to see it lad?'*

'Ready to see what?' I asked with a mixture of anticipation and apprehension, *'What's in the cabinet Paddy?'*

'Proof lad! Proof of all that I have told you to be true. Prepare to greet a saintly King.'

With that he opened the cabinets' double doors to reveal something that both amazed me and turned my stomach in equal amounts. It was the arm of King Oswald.

Day 2 - Bamburgh, UK
The Chintamani Revealed

I stood staring at the morbid scene, speechless and struggling to accept what I was looking at. An arm that was supposedly over 1000 years old which, apart from the lack of blood and gooey bits, looked like it could have been hewn from someone's body that very day.

'How is this possible?' I asked eventually, unable to take my eyes of it, *'It can't be real? There's no way that can be the arm of Oswald. There would be nothing but bone left after so many centuries.'*

'You still don't get it do you lad? It's the Chintamani Stone. Its presence keeps the flesh from decaying, just as it did to St Cuthbert's body in his coffin.'

'What?' I said in disbelief.

'The ring lad, the one there on his finger,' he said pointing to the hand, *'the stone within is a fragment of the Chintamani Stone.'*

A shiver ran over my body as the implication of his words fully sank in. After all the talk and all the history lessons, I was actually stood in front of a piece of this fabled stone.

With only the flickering light from the flame of Paddy's torch, and the candles he had lit it on the altar, it was hard to say exactly what colour the Stone was. Dark blue? Deep red? It even seemed black at some points. Maybe it was all of them in a complete contradiction of possibilities? Dull yet shiny, clear but cloudy, it seemed to change in appearance the longer I stared. Looking at it felt like looking through a window into the universe, as if the answer to every question could be contained within its crystal surface. It was all probably just a trick of the light though, amplified in my mind by the gravitas of the moment.

'You okay lad?' I vaguely heard Paddy say before his hand landed on my shoulder, jolting me out of my trance, *'You've*

been stood staring at that thing like a statue for about 5 minutes. I swear to God I haven't even seen you blink.'

'I'm fine, I'm fine,' I said shaking free of the moment, *'Just got lost in thought I guess.'*

'Indeed she can have that kind of effect on you. Beautiful ay? Now at last do you believe me?'

'I don't really know what to believe to be honest Paddy,' I admitted distractedly, still trying to tear my eyes away from the artefact, *'I mean yeah it looks convincing, and I'll admit that the mere thought of this stone being a piece of the Chintamani is very exciting, but what does it prove? How do I know that the arm isn't a fake? Do you really expect me to believe that a piece of stone could possibly preserve human flesh? How do you even know that it's a piece of the Chintamani? I mean I know there's compelling evidence to link it with the Stone of Destiny and all, but how have we jumped from Destiny to Chintamani?'*

The questions rolled out of me as if my tongue were a conveyor belt, trying desperately to make sense of it all.

'Holy Jaysus! You ask more bloody questions than a quiz machine on a Friday night down the pub,' he said with the tone of exasperation I was becoming familiar with. *'Alright, first off I don't really know "How" it preserves the arm, but then again I don't really know "How" my T.V. beams pictures right into my living room either. I just know that it does.'*

'Fair point,' I thought to myself.

'As for whether the arm is a fake or not, I guess I can't really know that for sure either. But then again, I would have to question the motive of the person who would go to the great effort of keeping this box supplied with a fresh limb every week in order to create a miracle that nobody gets to see. Who would the hoax be for? Unless of course you're suggesting that I went out this morning and butchered me some poor beggars arm in order to stage all this just for you? I guess that would explain why I was late picking you up wouldn't it? But I would ask you then, how do you suppose I preserved it? Ask yourself, where is the blood that should still be dripping from the soggy end? Where is the God awful smell that would hang around such a ghastly object?'

He did present some compelling arguments, but I just couldn't seem to let myself believe it.

'Okay, fair enough,' I replied, determined not to let him have last say this time, *'I don't think you've set this up ,but that still doesn't prove it's real. What if it were just a really good*

139

prosthetic? That would explain the lack of blood, the lack of smell and the reason it doesn't decay, would it not?'

He looked at me in frustrated disbelief before walking determinedly over to the cabinet, grabbing the arm, marching towards me and taking my hand.

'Here! You tell me if it's real enough for you!'

He thrust the thing into my hand and, despite having told myself it wasn't real, I had to force myself not to drop it and squeal like a girl in disgust. It certainly felt real.

'Okay, Okay, it's real, Christ! Here, just take it off me alright, I believe you.'

It was weird, if I had closed my eyes I'd have sworn that I was holding onto a real persons arm, one still attached I mean. The only difference was that it felt cold and almost leathery; as if the skin had dried out. But real skin it most definitely was. The way it moved under my touch was sickeningly unmistakable.

Taking back the morbid item, I could see his satisfaction. An almost cruel amusement at my reaction which appeared across his weathered face, cast in the light from his torches flame that seemed to flicker against a phantom breeze.

'Now you see,' he said, returning it to its resting place, *'It's not kept in a hermetically sealed container nor in a block of ice, so if the Stone isn't preserving it what the hell is?'*

When the last shiver passed through my body, and the urge to throw up subsided, I asked him the one question that still bugged me.

'How does any of this suggest that it is a piece of the Chintamani Stone though?'

He let out a long sigh and bowed his head in defeat.

'Alright lad, I suppose that's a fair enough question. Let me explain. During the reign of King Lha Thothori Nyantsen of Tibet, sometime in the fifth century, a chest is said to have fallen from the sky. Inside were four relics, one of which was a Charm stone. Now, this could have been a jewel, a crystal or even a gem, but what's important is what was inscribed on it; the mantra "Om Mani Padme Hum".'

At this point he held his hand up and said;

'And yes, before you ask, that is the very same mantra as what is engraved on your Amulet. The implications of this however, I have neither the time nor the energy to explain right now.' he added upon seeing I was about to say something.

His talk of the mantra that I instantly recognised had reminded me that it still hung around my neck and I had been about to say he could have it back. Robbed of the chance by his dismissive attitude however, I reluctantly held my tongue and let him continue...for now.

'Now the king did not understand what the objects were for, but still held them in reverence and kept them safe. Years later, there appeared two mysterious strangers at the king's court who explained to him the purpose of the relics and thus brought to Tibet the teachings of the Dharma. Again lad, don't ask as it is very complicated,' he pre-emptively cut me off once more, *'all you need to know is that those teachings became the base of the Buddhist religion, okay?'*

Again I kept quiet and simply nodded in frustrated response.

*'That "***maṇi***" stone, as it became known,'* he continued, *'is said to have been a magical jewel, one with the power to manifests the wishes of the beholder. Treasures, clothing and food could all be manifested it is said, whilst sickness and suffering could be removed and water purified all by its influence. Don't you see? If the stories of the Stone of Destiny are true then it possesses many of those same powers. A stone from the stars, beyond our comprehension to understand that can elevate men to greatness and even godliness.'*

I stood unspeaking, not really knowing what to say after all that, which prompted him to add;

'But if that is not enough for you, how about this? The Gaelic name for the Stone of Destiny is ***clach-na-cinneamhain***. *The Sanskrit name for the Chintamani is* ***cintāmaṇi-ratna***. *I don't believe in coincidences lad, I've seen too much in my life. What you must ask yourself now is do you?'*

I had to hand it to him, even if he was making it all up, the way he presented his evidence was incredibly compelling and I soon ran out of reasons not to believe him. Maybe I'm just easily taken in, but my excitement over his "proof" that the legends were true drowned out what little scepticism I had left. The quest Archer had begun couldn't have been a wild goose chase, the Stone and its fragments really where out there, I'd seen it for myself now. This left me with but one more question.

'So why didn't Archer take it?'

'Well lad, Archer was intent on finding the missing *Stones. This one isn't* missing *is it? It's right here, safe from unfriendly eyes.'*

'But what if they eventually dig up this vault?' I asked with a sincere concern, *'Worse yet, what if someone else stumbles upon the way to open the entrance?'*

'First off, the current Lord Armstrong has forbidden anyone from digging up this area under the pretence that, ruined or not, it is still holy ground. In actual fact, this was a mandate set down by the 1st Lord Armstrong. Likely he'd discovered the chapel's secret at some point and realised the importance of it remaining that way. And secondly, if anyone did ever just stumble down here they would quickly find themselves trapped with no way out.'

'What do you mean "Trapped"?' I asked as a dormant fear of being buried alive began to twinge, *'Surely you just go back out the way you came in right? I mean there must be a switch to open it from this side yes? How else are We supposed to get out?'*

He didn't answer my question, a response that instantly gave a feeling of foreboding. Instead he just handed me the torch and said;

'Go look for yourself.'

So I did. Squeezing back along the passageway, already beginning to feel slightly claustrophobic just at the thought of being trapped down there, I reached the hole we dropped in from and determinedly began searching for a switch. Running my free hand all over the stones, in hope of finding a pressure pad or a rope to pull, I was dismayed to find nothing but solid bare rock.

I heard a grinding sound followed by a click coming from back in the vault and, heading back down the tunnel, I found Paddy stood in the far right corner of the small room with a smug grin on his face.

'Any luck?' he asked, already knowing the answer.

'Alright, spill it! How do we get out of here?' I demanded, trying to hide my discomfort, *'I'm not stupid, no one would build a secret room that they couldn't get out of! There must be a hidden switch or something?'*

'I can promise you lad there is no switch under here that will open that entrance,' he answered.

The sound of his smugness, and obvious enjoyment at keeping me in the dark, was becoming incredibly frustrating.

'Okay then so what then, we phone Bob and he opens it from the outside for us?' I asked irritably.

'Well you could try that but I think you'll find that you won't get any signal down here.'

I checked my phone just to be sure only to see that he was right, "No Signal".

'Look Paddy, I'm getting a little tired of this now. I know you know there's an exit, so stop playing games and get us the hell out of here?'

'Very well then,' he said with a gratified look of achievement, *'As both Marker and Key ignore it not, for X isn't the only cross that marks the spot. When the Beast of Bamburgh guards the door, your salvation shall come from beneath the floor.'*

There came a long pause of silence between us as his voice echoed off the walls and faded away.

'What the hell is this, a poetry reading or something?' I was about to say, dumbfounded by the why he suddenly decided to throw me a riddle.

However, before I could, he stretched out his left arm and, without looking away from me, pulled down on a stone crucifix that protruded from the wall. I hadn't noticed it there before, but then I guess when I'd entered the room my attention had been instantly drawn to the altar. I noticed it now though. I noticed it slide a short way down the wall under his grasp until it clicked. That sound was almost instantly followed by another louder one as, over on the other side of the room, a hole opened in the floor revealing a ladder that dropped away into darkness. A part of me couldn't help but think that, despite the frustration and mild claustrophobia I had suffered, all of this was still really cool. I may not be Indiana Jones, as Martin had said, but I was starting to feel at least like his unwitting accomplice.

'Quickly now lad, drop that torch into the hole and get yourself down the ladder. Once I let go, the trap door won't stay open for long.' I was starting to see a pattern here.

I did as he asked and watched as the torch fell away, deeper and deeper down into the dark until eventually I could no longer see it.

'Christ! How far down does this thing go?' I asked in shock.

'Probably best I don't tell you lad,' he answered uncomfortably. *'Just concentrate on putting one foot below the other and you'll be down there before you know it. Mind you go slow and steady though, that is a very old ladder.'*

'Oh great, thanks for that,' I said with worried sarcasm. *'Filled me with a lot of confidence that has.'*

143

With no other option, I took one last look at the altar before stepping carefully down onto the ladder and reluctantly starting my decent.

I've never liked heights. Ever since primary school when they took us on an adventure weekend and I ended up embarrassing myself at the Abseiling wall; clasping on to my teacher and sobbing like a baby when I saw how high it was. The older I got though, the more adept I'd become at hiding my fears. In recent years I had actually begun seeking out opportunities to confront them, to the point where I'd rather grown to enjoy the adrenaline rush that being frightened produced. However, there on that ladder, it was a different story. I didn't know how high up I was and I couldn't see a bloody thing, having cast our only light source down into the abyss. The only thing between me and an unpleasant end was a rusty old ladder, built onto to the side of the shaft, upon whose rungs I could only just about get my fingers and tips of my shoes on. I wished I had a shoulder to cry on now.

Drawing in quickening breaths, I tried to focus on moving my hands and feet in alternating rhythms. It went well for a little while.

'How're you doing lad?'

As Paddy's voice echoed down from above, I looked up to see where he was. His own movements must have dislodged some lose rock for in that moment a small cascade of grit fell down into my eyes. I lost my grip.

I don't know how far I fell; I don't know how deep the shaft was. I scrabbled for a hand hold, grasped furiously for a way to save myself, but fear clouded any hope of clear thought and coordination. It wasn't a straight fall. I bounced from wall to wall in sharp jerking motions as my own body weight and force of gravity snapped my fingers away from every rung of the ladder I tried to grab.

Over the ringing of my own screams, I heard Paddy shouting the same thing over and over to me as I fell away into the dark.

'PUT OUT YOUR ARMS AND LEGS!'

I don't how many times he had to yell these words before I heard them. I'm not even sure that I even really did at the time, but whether consciously or not, they eventually sank in and I reacted.

In an effort to do my best impression of a starfish, I quickly found the bare rock walls of the shaft. Pushing all four limbs out as hard as I could to slow my decent, my cry of fear turned to

144

one of pain as the harsh stone tore at the skin on my hands. It was beginning to work, but not enough. I started to see a flicker of light beneath me. Time was running out and the ground was running up to meet me with fatal speed. In a moment of surprising clarity, I remembered just how narrow the shaft was. Bringing my legs up slightly, I leant back against the wall in an effort to wedge myself. Closing my eyes and gritting my teeth, I pushed out as hard as I could.

As the dust settled and the echoes of my pain dissipated into silence, I opened my eyes. It had worked. A little too well if I'm completely honest. It had hurt like hell, every bump and sharp edge dug into my back as my body went rigid and my knees locked. When I stopped falling, I did so with quite a jolt. I was wedged by the base of my neck and heels of my shoes in a very awkward and uncomfortable way. But at least I was alive.

'You alright lad?'

Paddy's voice was laboured and still some way above me, but it was good to hear.

'Yeah...I'm okay,' I groaned as I tried to wriggle myself into position from which to reach the ladder again, *'I'm a bit stuck though.'*

'Hold on, I'm coming to help.'

'I'm not going anywhere,' I replied with a strained sigh.

Suddenly the thought of sitting alone in the rain waiting for the next train home seemed a lot more appealing. If only I knew then just how much worse it was going to get. Why did I let myself get drawn further into all this?

'Paddy,' I called up to him.

'Aye?'

'Do me a favour,'

'What's that lad?'

'Don't fall.'

When Paddy finally made his way, tentatively, down to my position we found ourselves in a bit of a predicament. How was he going to reach down and pull me up without losing his own grip on the precarious ladder? In the end, he managed to safely wedge himself just above me, the way I had been trying to do, and reach an arm down for me to pull myself up on.

It took a while and no small amount of nerve and trust on both sides, but at last I was back upright on the ladder and continuing on down at a much slower and steadier speed.

Despite having taken a short cut down, what I thought must have been, a good portion of the way, it still took an uncomfortable amount of time before my feet finally landed back on solid ground. The only consolation was that Paddy seemed to be enjoying the decent even less than I was. I wondered if he still thought it a good idea to have brought me down here.

The feeling of finally being off that damn ladder was one of pure relief. My arms and legs where shaking so much from the strain of the climb that sitting down felt like heaven. As I waited for Paddy to join me, the adrenaline that had kept me going after the fall finally wore off and my whole body began to shake. It hit me then just how close I'd come to dying in that hole.

A combination of grunts and groans eventually preceded the old man's arrival as he stepped rather gingerly off the last rung.

'Jaysus, I'm getting far too old to be doing this kind of thing anymore. You okay lad?' he asked as he recovered himself.

'Yeah, just letting my nerves settle. That climb did nothing for my fear of heights you know,' I replied.

'You take all the time you need. I could do with a sit down myself after that,' he said, lowing himself awkwardly down next to me. *'Aren't you glad now though that you didn't bring your bag with you? Imagine how much worse it could have been with that thing tangled up around you.'*

'Well, considering that I have a number of painful cuts and grazes which could have been cleaned up an covered with the first aid kit contained in that bag, no, I can't honestly say I am glad I don't have it,' I replied quite flatly, looking over all my injuries to make it clear just how beat up I was.

'Ah, there's nothing on you but a few scratches. You'll be fine lad, though I don't mind telling you that I didn't think I'd be able to say that when I first saw you fall. You gave me quite a fright.'

'I gave you a fright?' the disbelief wheezed out of me as I searched for an appropriate reply to such a statement, *'Well I am terribly sorry for that, I shall do my very best to see that it doesn't happen again,'* I then said, deciding sarcasm was the way to go.

'Apology accepted,' he responded with complete disregard for my tone. *'Now, shall we push on?'*

I sat for a moment just looking at him with my mouth agape. His constant indifference towards my sarcastic remarks irritated me beyond belief, but by now I knew better than to waste my time arguing.

'Fine,' I sighed in submission, forcing myself up on wobbly legs *'So, where the hell are we now anyway?'* I then added as I gave him a hand up in response to his waving gesture.

'We're in what is called a Ley tunnel, running deep under the castle.'

'What's a Ley tunnel?' I asked slightly confused.

'A secret passage that links together prominent places. Some believe there to be a connection between them and the Ley lines of old.'

'What are Ley lines?' I then asked, now even more confused.

'They are proposed geographical alignments between sites of interest. Ancient pathways that channel energy from the Earth into monuments, megaliths and other sacred places,' he answered, as if channelling a text book definition. *'Often the term Ley tunnel is just used these days to describe old escape routes, medieval sewers and smugglers runs, rather than any specific spiritual place. This is because many experts believe that Ley tunnels are purely the creation of local folklore and are unlikely to exist physically at all. But with sites all around the UK, Europe, and even the world over, that have similar legends of such tunnels and links between sacred places, it's hard not to at least wonder if there ain't at least some truth behind them. The tunnel we stand in now can be called a Ley tunnel for it connects the sacred site of Oswald's Chapel, where his holy relics are preserved, and the church of the very man that blessed him.'*

'St. Aidan's Church!' I stated excitedly, *'That's where it leads too isn't it? That's how we get out of here.'*

'Well done lad,' he congratulated with little sign of any sarcasm, *'the tunnel ends in the grounds of the church where only a latch on our side of it can open a secret door.'*

'This is really cool,' I said with the excitement of a child who finds his grandad's old army gear in the attic.

'Worth a few bumps and scrapes wouldn't you say?' if a voice could sound like a smirk, his would have done so with these words, *'But, you should hear some of the other Ley tunnel legends. They are even more enthralling than this one.'*

'Like what?'

'Here,' he said handing me back the torch, *'I tell you as we walk.'*

A short way on from the ladder, we came to a T-junction. There I had to interrupt Paddy's stories, though I did so reluctantly; he had not been lying in what he said about them.

'Which way Paddy, left or right?' I asked, looking down two equally dark tunnels stretching off in either direction.

'What? Oh, erm, left lad. The exits down to the left,' he replied, stumbling out of his narrative.

'Where does that way lead to then?' I asked, pointing up to the right.

'That path runs down from the keep. It was added to provide an escape route out of the last strong hold of the castle should it ever fall. The king could be taken safely under the enemy's feet to the church, from where he could then be secreted away.'

'Awesome,' I thought to myself, *'I wonder if anyone still uses it?'*

We continued on walking down the tunnel in silence for a short time after that. Eventually, my curiosity got the better of me again though and I asked him to carry on with stories of the Ley tunnels.

'Well, up in Fife there is believed to be a Ley tunnel beneath Culross Abbey where it is said a man sits in a golden chair, waiting with treasures for any who manage to find him. Legends tell of a blind piper who decided to enter the tunnel at Newgate with his dog in an attempt to find the seated man. The sound of him playing his pipes could be heard as far as three quarters of a mile away it is said. His dog eventually found its way back out into the daylight, but the piper was never seen again. Some believe that he found the seated man and was awarded the treasure. They say the cost of such a trove however, was that he had to take the man's place in the golden chair until, one day, he too was relieved by another; hence why he was never found.'

'Come on,' I said disbelievingly, *'that one's a bit farfetched isn't it? The poor sod probably just lost his dog down there and starved to death when he couldn't find his way out.'*

'Okay, so some of the tales do lend themselves more to that of fairy-tale folklore I'll admit. But there are others that are more compelling, such as the tales of Glastonbury Tor. Many stories there are told about a series of tunnels running beneath the great Tor, the most famous of which being about one that links it to Glastonbury Abbey. The story tells of around 30 monks who followed this tunnel to the Tor of which only three came back out. Two were insane and the other struck dumb.

Nobody knows what they saw down there, and the fate of the other 27 still remains a mystery.'

After all the dusty history lessons he had imparted upon me over the last two days, this I was actually enjoying. With all the secrets, myths and legends, I couldn't help but get caught up in it, desperately wanting to head off to see for myself if any of them where true. Stupidly I told as much to Paddy, which got the poor guys hopes up again.

'See lad, that's exactly what I've been talking about. You've got the spirit of adventure. You were born to take on the quest that now stands before you. Having seen the truth with your own eyes, you must now know the importance of Archer's work?'

'It is amazing stuff Paddy, don't get me wrong,' I said before letting out a sigh, *'But it's just not me. I'm the type of guy that gets excited reading about these kinds of adventures, not the type that goes off and has them. I'm really sorry but, if you brought me all the way down here to try and persuade me to go, you've wasted your time.'*

'Well, you can't blame me for trying,' he said dejectedly, *'if your minds truly made up then so be it. We'll get out of here and I'll drop you off at the station like I promised.'*

I could almost feel the frustration and disappointment burn within his words, but my decision was final. I'd already had enough of an adventure to be able to go home with a good story to tell, and that's exactly what I wanted to do.

Once again we walked in silence, broken only by Paddy instructing me when the exit was just up a head. I was surprised at how far we seemed to have walked and, by the time I could see the tunnels end, I was definitely ready to get back up to the surface. I disliked being underground almost as much as I disliked being up high and, without any more of Paddy's stories to keep my mind occupied, the last few meters had gotten quite claustrophobic down in the dark.

What happened next I can recall very little of. I remember hearing Paddy shout *'LOOK OUT!'* in a tone of surprise and concern. A warning followed quickly by his hand pushing me forward, seconds before something hard and heavy struck the back of my head. At that moment, all lights went out.

Slowly I began to come too, groaning in protest as my body began to wake from a dreamless sleep with explosions of feeling. Opening my eyes, with all the effort of lifting heavy shutters, I was assaulted by an unexpectedly bright light and a terrible sense of déjà vu. Somehow, I got the feeling that I was no longer in the tunnel.

'Oh thank da Lord for that, you're awake lad,' came the sound of Paddy's voice, hazily through the mist, *'Doc! He's awake!'* he then shouted off to his side.

At first I could concentrate on nothing but the sense of re-living an earlier moment in the day; the painfully bright light was the same as was the headache trying to break out of my skull. But then an understanding of what Paddy had just said began to sink in.

'Doc? Paddy, where the hell am I?' I asked, trying once more to open my eyes.

As the world around me came slowly into focus, I managed to discover the answer to my own question.

'Why am I in a hospital bed? Paddy, what's going on? What happened to me? The last thing I remember is being in the tunnel and then –'

'– Shh! Quiet now lad, I'll explain later,' he interrupted me, seconds before a doctor came walking into the room.

'Well now how's my favourite patient?' the doctor said, in an overly cheerful manner.

He was a young Pakistani man, from the look and sound of him, and seemed very pleasant. I found it a bit difficult to understand him though at first, the strain of which only succeeded in hurting my head more.

'Favourite patient?' I asked confusedly, *'How can I be your favourite patient, I've only just woke up?'*

'Exactly my friend. You come in all nice and quiet, no fuss and minimum amount of blood. I examine you, patch you up and all before you wake. Ah, if only all my work was this simple,' he sighed.

'Wait, I was bleeding?' I said in shock.

'Oh yes, from numerous cuts and abrasions, but only a little bit from your head. I've cleaned out all your wounds and got you stitched up. You should be left with only minimal scaring.'

'You've given me stitches! Where?' I replied as the level of shock slowly increased in my voice.

'On the back of your head my friend, were you took the main trauma. Quite a nasty blow too I must say, going to leave one heck of a bump.'

'Am I going to be okay,' I asked, almost pleadingly.

'That is what I am going to find out now if you'll just sit up for me please. Okay, are you on any medication? Look up for me

150

please,' he asked, as he placed his hands on either side of my face and gently pulled down my lower eye lids.

'*No.'*

'*Are you allergic to any medications? Look down for me please.'*

'*No. Not that I know of.'*

'*That's good. Any prior head injuries? Turn your head to the right for me please,'* he said as he checked around my left ear.

'*No. Err wait yes, I have actually. I once had a large box full of butter fall off a shelf on to my head when I used to work in a super market. Oh and then another time I cracked the back of my head on a stone plinth as I was backing out of a low cupboard at home and stood up too quickly.'*

'*Did you pass out on either of those occasions? Turn to the left please.'*

'*I did with the butter, but only for about 10 minutes or so,'* I replied, trying to play down the seriousness of the incident, as you do when fearing the doctor might be about to give you some bad news.

'*Okay, any bleeding disorder or history of bad bruising or bleeding?'* he asked as he felt around my neck and the base of my skull.

'*No, no. Not that I can remember anyway,'* I said feeling a little uneasy.

'*Okay, now if you will just follow my finger with your eyes please,'* he said before passing his finger side to side, up and down and then in towards my nose.

'*Good! All is well I think. You've had a minor concussion but your reflexes are fine, your mental status seems fine, there is no injury to the neck and nothing to suggest a fracture to the skull. The small amount of bleeding indicates that the impact has caused light bleeding under the scalp but outside of the skull and will most likely form a large hematoma, or "goose egg" bruise. This here should help keep that down,'* he said handing me an ice pack, '*I see no need for you to have a CT scan, just observation for 24 hrs and a lot of rest. You should be yourself again in no time. Though I would suggest that from now on you try and be a bit more careful with your noggin. Anymore blows to the head and you will start to forget where you left your shoes,'* his attempt at humour was appreciated, if a little unsuccessful.

'*Thank you doctor,'* I said with grateful relief, '*am I okay to leave now then?'*

151

'Well, I would actually like to keep you here for a little while longer, just to check that all is well if that's okay with you?'

I could tell from his tone that it wasn't really a question and, feeling quite lethargic, I didn't really mind the idea of just laying back on the bed for a while.

'Now I know it may be difficult but I need you to stay awake for me and sit up,' he added, dashing that hope, *'we can raise the back of the bed up for you though so you can recline a bit. If you feel any dizziness or sickness then please don't hesitate to shout for me, otherwise just take it easy and you'll be out of here in no time.'*

As the door clicked shut behind him, I instantly turned to Paddy with demand of an explanation. It turned out that a stone had become dislodged and dropped from the roof of the tunnel, knocking me out, despite Paddy's best efforts to push me clear of it. He showed me the bandage around his arm where it had hit him after bouncing off my head, giving him a nasty graze. He had managed to drag me to the exit were he then phoned Bob to come and help. Together they were able to lift me out of the tunnel and into Bob's car. At that point Paddy insistently jumped into the driver's seat and sped me down to the Alnwick Infirmary. A journey which, apparently should have taken about 20 minutes, he somehow managed in 10. I don't even want to imagine how fast he'd been going. He'd told the doctor that I'd lost my footing on a stone stairwell and taken a nasty tumble. I suppose it was the best way to describe both the head injury and all the cuts and scrapes I'd sustained from my fall without having to explain what actually happened. Quite how he'd explained what had happened to his own arms, I never did ask.

By the time I woke up I'd been unconscious for just under half an hour he'd informed me, seeming somewhat relieved to see me awake. I'm sure I saw a slight look of guilt on his face though. I guess he now felt bad for taking me down there in the first place.

When at last I got the all clear to leave the infirmary, I found myself baffled upon stepping out of the front door. Though the doctor had said my head was fine, I was tempted to go back inside and ask for a second opinion as there seemed to be a distinct lack of light in the sky for the time of day it should have been.

'Jesus! How long were we in the tunnel?' I asked Paddy in disbelief.

'Why, what's wrong lad?'

'I'm a little confused is what's wrong. It was still light out when we went down there, now its pitch bloody black out here? I feel like I've just lost half of a day of my life.'

'Well at least we know the bump hasn't affected your keen powers of observation lad,' he said with a chuckle.

To be fair, I didn't quite see what was so funny about it.

'What time is it Paddy? Have I still got time to catch a train home?' I asked.

'No, you won't catch one now, but that's no bad thing as it turns out,' he answered with a smile, *'Come, I'll explain on the way back, but first we need to get ourselves a taxi.'*

We had to call for a taxi because Bob had been unable to wait with us, having already abandoned his post for too long in getting me down to the doctors. By the time we got back to Bamburgh and picked up Paddy's car, it was knocking on 9pm. On the way there, Paddy had explained how, after what the doctor had said about being under observation for 24hrs, he thought it best that I should go back to Lindisfarne and stay with him for the night so he could keep an eye on me. Initially, the thought of having to wait another night to get home did not sit well with me. But then knowing that it would be too late to catch a train now anyway, I found myself accepting his offer. To tempting was the thought of having a nice cosy bed to fall into after the eventful day I'd had. It felt so long since I'd enjoyed a proper good night's sleep.

'Okay Paddy, you win,' I conceded, *'I'll head home in the morning instead.'*

'Aha, good lad, you know it makes sense. I'll take you up to the station whenever you're ready tomorrow...but not before a good hearty breakfast.'

Leaving the castle, we thanked Bob for his help and began the short trip back to Holy Island. The wind had not let up and seemed even more menacing now for the darkness that hid its coming. A low rumble out over the sea resonated through my body as it travelled inland. The storm that had retreated during the day seemed now only to have done so to return back under the cover of night. I was suddenly quite glad that I was going to stay with Paddy and that his house was not too far away. It was time to get in, get warm and let the wind and the rain break futilely against solid walls.

During the drive, Paddy took it upon himself to enthral me with more tales of Ley tunnels and the history of the area. Most of it I just tuned out though; my head was banging enough already, despite the painkillers the doctor had given me. He talked so much that when the buzzing in my ears suddenly went quiet, I sat up and took notice.

'What's wrong?' I asked him as the car became lit up by lights flashing behind us, *'Why are you slowing down?'*

'The car behind has been following us since we left the castle and now they're flashing us down. Perhaps they've seen something wrong with the back of the car,' he said slowly, as if he didn't quite believe his own words.

A swell of unease rose in unison with a growing suspicion as I quietly questioned just who would want to stop us at this time of night. Looking into the wing mirror, I quickly found the answer to that question revealed as the car behind dipped its head lights and a flash of lightning illuminated the people within.

'Oh Shit! Shit! No Paddy, Paddy get us out of here, get us out of here NOW!!' I yelled, as a bolt of panic shot through my chest.

'Why, what's wrong lad?' he asked calmly.

'JUST DO IT! PLEASE PADDY DRIVE!!'

The unease I had felt exploded into full blown fear as I saw a figure getting out of the car behind and immediately recognised it to be one of the men who'd chased me from Penrith. Without another word, Paddy threw the car into gear and put his foot down, racing away from them in a screech of tyres.

'Are you going to tell me now lad why I just left half my bloody tyres on the road back there?' he asked with a forced calmness.

'It's the Masons!' I yelped, *'They've found me again.'*

'What? Are you sure lad?' he questioned, glancing back into his rear-view mirror.

'Bloody positive Paddy. It's the same two bastards that came to my house looking for me....how the fuck did they find me out here?' this last bit I said more to myself as I struggled to comprehend the tenacity of their pursuit.

'I don't know lad, but it ain't good for either of us.'

'You've got to get me out of here Paddy, please!' I pleaded to him with the restlessness urgency of a passenger desperately wishing there was an accelerator pedal on his side of the car too.

154

'Alright now lad, just calm down and let me think for a minute,' he said with a look of worried concentration. *'How sure are you that they didn't see you get on the train over here?'*

'What?' I had only been half listening to him as most of my attention was focused on look out of the reappearance of the headlights behind us.

'The train lad, are you certain they didn't see you boarding the train?' he stressed impatiently.

'Yes, I'm bloody positive they didn't,' I stressed back, *'What difference does it make anyway?'*

'The difference lad, is that if they didn't see you get on the train then there is only one other way they could have followed you over here,' he paused and turned his head to look at me, *'who knew you were coming here?'*

It took a moment for the meaning behind his concern to sink in. When it did, my eyes widened and I felt a knot in my stomach.

'No, no, you...you don't think they got it out of one of my friends do you? None of them would have given it up easily.'

My response was a mixture of denial and fear.

'I hope not for their sake lad, but these bastards didn't just appear out of thin air. Whatever it is that Archer's found, these guys really mustn't want anyone knowing about it.'

I was sure that no harm would have come to any of my friends, but I feared the possibility that I was wrong. I had only the naive belief that it was inconceivable to think that these men would "interrogate" them just to find me and get their hands on Archer's journal. It was naive because one doesn't have to look to far these days to find people doing a lot worse for a lot less.

As my head filled with terrible thoughts, one very selfish one reappeared and pushed its way to the front...why hadn't I just waited at the train station?

We raced ahead, gaining a good distance from our head start, before Paddy made an impossibly sharp turn at speed to send us screaming back onto the causeway road.

'What are you doing Paddy? This takes us back to Holy Island....it's a bloody dead end!' I practically screamed at him.

'Trust me lad, I know what I'm doing,' he shot me down, *'This has got to work,'* he added more to himself.

It wasn't long before the lights of our pursuer's car appeared once more in the rear-view mirror. I began unconsciously rocking in my seat, desperately willing us to go faster as we twisted and turned at dangerous speeds around the little country lane. When at last we made it down to the causeway, Paddy's crazy driving having re-gained a bit of distance between us and the Masons, my heart sunk as it came into view. The dark waters of the sea, thrashing in its violent battle with the now raging storm above, had already re-claimed it.

'Oh Shit, it's flooded, Paddy it's fucking Flooded! How was This a good idea?' I broke down as the rising panic finally reached its peak.

'Calm down lad, I was hoping for this,' he answered almost dismissively.

'What the hell are you talking about Paddy? They're right fucking behind us and we've got nowhere to go. What are we supposed to do, start swimming?' I was just shy of hysterical at this point, finding myself trapped, quite literally, between the devil and the deep blue sea.

'Not quite lad. You remember the snorkel?' he asked with a nod in its direction.

'Yes?'

'Well your about to see it in action.'

No sooner had he said this then he began to drive slowly out onto the causeway and into the deepening water.

'You might want to put anything valuable into your bags and then hold them above your head though,' he advised as the water started to surge over the bonnet, *'things are about to get a little wet.'*

Before I could question this advice, I felt water start to seep through the seals on the doors and flood the floor of the vehicle.

'Shit, Shit! Paddy, we're starting to flood?' I cried out.

'Yep. When they say a car's waterproof they mean the engine and electrics will stay dry, not us,' he replied calmly.

Trying to distract myself from the freezing cold water rushing in around my legs, I turned in my seat to see if we were still being followed. Sure enough the headlights of the Masons car crested over the hill and rolled down the water's edge. Holding my breath in the hope that Paddy's plan would work, I allowed a modicum of optimistic excitement to grow when I saw them roll to a stop and get out of the car.

'YES!' I exclaimed turning to Paddy and giving his shoulder a slap, *'It's working Paddy, your plan's working, they've stopped, they've........Oh Crap!'*

My jubilation was cut prematurely short as I turned back to gloat over our fallen enemy, only to see them back in the car and wading into the water.

'Scratch that, they're still coming. The water isn't stopping them Paddy?'

'Just wait lad,' he replied, still retaining his air of calm, *'a car like that ain't gonna get far in water this deep.'*

Watching with avid intent, I waited to see what would happen. As far as chases go it wasn't the most exciting as neither vehicle was going at any great speed. However, the tension involved more than made up for it. Every inch we made across the causeway was one closer to the safety of the island, but so too was it for our pursuers and the water flooding in was only getting deeper.

The storm outside was really raging now. Between the heavy rain shelling us from above and the explosions of spray erupting from the breaking waves around us, the wiper blades fought a losing battle to keep visibility clear. A couple of times I felt the vehicle lift slightly with the force of a strong wave and drift sideways, yet Paddy never once appeared anything but in control.

After what seemed like a painfully long time, we reached the tower about half way across. The water had risen up to my knees by this point and seemed to be flooding in a lot quicker now.

'Are you sure we're going to make it Paddy?' I asked with growing concern, *'The water's getting quite deep and we've still got a long way to go.'*

'Of course we are, this is nothing lad. Hardly wetting our toes yet,' he replied jovially, *'when it reaches up to my neck, then you can start to panic.'*

Feeling a little less than assured by his remarks, I looked back to check on our pursuers only to notice that they seemed to be getting further and further behind.

'Look!' I shouted, *'I think they've stopped,'* the optimistic excitement returning once more.

'Ha-ha! I knew their engine would flood eventually,' he blasted out victoriously. *'Now they've either got a nice cold swim to the life tower against the tide, or a longer one back to the shore. I dare say they won't be bothering us for the next eight hours.'*

My joy and relief over their inability to follow us was short lived as the later part of what Paddy had said slowly sunk in.

'But what happens in eight hours time Paddy? We're now trapped on an island with nowhere to go. What do we do when the tide goes back out and they can make it across?'

'Well lad,' he said with a foreboding tone, *'I do have a solution to that problem, but you're not going to like it.'*

'What is it Paddy? What aren't I going to like?' I replied, having completely missed the obvious.

'The only way off the island lad, that doesn't involve getting past those guys, is on a boat to Germany.'

Finding myself physically and emotionally drained from everything else that had happed that day, to this realisation I could but utter one response.

'Shit!'

Day 2 - Crossing the North Sea
A Storm Unleashed

There was little use in arguing at that point as my options were almost none existent. With the time until the causeway re-opened counting down like my last hours on death row, I had only two choices. I could either stay on Lindisfarne awaiting my fate, or I could take the boat to Germany and thereby effectively take up Paddy's challenge to follow in Archer's footsteps.

After reaching the other end of the causeway and emerging from the sea like a great leviathan, hissing water out of any gap it could find, we didn't stop driving until we reached Lindisfarne Castle.

'What are we doing here?' I asked Paddy, mildly confused at the destination.

'We need to get you off the island lad,' he said with conviction. *'My brother's anchored just off shore waiting for us. He will take you the rest of the way.'*

'Hang on a minute,' I said with affront, *'what makes you think that I've decided to go? Why do you assume that I have agreed to your plan when you haven't even asked me? For that matter, what the hell is your brother doing waiting off shore for us when he couldn't have known that we would be coming?'*

'Jaysus! That was a lot of questions in a very short amount of time,' replied Paddy, seemingly stunned by my bombardment of inquiries, *'I assumed that you would agree to go seeing as you know who is after you and to what lengths they will go to catch you. I figured that, unless you're completely stupid, you'll have realised by now that this is your only safe way off the island and probably the only chance you have of escaping them altogether. As for my brother, he's waiting off shore already because I asked him to this morning; just in case I was able to change your mind. A good thing I did too don't you think, otherwise you'd have been up the devils arse and no mistake.'*

159

I knew he was right. If these Masons had managed to find and follow me all the way to Bamburgh, then it's safe to assume they would never stop hunting me; regardless of whether I wanted nothing to do with their secrets or not. I knew too much already, and I doubted that they were coming just to give me a friendly warning. Still, I didn't appreciate his presumptuousness. He was trying to help though and there seemed little point in spitting feathers over things that had already happened. I *had* gone with him to Bamburgh, I *had* missed my train home and we *had* been cornered on the island by people I had a strong desire not to meet. What else now could I do but take the life line that Paddy had offered?

'*Fine, but you still should have asked me,*' I said quite childishly, reluctant to admit he was right again. '*That being said though, it still doesn't explain why we've come to the castle? How are we going get to your brother from here if he's anchored off shore?*'

'*We'll get to him by taking the small boat I have stashed away in the Kilns behind this Castle here. It's the one I use to fetch in the goods he sends my way. You see, there's nowhere for a boat the size of his to park up round here, the waters are just too shallow.*'

I sat quietly for a few seconds, watching as the weather outside the car seemed to be getting worse and worse. I began to wonder just how small a boat he was expecting us to go out there in.

'*There is one big flaw in this whole plan Paddy,*' I said as the thought suddenly came to me, '*How am I supposed to go to a foreign country when I don't have my passport? Stupidly, I did not think to pack it when I left home, but then nor did I think there'd be a need to,*' I added with a sharp tongue edged with sarcasm.

'*It's quite fortunate that you don't have it lad, as you'll be wanting to leave your real identity behind you anyway, just in case anyone tries to follow.*'

'*Christ's sake, I didn't realise I was going to have to become a sodding spy to do all this? How the hell do I leave my identity behind, I've only got the one?*' I snapped at him, '*What happens when I have to go through customs and they ask to see my passport, what do I say* "Erm, sorry, the dog ate it!"*?*'

'*Yes, you may want to try that one, right after they ask you why you came into the country on a smugglers ship!*' he snapped back, '*Have some sense boy. I can guarantee that you won't be seeing any customs agents where you're going. At least not until you leave Denmark, by which time my brother's contacts with have sorted you out with a new –'*

'– DENMARK?' I just about yelled, having almost choked on thin air, *'I thought I was supposed to go to bloody Germany?'*

'Ay lad, and you are, but my brother only sails to Denmark. You'll be making your way to Germany from there. Don't worry,' he said as a look of panic gripped my face, *'the German border's not far from where you'll be. My brother's assured me that his contact will be able to help you get to your destination. On that point, while I think of it, you will need to know where it is in Germany you want to go so you might want to be reading Archer's journal more thoroughly at some point.'*

'Haven't you read it?' I asked, not relishing the thought of getting lost over there if I couldn't find where to go, *'I thought you would know where I needed to go?'*

'I've read parts of it for sure, and I removed the page that mentioned your real name, but I can't do everything for you lad,' he said with mild irritation. *'You cracked the Amulet's code remember? Have a little faith in yourself. Trust your reasoning and you'll do fine. All that you need to know will be in those pages, Archer wouldn't have sent it were it not.'*

The thought of being in a foreign country by myself to find a needle in a haystack did not fill me with the sense of adventure I'd long sought, but it did present me with another question.

'Why is your brother going to take me the rest of the way Paddy? Where are you going to be?'

'Alas I can but get you to the boat lad. From there I must leave you and return as there are things I must see to, making sure those fellas back there don't follow you not least of all. I have done all I can to help you on your way. From here on out you must start your own journey. Just remember lad. Archer was no fool, he would not have entrusted this task to you if he thought you weren't up to the challenge.'

Sadly, I did not take from this the reassurance Paddy had meant it to give. Archer had met me for all of five minutes...how the hell could he know what I was capable of?

'What about my family though Paddy?' I asked, continuing my seemingly endless stream of questions, *'Those bastards know where I live. If they don't find me here then they might go back and try to force anyone who knows me into telling them where I've gone. And, what do I do about money? If I'm not going back to work I won't get paid. I have bills that won't stop*

161

just because I'm not there you know. And how will I afford to live over in Germany? The money I brought with me here has all but gone now and I can't afford to take out any more.'

'Have you forgotten about the money Archer left you lad?' he said, leaning back towards me after yet another failed attempt to get out of the car.

Reaching into his coat pocket, he pulled out a fairly hefty envelope which he then handed to me.

'Holy Shit!' I exclaimed upon opening it, *'There's got to be over a grand in here!'*

'Two to be exact,' he said offhandedly, *'and with it I actually have an idea that might solve your other problems. You see, Archer said in his letter to me that he would be leaving stashes of money with each piece of the journal, to aid you in your journey. Now, we know that there are likely to be three more pieces, the first of which should be somewhere in Germany. Therefore it's reasonably safe to assume that there will be another sizable sum waiting for you there. You won't need to spend any money as long as you're with my brother's friends, that I can assure you. So all you will need is enough to keep you going whilst you search whatever place in Germany you find indicated in your piece of the journal. With that in mind, if you want to keep only a portion of this first sum for yourself and send the rest back to your family, I will deliver it for you to make sure that they get it. How's that sound ? Say you take £500 with you and send home £1500, that should cover you for a good couple of weeks would it not? By then you'll have found the next stash and can send some more back, what'd you think?'*

I still couldn't get my head around what it was I was about to do. Everything seemed to be lining up just perfectly to leave me without a sound reason not to go; a suspicious man may have found it bordering on the unbelievable.

Whether by choice, fate or careful persuasion though, I had ended up in this situation from which there was no turning back and Paddy's idea did seem to offer a workable solution to my biggest concern. I only earned £200 a week stuck behind that bloody till at work, so sending £1500 of Archer's money back home would cover me for almost two months.

'Surely I'll be well and truly back by then?' I thought to myself.

'Will you definitely give it to them for me though?' I asked, knowing that whatever he said I had no choice but to believe him.

162

'What's the matter lad, don't you trust me?' he said, trying to hide the wounding in his voice.

'No, no, I didn't mean it like that,' I stumbled uncomfortably, *'it's just –'*

'– Well I will not tell you that you can trust me lad,' he interrupted, *'for you should never trust a man that says you can. Instead I will ask only that you think back and see if I have given you any reason not to.'*

In all honesty I couldn't think of a single reason not to trust this man, I'm not even sure what had made me ask the damn question in the first place. He had been nothing but kind and incredibly patient with me since we first met. Plus, he'd had that money for God knows how long since Archer had sent it to him. If stealing it was his plan, why would he have even told me about it in the first place?

I had no reason and, in truth, no choice. I couldn't afford not to trust him.

'Okay!' I said finally in defeat, knowing that it was pointless to fight it anymore, *'I trust you Paddy and I thank you for your offer. It would take a great weight off my mind knowing my mum would not struggle for money whilst I was gone.'*

'That's settled then,' he said with a smile returning to his face, *'Now, shall we go?'*

'But what am I going to tell people Paddy?' I asked, as my mind fell upon another obstacle, *'My mum thinks I'm just over here for a few days to see some friends, how am I going to explain that I'm now going to Germany? More to the point,'* I added, ignoring the pained sigh that emanated to the side of me as Paddy closed the door he'd managed to half open this time, *'what the hell do I tell work? Some of my colleagues know why I'm over here. My supervisor was good enough to give me this time off on short notice, but somehow I don't think she'd be happy with me not coming back?'*

He seemed to contemplate on this problem for a while before his face lit up as if the idea he had really did produce a light bulb.

'You were telling me earlier at dinner about your conservation projects and how you always wished you could go back and do more, right?'

'Yeees?' I answered with drawn out caution, wondering where exactly he was going with this.

'Well, why don't you tell your mum that you and your friends have been offered paid placements on one for a couple of

months? Tell her that you're sending some of the money they've paid you in advance back to her with your friend's father. That way she won't worry about you and will feel better because you're doing something you enjoy.'

'Sounds a bit farfetched, but okay, it might work,' I half-heartedly acknowledged, not entirely convinced yet, *'what then do I tell work though?'*

'Ah...,' he paused to think for a moment, *'...tell them it was all a test to see how resourceful you were for a competition you entered to win a place on the expedition... or something like that. Ask if it would be alright to take all of your holidays together this year as it is a once in a life time opportunity. Surly if they know what you're like they'll understand something like that?'*

In an insane way, the more I thought about it the more I had to admit that this didn't actually seem like such a bad idea. Anyone that knew me would attest to the fact that I yearned to be off exploring the world, so that part at least wouldn't be too farfetched. It would just be a case of whether or not I could make it sound believable; I'd never been much of a liar and the part about it having been a competition did push the realms of believability.

'What about the Masons, how do I explain them?' I asked, suddenly remembering the run in I'd had with them back home which resulted in Martin's "intervention".

'Okay,' he said with a drawn out pause, *'maybe just say that they were officials from the competition that were coming to explain the rules or something, and that there had just been a misunderstanding?'*

I decided that part might need some work, as they hadn't looked like the kind of people you would send to deliver a rule book. Plus I don't think I'd have had the heart to tell Martin that he'd pranged his car for nothing. Apart from that though, I decided it was a lie I could work with, and possibly even get away with, with a bit of luck. Unable to come up with anything better, it was all I had anyway. People would either believe it or they wouldn't. As I looked out into the elemental battlefield that lay ahead and thought of the danger that lay behind, I suddenly realised I had much more to worry about right now. How had it come to this?

Before I knew it, I had somehow found myself thinking of reasons to go instead of one's not to. It was one of those moments where it seems like you've made the decision to do something, although you're not fully sure how.

With my questions run dry and no more excuses, I grabbed my things and followed Paddy out of the car, wincing as the wind cut through my wet trousers with a cold that almost burnt my skin. We moved quickly around the side of the Castle and down to the Kilns by the beach, hunted by every raindrop that fell from above.

The Lindisfarne Kilns

With the ferocity of a growing storm, the weather seemed to be worse than ever, the brief respite we had seen at Bamburgh having long since been destroyed. As we ran for the cover of the Kilns we were bashed about on all sides by a wind that either couldn't decide which way it wanted to blow, or was just cruelly teasing us like a cat teases a mouse. One singularly stupid thought crept into my mind at that moment and came out of my mouth before I could stop it.

'Bloody hell, could the weather actually get any worse than this?'

With almost perfect timing, the sky directly above us was split by a huge fork of lighting quickly followed by a large and deafening thunder clap. Paddy turned and looked at me with an expression that said *'You had to say it didn't you!'* to which I acceptingly offered up a heartfelt, *'Sorry!'*

It took us no more than five minutes to reach the Kilns yet, by the time we got there, the pair of us were soaked to the skin. Needless to say we were both relieved to have made it to some shelter. As I stood catching my breath and trying to wring out my entire body, Paddy pulled out a torch, thankfully more modern than the one he'd had earlier, and instructed me to follow.

Heading in towards the back of the structure, I could see through the illumination he cast that we weren't the only one's who'd had the desire to get in out of the rain. We seemed to be sharing our shelter with a rather miserable herd of soggy looking woolly jumpers with legs, all huddled together.

'Here, give me a hand lad,' commanded Paddy, as he uncovered a small hard bottomed dingy with an outboard engine on the back.

'You have got to be shitting me!' I swore in disbelief, *'We can't go out there in this, we'll die. Have you seen the size of those waves?'*

As if on cue, another flash of lightening lit up the sky outside showing the sea thrashing about in a rage of water and white foam.

'Aye, she'll be a bugger to control in this alright, but we'll make don't you worry. It's not the first time I've been out in weather like this,' he said in a reassuring tone that failed to reassure, *'Come now, give me a hand to push her down to the beach.'*

I saw that the glorified life raft was sitting on a kind of trailer that would normally be hooked up to the back of a vehicle and towed. There was going to be no vehicle that day however. It was up to us to push it the 15+ meters down to the beach, from where we would then have to physically wade it out into the sea until deep enough to start the engine. After that would come the fun part of having to haul our, then soaking wet, bodies into the bloody thing. That is what Paddy should have told me we were doing for, as it was, I had to find all this out the hard way.

As we got down to the edge of the beach, with many a grunt and groan, the crashing waves sent cold, frothy water up to meet our feet. Paddy crouched down and began to take off his shoes and without question I followed his lead.

'Here,' he said, opening a compartment at the front of the boat, *'throw in anything you'd rather not get wet.'*

'Can I throw myself in there then?' I said sarcastically, not looking forward in any way to wading out into water cold enough to freeze an Eskimo; my exposed toes already beginning to go numb just from the lapping water.

'You go right ahead lad,' replied Paddy without missing a beat, *'Just make sure that your arse doesn't block my view when it sticks up at the front.'*

'Yeah, very funny,' I called back to him over the howling wind as I tucked away everything I had of value.

'At least I'm not having to hold it above my head this time though,' I thought to myself.

Little did I realise that I would soon wish I'd at least tried to get in that compartment. Yes I was already soaked from the ride across the causeway and drenched from the rain, so one might imagine it hard to get any wetter; but the worst was yet to come.

We positioned ourselves ready to lift the boat off of the trailer and I steeled myself ready for the plunge.

'Oh, before I forget,' yelled Paddy, as a strong gust of wind crashed against us trying to steal away his words, *'You'll be needing this.'*

He threw his phone over the boat towards me which, caught off guard, I then fumbled into the surf.

'Shit!' I cried out, quickly plucking the small brick-like object from the sea, *'I'm so sorry Paddy, I dropped it in the water. I wasn't expecting you to throw anything at me. It'll be buggared now.'*

'Don't worry lad, it'd take more than a little water to kill that thing. It's scratch-proof, water-proof, hell it's damn near bomb-proof and practically unbreakable.'

'But why are giving it to me? I've got my own phone,' I replied quizzically.

'Firstly, I'm only loaning it to you and secondly, is yours set up for international use?'

No was the simple answer. I hadn't been abroad since getting my current phone, my financial situation having gone somewhat south not long after buying it. It was a very handy device however, with all the bells, whistles and apps you expect from a smartphone these days. Sadly though, I realised that I would be unable to use any of them once I left the shores of Britain. I didn't have time to call my service provider to have it configured for international use for a start. But, more importantly, I knew there wasn't a chance in hell I'd be able to afford the ridiculous call charges it would incur, and God help me if I forget to turn off the data roaming; I'd probably end up losing my house.

With that in mind, I thanked Paddy for his generosity and stored the phone up in the compartment with the rest of my things; taking the time to make sure that any settings on my own phone that could cost me money abroad where disabled before turning the whole thing off. I knew I would need to turn it on again at some point to get a copy of my numbers from the phone book, but that would have to wait until I was back on dry land and out of the horrendous weather. Right then there were much more pressing matters to attend to.

The next twenty minutes were, in a word, chaotic. It took us about ten of them just to get the dingy out beyond the break waters and deep enough to start the outboard. Every time we made some headway another wave would come crashing into us, lifting us up of our feet and carrying us back a few paces. Then came the fun of trying to get into the damn thing once we were out deep enough.

Ever tried to climb up a slippery surface with wet hands? It's no easy task let me tell you. In fact, if I'm completely honest, it was a little bit frightening; treading water in a rough sea with a storm wailing overhead in the pitch black of night. It seemed like the further out we got the larger the waves became, crashing down on top of me trying to force me under and shake the vice like grip I had on the boats rope handles.

At one stage a large wave almost succeeded in this endeavour, nearly overturning the boat as it crashed into us, and managed to suck me down into the dark unknown. All my senses seemed to fail at once and I was left completely disorientated, but I clung to the boat like my life depended on it. Not knowing which way was up anymore though, along with the weight of my wet clothes, served only to make dragging myself back to the surface even more difficult. When I finally managed to break free and gasp for some air, I was almost instantly hit by another wave; stealing from me the chance to sufficiently fill my lungs. I started to panic as it happened every time I tried to catch my breath, sending sea water down my throat instead of air.

Somewhere in the turmoil of the moment I eventually lost my grip on the boat and, being unable to open my eyes long enough to search for it, felt like I was being swept away out to sea. In that moment, I truly thought I was going to die out there.

Suddenly, I felt myself being pulled upwards by the back of my belt. It was Paddy, hauling me ungraciously into the boat, along with about half a tonne of sea water that had soaked up into my clothes and flooded my lungs.

'Having problems were we lad?' he asked condescendingly.

'Of course I was having bloody problems,' I yelled at him through a splutter of sea water, *'I wasn't just letting myself drown for the hell of it!'*

As I lay on my back recovering from the ordeal, breathing deep all the air that my lungs could carry, Paddy kicked the motor into life and began navigating the waves. Taking us into what I can only describe as the outer ring of hell.

It was slow going for most of the way, as the unyielding waves seemed to toss us through the air as if our boat where a defenceless porpoise batted between two dolphins playing catch. It was like a nightmare that wouldn't end. The angry roaring of the waves and murderous claps of thunder, along with flashes of lightening that illuminated the sky and a wail on the wind akin to that of a banshee's cry. I clung to the boat for dear life, closing my eyes and praying to whatever Gods may be listening for an end to the torment of the sea.

The Morrigan

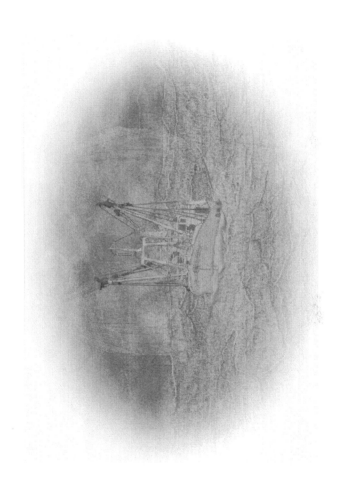

After what seemed like hours, my prayers were finally answered. Amongst the turbulent waves and streaks of light, I caught a glimpse of our destination. Ahead of us lay The Morrigan. Rising like a demon of the sea, high upon the waves, the outline of a large fishing boat came into view with an intimidating presence. Approaching it head on, the folded up rigging of nets and beams made it look like some kind of hellish giant bat waiting to ensnare us as we crossed the sea. Fortunately, my overactive imagination was soothed as I heard voices calling out to us, followed quickly by a long length of rope to be pulled in by.

'Steady yourself lad, this could get a little tricky,' warned Paddy.

A little tricky was the mother of all understatements. The fishing boat had a kind of winch thing for lifting a life raft in and out of the water, which we were trying to use with our dingy. If I'd had a pound for every time we almost capsized or crashed into the side of the larger boat, well I probably wouldn't be where I am now because I'd have been able to pay someone else to go on this quest for me.

When eventually we made it level to the deck, I climbed over the railing and flopped to the floor with exhausted relief; wishing desperately for the world to stop moving. I opened my eyes and was met by a great big shovel of a hand offering to help me up.

'Welcome aboard young fellow,' said the big jovial man attached to the hand, *'Captain Quinn and the fine ship Morrigan at your service.'*

Keeping hold of me whilst I found some semblance of balance, the man then looked past me to Paddy who was being helped up by another member of the boats crew.

'I see you finally managed to get some poor bastard to go off on this barmy quest of yours then brother?' he said.

'I see you're still introducing this heap of junk as being a "fine ship"?' Paddy answered quick wittedly, seeming to ignore his brother's comment.

'Don't listen to him son, this is a vessel well befitting her name,' said the captain with mock wounding. *'Named after the great queen Morrigan, the ancient Irish goddess of war, strife and fertility. Said to be the crow that flies above the warrior warning of his impending doom, she flies now above our quarry in much the same way,'* he added, his chest all puffed out with pride.

172

'Pay no attention to him lad, it's named after no god of war is this boat. The name comes from our Grandma, who gave him the money to buy the damn thing on the condition that he would name it after her,' Paddy interjected. 'It was just pure dumb luck that she was named after such a figure from Irish mythology and you know it,' he bantered back, deflating the captain where he stood. 'Although actually, thinking about it,' he added with a ponderous pause, 'the old coot shared a lot of traits with her namesake. She did nothing but cause war and strife within the family, and her arrival always heralded some kind of doom. My little brother here was the only person the sour old crone ever liked, may she rest in peace.'

'Ahaha! It's good to see you Aidan!' roared the captain, laughing cheerfully as he embraced Paddy in a bone crushing bear hug.

Standing proudly in a bright yellow fisherman's Mac he was almost the twin of Paddy, albeit a younger one with a bulkier frame, thicker beard and more muddled accent. If I hadn't already known, I could have easily guessed that they were brothers.

'It's been too long Finn,' responded Paddy whilst returning the reuniting grasp.

'That it has brother, but come let us get in out of this drizzle,' the captain said throwing his arm around Paddy, 'What news have you of my little girl?'

I watched as the pair walked towards a door that led inside and was about to follow, when something suddenly struck me.

'Wait! So your name is Finn Qui –' I called out after them.

'DON'T say it! Don't even think it! I was interrupted, 'Cap'n hates anyone bringin up his name. Call him Finn, Cap'n Quinn, or even just Cap'n, but never call him by his full name.'

Catching a brief glimpse of the man in question looking over his shoulder at me, I turned to see where the voice of warning had come from. Behind me was a short, stocky man with a salt encrusted mop of curly hair, dressed in dark waterproofs and leaning against the ships railing with a wry smile on his face. Without even asking his name I dove straight into sating my curiosity.

'Why?'

'Why do you think?' the man replied in a strong cockney accent, 'It's not exactly the greatest of names is it? Sounds like the punch line to a bad joke don't it?'

173

He pushed himself away from the rail to offer me his hand, seemingly unaffected by the rolling of the sea which had me stumbling about like a novice trying to balance on a surfboard.

'Graham Davey's the name, but most people just call me 'Gravy'. I'm what you might call the First Mate on this here tub. Bin with the Cap'n for twenty years now and probably know him better than his own brother there. If there's anything I've learnt well over all those years, it's that the man is a big friendly teddy bear until you ask him about his name, then he turns into a bear with a sore arse who will box your ears so you can't hear the answer.'

'And that answer would be?' I asked quizzically.

'Well, there have been many theories regarding this issue as the Cap'n never seems to tell the same version of the story twice,' he began in reply with a mock seriousness. *'Some are quite intriguing, and others downright ridiculous. But my personal favourite, the one that he confided to me when I became his second in command, goes something like this. When his parents got married and started thinking about kids, they made a deal that his old lady would get to name their first and his old man their second. Now his mother, bein an incredibly patriotic Irish lady, named their first son Aidan after the famous Irish saint, that bein your friend over there,'* he said with a nod toward the door Paddy had gone through. *'His father on the other hand had no intention of following suit when our dear Cap'n was born. He wanted to name him after the titular character of his most treasured book from childhood, a tattered old copy of Mark Twain's Adventures of Huckleberry Finn,'* he paused as his face scrunched into a "see where this is going" look. *'You see it was the only present he ever got from his old man, before the randy old git ran off with the milk maid and left his mother to take care of him and his three brothers. Fortunately for the Cap'n, his old lady managed to stop his father calling him Huckleberry Quinn. However, she couldn't stop him from then deciding upon Finn or she'd have been breaking their deal.'*

'Wow!' was my initial reaction, *'And I thought I had it bad being named after some goon from my Mum's favourite T.V. show.'*

'Aye, took a lot of punishment at school did poor Finn Quinn. Then again, I guess it was what made him into the man he is today. So maybe having a silly name isn't such a bad thing

when you think about it; builds a man of strong character and thick skin.'

'Thick enough that people have to be warned about how not to address him?' I said sarcastically.

'Na mate, you don't understand. It's not for the Cap'ns sake that I warned you, it's for yours,' replied Mr Davey with a smile. *'Welcome aboard the Morrigan,'* he added with a slap on the back before leaving to go about his business.

With the etiquette of the boat firmly in mind, I quickly headed in out of the rain. Stumbling from side to side trying to keep my feet, I made for the door that the two brothers had gone through but, by the time I arrived into the galley where they had been sitting, Paddy was just getting up to leave.

'Ah, there you are,' said the Captain, *'we were beginning to think you'd got lost.'*

'Just admiring the scenery,' I replied flatly, trying desperately to suppress the feeling of queasiness that washed over me with every rough wave that hit the ship.

'So lad,' said Paddy, standing before me now, *'this is where we finally part ways ay?'* there was a genuine touch of sadness in his voice, *'I have instructed my brother to look after you well and he's gonna introduce you to a friend of his when you get to Denmark who will help you get started. After that lad, it's all down to you.'*

'Great! No pressure then,' I thought to myself.

'Don't look so worried,' he added, obviously aware of the apprehension written across my face, *'It's no accident that brought you to this point. It's your destiny, whether you believe in it or not, to follow in Archer's footsteps. Everything you'll need to begin is in that journal, the rest you will soon find within yourself. I wish you the very best of luck and anticipate the day when our paths will cross again. Farewell my friend.'*

With a hearty handshake and a pat on the shoulder, he passed beside me and back out into the storm. I watched him disappear over the side into the dingy, and once again brave the furious waves as he headed back towards Holy Island. It filled me with a strange emptiness seeing him go as the reality of my situation suddenly began to weigh down on me. This was it, no turning back now. I felt like Bilbo Baggins heading out for Erabor with the company of dwarves, with home behind and the world ahead. I was going on an adventure. One I felt I'd been somehow powerless to refuse.

175

Focus on the horizon, someone had once told me, *If you feel sick, just focus on the horizon and you'll be fine.* It would have been sound advice had it been daytime and had I in fact been able to see said horizon but, out there in the dead of the night, I couldn't see a bloody thing. The sea itself was an invisible predator waiting to drag me down into its icy depths as the mighty sea god Poseidon unleashed his full unconquerable fury upon all who dare traverse his waters. At least, that is what it felt like as I hurled my guts over the side of the boat for the hundredth time.

That in itself was a task of surprising difficulty when restricted by a massive lifejacket squeezing against your stomach, which was itself held onto by a large fisherman ensuring that I didn't fall overboard. The worst part about it all though, was the fact that the crew didn't seem effected at all. Sure they were probably experienced seafarers but still, three of them had been playing poker in their cabins for god's sake...I mean, how in the hell do you play cards on a boat that never seems to sit at the same level twice?

After Paddy had left, Captain Quinn took me on a guided tour of his vessel showing me the galley, kitchens, cabins, wheelhouse, catch tanks and processing rooms, all whilst giving me a running commentary.

'Here in the north sea there are over 230 species of fish but mostly it's Cod, Haddock, Whiting, Plaice, Sole, Mackerel and Herring which are amongst the most commercially fished along with Norway Lobster, deep-water prawns and brown shrimp. We are mostly in the business of the old Norway Lobster however.'

'Is there a lot of call for lobster in England?' I asked as he showed me the catch they had made earlier that day.

'More than you'd think lad,' he replied, *'in fact I'd be surprised if you haven't eaten some yourself.'*

'God no, not me,' I scoffed, *'I abhor the eating of lobster. The way the poor things are killed, boiled alive just so they don't poison their own flesh, it's barbaric. All so some toffee nosed, insultingly ignorant, fat bastard can pay an obscene amount of money to eat the "so called" delicacy. We already farm plenty of animals for food that don't have to die in such horrific ways; it's an unnecessary waste to kill lobster as well.'*

Before realising, I had somehow managed to get up on my high horse and condemn the livelihood of the very man that was supposed to be helping me. Not the brightest idea I've ever had I have to admit.

'Have you ever had scampi lad?' he asked in a tone I had come to know as Paddy's *"I'm about to educate your arse"* tone.

'Yes, it used to be a favourite dish of mine when I was younger, why?' I admitted cautiously.

'Well, I don't wish to upset you and your delicate sensibilities, but scampi is made from the muscular tail of the Norway Lobster.'

I didn't know what to say. I felt stupid for unknowingly being an ignorant hypocrite and more so for lecturing a man about the morals of his job when, really, I knew sod all about it.

'Don't feel bad son,' he said with a smile, *'to be honest I don't much care for the killing of the poor creatures myself. Unfortunately though, the demand for them is too lucrative for a man like me to ignore in such economically uncertain times.'*

I appreciated his graciousness for not beating me over the head with my lack of knowledge and was very glad to be moving on. As he took me round the rest of the boat he reeled off a description that portrayed the love he had for it.

'Although she may look like an old Junker, the Morrigan is actually quite a modern vessel. She's what's known as a 36M Steel Beam Trawler, built in 1984 but renovated to my specifications back in 2007. I won't bore you with the details of the boats dimensions but it's enough just to say that she's been altered to look a lot smaller and slower than she really is.'

'For while we are still fishermen, a large portion of our time is now taken up with the...acquiring of certain products for people who really dislike having to watch their hard earned money disappearing into the bottomless pit that is the governments tax coffers. This being so, the finding of good secure hiding spots has been a priority in the ships renovation. We run on a modified MAK 6M 452 engine that my engineering officer there made a few "adjustments" to,' he said, pointing to a grubby looking man in dirty overalls who was swearing at a piece of machinery and hitting it intermittently with a large wrench. *'Somehow the clever bastard managed to take its standard 1600 BHP and almost double it. She is complete with motorised winches, electronic navigation, auto-pilot and Radar. Our communications range from basic radio and ship wide comms, to maritime distress systems and EPIRBs.'*

I didn't bother to ask what the last one stood for as my head was struggling to handle the information overload as it was.

177

'Then we have our fish detection instruments which are quite sophisticated if I do say so myself. Everything from echo sounders and sonar, to net sounders and catch sensors. Best of all is that most of it can be controlled from the wheelhouse, a paradise of buttons and switches all beautifully arranged around my chair from where I can practically play God.'

I had to give it to him it was a very impressive boat, once you looked past the rusty exterior that is. The pride in his voice as he talked was akin to that of a father showing off his son. So much enthusiasm did he have in fact that it wasn't long before the old Quinn family trait came out; the love of giving a good history lesson. He began with a brief synopsis of maritime history and the birth of the fishing trawler, something I might have found quite interesting had it not been for one thing....the onset of chronic seasickness.

Though I had been on plenty of boats before without ever becoming ill (more or less) I had never before been on one in the middle of a storm. The constant up and down, rise and fall, side to side rocking motion soon began to play havoc with my body. So rough was it that at one point, as I watched from the wheelhouse, the entire bow of the boat disappeared beneath the water as we crashed down off an enormous wave. It was a madness that seemed to never end.

With my balance thrown, my head swimming and my legs unable to adjust to the unrelenting movement, the captain's words started to wash in and out in time with the rolling of the waves themselves.

'The Trawlers of the North Sea can be dated all the way back to the 17th century when the British developed the Dogger, named after the Dutch word for a fishing vessel that tows a trawl. The area known as Dogger Bank was named so due to it being an area so often fished by the Dogger trawlers. They may have been slow vessels but they were very sturdy making them perfect for fishing in the rough conditions.'

By this point my head was spinning uncontrollably and, as the Captain spoke those last words that vocalised the seas current stage, I felt the contents of my stomach rise up suddenly into the back of my throat. It was only fortunate that, at the time, we had been walking out on deck, as I had a window of just a few seconds to throw my head over the side rail before erupting like a volcano. Just a shame I chose the wrong side of the boat.

There are a few things you should never do into the wind, but being sick has to top the list. Between watching the sea rise and fall right before my eyes and having the wonderful sensation of vomit blowing back in my face, that night quickly became one of the most unpleasant of my life. To make matters even worse though, every time I pulled my head back up above the rail, or the rolling of the waves lifted my side of the boat, all I could hear was Captain Quinn continuing his monologue.

Unperturbed by my situation he just continued to talk, happily holding on to the back of my life jacket as he did. Over the crash of the waves and the wail of the storm, I couldn't help but pick out odd words he spoke.

'Trawler designs changed from sail to coal-fired steam by World War I..........................many fishing trawlers were commissioned for use as minesweepers..........................During the Cold War many fishing trawlers were re-fitted so they could be used as spy ships..........................The beam trawl was used in the.......................... Sea by the.......................... from Grimsby and Lowestoft...................19th century.......................... rigid framework..........................ideal for towing behind..................................'

Then I was gone; his words eventually just becoming one muffled noise. I don't know how long I was out there in such a state, but it was long enough to feel like the life was draining from of me. My body became heavy and uncontrollable until I could support it no longer. Bereft of the energy to even be sick anymore, I crumpled to the deck and gave into exhaustion as the world spun away into a painful blur.

I don't think I passed out, but then I can't quite remember what happened between feeling like I wanted to die and waking up somewhere soft and comfortable, as if it had all been just a horrible nightmare.

As the morning sunlight kissed my eyes awake through an open port hole, I found myself in a large double bed that lay in a beautifully decorated cabin; an entire world away from where I had been the night before. Were it not for the now gentle rocking motion of a much calmer sea, and the occasional cry of a seagull, I'd have thought that I was in a five star hotel. The whole room was lined with a rich walnut effect wood panelling on the walls and furnishings along with a thick, warm carpet covering the floor.

179

Looking around the room I saw a walk in wardrobe, a half concealed flat screen T.V and a beautiful writing desk. The bed consisted of a wooden frame with rounded edges that housed the most comfortable mattress I've ever lay on, that dipped slightly into the middle to keep you from rolling out in rough weather. The whole effect was topped off by an impressive collection of old maps and maritime paintings decorating the walls; some of which I noticed bore Paddy's signature, a fact that led me to deduce I was in the captain's cabin.

Slowly swinging my aching body out of the bed, running my toes through the soft carpet bristles as they touched the floor, I forced myself to get up and made for my bags. They had been placed on a chair for me to the side of the bed and from them I picked out a clean change of clothes. Noticing a large towel draped over the back of the chair, I gathered that I was permitted the use of the cabins facilities to wash up. Investigating the en-suite bathroom, I found a neat compact shower and toilet that I wasted no time in making full use of.

As I dried off after a long, revitalising stand beneath the warm cascade of cleaning water, the irony of my situation came clear in my mind. In a matter of two days I had met two brothers, been sick in front of both and gotten into such a state that required them to carry me to a bed. I was definitely making a good impression upon the Quinn family.

Heading out of the cabin and down through the narrow corridors of the boats interior, I found my way into the galley where the crew were just sitting down to breakfast. Again, like the captain's cabin, the room seemed out of place to the exterior of the boat in a way I hadn't noticed the night before. A polished wood floor, cream leather seats around a dining table, and a kitchen that contained all the modern amenities you could possibly ask for in a compact, but no less effective, form. It was most definitely not your average fishing boat.

'Hey, Upchuck, how are you feeling this morning?' hailed Gravy upon noticing my arrival, *'You missed the best part of the storm last night you know. Must have been dead to the world to sleep through her,'* he added, indicated for me to take a seat.

'Christ! You mean it got worse?' I said sleepily as I gingerly sat down, feeling quite beat up from my ordeal.

'Aye didn't it just,' he replied, *'After carrying you into the Cap'ns cabin, we settled down to a hellish night being tossed about by gale force winds that must have reached, what, 45,50*

knots?' he threw the question out to his shipmates who all seemed to agree. *'Hell, it was one of the worst storms I've ever seen.'*

'This is probably going to sound like a really retarded question,' I said, distracted by a lack of understanding for nautical terms, *'but what is a "knot" exactly? I mean what does it equate to in miles per hour?'*

'A knot is a unit of speed equal to one nautical mile per hour, which is equal to exactly 1.852 km/h and so that would make it approximately 1.151 mph,' answered a man sitting down at the other end of the table.

'That there is Dom, our resident engineer and general know-it-all,' explained Gravy as I recognised the man to be the wrench wielding, Tourette's suffering man I'd seen during the captain's tour.

'Well someone has to bring a bit of intelligence to this fucking ragtag bunch of educationally stunted high school rejects,' retorted the scruffy looking man.

'Yeah, Yeah! Why don't you just go and calculate the square root of my arse!' bantered Gravy to a ripple of laughter from the rest of the crew.

After that, he proceeded to introduce me to the rest of the men and I spent the next half an hour getting to know them all whilst taking all their good natured jibes at my state the night before.

When breakfast was done and I'd braved a couple of pieces of toast, longing for the full English the guys were having but daring not chance it, I headed up to the wheelhouse where I was told Captain Quinn was waiting for me.

'Good morning Captain,' I offered as I entered the room, *'Thank you for helping me last night and for giving up your bed, it was most appreciated.'*

'Ah, top of the mornin to you son, glad to see you back up and on your feet,' he said, swivelling in his chair to look at me with a big friendly smile, *'You were in quite a bad way to be sure, but then it wasn't really the nicest of days to be arriving on board. Nearly lost you over the side a few times.'*

'Truthfully, the way I was feeling last night, falling overboard would have been a blessing,' I said as I rubbed my aching neck.

'Aye, I can believe that,' he replied with a chuckle. *'You know, the lads were even taking bets as to how long you could go on throwing up for.'*

Responding with a painfully embarrassed wince, I looked out of the window desperately searching for a change of subject.

'So, where are we headed?' I asked, gazing out into an endless mass of dark blue water.

'Well, weather permitting, we be headed for the port of Ringkøbing in Denmark. That's where we'll be taking on some "supplies" and I'll be handing you into the care of my good friend Soren. He's my "partner in crime" if you like and he'll be able to help you out with everything you need. All being well he should also be able to give you a lift into Germany when you're ready as he'll be needing to go on another supply run after this pickup,' he replied.

Don't ask, don't tell, I thought to myself on the mention of "Supplies". Although I trusted that a man of Finn's character would not be dealing in anything other than the smuggling of duty free goods, I liked him and his crew too much to want to risk finding out I that might be wrong.

'How long will it take to get there?' I queried, actually quite looking forward to it having never before been to Denmark.

'On a good day this crossing would take between 15 to 18 hours, depending on how hard we flogged the engines,' he said with a wink, *'but, with the full force of that storm kicking us in the face, we could barely make 12 knots last night. Which means that, in the 6 hours the bitch blew for, we were only able to cover about 72 nautical miles. All in all we've probably got about another 300 to go, so we should make port sometime tonight. It'll just depend on how we hit the lock.'*

'The lock?' I questioned.

'Aye, the Hvide Sande sea lock. You see if we get there just as the lock is in use, we'll be delayed a while until it's free again.'

'Well then, is there anything I can do in the mean time to work off the debt that I owe you all?' I offered to him in hope that I could make myself useful to pass the time away.

'That's a grand offer there son, I like your spirit,' he said with another big smile, *'Have a word with Mr Davey, I'm sure he can find you something to do. Good form lad.'*

Feeling quite buoyed by his enthusiastic response, I took my leave and went to find Gravy. Upon informing him of my wish he told me that, if I didn't mind undertaking a rather monotonous job, they were in need of someone to check all the fishing nets for any tears or tangles. Apparently the two youngest crew members, who should have been doing that job, had instead been playing rock, paper, scissors over who's turn it was all morning. Currently, they were drawing even in a best of twenty seven.

As entertaining as it was to watch the pure frustration they had with each other, growing to such a level that the rest of the crew were taking bets as to which one would throw the first punch, it wasn't getting the job done and the day was wearing on.

I accepted the task willingly and quickly got to it after a little instruction, grateful to have something to take my mind off the days ahead of me. It was actually quite a nice job. Sure if you did it for long enough it would probably drive you insane, but for those few hours it was great. I was out in the fresh sea air with a clear blue sky echoing above my head, and the bright golden sun reflecting up off the sea, creating a very fine day indeed.

Day 3 - Ringkøbing, Denmark
The Unavoidable Lie

Reaching the coast of Denmark, we made our way through the sea lock that Captain Finn had talked of earlier. As we passed through, Gravy took it upon himself to inform me of how the lock came to be.

'At one time the little town of Ringkøbing, across there on the other side of the fjord,' he said whilst pointing out over a massive lake that lay before us, *'was a very active fishing port. That was before the narrow channel that connected the fjord to the North Sea started to silt up, making it difficult for ships to pass through. In 1931 that problem was solved when this sea lock was opened. Unfortunately though, whilst this meant that easy access to the sea was once again possible, it also meant that Hvide Sande was then the perfect place for a fishing port and consequently Ringkøbing lost out. Quite fortunate for us mind as it gives us a nice quiet place to conduct our business don't it?'* he offered up as a happy ending for his tale.

A funny character was Mr Davey. He had a very dry wit and a perpetually unimpressed look about him; as if he was so world weary that nothing could surprise him anymore. He also had an impressively sarcastic tongue, one that even managed to rival my own. I think that's half the reason I took to him so well; you just couldn't help but like the man.

Once through the lock, it didn't take us long to cross the blissfully calm fjord and, with a mixed feeling of relief and sadness, our destination at last came into view. When finally we sailed into the sleepy little fishing harbour, we did so under the colours of an early evening sky. The extinguishing of the suns flame, as it slowly sank down to the sea in our wake, cast beautiful rays of pink, red, orange and gold over the gentle ripples of the water and across the vastness of the open sky.

184

The docks were filled with yachts and fishing boats, moored for the night against the back drop of a quaint townscape that created the type of scene you'd normally see in an oil painting. At the time though, none of that mattered to me. The only thing I cared about was getting off that boat and planting my feet firmly back on dry land.

As we congregated on the dockside, the crew getting excited about their evening plans, I noticed a man getting out of his car a short distance from us. At first I dismissed the observation, but then I saw him start walking towards us. Taking more notice now, I watched his movements with growing concern. My self-defensive level of suspicion towards everything forced me to think...what if he was with the Masons?

As that question passed through my mind, I suddenly became aware of the man's intimidating size. He was bloody huge! Before I had time start panicking however, Captain Finn, having also seen the man, called me over and introduced me to the Danish half of his operation.

'This is my good friend Soren,' he said.

'Pleased to meet you friend,' the man said in a deep jovial voice, one that gave a contradictory feeling akin to that of seeing a grizzly bear with a friendly smile. *'New member of the crew is he Finn?'*

If ever there was someone you didn't want to disagree with, this was him. Give him a big axe and a horned helmet and you'd have the most authentic looking Viking you'd ever seen.

'Not quite,' replied the Captain, *'but I'll explain on the way. You ready son?'*

'Cap'n,' interrupted Gravy. *'The lads and I thought we might take him out with us for the night to better acquaint him with the local area and such,'* he said with a cheeky grin.

'Aye, by all means boys,' he answered, *'what say you?'* he then directed at me, *'fancy a drink to help get your land legs back?'*

'I'd love to go for a few drinks with you guys,' I said in a remorseful tone, *'but to be honest, I don't think I could manage it tonight. I'm still feeling worn out from the trip over here and really just need to hit the sack. Thanks for the offer though Gravy, I really appreciate the thought.'*

'No worries mate, maybe next time then,' he replied with a touch of disappointment in his voice.

Bidding farewell to the crew as they headed out, I followed Captain Finn over to his friend's car and climbed in. The big man was taking us back to his house where I was to stay for a few days until he was ready to make his next trip down into Germany. I paid little attention to my surroundings that night; the promise of warm bed that didn't rock was too alluring for me to focus on anything else.

When we arrived, Soren kindly showed me to the spare room his wife had made up for me, after I respectfully declined the invitation to join him and the Captain for a night cap. Saying goodnight and goodbye to Finn, knowing that he would be returning to his boat after their business talks were over, I thanked him whole heartedly once more for his hospitality before calling it a day.

I awoke the next day to the most tantalising of aromas, drifting through the house like the beckoning finger of a seductive woman. Rising from the nest of comfy bedding I'd built around myself, I followed my nose down into the kitchen; still half asleep but determined to appease my already watering taste buds. What I found was a rather comely looking woman, whom I later discovered to be Soren's wife Gytha, cooking up a breakfast storm. Looking past her to the active stove I saw, with ravenous eyes, the source of those mouth-watering smells; a frying pan full of thick, juicy rashers of bacon.

'God Morgen!' she said, seeing me stood in the kitchen doorway, *'Come, please, sit down. I will make you a plate.'*

Her voice was very warm and welcoming. Her words reaching my ears wrapped in a pleasant Danish accent; albeit one with just enough authority edged into it to suggest exactly whom it was that wore the trousers in that household. Soren was a big man and had the look of a Viking, but Gytha, she had the look of a Vikings wife.

Breakfast was something to behold. In one sitting I could have consumed a whole day's worth of food, with pastries and cakes, chesses and cold meats, breads of varying varieties and the best parts of a Full English just for good measure.

'We weren't sure what you like so I have made little of everything. Please, eat as much as you like,' she said with a tone of acceptance I would expect for family or friends, but one that seemed quite odd aimed at a complete stranger.

She made me feel very much at home which, considering the circumstances, was a surprising comfort. So much so in fact that I had no problem in getting straight down to business and

186

loading up my plate with a bit of everything. I discovered a world of new taste combinations that morning I can tell you.

Just as I began to dig in to my incredibly unique concoction of food though, Soren came in from outside and said;

'Aha! I see my wife's cooking has tempted you out of your bed, and I see also that you have started without me.'

At first I wasn't sure whether or not I'd caused offence by eating without him, but then he broke out into a big smile and let out a bellowing laugh as he landed a massive paw down heavily on my shoulder.

'Don't look so worried friend, eat, enjoy. Breakfast is the most important meal of the day and nobody prepares a better one than my little strudel.'

I laughed out a sigh of relief before tucking back into the fantastic bacon buttie I'd been building with layers of cheese and salami on a sweet bread. After a good morning kiss for his wife, Soren joined me at the table and very quickly gathered up his own breakfast concoction.

'So, Finn told me that you are in need to go to Germany yes?' he asked as Gytha set down another plate full of succulent bacon beside me.

She might not have been the best looking woman in the world, but her skills in the kitchen more than made up for it.

'Yes that's right,' I answered, momentarily distracted by the bacons arrival, *'though I'm not yet sure exactly where in Germany I need to go.'*

'Well there is no rush. You are welcome to stay with us for as long as you need, right Gytha?'

'Of course. It is always nice to have another mouth to feed,' she said with a wink.

'It's a beautiful day out today,' he added after a while of silent eating, *'You should have a walk around our town when you are done with breakfast. Give yourself time to fully recover from what I am told was quite an uncomfortable journey for you.'*

'Thank you, that actually sounds like a good idea,' I replied. *'It would be nice to walk out on solid ground again.'*

'Finn also told me that you would be needing some identification documents?'

I froze with a pastry halfway between the plate and my mouth; not really sure how to react to such a statement.

'Do not worry friend, you will find no judgment here. Sometimes a man just needs to disappear am I right?'

187

I smiled and nodded in answer to this, not sure whether to be relieved or concerned about his attitude towards such a thing.

'So then, do you have a new name in mind?' he continued, *'I could give you one myself but, in my experience, a false identity is more convincing if you have come up with the name yourself. You are less likely to get caught out that way, if you get my meaning.'*

It's funny really because, although I'd never thought about giving myself a fake name before, one immediately came to mind. It was my grandad's name.

'Tom! I'd like my name to be Tom,' I said assertively.

'Okay, good. Now, what about the last name?'

This one I had to think about for a while, as the names of all my favourite fictional characters flooded into my head; Jones, Pitt, Drake, Croft, Vimes, Snake, Crowe, Underhill, Sparrow. Eventually though, I decided to keep it simple and just go with a jumbled up version of my own name.

'Keeldan! Tom Keeldan! That's the name I want.'

'Very good Mr Keeldan, I shall get that sorted for you, I will just need to take your photograph after breakfast. It will take a couple of days to come through so, as I said, take your time here and recover your strength. Once you know where it is you would like to go, I will take you on my way to acquire our good Captain's next order.'

With business sorted, we spent the rest of the meal exchanging the pleasantries of new friends getting to know one another. All the time I was there though, he never once asked what my real name was or what had brought me to his home. In many ways, this actually helped me relax without feeling the need to explain what even I didn't fully understand yet. To Soren and Gytha I was simply Tom Keeldan their invited houseguest. It was a pleasant fiction that helped me settle in to my new identity.

Not knowing where my next destination would be was a concern, but knowing I had someone to help me get there when I did was a big relief. I'd have had no idea how to get there myself so it was a safety net that took a weight off my shoulders.

With breakfast finished and my belly suitably stuffed, the rest of the day was mine to do as I pleased. Soren had suggested a few places to go and see if I did want a walk out, and loaned me some of their local currency to keep me going until I was able to change some of my own. The first place on his list was back down to the harbour to see the morning catch being hauled in and attend the daily fish auction. A look out of the kitchen window at the warm light of a new day's sun, caressing the roof tops of the village, was more than enough incentive to follow his suggestion.

Down at the harbours edge stood a red wooden structure were everything from salmon and sea trout, to flounder and eel were being bid on by crowds of people. It was actually quite an interesting experience walking around and seeing all the different catches; it left me craving a good old plate of fish and chips. The next stop on Soren's sights list was a walk down the Vester Strandgade to the Torvet, which basically meant following an old street up to the marketplace. I must say though it was a rather pleasant street to walk; the whole place felt like you'd stepped back into the 1800's or something. Dark red houses with white roofs lined the narrow cobblestone streets mixed with a variety of merchant shops.

As I walked, I passed a butcher's, a grocer's, a shoemaker's and a bike shop. But the place that really caught my attention was a little coffee shop whose window was full of ludicrously delicious looking Danish pastries; the type of sticky, gooey, crispy and creamy items that can make you fat just by staring at them. Despite having not long ago eaten my weight in breakfast, I really couldn't help myself from going in; I was sure there had to be at least a little room left for something sweet.

It was purely an investigative research mission of course. I had to ascertain if the coffee shops in Denmark where as good as the ones back home. I left half an hour later feeling very sticky, very gooey and very fat...a very good coffee shop indeed.

After having sampled a pretty generous selection of the local produce, I decided that I'd best try and walk off some of the calories that would be quickly settling themselves down into fatty deposits around my body. With that in mind, I headed to the edge of the town centre to a place Soren had called Alkjear Lukke. This turned out to be a beautiful park made up of an open beach-wood forest full of all kinds of stunning flowers; the names of which I hadn't the foggiest idea, but enjoyed the sight of just the same. I even came across a serene and picturesque pond inhabited by a rather boisterous gang of ducks, who had obviously discovered that a profitable living could be made from providing passers-by with entertainment...noisy entertainment. It was the perfect place to sit down, absorb some of the warming rays beating down from the sun's lofty home in a cloudless sky, and take full stock of my situation.

My peaceful rest did not last long however, as with time to relax and organise my thoughts I soon remembered that important thing I'd still forgotten to do. I hadn't called home.

Even as I dialled the number into Paddy's phone, a sense of dread coursed through me; suddenly losing all confidence in my "Conservation Project" story. No one would believe such crap. I knew I wouldn't if roles were reversed, but it was all I had. Taking one last deep breath, I pressed the "Call" button.

As it rang, the simple monotonous tone of an outgoing call seemed to grow louder and louder in my head whilst time seemed frozen around me. My heart almost refused to beat in anticipation of the sound ending with the muffled click of someone picking up at the other end. I knew I had to get this call out of the way, along with all the other calls I would have to make to friends, family and work; I didn't want people to be left worrying about me after all. But a part of me prayed that none of them would be home. The longer the phone rang, the more I started to believe that this might actually be the case. Then, just as I was about to give in to the urge and hang up, a connection was made.

'Hello?' came the familiar sound of my mum's voice, warming my weary heart.

'Hey Mum, it's me.'

'Me? Me who?' she said with a sarcastic aloofness.

'Come on Mum, stop messing about, you know who it is.'

'Well you do sound a bit like my son, but it's been so long since I last heard from him that I can't really be sure!'

'Okay, okay, I deserved that. I'm sorry alright. I know I said in my note that I'd call in a few days, but a lot has happened since then and time just slipped away from me.'

'Again! It's okay though, I'm used to being forgotten about,' she said with mock wounding.

'Come on Mum you know I wouldn't do it on purpose. I'm REALLY SORRY,' I replied, trying to project the sad face and stuck out bottom lip, that always used to generate forgiveness, down the phone.

'Oh Alright! I suppose I can let you off this time,' she responded with an exaggerated sigh.

It was all said in joke but the truth was, I really did feel bad about having only just got round to letting her know I was safe and well.

190

'Have you at least had good time over there?' she then asked me, *'When are you coming home by the way? Work rang yesterday asking as they hadn't heard from you and couldn't get in touch.'*

'Yeah...about that,' I started hesitantly, knowing that there was no going back from here on, *'I've got some good news and I've got some bad news.'*

The lie I told, in all its over thought complexity, seemed to eventually do the trick. My mum was nobody's fool, so either I had been sufficiently convincing in its telling or she simply had no reason not to believe what I said. In truth, neither of these possibilities makes me feel good about what I did.

You may notice that there is a page torn out of my journal here. You see, I originally wanted to explain the lie that I told and detail what I'd come up with and how I'd gotten away with it. But then I realised, what does it really matter? To clear my head of all concerns that might distract me from the task at hand, I lied to my family and friends under the pretence that I was doing it to protect them. That is all you need to know. What I said and how they reacted are of importance now only to my conscience.

What I will say however, is that the reason for the lie did seem to validate itself with that first phone call. One of the things my mum told me, as she brought me up to speed on what had happened since I'd left, was that another officious looking suit had come knocking at our door asking after me. I instantly assumed that it must have been another Mason, checking that I hadn't doubled back on his friends, and figured that it meant they would still be keeping an eye on the people who knew me.

I thought about how they could even have tapped the phones and been listening in on that very conversation; the silver lining to which would be that, having heard me lie to my mum, they would realise that she did not know where I really was and so would hopefully leave her alone. What I should have been doing right then though was paying more attention to the description she gave me of the man in question. It is an oversight that would eventually come back bite me in a very big way.

When I eventually hung up the phone, so very grateful now that Paddy had given it to me, I dove straight into another hour or so of calling everyone else. Having already established a coherent story in my head the rest of the calls were much easier.

It had come as somewhat of a confusing disappointment to those of them who'd known about the Amulet and the reason for my trip to Lindisfarne. Fortunately, with a few amendments to the lie, they all seemed to buy it. Either it didn't have time to fully sink in or my performance had grown suitably convincing, but no one questioned the gaping holes that would have appeared should they have but scratched the surface of my cover story.

My hardest sell was to my boss Ken. Asking at the drop of a hat to take my year's holiday entitlement was asking a bit much of him I have to admit. In all fairness, his concern was not that I was expecting too much from him but rather that it would be difficult to convince the company that they should make an exception to their two week limit on how many holiday days you could take concurrently.

Fortunately for me he was a great boss and he valued me as a good worker so, eventually, he authorised my leave and said he would deal with the powers that be. He did stipulate though that my five weeks holiday was all he could give me. If I wasn't back to work by then he would struggle to keep my job open for me.

I agreed this was fair and assured him that I would be back well before then...little did I know how difficult that promise would be to keep.

With all that out of the way, I then turned my attention finally to Archer's journal. I knew my destination was somewhere in Germany, but it was time to find out just exactly where. Only in those pages would I find the answer and so, with cautious excitement, I began to read.

Over the next few hours I enveloped myself in the journey he painted so vividly with his words. Each page was covered in sketches, notations and maps of each country he visited marked with the places he went to. Each of those places where then individually detailed with a smaller map and bullet points about what he found and the people he met. Every now and again he wrote about his thoughts on what had been happening and what he had found. He had even drawn some incredibly accurate portraits of the people he met on his travels. Most surprising of these was the first one. It was of me.

I thought back to our first, and only, meeting and certainly couldn't recall him sketching me or taking my picture. He must have had a type of photographic memory or something to be able to capture me so well.

The Beast of Bamburgh[x]

As fascinating as all his entries were though, I couldn't stop myself from skimming through most of them; impatiently wanting to know where it was I was to be going. I did stop again briefly though, to chuckle over the brilliantly grumpy expression he'd caught with his sketch of Paddy. This pause led to my eye being draw toward his entry about Bamburgh Castle and the piece of the Chintamani under the chapel. It wasn't clear whether Paddy had taken him to see it or if they had discovered it together, but what intrigued me most was the drawing he made labelled "The Beast of Bamburgh". I remembered that name from Paddy's riddle for finding the way out of the crypt, which Archer had also noted down...only his version had one extra verse.

> As both Marker and Key you must ignore it not,
> for X isn't the only cross that marks the spot.
> When the Beast of Bamburgh guards the door,
> your salvation shall come from beneath the floor.
> But guarded well the door must be,
> should the Beast be forgotten the light of day you shall never see.

Archer had written quite a lot about the crypt and this riddle, which he had found engraved on the altar in Latin. A part of me wanted to read it carefully and discover the trick Paddy had used to get us out of there, but I knew there were more pressing matters and so reluctantly moved on; telling myself I would come back to that page once I had found my destination. However, it would actually be quite some time before I ever returned to this mystery.

Archer's Stone of Destiny Symbol

From the things I read that day I was able to glean a better idea of what Archer's plan was. His aim was to find all of the fragmented pieces of the Chintamani Stone, his belief being that there had once been three main stones in the world. These were the Stone of Destiny that we believe came from Babylon (he'd sketched a symbol of this one that I noted was similar in design to the Chintamani one in the Amulet), the stone that was entrusted to Nicholas Roerich and, finally, one given to King Solomon.

Archer wanted to locate every piece of all three stones and re-unite them for a reason he did not fully detail; something to do with the ancient prophecy about the time of Shambhala.

His main focus had been Roerich's stone, but by a happy chance he'd discovered information that suggested the Stone of Destiny was hidden somewhere in England. Side tracked by this, he found himself on Holy Island where he met Paddy and learned what I have since learned. But rather than go in search of the main piece, he became intrigued by the links of a piece that went to Germany. This was the part I had to read carefully; the torn off end of my section of the journal beginning to loom close. A clue to my destination had to be there.

He didn't describe much of his journey into Germany, only that he had come through Denmark much as I was to do. As I read I couldn't help asking myself why he hadn't pursued the main piece. Maybe he'd had a good idea where it was in England and so decided to go after the loose ends instead. Or perhaps going to Germany was just a step in the right direction towards India where Roerich had died? I guess only Archer could answer that question. All I knew was that I was now following in his footsteps and so had to earnestly hope he knew what he was doing. Fortunately, the last few entries in his journal did shed some light on it all.

What now follows is Archer's account of why he went to Germany and what he found. I have transcribed it to the best of my memory as, regretfully, I no longer have the actual journal. Therefore some of the details may be slightly off, but it should still convey the general gist.

St. Oswald's head! Found within the coffin of St. Cuthbert whose remains had remained preserved at Durham Cathedral until sometime between 1104AD and 1827AD. It is my belief that the presence of the Chintamani Stone is what kept the body from decay and that sometime before the last opening of Cuthbert's coffin, which revealed only his skeleton in 1827, it was stolen. With such train of thought, I have discovered that no fewer than four other claims for the possession of St. Oswald's head have been made throughout history in continental Europe; Schaffhausen in Switzerland, Utrecht in the Netherlands, Echternach in Luxembourg and Hildesheim in Germany. It is with that knowledge that I have come to Germany and to the Lower Saxony city of Hildesheim. For it is here, in the treasury of St. Mary's Catholic Cathedral, that a head reliquary of St. Oswald is said to be enclosed within an octagonal German casket. My reasoning for choosing this site is thus. Of the four European sites, three are linked together by a thread of history; a thread held by St. Willibrord "Apostle to the Frisians". St. Willibrord was a Northumbrian missionary sent to Christianise the pagan north Germanic tribes of Frisia at the request of King Pepin, the Christian ruler of the Franks and father to the future King Charlemagne. It is known that St. Willibrord took with him some relics of St. Oswald, though how and why he came to possess them is a little less clear. I have found no detail as to what relics he took, nor where they came from; an omission from his history that I feel may hold more weight than what has been given to it. What if he somehow managed to retrieve the relics kept within St. Cuthbert's coffin? Perhaps he took the piece of the

Chintamani that lay within, which would then bring credence to the miraculous decaying of Cuthbert's body after all that time? It could be that I am filling in the blanks with my own yearning for a hidden truth to history, but it is with such information that I have drawn my conclusions.

Through his travels Willibrord founded many churches, one of which was a monastery at <u>Utrecht</u> where he established a cathedral and became the first Bishop of Utrecht. Later he founded his largest monastery at <u>Echternach</u> where he eventually died and was laid to rest. His Abby at Echternach enjoyed the patronage of King Charlemagne whose son, Louis the Pious, had the chapel of St. Mary built at <u>Hildesheim</u>. There Louis established the Bishopric of Hildesheim in 815AD and dedicated it to the Virgin Mary. According to legend, Louis found the site by accident when he and his entourage became horribly lost whilst out hunting in the woods of Elze. Upon realising there quandary, Louis ordered them to rest and a mass to be celebrated so that they could pray for rescue. For the mass, Louis hung a reliquary of the Holy Mary onto a rose bush to act as a focal point for their prayers. When rescue finally came, the form of which is uncertain, it is said that the servants forgot to retrieve the holy relic. When Louis noticed it missing he returned to the place of their prayer to reclaim it. However, upon doing so he found the relic to be somehow irremovably connected to the rose bush which he interoperated as a divine sign that a church should be built upon that very spot. So came to be the Chapel of St. Mary which, in 872AD, then became the foundation of the Hildesheim Cathedral. That rose bush is said to still grow there to this day; climbing up the apse of the

Cathedral. Rumoured to be over one thousand years old, it survived the bombing raids of World War II, which destroyed a large part of the Cathedral and surrounding city, and flourished to become a symbol of prosperity. Could it be that the relic of St. Mary was in fact the piece of Chintamani Stone brought by St. Willibrord? Could it be the power behind the rose bushes immortality and if so, do I have the right to take it? Legend has it that should the rose ever fail to bloom, it will signal the decline of the city. For now I will put such thoughts to the back of my mind and concentrate on finding the stone. But ignore such a decision for long I cannot, for the time may all too soon be upon me when the fate of the world must overcome the needs of the few.

In my mind this line of events, connected together so easily, seems too big a coincidence to overlook. Coupled with the fact that the Cathedral's treasury is amongst the largest and richest in all of Europe for Holy Relics, I can ill afford to miss the opportunity to investigate for myself. If the stone that travelled with Cuthbert's body did find its way into the hands of St. Willibrord, the casket at Hildesheim is surely its most likely resting place. This is my theory, one I hope to prove by opening the casket. Initially I was disheartened to find that both the Cathedral and its museum are closed until 2014 for renovation work. But with a bit of persistence, and a modest donation, I have managed to make an appointment with the curator of the museum for tomorrow to view the stored relics. I await it now with great anticipation.

The day has finally arrived! I made my way through the historic city, its streets lined with beautiful half-timbered buildings, and on to the Romanesque majesty of St. Mary's Cathedral. I could wax lyrical about the sights I saw and the marvel of both architecture and artefacts within and without, but alas I have not now the heart for my day has ended in the greatest of disappointments. Upon seeing the casket for myself I was sad to discover a grave error in my research.

The intricately decorated casket depicts both the kings Edward the Confessor and Cnut the Great along with St. Oswald. Often is the case of such head reliquaries that they contain the bones of more than one king, but often too is the fact that, in such circumstances, there is usually only a fragment of each king's remains within; pieces of bone whose origins are impossible to prove. I let my desire for the claim to be true come before conducting thorough research. I have since discovered there to be great discrepancies in the historical dates of the people and places I endeavoured to link. Such revelations have shed new light on the matter, making my theory quite unlikely. St. Willibrord died in 739AD and Louis the Pious in 840AD, but Kings Cnut and Edward died in 1035AD and 1066AD respectively. The casket is believed to be from circa 1180AD and therefore highly unlikely that it had anything to do with either Willibrord or Louis. Also, I considered not the fact that St. Cuthbert's coffin was opened at Durham in 1104AD to his still un-decayed body; a long time after the ending of Willibrord, Louis, Edward and Cnut. What I have done is to make the mistake of an incompetent researcher and follow clues based on belief not verified facts. Maybe the head of

St. Oswald never left Durham Cathedral? Maybe I have simply wasted my time in chasing a wisp of smoke?

Yet fate it seems has smiled upon me. My efforts have not all been in vain. Out of the ashes of my failure, a phoenix may be about to arise.

When I opened the casket, confirming my fears that the stone was not inside, the old curator laughed and told me that I had the same look of disappointment as what had crossed the face of Herr Himmler when he came to see the relic during the war. Pressing him on this matter, I discovered that the Nazi's had come to Hildesheim in 1938 seeking out Jews. During this time the head of the SS, Heinrich Himmler himself, took the chance to raid the Cathedral's Treasury and made a beeline for the very casket I now examined. Though he too had been disappointed with its contents, he had his men search the rest of the treasury and stole a number of ancient relics.

This story has intrigued me. For what purpose did the Reichsfuhrer[xi] of the SS come seeking the casket? I feel this is a lead that I cannot let lie as, from my earlier research, I know that the Nazi's had a strong interest in the legends of Shambhala and the Chintamani Stone. My journey must now take me through Berlin from where I will pick up transport onwards towards my final destination of India. But a longer stay in the German capital is in order I feel. This new mystery warrants a much closer look.

When I had finished reading I sat back, leaning my weight against my hands planted in the grass behind me. I wasn't quite sure what to make of it all really. Although Archer had discovered quite a lot, none of it left me with any specific clue as to where my destination should be. Berlin seemed to be the most obvious place of course; there would be little point in me going to Hildesheim after all. But where in Berlin should I go? I was left with a clue that gave me very little to go on. I'd read the journal with excitement, anticipating a moment of enlightenment that would put me onto Archer's trail. It was a moment that sadly never came. My only choice was to go to Berlin and hope that the Amulet would provide me with the next clue once I arrived. I found the link between one symbol and Paddy; perhaps it would be as easy to find the next. It was a plan that left more than just a shadow of doubt in my mind, but what other option did I have?

Returning to Soren's house I informed him of my newly discovered destination and in return he told me we should be able to leave in two days time. Travelling in his camper van he would drive me down to Hamburg where he would then see me onto a train going to Berlin. He did seem quite surprised at my choice of destination though.

'Not following your predecessor to Hildesheim then?' he questioned.

'No...Wait, what? How do you know about my predecessor?' I asked naively.

'What, you didn't think it was slightly strange that we accepted you into our house with no questions asked? Your friend, Mr Archer, came a year or two ago now, the same way you did; delivered across the sea by Captain Finn and the grand crew of the Morrigan. He told us little of his plans only that there may come a day when another would follow in his footsteps. It was his wish that we show that person the same hospitality we had him and offer any aid we could; for he would likely be feeling quite out of his depth. It is a request we were happy to oblige.'

I guess I should have realised this earlier, but I'd found myself too overwhelmed by my arrival in Denmark to really focus on anything other than wanting the comfort of a warm bed. Thinking back on things though, it had all been a little too easy. I later discovered that, had I taken more care in the reading of Archer's journal, it should have come as no surprise. As well as myself and Paddy, Archer had sketched Captain Finn and his crew along with Soren and his wife. He even talked briefly of his time spent with them. Something I could draw parallels to, especially in his opinions of Gravy and the cantankerous engineer of the Morrigan. I couldn't believe though that I hadn't seen it before, but I guess it is easy sometimes to become blinkered to anything but the goal you seek.

This explained the feeling of acceptance from the strangers I had met and, subsequently, the relaxed atmosphere that had lulled me into almost forgetting the huge task that lay ahead.

The fears and worries I'd had before leaving Holy Island hadn't plagued me that day. But with the finding of my destination, and the knowledge of my impending departure, a fear of the unknown all too quickly returned and my peaceful day was shattered. The next two days passed both too slowly and too quickly in equal measures with one part of me dreading what lay ahead and another wishing the days away until I could return back home with all this behind me.

Travelling with Soren in his spacious campervan should have been enjoyable; the journey required very little effort on my part, aside from making the occasional cup of tea. Unfortunately however, this wasn't to be. During the mammoth send off meal that Gytha had laid on for us the night before, I think I probably must have overindulged in something that didn't quite agree with me. Subsequently, I ended up spending most of the trip on the toilet in a rather pitiful state. Wretched as this situation was, I was somewhat surprised to find that it could get so much worse.

As we arrived at the border into Germany, our campervan was stopped and boarded by armed police. Forcing their way in, wearing body armour and carrying assault rifles, they were most definitely not friendly as they commanded us to step outside; an intimidating confrontation to say the least.

What made it truly unpleasant though was the fact that, at that precise moment in time, I was otherwise engaged on the lavatory and had been for quite a few hours. Being sat there for so long had resulted in my legs going numb which, combined with the feeling of being completely drained, resulted in a very difficult and embarrassing situation when the police forced me at gun point to get off the toilet and out of the camper.

The cop holding the rifle looked like your typical twitchy, trigger happy gun wielding moron who was just itching for a reason to shoot me as I tried to explain that I couldn't move. Fortunately Soren came to my rescue. Lifting me up, as I quickly yanked up my trousers, he carried me outside where we had to wait as they searched the vehicle. I can distinctly remember hearing Soren say out of the corner of his mouth;

'God I hope they search the septic tank.'

I tried not to laugh as I thought of how horrible it would have been in there after my recent activity; though I did silently pray that, if they did, it would be the moron with the itchy finger.

When I asked why they had stopped us, Soren explained that the police randomly searched vehicles like ours for drugs and illegal goods. Apparently the septic tank was a popular hiding spot for those involved in such illicit smuggling as it hides the smell from the sniffer dogs. Quite how he knew this he did not say and I somehow felt I didn't want to know. Instead we both waited patiently and quietly, enjoying the satisfying sounds of disgust coming from the men who had indeed got that nasty job.

When they eventually let us go, we climbed back into the camper and got on our way again. Soren admitted how glad he was that they'd stopped him then and not on his way back home. Then he would be loaded up with excessive amounts of alcohol and cigarettes, which would be rather difficult to explain away.

Determined not to resume my uncomfortable throne, I dug out some anti-diarrhoea medicine from my medical kit, curled up on a comfy chair with a blanket, and drifted off into an exhausted sleep.

When I woke, I did so to find us in Hamburg; camped in a train station car park as Soren prepared a tantalising breakfast. He told me that he'd been and booked a one way ticket to Berlin for me on a train that would be arriving in about an hour. This gave me plenty of time to come round and, feeling much better, get a good meal inside of me for the journey ahead.

That time passed all too quickly and once again I found myself heading off deeper into this strange adventure I had been caught up in.

Walking into the train station, I was astonished by its size and design. Being use to the small stations back home, the warehouse like building of metal and glass that was Hamburg Central seemed incredible and almost futuristic. It was also full of people and I was just glad that Soren had decided to escort me to my train. Had he not, I fear I would have become easily lost and probably ended up on the wrong one going in the opposite direction.

Shaking his hand and thanking him for all his help one final time, I dragged my weary body onto the train, found myself a seat and tried not to think of the task that lay waiting for me in Berlin. That was of course easier said than done and, as the train began to pull away from the station, I felt a faint touch of panic. I suddenly realised that, for the first time since Lindisfarne, I was truly alone.

Day 6 - Berlin, Germany
An Impossible Task

The journey took roughly two hours; a length of time I barely noticed for the train was bright, spacious, clean and, most of all, comfortable. Still feeling a little rough from my bad stomach though, realising that a large breakfast probably hadn't been the best idea, I settled down and drifted off into my book in an attempt to take my mind off things.

Before I knew where I was, the train pulled into a large glass domed tunnel of an equally modern looking train station as the one I'd left. Looming over the track, I could just about see a large sign that read;

BOMBARDIER
WILKOMMEN IN BERLIN

I didn't understand German, but I could definitely understand that sign. It told me I had arrived in Berlin. A feeling of dread quickly began to fill me. A fear over what might happen when I stepped off that train.

However, other than a rather unpleasant assault on my senses as hordes of people bustled passed heading off in all directions, nothing really happened to validate that feeling.

Squinting my eyes against the glare of the sun shining in through all the glass, and wincing at the echoy voice blasting out over the tannoy system, I made my way through the station towards its exit.

That was an adventure in itself as the place was built on three levels, with the top and bottom ones being the train platforms and the middle being the entrance, exit and shopping area. It probably shouldn't have been so difficult, and anyone that has been there would probably think I'm an idiot, but I just kept getting lost. It was not a good start to my time in Berlin. Sadly for me though, it wasn't about to get any better from there on out either.

When eventually I succeeded in escaping the labyrinth, I found myself stepping out into my own personal hell. Sprawling out before me was the city of Berlin. The CITY! Not a small island or village, but a city so vast that its buildings dominated the horizon in all directions. It finally dawned on me then, the reason for the feeling of dread building in the pit of my stomach.

In one unsettling moment the, true scale of my needle-in-a-haystack search for the next journal guardian was instantly summed up in a single word. Impossible!

Upon shaking off the initial shock, I decided that my only option was to ignore the size of the city and set out like I had done back on Lindisfarne; keeping my eyes open for any "signs" along the way. With that in mind, I picked up a map of the city, exchanged some money and headed east towards the city centre.

It wasn't long before I was hopelessly lost again; that is if you can become lost when you don't even know where you're going to start with. This wasn't like my trip to Lindisfarne. I was alone now in a foreign country whose language I did not speak and with no one at all to help me.

It was an odd feeling indeed. I'd always professed to enjoy being alone when I was at home; the peace and quiet of having no one in the house but me. I used to think that I was the type of person who didn't need contact with others. Loneliness was not a condition I thought I suffered from.

That first day in Germany was a new kind of loneliness though. It was an isolation from everyone and everything I knew and loved. I wasn't there on a holiday. I wasn't there to enjoy myself. I had a job to do and not a lot of time to do it, and in the back of my mind there was the constant threat of an unfriendly shadow lurking behind every corner; a single thought driving me on. I was still being hunted.

Loneliness aside however, the biggest problem facing me that day was the complete lack of both information and direction. All I had to go on was the symbols on the Amulet around my neck. Three symbols left, of which my next contact could be represented by any one of them. Assuming, that was, I had indeed come to the right place. I mean, it wasn't as if Archer had said, *'and here's where I met so-and-so.'*

The scale of the task was so much larger than before. Lindisfarne had been small enough to walk around in a day. Now I stood in the shadow of the German Capital. I'm certain I could have spent weeks there and still been unable to see it all.

In the end though, I steeled myself to the fact that I had to simply get on with it. One way or another I had to find the next contact. It was either that or give up and go home with my tail between my legs, and I hadn't come all this way to give up so easily.

That first day I walked continuously, from one side of the city to the other it seemed, exploring none stop; much as I had done on Holy Island. However, just as it was there, I lost the day to the disappointment of finding nothing. I had no idea where I was going, I just wandered down whatever road or street took my fancy. Past Museums and Cathedrals, through markets bustling with activity and parks devoid of life, save for the gentle movement of trees and the ripple of grass in the wind.

Every now and again I would find myself back alongside the river I'd crossed leaving the station. In one place, looking at the buildings along its edge, it was like looking at a timeline of the city; from the grand majestic architecture of a time when stone masonry was an art form, right up to the present day where class seems to have been replaced by glass. Not that I don't like modern architecture mind, the design of the train station was quite impressive after all. It's just that, to me, it always seems a bit soulless compared to the skill and workmanship that went into the stone archways, smooth columns, and intricate finishing's of the Neo-classical buildings.

Anyway, I guess what I'm trying to say is that Berlin, much like any other city in the world I suppose, had a very eclectic array of buildings that at least provided me with an interesting and intriguing place to be lost in. For despite all my wanderings, hours and hours of aimless walking, I still had absolutely no idea what the hell I was looking for.

I kept hoping that I would suddenly be drawn towards a place again, just as I had been towards the Ship Inn. I concentrated hard on keeping an open mind and staying receptive to any kind of sign; praying that this would indeed be the case. Yet the harder I looked the less I seemed to find. It was folly. Given that I couldn't even narrow my search down to a single area within the city, the task I'd been charged with seemed ever more one of impossible odds.

The sleepy blanket of night crept up on me all too quickly that day and I found myself in desperate need of a place to stay. As I abandoned my hopeless search, I began looking instead for a

208

cheap B&B or hostel that had vacancies. In the process of this, I ended up wandering past an old run down looking building that appeared to have a bar of some sort down in its basement.

It caught my attention for two reasons. First off, I thought it quite unusual; an underground pub not being something you come across every day. But it was more what heard than what I saw that intrigued me. As I walked slowly by, my ear was caught by the words of a song drifting out on the night breeze.

♪ *This is all the heaven we've got, right here where we arre,*
In ourrrrr Shangri-Laaaaa ♪

What at first just seemed to be words from a beautiful ballad, suddenly burst into my head like a firework of realisation. Shangri-La! That was another name for Shambhala! Archer had told me that when we first met.

'It can't be a coincidence,' I told myself, *'this has to be the sign I've been waiting for, the guardian of the next journal piece must be inside.'*

With that, ludicrously flimsy, thought firmly in place, I followed the music down into the bar with great anticipation.

It looked every bit the typical dimly lit, almost smoky, movie scene bar where a big brawl would break out. Mostly this was probably due to the fact that, from what I saw as I walked in, it seemed as though that was exactly what had happened. There were upturned tables and chairs scattered all over the place, while broken bottles and splintered pool cues lay in abundance; though, interestingly enough, I could see no sign of a pool table. Sat in the centre of all this chaos, just in front of a sort of stage area, were a small group of musicians; playing their instruments whilst one of them sang.

I stood there, a little way in from the door, and watched them unnoticed for a while, enjoying the rest of the song that had drawn me in. The harmony of instruments playing in support of the man's haunting voice combined to create an amazing sound that seemed to resonate through the air. I could have stood and listened to them all night.

Sadly however, after that particular song ended, my enjoyment was quite rudely interrupted.

'Haben wir gescholssen,' came the voice of a barman who seemed to appear from nowhere.

'Excuse me?' I asked, *'I-no-sprekenzy-German,'* I then added rather pathetically as way of an explanation.

209

'*Ah! You're English then? I'm afraid we're closed mate,*' he said in a cockney accent that seemed far happier articulating words in English, '*Did you not see the sign outside?*'

In truth I hadn't, having been far too excited by the prospect of what I might find within to take any notice of a sign. The barman practically had the word "Hooligan" tattooed across his forehead. I half expected to see "Love" and "Hate" written across his knuckles as they aggressively gripped the handle of the brush he was using to sweep up the mess.

'*I'm sorry,*' I said eventually, '*I didn't realise. I heard the music from outside and had to come and listen. I'll go now though, sorry for the intrusion.*'

Dejectedly, I turned around and began to walk back to the door. In all honesty I think at the time I was more disappointed about not being able to stay and listen to the music than not having a chance to search for my next clue.

'*Hold on there a minute,*' said the man who had been singing, '*The lad's come down here to hear us play. We should be honoured. What's the harm in letting him stay? It's not like you couldn't use the custom is it Rob?*' he added, gesturing around the room.

'*Ah what the hell, why not,*' replied the barman quite flippantly as he returned to tidying up.

'*Come lad, pull yourself up a stool and let my friend here pour you a drink, it's on me,*' the singer said to me, before looking to the barman. '*Just put it on my tab eh Rob!*'

'*Yeah, Yeah, you guys and your bloody tabs. Let in a new customer and don't even get to see any bloody money for it. I have bills to pay you know!*' the barman grumbled.

'*I've got some money with me, I don't mind paying,*' I offered, feeling a bit awkward.

'*Don't worry about it, Rob's just in a grump because his "English Theme" bar has been trashed again in a brawl that broke out.*'

'*Thought when I left London I'd left behind this kinda shit,*' Rob muttered sullenly to himself, '*the only thing that's bloody changed is the language and the currency. Sodding drunks are the same where ever I go.*'

Taking my drink gratefully from the moody barman, I picked up a stool and set it down in the space made for me within the musicians circle.

'*What's your name friend?*' asked the singer.

'Da..,' I managed to stop myself and cleared my throat to cover the stumble, *'Tom. Tom Keeldan.'*

So thrilled by the invitation to join them had I been, warmed by having found some English people in this foreign place, I'd almost forgotten my new name.

'Good to meet you Tom,' the man said, extending out his hand, *'I'm Richard and these here are my band mates Steve, Johno, Mark and Danny,'* he added, introducing me to the rest of the circle.

'I can't tell how relieved I am to have found some English people,' I told them truthfully. *'It feels like forever since I left home.'*

They asked where I was from and, by strange coincidence, it turned out that Richard was from a place called Greystoke, which was all of about 10 minutes outside of Penrith. We went on to discover that we both actually frequented the same pub there and had quite probably crossed paths before without noticing.

Normally I didn't like classing myself as a Cumbrian. I was a born and bred Liverpool lad until my family moved north when I was about 12. I'd never really fit in with the country folk of my new home, and the small town mentality, where everyone seemed to know everyone else, had never being of great appeal to me. As such, I clung to my roots like a drowning man to a life raft and refused, even after fifteen years, to class myself as Cumbrian.

That day in Germany however, I was only too glad to do so. It was worth it to have the feeling of a common bond with someone so very far away from home. After the day I'd had, spent lost and homesick in a foreign country, I couldn't have found a better remedy if I'd tried.

The evening soon disappeared into the early hours of the morning as we talked and drank, then they played some more songs before we drank and talked some more. It was one of the most enjoyable evenings I'd had in a very long time.

As the light of the rising sun began to filter in through the windows, the lively drunken atmosphere had turned into a more placid melancholy one as we all began to talk of our plans beyond that night.

'So what's really brought you all the way out here then Tom?' asked Richard, obviously having seen right through the,

admittedly transparent, "Backpacking Holiday" story I'd told them earlier.

With the alcohol having dulled my defences, and filled me with a desire to share my burden with someone, I decided to tell them the truth. It turned out to be rather a fortuitous decision.

Over the next half hour or so I recounted my tale; from meeting Archer to arriving there in Berlin. As I did, Richard and the other guys listened with the kind of avid fascination that only a certain degree of drunkenness can bestow on people.

With the close of my story I sat back and waited for the barrage of questions that where sure to come. To my surprise however, there was but one.

'Ah Tom, that's fantastic! What a story to tell,' said Richard with a sincerity that seemed a surprise even to the words he spoke, *'So what are you going to do next? How are you going to find this next journal piece?'*

'Well, you see, that's the thing...I have absolutely no idea.'

I explained how I had been wandering around all day without finding any clues and of how I couldn't even work out which symbol on the Amulet was supposed to help me. I told them of how I'd foolishly come down into the pub upon hearing the Shangri-La song in the hope of finding some answers; believing it to be some kind of sign.

Curiosity, along with the desire to help me I guess, caused Richard to ask if he could see the Amulet. It was a request I willingly obliged, desperate for all the help I could get.

'Wow! That's some rock in the centre there isn't it?' he said as I handed it to him. *'What a beautiful colour,'* he added as his eyes lingered over it.

'What are all the pictures supposed to be?' asked Johno, as the Amulet got passed around.

In answer to that question, as I cautiously watched it pass from one man to the next feeling oddly bereft of its presence around my neck, I went on to explain what each of the four symbols on show represented.

It was then, upon revealing the name of the symbol on the bottom right hand side, that the breakthrough I had been looking for finally arrived.

'Wait! Sorry! Did you say that one's called the "Victory Banner"?' asked Richard.

'Yes,' I replied, *'Why?'*

'Well, this may just be a coincidence Tom but, if you're looking for a link from that Amulet to a place here in Berlin I

think you've just found it. The Victory Banner was the symbol used by the Soviet people to celebrate their victory over the Nazi's during the Second World War. It was made on the battlefield and was the first flag to be raised at the fall of Berlin by three Soviet soldiers up on top of the Reichstag building.'

'The Reichstag building? What's that?' I asked trying to keep a modicum of composure about myself, as the excitement of being on the verge of a breakthrough began to grow.

'It's a government building, still in use today I think,' he said in reply, 'But more than that, it is a landmark of this city's turbulent history. I personally couldn't think of a grander place in all of Berlin to have as the destination for such a journey. If the person you must find is represented by one of these symbols, then I'd bet a pound to a penny that the Reichstag is where he'll be.'

Filled with a euphoric sense of elation and relief, as the thought of having finally found my next destination set of explosions of excitement within me like a Roman Candle firework, I grabbed Richards hand to shake in grateful thanks but ended up pulling him off his stool and into a great bear hug.

'Thank you Richard!' I said with a big smile, 'Thank you, thank you, thank you! You've just made my day,' I added through joyful laughter.

'Happy to help Tom,' replied Richard, a little stunned by my expression of gratitude, 'I just hope it does turn out to be the place you are looking for or else I'll feel bad for getting your hopes up this much.'

'Oh, it has to be!' I said with an unusually unsinkable optimism, 'I don't believe in coincidences anymore, especially not ones this big.'

It was probably the amplifying effect of the alcohol making me see things that weren't really there, but I was just so excited to have unravelled the next part of the Amulets instruction by following my instincts. It felt like it was all meant to be.

After a few more rounds of celebratory drinks, everyone having been buoyed back to life by the excitement of my story, our night of merriment and discoveries did at last come to an end. I was offered a room above the pub where the guys were also staying, for what was left of the night, and a lift on to my destination the next day.

Richard explained that they would be heading past the Reichstag building on their way out of Berlin so it wouldn't be

213

any trouble for them to drop me off along the way. Both of these offers I accepted gladly before turning in and drawing close to the rollercoaster ride that had been my day.

That night, as I passed into a drunken slumber, I found myself plagued by a recurring dream...the city of light. Once more I ran through the darkness, pursued by a hidden nightmare, until the city stood before me again.

So bright was the glow that I could only make out the faint shapes of buildings and, what looked to be, strange vehicles flying in the sky. The light was strong but it didn't come from the sun, it was somehow purer. It appeared to radiate out from the city itself and fill a giant cavern that I sensed more than saw. It was beautiful.

Having had this dream before I expected the world around me to be rocked by an earthquake again, as it had the first time, but it never came. Instead I simply heard a gentle voice blowing toward me on the wind. It was the same voice I'd heard in the dream I'd had the night before I'd left home but, just as then, I still could not understand what it was trying to say. I called out to the wind, asking the voice to speak clearer, asking it to identify itself and tell me what it wanted. In response to my questions however, the city of light simply began to fade away.

Suddenly, as can only happen in dreams, I found myself back at work staring out the window across the forecourt watching my life pass me by as I had done so many times before.

I watched, with inexplicable interest, a crow that was perched high up on the top of a spindly, leafless tree. It was night time and a full moon rose up, quite eerily, behind the bird as it cawed into the darkness. The more I watched it, the more I began to get the feeling that it was watching me back.

I turned away to do some work, but felt drawn to look back out a short while later. The crow was still there, only now it was closer. It had hopped from the tree down onto a low wall ahead of it.

Choosing to ignore what was a completely normal scene, despite the slight feeling of unease that crept up my spine, I turned away once again.

I then saw the crow move out the corner of my eye and looked out to see it even closer now, sitting on top of a pump. This somewhat sinister take on a children's game continued on for a while, with the bird getting closer and closer each time I turned my back until, at the final glance...it was just outside my window.

The shock of seeing the creature so close, starring right at me with large, almost human eyes, forced me out of the dream and back into the real world.

Sitting bolt upright on my fold out bed, I looked around to see that I was still in the company of the musicians who all slept soundly. Relaxing back into my bed I tentatively let sleep wash over again, hoping that the dream was not waiting for me to return this time.

Though I'd never dreamt about it until recently, the scene with the crow sitting in the tree across the forecourt was one I'd seen many times. I had even once commented, jokingly of course, that I felt the bird was watching me sometimes.

I'd always felt a little uncomfortable around crows, there's something about the sound of their cawing and the way they seem to just lurk about that I find unnerving. My sister, who was in to all that dream analysis rubbish when she was younger, graciously decided to inform me of how being followed by a crow in your dreams can be a sign of an enemy drawing close.

The fact that, back then, it was something I was seeing when I was awake allowed me to ignore such a ridiculous idea. The fact that I was now seeing the same thing in my dreams however, left me feeling rather unsettled.

Upon rousing in the morning proper, once hangovers had been nursed and stomachs cautiously filled, I joined the guys in saying thanks and goodbye to Rob the barman before loading up their van and taking off through the heart of Berlin.

Along the way the guys talked about how this had been the midway point of their tour and told me of the places they intended to stop at on the way back home to England. I listened with only half an ear to them that morning though. Not out of disrespect but rather a preoccupation with my growing excitement.

I stared out of the window and let the city pass by in a blur; feeling quite sure that I'd seen enough of it during my previous day's wanderings. Occasionally though, my eye was caught by a few familiar sights.

'Richard? Where is the Reichstag building exactly?' I asked quizzically.

'You came by train didn't you?' he said, answering my question with another question.

'Yes. Why?'

'Well, and you'll kick yourself when I tell you this but, it's almost directly opposite the station on the other side of the river. You could have been no more than about a 10 minute walk from it.'

'Typical,' I thought to myself, *'Bloody typical.'*

The one place in all of Berlin I'd wanted to get to and I'd probably walked right past it. True I hadn't known it was the place I was looking for back then, but that wasn't the point.

It made me think though. Meeting Richard had just been pure dumb luck, and him knowing about the victory banner unpredictable. Archer couldn't have possibly anticipated such a thing, so how had he expected me to find the Reichstag building without relying on me already knowing about the Russian flag thing? Perhaps I had missed a clue or something. But then I didn't have a letter this time that could have contained a cryptic clue and surely the first one couldn't have contained anymore?

I decided not to worry about it too much for the time being as, if this building turned out to be the right place, then all would be well. The question still nagged away in the back of my mind though. I had never been THAT lucky before!

The traffic on the roads was quite heavy that morning and it must have been about twenty minutes before, upon passing alongside a large wooded park, I saw a colossal building emerging through the trees. A palace of stone columns and towers that sported imposing statues; standing proudly upon lofty perches and gazing out over the whole city. No grander place for such a meeting he'd said. I couldn't have agreed more.

The van pulled up opposite the grandiose entranceway that led into the Reichstag building and, sliding open the side door, Richard let me out.

'Well Tom, here we are. It's been a real pleasure to meet you and I really hope you find who you're looking for in there,' he said, shaking my hand, *'the best of luck for the rest of your journey too.'*

'Thanks again guys, for everything. I hope you enjoy the rest of your trip and have a safe journey home,' I replied, shaking hands with the rest of them as I did, *'Who knows, perhaps luck will strike twice and we'll meet again one day,'* I added, reluctant to see them go.

'I'm sure we will Tom. One day we'll find ourselves both back in the Boot and Shoe with many stories to tell, and on that

day I'll be keeping a pint waiting for you. Until then though, look after yourself.'

With that, he slid the door shut and I was left alone once again; waving goodbye to my new friends far too soon.

Shaking off the fresh chill of loneliness, I focused my attention back on the job at hand and set off towards the steps that I prayed would lead me to some answers.

The Reichstag Building

The building towering above me was incredible; a marvel of highly skilled workmanship and masterful design. It comprised of two wings that stretched out in symmetry of each other. Both ended in towers rising up higher than the main body of the building to display the boldly coloured national flag flying regally in the breeze. At the point where these two wings joined, stood a structure that resembled a Pantheon of Ancient Greece. Six ornate columns, holding up an elongated isosceles triangle roof structure that acted as a porch in precedence to the wall of glass that was the buildings front.

The triangle contained some sort of relief, embossed into the stone, of people standing either side of a shield; symmetrical in shape though not in depiction. Underneath this were the words "DEM DEUTSCHEN VOLKE" boldly carved into the facade.

Above all this, in a joining of the historical with the modern, sat a spectacular dome of glass and shining steel glinting in the rays of the sun. With its brickwork and glass, columns and statues, the place looked like it should have been a museum or something. Instead it is criminally wasted in service as a governmental building, albeit one partially open to the public as a tourist attraction. Such a shame!

As I walked through the main entrance, I was astonished to see the grand architecture of the outside give way to an almost complete contrast of modern design. The best way I can describe it is sterile and minimalist. Large pieces of pointless modern art hung from otherwise featureless, and colourless, walls. It was like walking into a different world.

The dome on top of the building and the glass entrance was okay, it gave a feeling of moving with the times without sacrificing the soul of the original building work. But the interior, whilst being great for the offices of say a law firm where pretentiousness and a feeling of cold clinical dealings is quite apt, did not fit in a building that should have been a monument to its cities history.

Looking around with distaste, my eyes fell upon a guard at the main desk who seemed to be watching me with some suspicion. I shrugged it off as just being part of his job to observe all visitors and proceeded to wander round, hoping to stumble upon my contact. Before long though, I began to feel that, after all the excitement of anticipating what I would find there, it wasn't going to be just the interior design that disappointed me. Perhaps this wasn't the right place after all?

Eventually I headed up into the glass dome that I'd seen from the outside; more out of curiosity than anything else. At its centre was a mirror clad funnel that seemed almost to ripple out into a spiral walkway that spun round the inside of the dome taking you to the top. The overall effect made it look to me like a giant water fountain frozen in time, from where you could get a spectacular panoramic view of the Berlin cityscape. It was quite breath-taking.

Sadly however, it began to appear as though a spectacular view was to be the only thing I would find there that day. I'd seen nothing that could have guided me to the next guardian or given a clue as to where they were; no paintings that caught my eye or old men sat in corners to talk to.

Pretty soon I found myself with little option other than to concede that this was obviously not the place I was meant to be. With that dejected defeatism settling into my mind, I made my way back towards the entrance; ready to give it all up as a bad job.

'Entschuldigung! Excuse me Sir!' a voice called out from behind as I approached the main doors.

Glancing over my shoulder to see what was going on, I saw the guard form the front desk approaching me at an officious speed.

'Englisch? Deutsch?' he asked.

'Yes, I'm English,' I replied cautiously, *'can I help you?'*

'I must ask that you come with me please Sir!' the man replied...it wasn't a request.

'Why? Have I done something wrong?' I asked with a growing concern.

'Please. This way,' again this was not a request.

Every fibre of my body screamed to get the hell out of there. Something just felt very wrong about the whole situation. But, before I could even think of doing a runner, two more guards appeared either side of me, leaving little choice other than to follow as asked. What had I gotten myself into?

I was led off towards, and then through, a door marked with a no entry sign. This opened up into a long corridor that seemed to stretch out endlessly before me. At the far end of it I was ushered into a room, devoid of any features save for a table and chair, and instructed to take a seat.

'Wait here!' said the chief security guard before shutting the door on me without even the courtesy of an explanation. It was then that I started to panic.

'What have I done? Am I going to be arrested? Did they somehow discover that I have a fake passport?'

All these things went through my mind as I waited alone in that room, before coming to settle upon one singularly disturbing thought. Had I just walked myself into a trap?

As paranoia began to reach fever pitch over the possibility that these men belonged to a branch of the Masons, I heard the "click" of the door handle being turned signalling their return. This was it!

'Sorry to keep you waiting,' said the tall, athletic looking man that entered the room, *'My name is Sebastian Reinhardt. My apologies for the rather clandestine escort you received just now. I instructed the guards to detain you and contact me immediately should you ever show up here, but I negated to tell them why.'*

Having expected to see another man in uniform coming through the door, I was more than a little surprised by the person now standing before me. This was a well-educated man, in his mid to late twenties as far as I could tell, smart in apparel with a cool air of confidence about him and incredibly fluent in English; only a soft accent showing through on certain words to give away the fact that he was in fact German.

He wore a tailor made black suit with a light blue shirt and an understated tie that contrasted well against his short blonde hair, glacial blue eyes and angular features. I wouldn't normally pay this much attention to another man's appearance, but this one evoked a very strong first impression.

If Hitler had been alive today, this guy would have fit perfectly into his Master Race, let's just put it that way.

'I am sorry but, I did not catch your name?' he said diplomatically after an uncomfortable pause.

'That's because I didn't give it!' I answered sternly, *'Do I know you from somewhere?'*

'No, no, I am quite sure we have never met before,' he replied with a smile that was both pleasant and unsettling in equal measures.

'Then pardon me, but why the hell did you have the guards looking out for me?' I demanded with a peevish tone.

'Simple, you are a friend of Archers are you not?' he said with a look of surprise.

'How did you know that?' I asked him with suspicion.

Yes the thought crossed my mind that he could be the person I'd been looking for, but I wasn't about to trust a man that had me dragged away in public like a criminal until I knew for sure.

'My apologies again, I naturally assumed that you would know how this whole thing worked. Please, allow me to explain.'

He went on to tell me how Archer had sent him a letter about one month earlier with a very detailed sketch of my face and a cryptic riddle that, once deciphered, read;

'A friend will seek you in a public place,
Where a Victory Banner overthrew the Master Race'

He figured the Victory Banner link to mean the Reichstag building much as Richard had done and, being unsure of when I would arrive, he circulated my picture around to the guards in anticipation that it would be some time soon.

'If you really are a friend of Archers, and he informed you to meet me, then you must also have received something else,' I probed vaguely, wanting proof that he was who he claimed to be.

'Very cautious, I like that. Quite befitting an attitude considering the parliamentary history of this grand building,' he replied with a wry smile. *'Of course, what you are referring to is this!'*

He placed the briefcase he had been carrying down onto the table and opened it, with a synchronised clicking of the spring loaded locks. From it he then passed me an already open parcel.

Hesitantly I took it from him and reached a hand into the packaging. With surprised excitement, I pulled free the object within; wanting to see it with own eyes and confirm it was what my hand had felt it to be...the second piece of Archer's journal.

<u>Day 7 - Berlin, Germany</u>
Himmler and the Holy Grail

As my mind raced with questions for the man sat before me, and my eyes revelled in the chance to glance through the next part of Archer's journal, my mouth completely failed to articulate anything coherent.

'My reaction was very much the same when I first opened the parcel,' he said as if to acknowledge my pains.

'I have so many questions, I just don't know where to start,' I managed to say eventually, *'How did you and Archer meet? Why did he send this piece to you? What is your connection to his quest? Did he find what he was looking for here in Berlin? Where did he go from here?'*

'I will answer all those questions and more Mr...?'

'Keeldan,' I said offhandedly in response to the implied pause. I quietly commended myself for having instinctively remembered my new name this time though.

Mr Keeldan, but not here,' he continued. *'Please, come with me and we shall go somewhere better suited for such discussions.'*

Something about the way he said this suggested that he had a good reason for it; one that I shouldn't question.

I followed him out of the building and into the street; noticing the look of suspicion still present on the guards face as we passed back through the entrance hall.

Relieved to see the light of day once again, I watched as my new acquaintance flagged us down a taxi.

'Where exactly are we going Mr Reinhardt?' I asked as one pulled up alongside us.

'To the place where I met Archer, Mr Keeldan,' he answered whilst opening the back door of the car for me, *'and please, call me Seb.'*

'Thank you,' I said in response to his friendly gesture, *'I'm Tom.'*

'Staatsbibliothek unter den Linden bitte!' he said to the driver as he got in behind me. *'The Berlin State Library,'* he added in English for my benefit, upon seeing the slight look of puzzlement on my face. *'Well to be more precise, it is House 1 of the State Library that we go to. The whole thing is actually spread out over several sites around Berlin. Where we are headed is a building originally known as the Prussian Royal Library, located Unter den Linden; a boulevard named for the trees that line it.'*

'What does "Unter den Linden" mean?' I asked as we left the Reichstag building behind us and headed back in towards the centre of Berlin.

'Literally it means Under the Lime trees, a description I think you will find is rather accurate.'

Looking out of the taxi's window upon Seb's prompt, I soon saw what he meant. We were driving under a canopy of heart shaped leaves belonging to a seemingly endless line of lime trees that stood before buildings of grand architecture. It was a perfect example of man and nature coming together in a beautiful moment of peace.

Moments later we arrived in front of the library and I found myself wondering if the taxi had been all that worthwhile considering the short distance it had taken us.

As I stepped out of the car, a sense of familiarity hit me upon surveying the building that rose up before me.

'Magnificent is it not?' said Seb as he arrived at my side, *'Built between 1908 and 1913, its Neo Baroque architecture is very similar to that of the Reichstag building, as no doubt you have noticed.'*

He wasn't wrong. Whilst not quite as grand as the Reichstag's, the entrance to the Library was framed in a similar "Pantheon-esque" styling. In retrospect though, the Library building was quite different in the fact that its columns, of which there were only four, were built into the wall rather than freestanding, and in-between them stood three arched gateways that led through to an inner courtyard.

From where I was stood, that which lay beyond had the look of a secret garden. Its walls were thick with a crawling ivy that stretched out of my sight, and in front of them sat a large circular pond, dominating the centre of the courtyard, with only the dancing of a water fountain to disturb the scenes serenity.

224

'Shall we?' came the gentle nudge of Seb's voice as I realised I'd been stood staring at the building like an idiot.

Following him through the central archway into the library and then on to the secluded table he led me to, I took a seat opposite him and waited expectantly for the explanation he promised me.

'What do you know of the Holy Grail Tom?' asked Seb, wasting no time in getting down to business.

'It's supposed to be the cup that was used by Christ at the Last Supper, the one that was subsequently used to catch his blood after the Crucifixion if I remember right. Isn't it meant to have had great healing powers, been protected by the Knights Templar and greatly sought after by the Nazi's,' I replied, exhausting my full knowledge of the subject within a few breaths, *'or was that perhaps just in the Indiana Jones film?'* I added as an afterthought.

'Well yes, it is as you say, in the Sunday school biblical version of the story anyway,' he said with a slight look of surprise, suggesting he had been expecting something more from my reply, *'But the story of the Grail actually has its origins in much less holy times.'*

By this point I'd come to accept that history lessons were going to be a big part of this journey, and already the signs of one about to begin were becoming quite clear to me. As such, when Seb drew the tell-tale deep intake of breath, I readied myself for another one.

'What I am about to explain to you is the highlighted version of the research conducted by myself and Archer. In an attempt to keep it as short and concise as possible, I will omit certain things that are not crucial to the telling of the tale. The truth of our findings and the credibility of the links we made are as yet untested. That is the trial we two shall face, once I have brought you up to speed on my research and you have done so to me with yours.'

The strong pull of boredom already began to lay a heavy glaze over my eyes, and he hadn't even properly started yet. That was however, until his last statement sank in. Suddenly I found myself feeling like the idiot who turns up to class as the only person who hasn't done the homework. What research was he expecting me to have done?

'Okay, where to begin?' he said ponderously, *'Do you know the legend of the Fisher King?'*

Hoping this was a rhetorical question I merely stuck out my bottom lip, raised my eyebrows and shook my head in response.

'Well...' he started before pausing mid speech. *'Actually, perhaps it would be best if I were to first explain to you how Archer and I met?'*

He seemed to say this more to himself than to me, before nodding in agreement to his own suggestion.

As intrigued as I was about how they did meet, and relieved at the postponement to the history lesson, I couldn't help feeling a little bit cheated. Who the hell was the Fisher King, and what was the legend surrounding him?

I doubt it actually would have bothered me any had he not decided to segue into another story without explaining the first but, as I hated things being left unfinished, it felt like an itch I wasn't allowed to scratch.

Before I could put forth any kind of protest though, he began to talk again. I knew these questions would niggle away in the back of my mind until answered but, for the time being, I would just have to let it be.

'It seems an age ago now since I was sat here in this library with Archer. Thinking about it, I suppose it has been. It must be almost two years now since we met. I had been coming here on a regular basis at the time you see, conducting research into an old castle in the town of Buren where I grew up. As a child I had loved this castle and so was dismayed upon discovering, in later life, that it actually had a rather dark secret surrounding its name. You see Castle Wewelsburg had once been occupied by the Nazi's and, more specifically, Heinrich Himmler the head of the SS.'

The sound of that name instantly grabbed my attention. I remembered then how it was in search of information about Himmler's interest in the Oswald head reliquary that Archer had decided to stay longer in Berlin. Finally I was going to find out how all this was connected.

I couldn't quite put my finger on it at the time though, but I somehow felt that Seb was holding something back from me.

'It was pure chance that I happened to be here on the very same day that our friend showed up,' he continued. *'Taking little notice of him initially, due to his rather scruffy appearance, I was surprised to overhear him asking a librarian if there were any books about Himmler's interest in ancient relics; something which prompted my curiosity. It was this that brought us together. My findings had also led in such a direction you see,*

226

and it left us needing many of the same books. For a time we simply acknowledged one another whilst otherwise keeping to ourselves. Eventually however, my curiosity got the better of me and I had to know what his interest in the subject was. I introduced myself to him and explained how I could not help noticing that we seemed to be researching the same subject. I then suggested that, seeing how we both had been reading books the other needed, perhaps we could combine our findings and assist each other. To cut a long story short, that is exactly what we did. Over the next few days we became quite inseparable as we realised more and more how much alike our interests were. I offered him a place to stay and in return he told me of his quest for Shambhala.'

Something happened to me upon hearing this; something that was most unexpected. I felt jealous. I can't fully explain why, but knowing that Seb had spent so much time helping Archer with his research made me feel extremely envious. It's strange because I never got that feeling when hearing about Paddy's time with him? Perhaps it was some kind of primal territorial thing, another young male being seen as a competitor. A competitor for what though I'm not quite sure.

I had only met Archer once, and for a relatively brief amount of time, yet there I was feeling the pains of a child whose sibling has had more attention from their father. Quite sad really, now I come to think about it.

'When he told me of his discoveries at Hildesheim,' Seb continued, oblivious to the fact that every word he spoke was feeding the green eyed monster that grew within me, *'a revelation hit me like a bolt of lightning......I knew what Himmler had been searching for!'*

'Was it a piece of the Chintamani Stone by any chance?' I said sarcastically, *'Not much of a revelation that mate.'*

'Perhaps not,' he replied, mildly disgruntled by the tone I had taken. *'But what if I was to tell you that the piece he sought was otherwise known as the Holy Grail?'*

My jaw almost hit the floor when he told me this. I suppose really I should have foreseen the connection, considering Seb's earlier question, but instead his words left me reeling in an attempt to make sense of it all.

'You expect me to believe that Himmler thought the Cup of Christ was contained within St. Oswald's head reliquary?' I scoffed at him, trying desperately to appear doubtful and astute.

'Only if you are a fool!' he fired back, shattering that attempt, *'Otherwise I would expect you to know the difference between the Cup of Christ and the Holy Grail.'*

'I'm sorry,' I stated more as an objection than an apology, *'maybe something has been lost in translation here, but what the hell are you on about?'*

'You know Mr Keeldan,' he said as he shot me a hawk-like stare, *'I am beginning to question your involvement in all of this. What exactly do you know? Better yet, perhaps you should tell me just how it was that YOU met Archer?'*

Somehow things had all too quickly gotten out of hand. Our initially friendly opinions of each other were rapidly eroding. I found myself in the situation of having to recount my meeting with Archer before Seb would reveal anything more. It did not go well!

'So let me get this straight. You work at a filling station, stacking shelves and serving behind a till all day? And Archer chose You *to send the first piece of his journal to?'* this was a statement more than a question, spoken in a tone of scorn that I doubt Seb had even tried to hide.

I guess he'd expected me to be some kind of history buff like him, or someone with a skill set crucial to the quest. If that was the case then I suppose it must have come as an earth shattering disappointment to learn that I was in fact a nobody; someone just randomly caught up in something far beyond his own understanding.

Despite this, I was still deeply offended by the way he began to look down on me from then on. I only wish there had been some strong reason I could have thrown back at him as to why Archer had chosen me to follow in his footsteps. But in all honesty, that is a question I still don't really know the answer to myself.

'I may work in a petrol station,' I began in response, *'but that is not who I am. I bet even you have had to work some crappy jobs at some point in your life, so maybe you shouldn't be so quick to judge me,'* I was trying my best to keep my temper here, and I was pleased that I had managed to do so thus far without reaching over the table to throttle the condescension out of him.

'Whatever his reasons,' I continued, *'Archer did choose me and now I'm here. True, I don't know much about the Holy Grail, but then is that not perhaps why Archer arranged for us to meet?'*

228

As disillusioned and irritated as he was, I think Seb saw some sense in what I'd said. I think he was also just grateful for the chance to distract himself from the unsettling questions that were probably flying around in his head at that moment.

'Fine, I will try to explain it in simple terms for you,' he viciously conceded. I bit my tongue.

Taking a moment to compose himself and rein in his scorn, he drew in a deep breath before picking up where he'd left off.

'During World War II, the Ahnenerbe Forschungs-und Lehrgemeinschaft was created with the purpose of using scientific methods to bend history and archaeology to suit the Nazi's racial and cultural policies. There has been much debate as to the truth behind what this society actually did but, from my own research, I believe that it was tasked with the finding of historical, and arguably mythical, objects that could have given the Nazi's an advantage over the Allied Nations. As a founding member of the organisation, Hienrich Himmler used his power as head of the SS to achieve these goals by any means necessary. Of greatest importance to him was the finding of the Holy Grail. So fixated did he become that it is said he may have even had a special room set aside for it within Wewelsburg Castle, the headquarters of the Ahnenerbe.'

Perhaps it was just my desire to believe in a more exciting truth to our history than what was contained within the dusty old books we take for fact, but I found myself willing to accept that this theory was at least possible, if though not all that probable.

'I still don't get though how this links the Holy Grail to Oswald's reliquary, or why I'm supposed to know the difference between it and the Cup of Christ?' I interrupted him.

'Okay look,' he replied, fighting back his growing impatience *'The Cup of Christ is not the only, or even the first, version of the Holy Grail story. It was not until the end of the 12th Century that the Holy Grail even became connected to Jesus and Christianity, when it was referred to by Robert de Boron in his literary work "Joseph d'Arimathie". It was he who suggested that it was the cup used to catch the blood of the Christ. An earlier story of the Grail came in the form of a great medieval German romance by the poet Wolfram von Eschenbach. In his story, "Parzival", he tells of the Grail described not as a cup or chalice but rather as a stone that fell from heaven.'*

This wasn't the first time I had heard of such a stone!

'But surely that is just a fictional story is it not?' I queried, genuinely intrigued by what he had told me, though determined not to give him the satisfaction of knowing that.

'Yes, I suppose it could be, just as the bible could be just a series of fictional stories, yet half the world believes blindly in the words contained within that book!' he wasn't going to get an argument out of me on that one. *'Fiction or not, what you choose to believe is irrelevant. The fact of the matter is that one man did believe in the Parzival legend and became obsessed with finding the Grail. A man by the name of Otto Rahn.'*

'Who?' I asked.

'Do you know nothing at all about history?' he snapped quite aggressively at me.

'Afraid not, they don't teach that kind of stuff in shelf stacking school,' I replied with dead pan sarcasm.

'Fine! I guess I will just have to explain this to you as well,' he said, seeming to have completely missed the tone of my words.

'Otto Rahn, the great German researcher, was a known and dedicated Grail seeker. Interested in the legends of Parzival and the Holy Grail from a young age, Rahn went on to study the Catharism movement and the massacre at Montsegur at the suggestion of his University professor. It was there that the legends really came to life for him. He argued that there was a direct link between Wolfram von Eschenbach's Grail story and the Cathar Grail mystery. He believed that the village of Montsegur in the Pyrenees Mountains, where the remains of the last Cathar fortress to fall during the Albigensian Crusade still stands, was in fact the Grail Castle referred to as Monsalvet in Eschenbach's story. One reason for this was that both place names have the same meaning, "Safe Mountain". This, along with many other similarities Rahn discovered to the tale of Parzival, convinced him to go there in search of the Grail itself.'

'Whoa, whoa, whoa, slow down,' I interrupted. *'Who were the Cathars? What was their Grail mystery and what was the Albigensian Crusade?'*

'Um Gotes Villen!' I think was what he said; something I took from his tone and gesture to be an expression of exasperation as he got up and walked away to gather a series of books from the surrounding shelves, *'Here, read these!'* he said throwing them down onto the table before me, *'If I had wanted to teach empty headed shop workers I would have become an educator in a state school. I do not have time to explain*

everything to you so, if you want to know more, start reading. Archer went into great detail about our findings in his journal so you might want to check there too. Now, if you have no educated questions to ask, I will move on.'

This guy was really beginning to get up my nose. He'd instantly assumed that I was a brainless moron simply because of the job I had been doing. It was all I could do not to get up and slam his head into the table.

'In 1933,' he continued, staying stood up and pointing to one of the books now on the table, *'Rahn wrote his first book entitled "Crusade Against the Grail", the publication of which brought his work to the attention of Herr Himmler. Intrigued by his take on the Grail legend, Himmler seduced Rahn into joining the SS. Do not judge him for this though,'* Seb instructed upon noticing the distaste written across my face, *'it was a move he was uneasy about making. But, as he said in his own words, "A man has to eat. What was I supposed to do, turn Himmler down?" Such a decision would have been unwise I believe. Himmler was obsessed with the occult and even had plans to turn the SS into an elite Knightly Order, akin to that of the Knights Templar. In addition to this he sought to turn Wewelsburg Castle into a place of initiation and a spiritual centre for Nazi paganism and occult practices. He was so fanatical about it that he even planned to take over the whole town of Buren, turning it into a community for members of his order and their families. This was a vision he was only able to partly realise I am happy to say,'*

I really wanted to query what he'd meant by this, but I decided it wasn't worth the grief.

'Rumours abounded for decades that Rahn did in fact discover the Grail and that it even sat in the special room set aside for it at the castle. Many historians dispel this as pure myth however, mainly due to Rahn having once written that he believed the Grail must have perished with the end of the Templars back in 1307. A compelling augment it may be, but then why would the man waste so much time and effort exploring old Cathar ruins only to then give up so quickly and say that the Grail was lost with the Templars? Is it not possible that he did this to protect the true location of the Grail as any real Grail Knight should?' his raised eyebrows and head tilted to one side, looking down at me over imaginary glasses perched on the end of his nose, suggested that he expected me to think on this, despite it being obvious from the tone that the question was rhetorical, *'The truth of what he actually found at Montsegur*

231

may never be known but, Grail or not, it is said that he did find a large crystal stone that was eventually given over to Himmler. It is for this reason that I believe the castle is worth checking out.'

'Which one?' I asked, slightly confused.

'What do you mean "which one"?' he snapped, *'Wewelsburg castle of course, is that not what I just said? The object that Rahn found in Montsegur was eventually turned over to Himmler whose base was Wewelsburg....what point would there be in going to Montsegur?'*

'Alright, jeez! I only asked a bloody question for God's sake.'

'Yes well, in future, please refrain from asking stupid ones,' he said quite spitefully, his eyes closed in exasperation whilst he rubbed the centre of his forehead as if to ward off an approaching headache.

'Okay then, if Rahn did find the Grail, why would he give it over to Himmler if his aim was to protect it?' I asked superciliously.

'Well...,' he paused, his eyes opening suddenly to a quizzical look across his brow. *'Actually, that is quite a good question,'* he then added, seemingly rather surprised by this. *'It is the same one I asked myself in fact. Unfortunately though, there is no definite answer. I do however have my own theory about it. You see in 1939, after an argument with Himmler, Rahn requested dismissal from the SS. Shortly after this, he was found dead on a mountainside in Austria to the official ruling of suicide,'* by this point he was leaning on the table and had landed a heavy finger vertically down upon Rahn's book deliberately with the last few words of the sentence.

He then stood back up straight before continuing on with a wave of his hand. I got the feeling that he took this man's fate quite personally for some reason.

'After his death it came out that he was openly gay and that it was over such matters that he had argued with Himmler. An argument that they say led to him leaving the SS and taking his own life in shame. This I do not believe!'

He let this statement, having taken care to highlight each word as he spoke it, hang in the air for a moment as if to highlight his resolute stance over it.

'From what I have read about the man, gay or otherwise, he was not the type to commit suicide. An opinion I am not alone in having. The tales of his amazing life were of great public interest and as such many rumours grew surrounding his death amongst

those that refused to believe such an enigmatic end for this man to be possible. The most prominent of which were the ones suggesting that he was actually murdered by the SS for wanting to leave. Quite a believable possibility would you not agree? My question is however...what if he was murdered, not for leaving, but rather for withholding the location of the Grail from Himmler?'

I had to admit, he did present a very compelling argument. Maybe one not good enough to stand up to scrutiny by a historian, but one that was definitely plausible enough to get my excitement bubbling and make me want to check out this castle too; just in case there was a chance his theory was right.

'How much of this did Archer discover with you?' I asked.

'Not a lot in truth,' he answered with a far-away look. *'Upon learning of my interest in the subject, and the connection I made to the Holy Grail, Archer asked if I would be willing to conduct further research into the story for him. Obviously I jumped at the chance; with my curiosity and desire to discover more already running at fever pitch.'*

'Why would he do that though?' I voiced, unable to understand Archer's reasoning.

'What do you mean?'

'Why would he pass this onto you? It just seems odd to me that if Archer had good reason to believe the Holy Grail did exist, and that it was indeed a piece of the Chintamani Stone, why would he not want to follow up on the clues himself?'

'You know, I asked him this question myself,' he replied, with an almost impressed tone. *'What he said to me was that the finding of the Grail, although it would be a major discovery, would still only be one piece of the puzzle...one part of the greater Stone. He believed that the chances of it still being at the castle were slim at best, but he also felt that no clue was small enough to be ignored completely and so was still worth investigating. I got the feeling that he was intently focused on finding a major piece, the one he thought had been given to Nicholas Roerich, and was content to leave the tracking down of the smaller pieces to people he found worthy enough to trust with the responsibility.'*

Although he didn't say it, I could see in his smug face that he was full of himself for being such a person. What he said did make some sense though. It would be wise of Archer to have delegated to others the tasks that would distract him from his main search. Who knows how many more people Archer had requested assistance from?

In the back of my mind though I couldn't help wonder if there was more to it than that. The logic here would be that Archer was dedicated to finding the primary pieces of each Chintamani Stone. If this was true however, then why would he not have pursued the Stone of Destiny? What was so special about the Roerich piece that made him so obsessed with finding it?

My excitement at the revelations presented to me soon eclipsed any worries I was having however, and I wasted no further time in asking what Seb thought our next move should be.

'OUR next move?' he said with an unfriendly emphasis on the "OUR", 'Since making MY discoveries, I have long desired the chance to explore the castle for evidence that would support my theory. But as I will have to practically break in to get to the necessary areas, it is something I can not do alone. Impotently,' I'm hoping that wasn't the word he meant to say 'I have watched these last two years pass away, able only to further my research through books. It is an avenue I had just about exhausted when the letter from Archer arrived foretelling of your coming. As my excitement grew at the thought of meeting another one of his researchers, I set about plotting a way into the castle.'

He'd walked back around to the other end of the table by this point and sat somewhat forlornly down in the chair that awaited him.

'Finally my time had come...or at least so I thought. I expected Archer to send me some one of use, but instead he sent me you! Our next move? There is no "our", no "us". There is now only me and my wasted time!' slumping quiet sulkily back into the chair, he looked away from me and waved a dismissive hand as spoke his next words, 'Honestly, I do not know of what use you could even be. It's not like I even have a car that you could fill up for me.'

I'm not sure what rattled me more, the fact that he had insulted me again or that he had seemingly done so without specific intention; rather like he was just stating the obvious. Either way, he had just pushed one button too many.

'Now you listen to me you pompous, stuck up, sack of shit,' I growled in as low a tone as I could manage, having not forgotten our current surroundings 'I've had to run from my home with members of the Freemasons hot on my heels, been fed an endless

234

stream of bloody history lessons, almost died falling down a long dark shaft, got knocked unconscious by a falling stone, forced to flee from my country, tossed about like a rag doll on the bastarding sea and faced with finding a needle in a bloody haystack alone in this sodding city of yours all because a man, I stupidly took in out of the cold one night, decided, for some unknown reason, to send ME a piece of his bloody journal,' I paused to suck in a fresh lung full of air, having forgotten to do so during that little tirade, *'and now, on top of all that, you think that you can sit there and insult me because things haven't quite gone how you would have liked? Well I'm sorry but I'm gonna have to disappoint you once more because I didn't come all the way out here just to take your shit.'*

With that weight finally off my chest, I allowed myself a brief moment to breathe whilst taking pleasure in the look of surprise on Seb's face at my outburst.

'If you want to help Archer, as I do,' I continued in a slightly calmer, yet no less pissed off, tone of voice, *'you're just going to have to make peace with the fact that, for now at least, we are stuck with each other. You need me to get into that castle, and I need you to help me figure out Archer's next step. Accept that and let's move on!'*

Sitting myself back down in the seat I had practically leapt from, I relaxed my body, calmed my temper, and said in a more patronising tone than maybe was necessary, *'Now, I'll ask again. What is our next move?'*

Day 7 - Berlin, Germany
Amongst Thieves

I suppose reluctant is as good a word as any to describe Seb's acceptance of my terms. A growing dislike of each other aside though, he did eventually swallow his pride and begin to explain his plan. I say explain, but in truth he barely gave me enough detail to pass as an overview; purposefully keeping the finer points of it to himself just to irritate me and show who was in charge.

'Where are we going then?' I had asked as we made to leave the library.

'The train station,' was his flatly spoken answer...you see what I had to deal with?

'I must stop by my apartment first though to collect a clean change of clothes and some toiletries,' he informed me. *'It is a hygiene thing, you probably would not understand,'* he then added in a tone that turned the otherwise innocent words into an insult.

Either he was a clever bastard, who knew how to insult in a way that was hard to react against without losing your temper, or he was just an incredibly rude man. Either way, I knew I couldn't allow myself to rise to the bait.

As we left the building I was too busy trying to control my temper, by imagining what we might find at this castle, to notice the two rather thuggish looking men skulking in the shadows of the archway ahead. Almost bumping into Seb as he stopped dead in his tracks, I sensed more than saw his whole body tense up as the men stepped out in front of us. He looked like a rabbit caught in headlights; knowing he should run but physically incapable of doing so.

Not only did they manage to effectively block our way, but they damn near blocked out the sun too. They were both almost as wide as they were tall...and boy where they tall. I consider

236

myself to be quite a well-built man of above average strength, but against those two I felt like a matchstick.

I couldn't understand what they said to Seb, speaking to him as they did in German, but their body language and expressions where unmistakable. Mr Reinhardt was in trouble and these men were here to give him and unfriendly warning.

Struggling to keep his composure, Seb managed to tell them something that caused one to smile sinisterly and the other to give him an unsettling pat on the shoulder before turning round and heading off back wherever they had come from.

As his body unclenched and he wiped the nervous sweat from his brow, I asked him what it had all been about. At first he seemed reluctant to tell me but, after seemingly being unable to come up with any plausible lie, he eventually confessed.

I was surprised to thusly discover that this confident man, with his expensive suit and executive briefcase who'd looked down on me for being a mere shop assistant, had a rather serious gambling addiction; one that had run him up a lot of bad debt with even worse people.

The two heavies we had just encountered were the right and left fists of a particularly nasty loan shark, whom had grown impatient with Seb's debt and wanted his money back. To say I was surprised at his confession would be an understatement as, despite what I thought of him, I'd never have taken him for a compulsive gambler. To say I took no pleasure from it though would be a lie.

As we walked on to his apartment, he seemed to feel the need to explain what had happened; as if to convince me that the gambling was all in his past. Against all the odds, I actually found myself feeling rather sorry for him.

'I was young and I was stupid. A boy attending university with an attitude to rebel against everything. I had become infatuated with a girl in my building and we eventually began to date. It was she who introduced me to the temptations of gambling and...other things. One bad bet led to another until, before I knew it, I had lost a year's worth of tuition money. I could not bear to tell my family for the shame of it, and so instead I took out an ill-advised loan from someone whom I was assured would be discreet about it. And now here we are, an ugly past has finally caught up with me,' his head bowed down in regretful sorrow as he spoke.

'Why has he only just come after you though?' I asked.

'Because part of our deal was that I would not have to pay the money back until I finished my studies and started earning. I naively thought this was a generous offer. The thing is, my life grew ever more complicated and the time to pay up never seemed to arrive. Foolishly I thought, having not heard from him for so long, that he had forgotten about me and my debt. I started to spend the money I earned without putting any savings aside. That childish naivety has cost me greatly.'

He went quiet for a while, his hands in his pockets and head hung low as we walked in silence.

'With the debt I owe and the interest he has added to it, I have now only one of two choices, either pay back the whole debt in one lump sum of €21,000 or make monthly payments of €1000 for the next two years,' he added dejectedly, *'and to think, I only borrowed €3,000 from him.'*

'Jesus Christ!' I said with a burst of shock, *'What kind of interest rate is the guy charging? Surely that's illegal? Can't you go to the police about it or something?'*

'And say what, that I am being charged an extortionate rate of interest on a loan I signed an agreement for?' he snapped back, as if offended by my "stating the obvious" comment, *'No, there is no way out other than to pay him what he asks.'*

'Can you afford to pay it?'

'Of course I can,' he said assuredly, though his eyes lacked the conviction to back the words. *'It is just the imposition of having to decide whether to pay the full amount or the monthly instalments.'*

The tone in his voice wasn't as confident about it as I believe he'd intended either, but I also got feeling that the conversation was over and that I'd best just leave it at that. After all it wasn't my problem... or so I thought!

Arriving at Seb's place, both our days were about to get much worse.

He lived in a rather posh looking apartment block that was situated far enough out of the city centre to be away from the night time noise and daytime congestion, yet close enough to be within reasonable walking distance just the same.

'Where was Archer going?' I asked him completely out of the blue as we headed towards his building.

'Excuse me?' he replied in a mild state of bewilderment.

238

'Where was Archer going when he left Berlin? I asked you about it back in the Reichstag building and it just dawned on me now that you never actually told me.'

'Oh, it must have slipped my mind,' he said innocently, *'Let me see, he said something about following a lead he had discovered on the trail of Nicolas Roerich. Some Russian historian with an ungainly name.....Dos?....Drov? Ach! What was it?'*

His face creased in irritation as he tries to recall this man's name.

'Aha! Dostchevsky! That was it,' he suddenly blurted out with satisfied relief, *'Dr Levendrov Dostchevsky. He is apparently some expert on the subject who Archer believed could help guide him in his search. I think he worked at a museum in St. Petersburg, if I remember correctly.'*

'Which museum?' I asked excitedly.

'Ermm...it was...,' he paused as that look of irritation passed across his face again and he once more tried to rub it away with a finger pressed in the centre of his brow, *'...Oh how am I supposed to remember that, it was years ago?'* he then snapped with a flap of his arms, *'If you want to know then check his journal, I am sure he would have detailed such things.'*

I wasn't going to hold my breath on that. Likely the next piece would end with but a hint of his next destination as did the first. I decided to check it later on when I had a bit more time though, just to be sure.

As we walked into the lobby area of the building, Seb commented on the fact that the security guard wasn't at his post before dismissing it as being of little importance. Taking the elevator up to his top floor apartment, we hardly spoke other than to exchange pleasantries about the building. That was until the doors opened.

'I consider myself to be quite lucky to have found this place I must admit. It is the perfect location for...Scheizer!' he cursed, stopping mid stride as if having hit an invisible wall.

A double take of what lay ahead left him wide eyed and motionless. I could hear his body tensing through the creek of his briefcase handle as his grip around it tightened.

'What's wrong?' I asked, before following his gaping stare to a door that was ajar.

'My door is open. I never leave it unlocked!' the panic in his voice confirmed what my mind had already concluded. Someone had broken into his place.

Suddenly the absence of the security guard down in the lobby became very important, suggesting that this wasn't just your average burglary. Cautiously we inched closer to the door, uncertain of what we would find inside.

Standing at either side of the door, I gave Seb a nod to push it open. As it swung slowly upon its, thankfully silent, hinges, the two of us held our breaths in anticipation of discovering someone still inside. Peeking around the door frame, we saw that the place had been well and truly trashed; the sight of which understandably sent pained looks of shock across Seb's face.

Feeling wholly sorry for him, this being something I wouldn't wish even on my worst enemy, I decided to go in first and quietly look around.

Quite why I was putting my neck on the line for him I soon began to wonder and almost instantly regretted. Images of a possibly armed and dangerous assailant hiding in wait for me began to play on my mind. Despite this, and the possible inappropriateness of the thought, I couldn't help but marvel at the apartment I was walking through. It was huge! Apart from the mess caused by the break-in, it looked like the penthouse suite of an expensive hotel.

A sudden thought crossed my mind, as I nervously went from room to room hoping not to find anyone. I actually knew nothing about this man whom I had so readily accepted as an ally, based purely on him having a piece of Archers journal and a believable story about how they met. What did he do that afforded him such an impressive apartment but left him struggling to pay off a loan shark?

'Anything?' Seb asked having crept in right behind me, causing me to near jump out of my skin.

'Jesus Christ! You frightened the shit out of me!' I yelped.

'There does not look to be anyone here now,' he added, completely ignoring my remark.

'No, whoever it was looks to be long gone and has left no obvious trace,' I agreed as my heart rate slowed back down. *'But what the hell were they after?'*

'What do you mean? Look at this place! They were clearly here to rob me!' he barked impatiently.

'Then why haven't they taken anything of value?' I replied sharply, *'True, I don't know what you had in here to start with.*

240

But unless you had some other stuff worth more than the expensive looking computers, flat screen T.V, stereo system, iPod and Blu-Ray player that I've seen lying around this place, I would say that whoever did this was looking for something in particular.'

'Or maybe they just got distur...' he began to say before his face dropped and his eyes became fixed on one room. *'Nein, bitte nicht so!'* he pleaded to himself before dashing away in its direction.

'What's wrong?' I was left asking the empty space he had seconds ago been occupying.

Deprived of an answer to that question, I followed him into the room which, from the parts of it not thrown all over the floor, I took to be some kind of study. There I found Seb desperately digging through the mess whilst babbling to himself.

'What's wrong?' I asked again, 'What are you looking for?'

'My money!' he cried out, looking up at me with an alarming amount of genuine fear and panic on contorting his face, *'The bastards have taken my money!'*

At this point I noticed that he was holding an empty shoe box in his hands and the first thing that came into my head was;

'You seriously kept money in a shoe box?'

Admittedly this was probably not the most helpful of comments to make right then, but seriously, who does that?

Fortunately he didn't seem to have heard what I said, or perhaps he just chose to ignore it, as he leant his back against one wall and forlornly sunk down to the floor. Feeling an unexpected sense of pity for the man, I crouched down near him and asked, in a supportive tone, what was going on.

'It is the money I had put away and could have used to pay Kruger his first instalment. That is what has been taken. What is worse, I think I know who it was that took it.'

'First off, who is Kruger and secondly who do you think stole the money?' I asked, bracing myself for the short tempered response I was sure he'd give.

'Kruger is the loan shark that holds my debt,' he replied without even a hint of anger or impatience in his voice. This must be really bad I thought to myself, *'And I am quite sure it was his thugs that did this.'*

'What, you mean the two walking brick walls that cornered us before?'

241

'Yes. I knew something was not quite right by the way they smiled when they said they had missed me at home today. Now it all makes sense.'

'But why would they do this?' I asked naively.

'Why do you think?' his voiced was laced with despair and defeat written across his face, 'This is part of the late payment fee. First they start by breaking your property and then, if you still do not pay up, they start breaking you. It is a double blow too as, in order to make the full payment, I was counting on being able to sell some of my possessions; the possessions that now lie broken and damaged all around me.'

'I'm sorry, I don't understand,' I began to query as politely as I could. 'If you planned to sell some stuff to pay off the loan in full, why then did you have money set aside for the first monthly instalment?'

'Because his first warning that payment was due came only days ago and I knew I would not have time to get the full amount together as quickly as he would be expecting. I planned to pay the first instalment to buy me some breathing room and take it from there.'

'Well okay then, now that they have the money back, surely that's at least bought you more time?' I offered optimistically.

'Do not be stupid!' he spat, barely lifting his head out of his hands to look at me, 'Kruger will just consider it a back payment of interest. He will still want more money and if I do not pay he will expose my association with him to the papers,' this was an odd statement I thought, 'They have given me three days to make a payment or else. Without anything to sell, and my money gone, I am screwed.'

'Not to sound cold hearted or anything, but so what if he does? Who's going to care about your gambling problem?'

'You do not understand Tom, I am a politician. One who has a good chance at running for office in the next election. Something like this getting made public could ruin me!'

Of all the things he could have said to me at that moment, revealing that he was a politician was the last thing I ever would have suspected.

'Aren't you a bit young to be running for government?' I stated, not sure what else to say.

'That is the whole point. People are tired of having the same old out dated politicians running the country. It is time for a change and many people are already intrigued by the thought of a younger, more modern thinking man being at the helm.'

242

There was something about all this that just didn't quite add up. There he was giving me the full campaign speech and all I could think of was why, if he is so determined to keep a clean image, was he willing to break into a Castle in order to help Archer? Something wasn't right.

Admittedly he did have the right kind of stuck up, self-important attitude to be a politician, but in no way could I see him as the leader of a country.

Putting that feeling aside for the time being, I decided to throw him a life line.

'Look, I'm guessing that Archer sent some money, along with the journal, to give to me just as he did with Paddy, Yes? If it's that important for you to pay off this Kruger guy then let's use some of that money and pay the first instalment so we can get on with our mission.'

The feeling of benevolence I had at being so generous soon faded as I saw the sheepish look on Seb's face.

'What's wrong?' I asked with growing dread.

'The money that has been stolen WAS that money!'

For a moment I was speechless. I couldn't believe what I was hearing.

'You're shitting me right? What, so you just decided that you were going to use money that wasn't yours without even asking, is that it?'

'Look, I did not know if you would ever show up and Archer gave no specific instruction as to what the money was for. I am the one that has spent the last two years doing all the leg work so back off,' he threw the empty shoe box aggressively against the far wall before slumping back against the wall, never once turning to look at me.

'Archer sent the money to me and my need for it was greater than yours. It's that simple!' he concluded as if to suggest that he'd been well within his right to do so and who was I to challenge him.

'Well, that's just fantastic then isn't it!' I growled in a short, sharp, agitated burst, *'What the hell am I supposed to do now without that money?'*

'What does it matter, you had just offered it to me anyway?' he replied in a tone that suggested he thought my sudden upset was somewhat hypocritical.

'No! I offered to let you use SOME of it to pay off your debt. How much did he send you, £2000 was it? You would have needed, what, around £900 pounds with the exchange rate? That

would have left me with just over a grand. More than enough to get me wherever it is I'll need to go in search of the next piece of the journal.'

I could feel the veins in my neck start to pulse as the blood passing through them began to boil.

'This was not supposed to happen,' he said as if that should have made it all better. *'Look, I have to call the police and report the break in or questions will be asked. I will sort this out after they have been but, until then, you must play along and say nothing about Kruger or his men to the police okay?'*

Despite his brash attitude, there was a genuine pleading in his voice that tempered my anger. After a moment of clear thought, I realised that there was little I could do now but trust that he would keep his word. Being angry at him and stomping my feet wouldn't change what had already happened.

'Fine, but this isn't over,' I warned him.

'No Tom! No it is not!'

Day 7 - Berlin, Germany
A New World Vision

As Seb set about reporting the break in to the police, I decided to leave him to it and go see if I could find out what happened to the security guard he had mentioned on the way up. In truth, I think I just wanted an excuse to get away from him; still fuming over his intention to use my money without my permission.

It suddenly dawned on me that it wasn't just faith Archer was putting in me to help him, but a lot of money too. I hadn't really thought about it until then but it seemed odd to say the least. I suppose the selling of his family home and all the possessions he no longer needed would have left him very well off but still. At two grand per guardian he would have potentially left me £8000 to facilitate my participation on this quest. Surely with that kind of money to throw away he could have found someone more skilled and suited to it that I?

Arriving back down in the lobby, the mystery of the missing guard was soon solved upon hearing a groan emanate from behind the reception desk. Relieved that I wasn't going to be discovering a dead body, I quickly followed the sound and found the man in question slumped on the floor with his back against the desk, slowly coming round.

Unsure as to whether he could speak English I purposefully kept my voice calm and soothing as I spoke to him whilst putting a hand on his shoulders to show I was there to help. It may sound daft and overly cautious, but then the man did have a gun holstered on his belt. I guess politics is a volatile enough profession as to warrant a high level of security. Although, if I were Seb, I'd have been thinking about employing someone to guard the guard from now on as he obviously hadn't proved too difficult to overpower.

Somewhat surprisingly, it turned out that the guy was actually South African, so communicating with him was not a problem once he finally came too. A quick check of his head

245

revealed that he had been, as I'd suspected, hit from behind and knocked unconscious. There was no bleeding, but an already forming lump suggested that he would have one hell of a bruise; something I could relate to as the memory of my own recent head trauma almost brought me out in sympathy pains for him.

Despite suggesting he should maybe get checked out at a hospital, the guard insisted that he would be fine and asked only if I could fetch him a glass of water.

It wasn't long before the sound of sirens approaching indicated the imminent arrival of the police, for which Seb had joined me down in the lobby to meet them. The place soon became a hive of activity as the apartment was picked over by detectives and crime scene specialists looking for evidence left by the robbers.

I kept out of the way as much as possible, opting to stay with the guard until a medic arrived to check him over. Once assured that he was okay, I eventually left him and took the elevator back up to Seb's apartment where it seemed the police where just about finishing up.

I asked Seb if they had found anything but, before he could answer me, he became distracted by the arrival of an important looking man in an expensive looking suit. The expression on Seb's face was a mixture of surprise and irritation as he pushed past me to confront the mystery man. He was larger in frame than Seb but otherwise seemed to have that same "Master Race" blond hair, blue eyed, chisel featured look that I was beginning to think of as "Classic German".

'Like bloody clones, these buggers are,' I thought to myself, abhorrently imagining a world where Hitler had won the war and everyone looked like that.

They spoke in German, so of what I cannot say for sure. I did roughly get the gist of it though simply from their body language as Seb looked to be squaring up to the other man. Too friendly to be enemies and yet I doubted Seb would have called him a friend from the awkwardness of the situation.

They continued to converse in German until the larger man gestured toward me with a questioning nod.

'Oh! Apologies! How rude of me,' Seb responded with an overacted sincerity, edged with a not so subtle derision, as he motioned for me to join them, *'Tom Keeldan, let me introduce you to the, newly appointed, President of the Federal Office for the Protection of the Constitution, Anton Reinhardt...my brother!'*

Well, at least that cleared up the reason as to why they had looked so alike; I just wish I had considered that possibility to begin with before going with the bigotedly stereotypical "Classic German" idea. The reason why I hadn't done this posed questions I don't think I really wanted the answers to.

'A pleasure Herr Keeldan,' the older man offered with a slight, yet officious, bow and a much stronger accent than Seb's.

'Likewise,' I said in return, offering a hand that was quite purposefully ignored as the two returned to their attentions back to one another. This time however, they conversed in English upon Seb's prompt; which I took as being for my benefit.

'So, what is it I can do for the head of the Domestic Intelligence Agency today?' asked Seb, still in a derisory tone.

'Sebastian! You do not think the head of an extremist political group can report a break in without us knowing about it do you?' replied his brother in a viciously playful manner.

I was beginning to get a picture that painted the reasons for the bad blood between the siblings. I had known Anton for less than a few minutes, and already I thought he was an arsehole. He obviously held a position over Seb which he seemed to make no effort to hide......although calling Seb the "head of an extremist political group" had concerned me a little.

'Why are you here Anton?' Seb fired back with a more direct, and almost accusational, attitude.

'I was head of state police here remember? When I heard about the robbery I came to check my little brother was okay. Is that so wrong?'

'Well, thank you for your concern but, as you can see, I am fine so now you can leave.'

At this point, Seb turned his back on his brother and began to walk away.

'Sebastian!' Anton commanded with halting force, *'Do not turn your back on me. You will listen to what I have to say.'*

'And what is that?' Seb snapped back round to face him with seething defiance, *'What words of wisdom have you come to offer me brother?'*

'I warned you this would happen should you go public with your views. The people will not stand for it and I can no longer protect you!'

I felt like a rabbit caught in the headlights as this family drama unfolded before me.

'I do not need your protection any more than I need your opinions,' Seb almost spat the words.

247

The grinding of his teeth and twitch around his mouth suggested that Anton was now becoming riled.

'*You may not, but what about your friend? Does he know what he is getting himself into?*'

'Get out!' Seb snarled.

'*Does he know he is involved with a Neo-Nazi, the leader of a right wing organisation deemed a threat to the constitutional order of this country? Does he know that?*'

'Get Out Of My Home!' Seb barked this time, his nostrils flaring as he flung an arm aggressively towards the door.

'*Does He Know?!*' repeated Anton, raising his voice to match Seb's.

'*I SAID GET OUT OF MY HOME!*' this raging demand was followed by Seb's fist flying into his brother's jaw with a force that noticeably unbalanced the larger man.

The whole room held its collective breath as neither I nor the remaining police officers could believe what had just happened. As time seemed frozen I watched the scene with morbid fascination, half expecting a fight to break out at any moment; one which I did not relish the thought of being in the middle of.

Thankfully, and quite surprisingly, Anton did not retaliate. Instead he simply raised a hand up to his busted lip and, with an unnerving level of calm, shot Seb a look of disgust.

'*Father was right!*' he said, dabbing at the small trail of blood running from his mouth, '*You are an ungrateful bastard!*' Then he turned and left.

I think Seb had also been expecting a retaliating punch from the way his body had tensed up but, from the look on his face, it appeared as though his brother had landed a much more painful blow with his parting words.

The rest of the apartment emptied rather quickly in the wake of Anton's departure, the police officers obviously feeling a little awkward about what they had just witnessed, and soon we were left alone.

Before I could say anything to Seb though, he disappeared in the direction of the kitchen with a face like thunder. This was shortly followed by the sound of smashing glass and, what I can only assume, was a lot of angry swear words.

Tentatively following him through, I found him slumped on the floor, leaning against a cupboard and holding a half broken glass filled with a liquid that smelt like a strong brandy. Looking up at me as I approached, I could see his eyes were red with the tears he was trying to hold back.

'What was all that about?' I asked as gently as I could, not wishing to upset him further but feeling in desperate need of some answers, *'Why did he call you a Neo-Nazi Seb?'*

'Because that is what the mainstream media and our political opponents have labelled my party out of pure ignorance,' he half sobbed.

Somehow I got the feeling that this wasn't the reason he was upset. Something in Anton's words seemed to have really struck a nerve.

'We stand for the interests of the German people and for Germany herself,' he went on to explain, *'We offer an alternative to the black and white choice between Liberal Capitalism and Communism. For this we are labelled as a "Far Right Successor to the Third Reich" by short sighted fools who wish to discredit our policies for fear of the support we have already begun to gather.'*

There was an exhausted tone in his voice, as though he was growing tired of fighting against the tide of opposition. As he took a large swig from the broken glass, I knew I had to prompt him for more.

'What cause do they have for such allegations though? I mean, the title of Nazi is not something usually thrown around lightly.'

'Look,' he replied whilst sliding me the brandy bottle across the floor, *'I doubt that you will understand this, but here in Germany we run a Federal Parliamentary Republic with a multi-party system; similar to your coalition government. It has been dominated since 1949 by the Christian Democratic Union and the Social Democratic Party of Germany. It is through them that we were led into the European Union and have now lost much of our national identity,'* he wiped his eyes and leaned his head back against the cupboard with a scornful sniff of this nose.

'They try to turn Europe into a single state where everyone is equal and everyone is the same. But we say this is wrong! We acknowledge the unpleasant but true fact that people are unequal products of their societies and environments, governed by the natural laws were the strong will always rise above the weak. Survival of the fittest, it is how life works in nature and so should work for us to,' I didn't like where this was going. *'Yet, here in the western world, this fact is painted over and ignored as those in charge try to tell us that all men are equal and*

should live as one. It is a fantasy for the perfect world; one in which we sadly do not live in. This is a truth all men know but many pretend not to believe, and it is through their ignorant naivety that we are called Nazi's and deemed a threat to democracy.'

'I'm sorry to say this Seb,' I said uneasily, after taking an awkward swig of the brandy, knowing that what I was about to say would likely anger him, *'but, from what I have just heard, I can easily understand why you are seen as such. Your party comes across as supporting the ideals of an authoritarian leadership?'*

'Exactly my point!' he expelled with a theatrical wave of his arms, *'You jump to conclusions because you do not understand. Dismissing ideas because you have been told they originate from the minds of evil racist men. We do not want to abolish the parliamentary democracy, or the democratic constitutional state. We are not Neo-Nazis trying to bring back the totalitarian regime of the Third Reich, just some of its ideals.'*

The calm and immaculately presented man I had met earlier that day was not who now sat before me. His hair had become dishevelled from repeatedly dragging his hands through it, his shirt unbuttoned around the neck and his tie pulled away to one side. His mere tone of voice displayed a level of agitation that suggested he was tired of people not seeing the world the way he did.

'It is true that the Nazis became an evil regime,' he continued, motioning for me to slide the brandy back over, *'but that does not mean all of their ideas were wrong. We do not believe in the idea of a "Master Race", but we do believe that not all people are equal and therefore cannot be expected to live peacefully under one rule. The idea of a multi-cultural society is unrealistic, fanciful and deeply flawed. It is not just religion that separates people but their lifestyles, beliefs, morals and intelligence, all of which differ between races and societies. Trying to force everyone to live together under one law is ludicrous.'*

He paused to take a swig before using the bottle as an extension of his arm to point at me.

'Just look at your own country for example. Despite your governments best efforts to unify the multitude of races living in the UK, you now have a More segregated society where whole cities have been practically taken over by the so called "ethnic minorities". It is a situation that has bred, and with continue to

250

breed at an ever alarming rate, new generations torn by racial inequality and intolerance.'

'I suppose that is a fair enough point of view,' I reluctantly acknowledged, not wanting to be completely dismissive of his opinions, *'but then how do you think that could be changed?'*

'What if cities where divided into quarters?' he answered in a self-indulgent tone of implied wisdom as he slid the bottle back towards me, *'Individual areas for each race and culture with a central unified area in-between. Can you imagine how much better things would be? Everyone would then have the choice of being separate in their own district if they wanted, or mixing together with other races in the central areas. Each nationality could then grow to its strengths with businesses in each quarter not having to worry about employing unsuitable people just to prove they are equal opportunities employers.'*

'Wouldn't that just lead to more unrest though?' I asked, struggling to grasp the over simplistic view he had on the state of the world.

'What do you mean?'

'Well not all cities have an equal number of people for each nationality that may be residing there for one. Some will always need more room than others, what happens then?'

'Well of course it would not be a strict line divide, there would obviously be some bleeding of residents between the districts, but surely you get the idea?'

A poor choice of words I thought, one that probably said a lot more about his plan than he intended.

'Oh yes,' I began in a borderline sarcastic reply to his question, *'I get it alright. I get that what you are proposing would only serve to substantiate the already growing divide between the nationalities of the world. Instead of a whole city working, for the most part, as one, you would have divided settlements working for themselves. You would have competition between the races, then you would have jealousy and elevated racism....and then you would have violence.'*

'It is not racist,' his voice cracked with anger as a tense jerk snapping through his whole body, *'just an acknowledgment of the unfortunate and ugly truth that governs the human race. We are all human, but we are not all the same. We can not all cohabitate in large numbers for long periods of time without it leading to unrest. How many times does history have to show us this before we take notice? If you force a man into a situation he does not like, he will reject it even if it is for his own good. But if*

251

you allow him the choice to approach it by himself, he will be much more open to accepting new wisdoms. Imagine a country where anyone could live but only the national people would be eligible for state benefits for example. What would be wrong about that?' there was almost a pleading edge to this question, *'Why should foreigners, fresh off the boat, be granted the same rights as the people who were born and raised in the country? Why should they get preferential treatment? Surely an Englishman like yourself can understand where I am coming from?'* he said, doggedly searching for some common ground to establish a foot hold.

I remained silent and looked away, feeling slightly ashamed that I could not whole heartedly disagree with him here. Much of what he said seemed to echo words I had often spoken myself. When I said it however, it was merely the ranting of a frustrated man that hadn't he power to change what annoyed him. Hearing Seb say these things though, a politician who could change things if elected, unsettled me deeply for it was hard not to see them as anything but fanatical.

'It is through the softness of your immigration laws that your economy has become so unstable,' he continued in the absence of my reply. *'Money earned in the UK is not getting put back into the economy as it should be, because a large chunk of it is being earned by foreign workers who send it back to their home countries. And what about the inequalities within your legal system?'* he added animatedly as I once again gave him possession of the bottle, *'Can you honestly say you enjoy living in a country where foreigners can come and claim your house under squatters rights simply because you are not in it at the time?'*

'No of course not,' I replied, wincing as I tried to calm the anger that very issue elicited within me, *'but it is not just foreigners that can do that is it!'*

'Of course not, but it is only in speaking out against "them" that you would be called a racist. How does that make sense?'

I guess he did have a point there; we do have some pathetic laws in England I had to admit.

'You see,' he began again after a dramatic pause, *'it was over such issues that support for the Third Reich originally came about. Their popularity rose quickly because their policies stood against this kind of madness. Yes they took it too far and yes they became a murderous dictatorship, but that does not mean their ideas where wrong, just their execution.'*

252

I found myself somewhat speechless to all this. I couldn't make my mind up whether his ideas had merit or were just plain crazy. Yes, I could admit some of what he said rang true about the way things were back home, but could I really condone the belief that Nazi policies were revolutionary ideas that simply became twisted by the men enforcing them?

A storm of questions soon began popping chaotically into my mind. Could I trust a man with such extreme beliefs? Surely Archer could not have known about any of this or else why would he have accepted the man's aid? Or was I maybe condemning him out of hand as others had for fear of admitting he could be right?

Before I could form any kind of order to these thoughts though, I was distracted by the sound of Seb's voice beginning to speak again.

'The sad thing is,' he said as the fire within him seemed to extinguish some, *'Anton was right. Through an eager desire to gain support and approval from both the German people and from my father, I ended up presenting our party as an extremist one in the shadow of Hitler. For a politician I am a terrible public speaker,'* he admitted with a deflating sigh, *'I can never seem to explain things right as they are in my head, instead they always come out wrong and turn people away. It is frustrating because I can see what is being allowed to happen, not just to Germany but to the whole world, through the inaction and assumed superiority of the Union.'*

'Which union?' I asked just to clarify.

'The European Union of course, who else?' he snapped.

'I was just asking Seb, no need to bite my head off. You could have been talking about anything for all I know. I'm not well up on politics.'

'Well I wish I could say that was a big surprise,' he said with a roll of his eyes and shake of his head, before returning to his speech. *'The "European" Union,'* he began in an exaggerated tone meant to insult, *'should be abolished in my mind. Integration in to it weakens national identity, sovereignty and values, whilst its bureaucratic nature undermines democracy as a whole. Their policies are directed to the benefit of European business rather than the well being of its people. The more countries that fall to the Union, the more power there will be in the hands of those not easily subjected to democratic control. Hell, they even passed a law that allows them to suppress political criticism aimed at their institutions and leading figures,*

and no one seemed to object. In one move they swept aside 50 years of European precedents on civil liberties and they have the nerve to call me a Neo-Nazi! They have basically given themselves the right to silence free speech if they do not like what you are saying.'

I was in the dark a bit here. He could have told me anything about what happened in the world of international politics and I wouldn't have known if it was true or not. If what he said was true though, it seem like a very disturbing misuse of power. I really wished I'd picked up a newspaper once in a while back home and actually read about what's going on in the world.

'They are bringing in Communism and presenting it as global democracy and nobody notices,' he continued. *'The thing is, that is not our biggest problem. Whilst the EU sits up on its lofty throne, admiring the position of power it holds, it has become blind to a shadow approaching from the Far East. As the economies of the west suffered great blows in the recession, and our attentions were focused on the threat from the Middle East, China has enjoyed a boom that has seen them rise to become a new world super power.'*

'China? I thought they were a relatively poor country?' I said, finding myself obviously ignorant of world economics as well.

'The people, yes. The country, no,' he replied with a resolute shake of his finger. *'Through tactical investments in Europe, Africa and the USA, the Chinese have moved themselves into a position from where they can hold the world to economic ransom. Blinded by belief in its own strength, the EU has now made the assumption that if it is nice to China, expanding the trade between our countries, welcoming their investments, and allowing them an equal voice at the International Democratic table, whilst looking the other way over its many Communist ideals that should otherwise prevent it from doing so, China will become our "Friendly Giant". But whilst it may be better to sit at the devils side than in his way, the devil by definition can not be trusted. The longer we sit and pretend that all will be well and that China is our new friend, the more time they have to methodically move pieces on an international chess board that will see the end of Western world dominance in the next twenty years.'*

'Surely you're being more than just a little paranoid here,' I said in response to his conspiracy theory, accepting back the dwindling contents of the brandy bottle.

'You think so?' he questioned with raised eyebrows, feigning surprise, *'Well then would it change your mind to know that China has already been expanding their own economy through the purchasing of large amounts of U.S. treasury bonds, under the guise of "helping the trade deficit"? Or that now they are trying to do the same in Europe? How about the fact that they have even been ploughing money into the development of countries such as the Congo to help them build roads and work themselves out of poverty?'*

'Hmm, I see yes. Helping poorer countries get themselves out of poverty is a terribly dastardly plan,' I replied with a dry sarcasm.

'I am glad you see this too,' he said, either not having understood my tone or simply choosing to ignore it. *'On the outside it seems like a very noble and humanitarian thing to do, but if that alone does not set off alarm bells about the Chinese, I do not know what will. The real reason behind the move is that, in return for their investment, the Chinese have secured exclusive rights to the Congo's diamond mines which could eventually bring them control over the entire diamond market. All these things and more are going on right under our noses, and still the Western leaders think they are in control,'* he scoffed as his gestures appeared more and more animated after every pass of the bottle.

He was up on his soap box with a captive audience to engage and enlighten. His emotions seemed to run a little too close to the surface for this to have been his profession though.

'Okay, let's just say for arguments sake that I do believe all this,' I said, offering him a bone, *'why is China becoming a super power such a bad thing?'*

'Because they are not a democratic country, and they never will be,' he said in a forceful tone. *'To them the needs of the individual matter not in comparison to needs of the state. As a race, they have existed for over 3,000 years under an authoritarian rule where the concepts of "human rights" and "freedom of speech" are mere words that can be swept aside. They will never change and they will never agree to compromise. Should they replace the western nations as the dominant world power, we will enter a darker period of human existence than any have known before!'*

'Jesus man! You could drive a puppy to suicide, you know that?' I said, sliding the brandy bottle back along the floor to

him for the last time, *'You best have this back before I attempt to slit my wrists with the glass.'*

Catching the bottle, a look of amused acceptance crept across his face as he raised it to his lips.

'I know it is hard to believe from all that I have just said, but truly I am not a Nazi,' he seemed at pains for me to believe this if nothing else, *'In truth, I am not even sure I can call myself a politician anymore either.'*

'What do you mean?' I asked, baffled by this statement.

'I resigned my leadership two weeks ago after having come to odds with some of the party's more "influential" supporters.'

'What happened?'

'Let us simply say that there are some who would see us bring back more than just a few of the Nazi's ideals,' he replied with a look of regret about him, as his shoulders drooped and he wiped at his face with the arm that was holding the brandy bottle. *'I guess my only hope for saving the world now rests in helping Archer complete his quest and in believing it will bring about the prophesised time of great peace.'*

'Well okay then,' I said with a slap of my thighs, desperate to leave behind this unsettlingly odd conversation. *'Sitting around here putting the world to rights isn't going to get us far in achieving that goal is it? So, let's put this, rather disturbing, incident behind us and get moving. Now, what's our next move?'*

'Simple,' he said as he accepted my hand to help him up, *'I am going to have to ask my father for some money.'*

256

Day 7 - Berlin, Germany
Histories Rewritten

I purposefully forced myself into adopting a friendly attitude towards Seb for the time being; despite still having doubts as to whether I could trust him. There were too many questions left unanswered, like why, if he was no longer running for government, was he still worried about Kruger taking their dealing to the papers and what had been his interest in this castle and Heinrich Himmler before Archer came along? However, it seemed like trusting him for now was the only way to further my own quest as, like it or not, I did need the man's help.

As he dug around in the mess looking for his telephone, eventually finding one end of a cable and following it to a buried handset, I decided to ask him about his father. All he would say though was that the man was a retired Army General who had made his fortune in the stocks and shares market. A bit of a bastard from what I understood, but likely our best chance of replacing the money "we" had lost.

Unfortunately, the phone call he made got us nowhere. Seb's father refused to help him during a conversation that had quickly turned into a blazing row. This resulted in Seb eventually slamming down the phone and throwing it across the room; ripping the cable from the wall in the process. At the time I thought it probably best not to pry too much into the reasons for his father's refusal. All he said was something about his father wanting to teach him a lesson.

Before I could ask what we were going to do next, Seb reached into his jacket and produced a mobile phone along with a plain white business card showing a single contact number. Without looking at me, he began to dial and simply said;

'He leaves me no choice!'

What followed was probably the shortest phone call I'd ever witnessed. After no more than half a dozen words, spoken in German, he hung up and turned to me with a wincing smile.

'Do not worry Mr Keeldan, you will have your money back within the hour, and I will have enough to leave all this behind me.'

He told me very little about the person he had called, saying only that it was someone willing to pay good money for certain family secrets of his. His lack of concern about the person's motives did worry me a bit, as it suggested that he was either holding something back from me or that he was just too blinded by some kind of childish revenge against his father to care. What bothered me most though was the feeling that it was likely a bit of both. What was he getting us into?

He had arranged to meet the mysterious contact at a cafe back in the city centre an hour later. With some time to kill before then, Seb went and changed out of his suit and into a more casual, yet still annoyingly smart, attire. He then set about picking through his belongings in an attempt to pack the bag we had come to his apartment for in the first place.

Whilst making an effort to help him tidy up, I desperately tried to glean more information about his contact, asking him what kind of information the man wanted so badly that he was willing to pay so much money for. Initially Seb looked to be quite uncomfortable with the question, as if reluctant to tell me something he thought I wouldn't understand. I could almost see the battle of conscience playing out behind his eyes. Eventually, common sense must have won out as he decided to tell me the truth.

'He wants to know of my great grandfather,' he admitted.

'Why?' I asked in a puzzled tone, *'Who was he?'*

'He was...a....' he began slowly before letting out a deep sigh, *'he was a powerful officer in the SS during World War Two!'*

My mouth practically dropped open in amazement at his revelation. It really didn't do my willingness to trust him any favours.

'The SS? Hitler's special police?' merely speaking the words sent a shiver down my spine, the name alone being enough to recall the atrocities they committed, *'I can see now why you were so reluctant to admit such a thing. I'd feel ashamed about having such a monster present in my family tree too!'*

It may be unfair to label all Nazi's as being evil, but in regards to the SS, I believe it is simply a factual statement.

'You see nothing', he sneered, lip curling in line with a scowl as he look back at me over his shoulder, *'You understand nothing about my family and you have no right to speak as such.'*

This brought a halting end to our conversation as he turned away leaving a tension hanging between us. I suppose his reaction was fair, I had spoken ill of his family and therefore understandably offended him. If the roles had been reversed I'd probably have hit him for such an insult.

Still, it bothered me that he would defend a member of the SS; family or otherwise. The more I learned about my companion, the more I feared that Archer had been unwise in choosing to trust him and the more I began to question whether I should be so eager to do the same.

As it was, I had little choice other than to have faith in the old man's judgment and go along with it all for now...It didn't mean I had to like it though.

The skies had darkened that afternoon and a dreary rain began to fall as we left Seb's apartment for that oddest of meetings. At the sight of the weather, and conscious of the time, we called for a taxi to take us back into the city for which I was glad. Not for care of keeping dry was that joy, but rather due to an almost audible rumbling from my stomach; one which reminded me that lunch time had passed me by without a crumb since breakfast.

It seemed such a long time ago since I'd began the day with the musicians. As it turned out, it was only about to get much longer.

I can remember the look of the little cafe as the taxi pulled up across the road, its open glass front preceded by an area of metal tables and chairs protruding out into the street. The smell of fresh coffee drifted across to us as we waited to cross the busy road each time someone opened the door.

I suppose it was much the same as any other cafe you could find upon entering, a counter strewn with coffee machines, cold drink dispensers and an array of tasty looking cakes and sweets, but then it did have a distinctive feature that stuck in my mind. It was the way the seating area was made up that was different, with "American Diner" style booths taking the place of regular seating to give the place a very comfy and welcoming feel.

Arriving there ahead of time, Seb suggested that I take his bag and sit at another table out of the way before his contact came, in order to keep an eye on things just in case something went wrong. Feeling the James Bond theme creeping into my head at the chance to be all spy-like, I picked up a newspaper left on one of the tables and sat away in a corner, with a good eye line on Seb's chosen table, pretending to read. I say pretend to read because, regardless of my intention, I had about as much chance of being able to actually read the paper, it being a German one and all, as I did of understanding Quantum Physics.

After a short but agonising wait, wishing I'd bought myself a piece of cake or something before sitting down and eying every passer-by with undue suspicion, I spotted a man walking past the front of the cafe towards its door. Trying to covertly keep my eye on him, I watched as he entered and made a bee line for where Seb was sat.

'Here we go,' I thought to myself.

If I'd had to describe him in one word, it would be sleazy. Dressed in a smart suit and a nice over coat, he had jet black hair that had been gelled so flat it looked more like a skull cap, along with an almost sinister greasiness to his skin. He looked more like businessman than a historian; an observation that served only to add to my concerns.

As he sat down opposite Seb, ignoring the hand offered to him in welcome, I found myself analysing his appearance further like a Sherlock Holmes wannabe. He wore a thick overcoat, despite it being reasonably warm outside? He chose not to take off his sunglasses, despite now being indoors? He left his gloves on and seemed intent on not touching anything or anyone? His shoes and the bottom of his trousers seemed dry, despite the ground outside being wet, suggesting that if he had walked here he hadn't walked far.

Watching them converse, a memory sprang to mind of the time my sister's boyfriend dressed up as a hit-man for a fancy dress party; he had looked almost identical to this guy. Initially the thought made me chuckle to myself, but then it began to play on my mind. What if that's what this guy was?

Maybe he had made up the story of needing the information just to get Seb to meet him. Maybe it had been him that trashed Seb's place? Perhaps he had a political agenda or maybe he'd been sent by the loan shark? Then another thought crossed my mind. What if he was sent by the Masons, who'd somehow found out that he'd been in contact with me?

For a brief moment I was filled with a sense of panic, not knowing what to do for the best, but thankfully common sense soon kicked back into action and pointed out all the flaws in my "hit-man" theory. The biggest one being that, if he was planning to kill Seb, or myself, why would he have arranged to meet in a public place where there would be plenty of witnesses? No, thinking sensibly, I very much doubted he was a hit-man; but that didn't stop me from being increasingly suspicious of him all the same.

Then I saw something that damn near made my heart stop beating. The guy reached a hand into his jacket!

Time seemed to slow down as I thought I could see the shape of a gun being pulled from a concealed holster. I always believed that in a situation like that I would spring into action, go hurtling towards the aggressor and wrestle the gun from their hand to save the life of whomever it was aimed at. Sadly for me, that was the moment I learnt that I was no hero. I just sat there frozen with fear and panic, like a rabbit caught in the headlights, incapable of even calling out a warning to Seb.

Incredibly, he didn't even seem to be reacting to the situation at all...and then I saw why. As the man's hand emerged out of his jacket and reached over to Seb, partially revealing an odd looking tattoo on his wrist, I saw that it was holding a wad of money, not a gun.

Breathing out, for what seemed like the first time in about 10 minutes, I felt relieved yet incredibly stupid. I was no spy, I was no hero. I was just a fool with an over active imagination and a possum like danger response.

After that little bout of excitement, the meeting effectively came to its end. The man stood up to leave but before he did, he leant in closer to Seb and whispered something to him that made my companions face drop and his eyes immediately darted towards me. If it wasn't for the fact that I assumed they'd have been talking in German, I'd swear that I saw the man's lips say *'we'll be watching.'*

I can't tell you why, but that moment unnerved me more than when I'd thought he'd had a gun. Something just felt wrong about it all.

I stayed hidden behind my paper and watched the man depart, making sure he had definitely gone before I moved. When I was content that the coast was clear, I joined Seb at his table where he'd remained seated and looking quite shaken.

'What's wrong? What did he say?' I asked pressingly.

'Nothing, nothing,' he dismissed, shaking his head as if coming out of a trance, *'I agreed to get him what he wanted in*

261

exchange for some money up front. He accepted my terms and we now have Archer's money back.'

'Seriously? He just gave you two grand like that, as if it was loose change to him?' I asked sceptically.

'He is willing to pay me €20,000 to complete the job,' he stated quite easily, *'I actually think that two thousand is just that to him.'*

'Are you shitting me?' I asked, dumbfounded by the statement, *'He's going to pay you €20,000 for information about your Grandfather.....and that doesn't worry you at all?'*

'Why should it?' he answered flatly with a look of indifference, *'What concern is it to me, or you for that matter?'*

'Look I don't want to sound like I'm pointing out the obvious here, but what if the information he wants contains secrets that could hurt your family?'

'It is of no consequence, I do not care what shame it may bring down upon my family name. I will be too busy sitting on a beach and sipping on cocktails to care.'

It didn't take an expert psychologist to see that there was something more to all this than what Seb was telling me. He was either a really bad liar, or the man had really spooked him. His unspoken words screamed out in opposition to those he had spoke. However, I knew there would be little point in pressing him further. If he didn't want to tell me what happened there was nothing I could do about it so, for the time being, I decided to let the subject drop. After all he was right, what concern was it of mine?

'Well, seeing as how you've obviously thought this all through,' I said sarcastically, knowing that my sarcasm would wash right over him, *'what's our next move from here? Are we going after the Grail or this guy's information first?'*

'Well, luckily,' he replied, sounding quite happy with himself as he pushed himself up from his chair and collected his bag from me, *'We find ourselves in the fortunate situation of being able to do both at the same time.'*

'What do you mean?' I asked slightly confused.

'Well, the information we need will be found at my family home. My family home is located in the town of Wewelsburg, and it is in the town of Wewelsburg that we will find our Grail Castle. So you see Tom, luck seems to be finally on our side.'

262

On leaving the cafe we jumped a taxi again and I soon found myself arriving back at Berlin Central Station; only this time it was to catch a train not to leave one.

Trusting Seb to sort out the tickets, I went in search of some snacks having realised that, in all the excitement, I'd still forgotten to get something to eat back at the cafe. As it turned out though, this was actually quite a fortunate thing as, along with a bag full of pre-packed sandwiches, cheese and onion crisps and cans of Diet Coke, my need to forage for food saw me unearth an English newspaper of all things.

Overjoyed at seeing words I could actually understand, I wasted no time in turning to the sport section at the back to check the week's football results. As a lifelong supporter of, what I still believe to be, my home team, I longed to know how Liverpool were getting on.

Sadly, the team had recently suffered a run of poor performances, and worse results, that had left them floating down in the middle of the league table. It was a run that I was frustrated to see had yet to be broken. But, through thick and thin a true fan supports his team and, as the number 8 shirt stashed at the bottom of my bag suggested, I am as true as they come.

I'm never quite sure why I always packed that old shirt, but did so wherever I went. It did come in handy for wearing to the gym on holiday or having a kick about with my mates. Quite why I thought it might come in useful on this trip though I have no idea.

****

It's funny how, sat here alone in the dark, I find myself wishing that I'd made more of an effort to see them play when I had the chance. To hear the sound of 40,000 voices singing in unison once more. You'll never walk alone, that is what they would sing. A song whose words, now more than ever, have come to hold a poignancy that strikes at my heart.

I can remember how the words would ring in my ears as I sat in the stands at Anfield and it fills me with a strange sense of pride. In a world of ever increasing differences and fewer tolerances, it's a wonderful feeling to be surrounded by thousands of people who, even just for 90 minutes, have a common interest, passion and pride. It's hard for many to understand, but that is the true beauty in the beautiful game.

Such memories seem to dwindle into dark nothingness now though. I try to hear the words again, but all that's left is the deafening sound of silence. What hope can I hold in my heart anymore?

I'm finding it harder and harder to keep my emotions in check of late. The simple act of remembering being at a football match is seemingly enough to send me into a tearful depression. If anything, it was thinking about my football shirt that hit me hardest. See, it wasn't until I wrote about it that I recalled I no longer have it.

It's not so much the shirt itself, but rather the reason I no longer have and the realisation that I now have nothing left to remind me of the life I had before all this. I guess the weight of all that has finally knocked the wind out of me. My emotions are fragile and I feel my sanity is too. I've been seeing things of late. Seeing things that can't exist and hearing sounds that can't be real; whispers in the dark, movement in the shadows. Perhaps here in my solitude it is just becoming harder to tell sleep from awake. Perhaps these things are simply the remnants of vivid dreams maybe, I don't know. For now I can rationalise it all away as just my mind playing tricks on me. But should a time come when I can no longer tell what's real and what's not, my story will fail. I will fail, and all of this will have been in vain.

Loneliness is beginning to weaken my mind, I can feel it. I don't want to be alone anymore. I mark this as my 26th day without any human contact, barely enough food or water and only this single dusty light bulb to keep me out of the dark. I don't know how long it takes the average person to snap in solitary confinement. Perhaps 26 days is hardly anything to some. Perhaps I'm not as strong as most other people. I just don't want to be alone anymore. I don't want to end up like Mr Thatcher.

A part of me thinks that it's a good idea to write down these feelings as it may help to keep me sane, and in a way it is working. Through doing so I can see that I must now try to steer clear of memories that lead me to thoughts of home and the things I will never have again.

These irrelevant breaks are a hindrance to both the flow of my telling and the strength of my mind. I have to keep it active, have to try harder to remember everything that has happened.

It's the only way to ward off what I now fear to inevitably be my fate. Time is of the essence. I must continue.

****

Sat on the train to Wewelsburg, facing Seb across a table, a niggling question had finally come to the surface.

'Why were You *researching Himmler's life?'* I asked him.

'What?' he asked in an uncertain tone as the lines on his forehead fell into deep furrows, suggesting I'd just pulled him away from an important thought.

'I understand why Archer was at the library researching Himmler's life, but why were you?'

'Have I not already explained this to you?' this he said more as a statement of irritation than a question, *'I wanted to learn about the dark history that stained the castle I had loved as a child.'*

'Yes, I know that part,' I said, my own tone turning now to one of exasperation, *'but* why *did you want to know?'*

It's hard to tell for sure, on a face that rarely showed any emotion other than contempt, but I'd swear that I actually saw a small glimmer of surprised approval in response to this question. Sadly however, his words did not quite reflect this.

'I suppose I should commend you for not being as stupid as I thought, but then it has taken you almost the whole day to ask me that question. Slow instead of stupid. I am not really sure it is much of an improvement,' this biting remark came served with side order of scornful derision that I was not about to stomach.

'I tell you what,' I said in a low threatening tone as I leaned in towards him, *'you keep insulting me like that and we'll get to test just how slow I am when I attempt to lodge my size 11 foot up your sausage loving arse.'*

I don't think he quite got the inference I made, but the insult seemed to work all the same.

'Now,' I continued, calming the temper that had risen in my words and leaning back in my seat, *'how about you try answering my simple question like a civil human being for once?'*

'Well,' he began, trying unsuccessfully to show disinterest to the threat of violence as he shifted uneasily in his seat, *'if you must know, it has been my belief for some time now that there was more to the history of the Nazi's than what the history books tell us; something about Hitler that just did not quite add up.'*

265

Drifting off into another conspiracy theory, he seemed to relax again and took on the animated gestures he repeatedly appeared to adopt when talking about things he felt passionately about.

'How could one man convince so many to commit such acts of evil as what was brought about during his rule?' he asked as his eyes narrowed beneath a frown of incomprehension, *'Why did so many follow him blindly? These questions agitated my mind, with no satisfactory answers given in the accepted records of that time, until a point came when I just had to investigate further for myself. Through my early research I discovered that, in his youth, Hitler had not been the evil man depicted in history. In fact he was a poor man who suffered many hardships which turned him into a man of strong views and opinions; a condition that can be seen in young men all around the world,'* he offered in a higher tone that seemed almost to direct the statement at me personally. *'When frustration and anger mix with testosterone fuelled desires of rebellion, what you get is that which is often referred to as the "hot headedness of youth". A natural part of male growth and maturity, not an indication of an evil man,'* I suppose he did have a valid point there, one that found echoes of my own past. *'After serving, and being wounded, in the First World War, Hitler became disillusioned with the countries leaders and believed he had the ability to become a stronger ruler and lead Germany out of its post-war crisis. It was with this goal in mind that he joined, what would become, the Nazi Party in 1919 and quickly rose up to become its leader by 1921. At this point, whilst he was a confirmed anti-Semite, he was still not what you could call evil.'*

'Hang on!' I stopped him, not quite sure I believed what I was hearing, *'Are you seriously trying to suggest that one of the most hated men in human history was actually a good man? You just admitted that he was openly racist, and that he hated the Jews, yet now you're trying to say that he wasn't evil?'*

He didn't react immediately, looking rather like he was pondering just how to answer me.

'Can being a racist really condemn you as an evil man?' he asked in a more hushed voice, leaning closer to me having noticed the attention our discussion was drawing from other passengers, *'Can you honestly tell me that you have never had a racist thought; that not once have you ever in your life judged another by a racial stereotype?'* his left eyebrow lifted in unison

with his tone of voice and managed to somehow turn the moral table on me.

I found myself slightly floundered by this and stumbled, unable to give him an immediate answer. I couldn't deny that I probably wasn't the most politically correct person in the world. To my shame I had been known, on more than one occasion, to have a bit of a rant about certain ethnic groups taking jobs and money away from us, or certain faiths being a bad joke and the cause of the world's problems. But it was never more than harmless ranting. It didn't really make me a racist did it?

His question left me looking into a mirror of hypocrisy, and I disliked the reflection I saw. If being racist can indeed condemn you, where is the line of evil drawn?

'The only difference between a racist and a political dictator is power,' Seb continued, almost as if to answer the question in my head. *'Power and people who will listen. Very few of us would have the ability to rise above the corrupting effect that total power can bring.'*

We sat quietly for a brief moment after this. I think Seb was watching me and enjoying the sight of his arguments gaining ground. However, it was not in consideration of his beliefs that I sat in silence, but rather in contemplation of a question I found most disturbing...what would power do to me?

'That being said,' he began again, suddenly breaking the silence, *'there is a difference between a political dictator and a truly evil man. Racist or not, at the time of becoming leader of the Nazi Party, Hitler was still just a man, no more evil than you or I.'*

'What changed him then?' I asked distractedly, having lost some of the wind from my sails.

'Prison,' he replied flatly, *'In 1923, Hitler was imprisoned for one year after a failed political coup. Following this he quickly gained support by promoting German nationalism, anti-Semitism, anti-capitalism and anti-communism with charismatic oratory and astonishing personal magnetism. It seemed that suddenly he could transform crowds into hysterical worshippers and mesmerise even the strongest of men into a frenzy of emotion. It is as if his natural ability as a leader was somehow dramatically enhanced to the point of almost being able to brain wash people. Where did this change come from?'*

I sensed that this was a rhetorical question, and was relieved to see that he didn't expect me to answer in any way. However, he also looked to be at pains with it himself, suggesting that it was one question which even he couldn't yet answer.

'On the whole this question still baffles me,' he continued, validating my assessment, *'however, as I delved deeper into the history of the Third Reich, something began to stand out. Behind every decision and action that Hitler made, there seemed to be a marionette like string leading back to one of two men; Martin Bormann, Hitler's private secretary and party chancellor, and Heinrich Himmler, head of the infamous SS.'*

He leaned back away from the table and folded his arms before continuing.

'Himmler was Reichsfuhrer of the SS, Chief of the German Police, Minister of the Interior and one of the leading members of the Nazi Party. He oversaw all internal and external police and security forces, including the Gestapo, and rose to become the second most powerful man in Nazi Germany. If there was evil in the Third Reich, then this man would have been its origin,' he leaned back in close and pointing a finger at me as if to emphasis this last statement. *'Even from as young as ten years old he showed signs of having a twisted mind. He attended a school where his father was principle and was used by him to spy on and punish his fellow pupils; a duty that, by his own admittance, he took great pleasure in. Obsessed with war and the idea of becoming an officer, he was given, through his parent's connections, to training with a Bavarian regiment upon leaving secondary school in 1918. It was a very short lived position though as it was only later that year that the First World War ended with Germany's defeat.'*

'1-0 to us,' I thought, quite childishly, to myself.

'He kept meticulous diaries of his life from a young age,' he continued with an almost pained admiration in his voice, *'and, from reading many of them myself, I learned of his membership to a German occultist group calling themselves the Thule Society. A group most notable for being the organisation which sponsored the political party that Hitler later turned into the Nazi Party. Their primary focus was to propagate their belief of a coming "German Messiah", someone who would redeem Germany after its defeat in the First World War, along with the idea that the German people could claim ancestry to the ancient Aryan race.'*

'Who were the Aryan's?' I asked, genuinely interested by a side of history I had never heard before.

In response he just let out an irritable groan, in time with a rolling of his eyes, before saying;

'How stupid of me to assume that you would know anything about German history! Well, putting it as simply as I can, the Aryans were a race of people thought to be descendants of the ancient Atlantians. I know Archer wrote of them in his journal so, if you want to know more than this, I suggest you look in there.'

Against all odds, I actually found myself missing Paddy in that moment. As much as I moaned about the old grump's history lessons, at least he had always taken the time to explain things to me. The jury's still out though on whether or not he was any less irritable though, but at least he wasn't as obnoxious and condescending.

'So now, where was I?' Seb asked, as if only to accentuate his annoyance at being interrupted, *'Ah yes, the German Messiah and the Aryan race ancestry. The latter of these two Thule Society objectives stemmed from a theory popularised in the late 19th Century, when eastern mysticism and occult religions gained great interest. During this time the teachings and beliefs of the Russian mystic and spiritualist, Madame Blavatsky, really came to light. She believed that Europeans were descended from a race of "angel-like" creatures known as Aryans and claimed that they had used mysterious psychic forces to build the pyramids, Atlantis and a network of cities beneath Antarctica. She also believed that the descendants of this race were to be found in the Himalayas and that their sign was the swastika.'*

'The Swastika?!' I said with aghast bluntness, *'You're telling me that the builders of the Pyramids, and Atlantis, were actually Nazis?'*

'It truly seems your ignorance knows no bounds,' he sighed half to himself whilst slowly shaking his head and rubbing that favourite spot between his eyebrows. *'No! The swastika was originally the ancient Hindu symbol of good luck. It comes from the Sanskrit word "svastika", meaning a lucky or auspicious object, and often is presented as a mark made on persons and items denoting good luck. It was only during the late 19th Century that it came to be seen as an important religious symbol of the Aryan race; through archaeological findings associated with the ancient migrations of Proto-Indo-Europeans. As this belief gathered ground through on into the early years of the 20th Century, it was inevitable that the Nazi party would adopt the symbol due to their beliefs in an "Aryan Master Race".*

269

Many variations of the symbol have existed the world over and all throughout history, yet now it is seen merely as a symbol of Nazism, fascism, racism and the horrors of the Holocaust. Truly it has become unfairly stigmatised and made taboo in the western world because of this, so much so that it has even been outlawed here in Germany.'

His voice fell silent and his gaze drifted away into space as a look of aggrieved sadness washed over him.

'I actually didn't know any of that,' I admitted genuinely, *'but, as fascinating as it is, what does any of it have to do with Himmler?'*

'Sorry?' he said as if his mind had drifted away in thought, *'Oh yes, well I was just getting to that before your interruption actually. See, the beliefs put forward by Blavatsky were reinforced by Edward Bulwer-Lytton in his science-fiction novel "The Coming Race". In it he told of a strange people called the Vril-Ya, living at the centre of the Earth, who wielded a fantastic power which they used to propel flying saucers. Though popularised through his adventure story, all of these ideas would have remained the fantasy of mystics and cultists had it not been for the ending of World War 1. Through the chaos and violent anarchy that was post war Germany, came the extremist politicians and cultist leaders battling for power. Thus came also the rise of the Thule Society.'*

He paused to take a swig of water. I don't doubt he needed it to re-hydrate his mouth after all the talking he did. Besides, I realised then that neither of us had really had anything to eat or drink since polishing off the half bottle of brandy between us. It was time to break out the sandwiches.

'Now,' he continued with a half chewed mouthful of food, *'I do not know whether Hitler actually attended any meeting of the Thule Society, or if he just became unknowingly connected to it through his rise, and their interests, in the Nazi Party; there are many conflicting accounts on the matter,'* he swallowed and thankfully didn't reload before starting his next sentence, clearing his throat with a short cough. *'What I do know however, is that members of the society were quick to spot the fiery young man's potential and exploit his incredible personal magnetism. It is well known that Hitler was fascinated by the occult and was obsessed with finding ways of using astrology, numerology, psychic medium-ship, hypnosis and water divining to further his pursuit of power. Therefore, I feel his association with the Thule Society is not that hard to believe.'*

270

I wasn't sure I could agree with him on that. It seemed to me as if he were basing his theory on an assumption for which he had no real proof. This to me did not bode well.

'*According to my research,*' he continued, '*it was through this association that Hitler met the men who would help him take power and wage the Second World War; Heinrich Himmler, Rudolf Hess, Martin Bormann, Dietrich Eckart, Alfred Rosenberg, and Hermann Goering. All of them members of the occult society and all of them (bar one) came to occupy key positions within Hitler's Third Reich. Goering was Commander of the Luftwaffe, Rosenberg became Minister of the Third Reich, Bormann, Chief of the Nazi Party Chancellery, Hess became Deputy Fuhrer and Himmler the head of the SS and Gestapo. Only Dietrich Eckart failed to join them having died of a heart attack shortly after the parties failed coup in 1923. Hitler actually dedicated the second volume of his book, Mein Kampf, to his fallen friend,*' he added quiet offhandedly, as though it was simply a matter of interest.

I really did get the feeling that he must have just liked the sound of his own voice sometimes, as some of the things he told me were trivial at best. Then again, I suppose one should wonder why, if trivial, I have still seen fit to write it down? Perhaps I just like the look of my own hand writing?

'*Of all these men, Himmler seemed to be the most ambitious and power-mad,*' he resumed after another mouthful of food. '*It was his extreme anti-Semitism, and eagerness to commit genocide in the name of purifying the Aryan race, that brought about the Holocaust. His theology has been defined as Ariosophy; his own religious dogma for the racial superiority of the Aryan race. In 1923, Himmler took part in Hitler's Beer Hall Putsch political coup, helping to plant the seeds of their later friendship through which Hitler was exposed to the Ariosophic world view. The anti-Judaic, Gnostic and root race teachings of Theosophy came to have a, still unacknowledged, influence over Hitler's impressionable mind.*'

'*Impressionable?*' I scoffed, '*You're making the bastard sound like some kind of victim here?*'

'*That is because I believe he was just that,*' he scowled, pounding the table with the tip of his index finger, '*a victim of manipulation, and if you will let me continue I will explain exactly why.*'

'*I can't wait to hear this,*' I thought to myself.

271

'After joining the SS in 1925, Himmler rose to become its leader by 1929. At that time the SS had only around 280 members and was little more than an elite battalion of the much larger Sturmabteilung. By 1933 however, Himmler had successfully swelled the organisations numbers to around 52,000; enforcing strict membership requirements ensuring that all members were of the Aryan race ideal. The leader of the Sturmabteilung, Ernst Röhm, was then a threat to Himmler and his SS. This caused Himmler to use the influence he had over Hitler and persuade him that Röhm was intent on undertaking a coup against him. Trusting the words of his close friend, Hitler ordered Röhm to be executed, along with others deemed to be his personal enemies, in what came to be known as the Night of the Long Knives. The very next day, the SS became an independent organisation answering only to Hitler. From here they went on to organise and administer the regime of concentration camps, with Himmler opening the first one at Dachau on 22 March 1933. He was the main architect and overseer of the whole Holocaust, using mysticism and his fanatical belief in the Nazi ideology to justify the horrific mass murder of millions.'

He let this hang in the air for a moment having leaned in close and fixed me with an intense stare. Eventually he reclined back again and continued with a meaningful wave of his hand.

'It was Himmler, not Hitler, who inspected the camps, the result of which saw the Nazis searching for new and more expedient ways to kill, culminating in the arrival of the gas chambers. He saw them as a way to terrorise the people into accepting Nazi rule.'

The mere mention of gas chambers sent a chill down my spine as harrowing memories of watching Schindler's List in my youth drifted through my mind.

'It was also Himmler who wanted to breed the master race of Nordic Aryans. He believed he could engineer this through the eugenic selective breeding of the German populace, and be successful within several decades of the end of the war. HIS idea, not Hitler's,' Seb stressed, before taking another a sip of water. *'You see, central to the Nazi ideology was the establishment of a thousand year Reich through the creation of a new religion based on Aryan mythology. With this in mind, Himmler set up an occult research bureau, known as the Ahnenerbe, and instructed it to prove German racial superiority by linking them to the ancient Aryans. He also hoped to uncover*

272

any and all lost mythical artefacts that could aid in their cause. Artefacts such as the Holy Grail.'

As exciting a prospect as learning about the Holy Grail was, I was intrigued to know what other artefacts they had sought. Before I could ask the question though, I quickly remembered whom it was I was talking to and decided it wouldn't have been worth the grief of interrupting him.

'All the time he was there pulling the strings,' Seb continued, *'it was even Himmler who masterminded the false flag project in 1939; to create the appearance of Polish aggression against Germany used to justify the invasion of Poland,'* his tone kept growing in pitch as if he was pleading with me to accept what he was saying. *'It is even recorded how he once wrote that, if Germany did not soon go to war, he would go to another country to seek battle, and that is just what he did. So you see, while it can be in no doubt the truth of the horrors committed under Hitler's rule, I believe the man himself was little more than a pawn. A figure head of the Nazi party controlled from behind the scenes by Himmler and the Thule Society. For all his charisma and prowess, Hitler was a gullible man easily lead by those that would tell him what he wanted to hear; that he was the Messiah destined to lead Germany to glory.'*

There was a moment of silence as Seb let his words settle and I tried to make sense of it all. The problem was, it didn't make sense to me.

'I'm sorry but, figure head or not, Hitler still allowed the atrocities of the Holocaust to be committed in his name. In my book that makes him as evil as those he led,' I told him, feeling somehow sullied by having even been a part of this conversation.

'Have you ever heard of the Milgram experiment?' he countered with apparent randomness.

'No! Why?' I then asked, ever so slightly blindsided by the sudden change of subject.

'It was a social experiment conducted by a psychologist at Yale University in the 1960's to study human obedience towards authority figures. It measured the willingness of participants to administer ever increasing levels of electric shock to a subject that they could hear but not see. They were told it was to discover if shock therapy could stimulate faster learning, when in fact they themselves were the subjects; flicking switches that triggered pre-recorded actors responses to the varying shock levels.'

This did actually ring a bell once he began to explain it. I'm sure Daren Brown had done something similar on one of his T.V. shows.

'Each was given a low level shock to show them what they would be administering should their "subject" give the wrong answer to any of the questions they would ask. Its goal was to see just how far people could be pushed by an authoritative figure to perform acts that conflicted with their own conscience, simply by being commanded to do so and reassured that they would not be held responsible. The shocks administered would increase in 15 volt increments up to an extremely lethal dose of 450 volts. Despite many of the participants expressing their discomfort at doing so, the results of the test showed that 65% of them continued through till the end of the experiment; knowingly administering a shock that would have killed their subject. This experiment has been repeated many times since then and each time it produces consistent results. If you are kept from seeing the effects of your actions, your mind can tell you it is not real or it was not your fault. Sixty five percent of all people tested were susceptible to this kind of impressionism. Does that then make them evil? Weak minded and easily led perhaps, but not evil by any definition, would you not agree?'

'Well, I...I guess not, no,' I stumbled in answer, not really sure what I thought about it to be honest.

'Of course not,' said Seb jumping on my agreement, disregarding any lack of conviction I might have showed, *'and so is it then so hard to believe that Hitler was such a person, someone easily led?'*

'Well no, I suppose it isn't,' I replied, still unsure of how I should feel about the subject, yet sensing I had been expertly bamboozled into agreeing it was possible, *'but just because he could have been, doesn't mean he was. I mean just look at all of the atrocities associated to him.'*

'Argh, is that not what I have just been explaining to you?' Seb replied with a frustrated groan as he threw his hands up and then dragged them back over his face. *'It was* Himmler *that oversaw the entire concentration camp system,* Himmler *that controlled the SS and Gestapo. All the evil acts attributed by most to having been Hitler's doing, were in fact committed, or at least organised, by Heinrich Himmler. Hitler was just a puppet to be dangled in the public eye as the face of it all. Yes his inactions still condemn him as a war criminal, that I do not dispute, but they too are his biggest crime; inaction and a blind*

274

trust in the men around him. He was a clever man that let himself be used by those who would fuel his self-important messiah complex; a short sightedness that many great men in history have also suffered from.'

Though I still wasn't convinced by his wild theory, I had to admit that I was beginning to have doubts as to the reasons why. Were his arguments implausible, or did I simply condemn them as such because society had conditioned me to believe that any challenge to the approved version of history could not possibly be true?

'Okay, let's just say for the moment that you are right about all this, let's say that Himmler was the big bad guy behind it all, why then hasn't anyone one else seen this truth? Why has history laid most of the blame on Hitler?' I asked, desperately trying to throw him a bone and cast off any thought of narrow-mindedness on my part.

'Why when your football team loses does your country blame the manager?' he countered.

'Wwwhhat the hhhell has that got to do with Anything?' I replied in long drawn out words of bewilderment.

'Everything Tom. It is about the mindset of the masses,' he said with a greasy look of superiority. *'People always need someone to blame when things go wrong, and it is easier to blame one person than a whole group. The manager gets the blame because he is in charge, yet it is the players on the field who win or lose the game. The same constitutes for governments and politics. Fault can be found in entire political parties, yet only the leader is ever remembered in history as they are the figure head. Just look at your Margret Thatcher,'* I guess he did have a point there. *'Himmler was seen for the evil bastard he was but, as memories fade, the masses only recall the leader of the Nazi regime and so cast all blame on him.'*

It was really beginning to wind me up the way he tried, when he could be bothered, to explain things to me. He spoke as if he believed he was turning universal wisdoms into a language that a layman like me could understand.

It is obvious to me know that he'd observed me reading the sports section of the newspaper intently and thus decided football would be a good analogy to "get through to me", but that doesn't help me think of him as being any less arrogant.

'Seriously Seb,' I responded in a dry and peevish tone, *'you could have just said that Hitler was a figurehead and I would have understood. That's all you had to say, figurehead.'*

'Well you did not seem to grasp the concept when I first talked of it, so I thought you must need it explained in simpler words,' god I wanted to hit him, *'At least now you understand though. The fact that Himmler managed to indoctrinate the SS with an apocalyptic idealism, leaving them without guilt or responsibility and able to rationalise mass murder as being a form of martyrdom, shows the twisted nature of the man who was the true evil behind the swastika.'*

'I said I understood what you were saying, not that I agreed with it. I still cannot see why, if you're so convinced it is true, that no one else I've ever heard of has put any faith in such a theory?'

'The facts are there for all to find, but you have to search behind the cloak of blame cast around Hitler by lazy historians. Your belief that there was evil in the Reich is sound, but it has just been misplaced.'

'What difference does it make though?' I asked with growing frustration.

'The difference Tom is that I believe Himmler had a plan in which Hitler was just a pawn. I believe the evil that drove him was beyond that of what Hitler could have conceived,' his voice dropped down to a conspirators whisper as he eyed the rest of the carriage suspiciously, *'An evil I now believe was fuelled by his possession of a Chintamani Stone piece!'*

'What do you mean "fuelled by"?' I asked, quite surprised by the statement yet managing to mirror his cautious tone.

'Well, from what I have learned of the Stones, I believe they have the power to enhance a person's natural strengths.'

'Enhance their natural strengths?' I repeated back at him in a slow patronising tone, feeling that this was one stretch too far for me to find believable.

'Yes,' he replied, as though he couldn't understand the reason for said tone. *'For example, if you are a naturally strong person, being in possession of one such stone can make you stronger, or if you have a good memory, it can make it better. So, if say you had a naturally gifted ability to out think those around you, having a Chintamani Stone could make you become an incredible tactician,'* I couldn't believe what I was hearing. It felt like I'd just fallen into a Marvel superhero comic or something. *'Throughout all my research I have found the stories of the Stones to be linked to history's greatest figures. Those that, for good or evil, stood above the rest of their fellow men to become something more. Take your St. Oswald for example, had*

276

you not known of his possession of the Chintamani Stone, how would you have explained his remarkable healing powers?' Okay, so he did have me on that one, though I still wasn't sure I really believed any of that either, *'I believe that it was the presence of one such stone in Nazi Germany that brought out the evil traits that defined its leaders; none more so strongly than in the Reichfurhur of the SS.'*

'Alright then,' I began to reply, morbidly curious as to where all this was going, *'so you're saying that Himmler found the "Holy Grail" and that its presence within their ranks caused the Nazi's to commit the atrocities of the war, Yes?'*

'More or less, how else could men be so evil?'

The naivety of this response actually caught me off guard and left me wondering...could he really believe that there had to be a reason for people to be evil?

'Anyway,' he continued, *'that is why I was researching Himmler and that is why I have come to aid Archer in his quest. His knowledge has given me many answers already and now I am certain that the final pieces of the puzzle lie in wait for us at Wewelsburg Castle.'*

'Don't get me wrong Seb, I think it's an intriguing theory' I said, trying to remain politically neutral, *'but then, as you have so eloquently proposed, I am no scholar. The facts and information you have presented would be easy for me to believe as I don't know enough about the history of that time to argue otherwise. The only problem I do have is, if it is how you say and the Nazi's did find the Holy Grail...why did they lose the war?'*

Seb started as if he had an answer to this, but then paused as a brief look of uncertainty crosses his face, *'Well, that is what we need to find out!'*

This brought an end to our conversation, as Seb leaned back into his seat and stated that he was going to rest his eyes a while before our arrival at the first two change over's we had to make.

The day had grown old without me really noticing. Shadows from the east had long ago retreated and left the land to those now encroaching in from the west.

Watching the world pass by in a blur out of the window I too felt tired. The last few hours had been mentally exhausting after all, but too many questions had been raised in my mind to allow any kind of rest. Questions about Himmler, about the Ahnenerbe and the Thule Society, about who the Aryan's actually were, and why after all of Seb's explanations did I still not know who the bloody hell the Fisher King was?

That question, above all else, had bugged me ever since he brought it up back in the library and never answered it. Come to think of it, leaving questions unanswered seemed to be a recurring issue with Seb. He had said that he found it difficult, despite being a politician, to verbalise his ideas; perhaps this is what he meant? Perhaps this is why his theories had felt thin and sometimes inconsistent. Or perhaps the sheer amount of information he produced had simply overwhelmed and confused me. Either way, there was something about him that made me feel very uneasy. First he'd admitted his Grandfather was in the SS and then he tried to convince me that Hitler wasn't the monster the history books condemned him as, saying instead that he was somehow brainwashed by the power of the Holy Grail and exploited by Himmler. No matter how many ways he tried to persuade me of this "truth", something inside just made it feel all wrong.

Arriving in Germany I had longed for some company to share the weight of the task I was faced with. As that train sped me on towards a place where the evil heart of Nazi occultism had apparently once beat, its gentle rocking threatening to eventually swallow me into a dark sleep alongside a man I feared untrustworthy, I found myself longing instead for the return of loneliness.

Day 7 - Wewelsburg, Germany
What Kind of Castle doesn't have
Tapestries?

Our journey made the first of its two changes at the Hannover Central train station where we switched from the main intercity lines on to the S-Bahn. This, Seb explained to me, was the suburban railway that linked the outlying towns and villages to the city centre. All I knew was that it meant we went from the modern comfort of the Intercity express to what I can only describe as something you would expect to see in a Lego train set. It was bright red with a chunky white outline round the bottom half of each carriage and almost boringly square in shape.

Despite this change in comfort however, I was somewhat relieved when it came. Having spent the last hour and a half on the previous train listening to Seb, becoming ever more worried about his opinions, the forced break of having to switch trains was a welcome reprieve.

The connection we picked up was heading to a place called Paderborn, from where our final change was to take us by bus on to the village of Wewelsburg.

As I settled into my seat as best I could, I finally took the time to have a more thorough read through the second piece of Archer's journal. An excitement had burned within me to see what Archer had done next after Hildesheim ever since Seb had given it to me. Yes I already had a basic idea from what Seb had told me, but I knew there would be more. I knew in Archers writing I would find the answers that Seb had not explained. I also hoped that seeing me so preoccupied, would dissuade Seb from striking up any more disturbing discussions. Fortunately, the faint sound of snoring next to me indicated that my companion had almost instantly resumed the "resting of his eyes"; something I took to be a great blessing. Had I known what was to come later that night though, I probably would have been following his lead.

As I began to read, the first thing that really caught my attention was Archer's detailing of his meeting with Seb, which did at least confirm the truth of Seb's involvement; though I'm not exactly sure whether this made me feel better or worse. There was a sketch of him too but it had an unfortunate stain over it that obscured much of the face. Though I couldn't clearly make his features out in it, the silhouette was recognisable enough I felt.

Archer talked of how comfortable he'd felt leaving Seb to follow up on the Holy Grail piece, describing him as "a brilliantly competent young man with knowledge and wisdom beyond his years".

'Wasn't wise enough to avoid his gambling problem though was he?' I thought spitefully to myself, as I looked over at the sleeping idiot.

It was admittedly a very childish thought to have had but at that time, reading what Archer had written about him, I was once again feeling quite jealous. However, what the journal also confirmed was that Seb had been lying to me just as I'd suspected. Either that or he'd just given himself way too much credit as, despite what he had told me, Archer had in fact done a massive amount of research into the Himmler/Holy Grail link. The old man was not one to steal the glory of others, so the lack of credit given to Seb through much of the research reconfirmed my caution over allowing myself to trust him.

The depth of research in the journal was quite incredible to read. Through it I learned of the Parzival story Seb had mentioned, the links that connected it to the Chintamani Stone, details of who and what the Anhernbe and Thule Society were, and I even got to finally discover who the bloody Fisher King was.

What follows are the, highly edited, parts of his research that I believe crucial to the understanding of my tale. As much as I'd like to, I feel I no longer have the time or the patience to recount all of his writings word for word. Instead I shall just cut straight to the most interesting parts.

The Parzival Link

Parzival, a great medieval German romance by the poet Wolfram von Eschenbach. The story told within its pages is that of the titular character, the Arthurian hero Parzival, and his quest to find the Holy Grail. It is a marvellous literary work illustrating the journey of a young man who overcomes his youthful ignorance and selfishness to become a hero of empathy and great wisdom.

Though this paragraph gave a quick answer to the question that had been Parzival, what interested me the most was how similar the description of the stories hero seemed to Archer. An image of my mysterious friend was the first thing that came to mind as I remembered his story of being a hot-headed arrogant youth and the journey he took to becoming the enlightened and peaceful man that I'd met.

'Perhaps the similarities show a formula for growing a Grail Hero,' I thought to myself...a somewhat encouraging thought in light of my own life.

Where Parzival becomes more than just another Grail quest story however, is with the author's description of the object itself. In his story, Wolfram proclaims the Grail to be, not a cup but rather a 'Stone that fell from Heaven'. This is almost identical to the description given of the Chintamani Stone in the Tibetan teachings I have studied. For his claim, Wolfram cites the authority of a French poet, Kyot the Provencal who, he claimed, found a long forgotten Arabic manuscript written in Moorish somewhere around the municipality of Toledo in Central Spain. It was said to have been written by the Muslim astronomer Flegetanis, a descendant of King Solomon, who found the secrets of the grail written in the stars. However, many scholars have come to doubt that Kyot is anything more than a work of fiction created by Wolfram to silence his critics of the time.

Yet such a discrediting dismissal does not sit well with me upon reflective contemplation of the subject. Parzival is Wolfram von Eschenbach's adaptation of the earliest written account of the quest for the Holy Grail. This being Chretien's de Troyes unfinished fifth romance 'Perceval, the story of the Grail' which was written sometime between 1181 and 1191 during the height of the Crusades. In this telling, the Grail itself is never referred to as 'Holy', it is simply described as a golden grail used as a serving dish. Not the cup of Christ then? No, in fact it wasn't until the end of the 12th Century that the Holy Grail even became connected with Jesus and Christianity, in Robert de Boron's work 'Joseph d'Arimathie'. Boron identified the 'Rich Fisher' as the founder of a line of Grail keepers that eventually was to include Perceval. The Rich Fisher, so called because he is said to have caught a fish eaten at the Grail table, was a man called Bron who Robert de Boron claims was the brother-in-law of Joseph of Arimathea; he who used the Grail cup to catch the blood of the Christ. As the story goes, Joseph founded a religious community that eventually arrived in Britain unto the Valleys of Avalon (an area many believe to be where the town of Glastonbury now stands). Here the Grail was entrusted to Bron until the rising of King Arthur and the coming of Perceval. Interestingly, in Chretien's story, the keepers of the Grail were two; the Wounded King, father, and the Fisher King, his son.

Is it not likely then that, just as Eschenbach, Boron was greatly influenced by Chretien's work? Wolfram greatly expanded the original story, reworking the nature of the Grail and the community that surrounds it. What if Boron was himself influenced into reworking the story also? What if his task was to link a mystical, and highly sought, treasure with the story of the Christ? Is it so inconceivable to believe that such a thing might be done? Indeed it would have created a golden carrot to be dangled in front of any reluctant would-be crusaders by whomever might have had the strong desire to send them off to the Holy Land. Could it then also be possible that Parzival, commonly dated to having been written in the first quarter of the 13th Century, was Eschenbach's attempt to retell the story the way it was? His attempt to tell the truth!

By linking his Grail to the Muslims and a descendant of King Solomon, Wolfram would not have won any favour with Rome; rather he would have instead landed himself with a powerful enemy. I have come to believe through my research that Kyot the Provincial was in fact real and did in fact find an ancient manuscript as Eschenbach claimed. I also now believe that for his troubles he was later erased from history to discredit any theories such as the one put forth in Parzival. After all, it wouldn't be the worst thing done in the name of protecting the Christian Faith!

This theory was right up my atheist street. If the grail did in fact exist before the cup of Christ, then it would prove that my thoughts about religion were true. That the dogmatic faiths use religion as a tool to control the masses through made up stories; or at least greatly exaggerated ones. There is no room in the modern world for such blind belief in my opinion and each new generation seems to be waking up to this simple fact more and more.

The next section in the journal that really caught my eye was about Archer's research into the rise of Himmler's own religion.

283

Theosophy was a movement founded by Helena Blavatsky and Henry Olcott at the end of the nineteenth century whose philosophy took inspiration from Indian culture. Blavatsky argued that humanity had descended from a series of 'Root Races', one of which she named the 'Aryan Race' whom she believed originated from Atlantis.

She used 'Root Race' as a technical term to describe human evolution over the large time periods in her cosmology. She claimed that there were modern day inferior peoples who are an offshoot of the Aryans that have become *'degenerate in spirituality and perfected in materiality.'* A key example of this she claimed where the Semitic peoples. Of course, such claims instantly cause one to form the opinion that she was a racist. Despite this however, Blavatsky's admirers claim that her thinking was not connected to fascist or racialist ideas, asserting that she believed in a Universal Brotherhood of humanity and wrote that *'all men have spiritually and physically the same origin'.* She also wrote that *'mankind is of one blood, but not of the same essence'.* Her explanation for this was thus;

'The intellectual difference between the Aryan and other civilized nations and such savages as the South Sea Islanders, is inexplicable on any other grounds. No amount of culture, nor generations of training amid civilization, could raise such human specimens as the Bushmen, the Veddhas of Ceylon, and some African tribes, to the same intellectual level as the Aryans, the Semites, and the Turanians'

Whilst she may not be seen today as having been 'politically correct', those who have studied her work would agree that, right or wrong, her ideas were based on research not racist beliefs. She was no Nazi, this is a certainty, but one has to agree it is not hard to distinguish the many similarities in their beliefs. This however is due to a certain Guido von List who took up some of Blavatsky's ideas and mixed her ideology with nationalistic and fascist ones. His system of thought became known as Ariosophy.

It was believed, in Ariosophy, that the Teutonics were superior to all other peoples because, according to Theosophy, the Teutonics (or Nordics) were the most recent sub-race of the Aryans to have evolved. It was such views that then fed into the development of the Nazi ideology. According to the adherents of Ariosophy, the Aryan was a 'master race' that built a civilization which dominated the world from Atlantis about ten thousand years ago. This alleged civilization declined when other parts of the world were colonized after the 8000 BC destruction of Atlantis; which they claim was the result of genetic dilution caused by the inferior races, such as the Semitics, mixing with the Aryans. Yet, traces of their civilization were left in Tibet (via Buddhism*), Central and South America and even Ancient Egypt. These theories affected the more esoteric strand of Nazism.

It was principally for this reason that Himmler was interested in Buddhism and his institute the Ahnenerbe sought to mix some traditions from Hinduism and Buddhism into their religion. He even sent expeditions to Tibet as part of his research into Aryan origins. Could this have been a cover to hide the fact that he was really searching for Shangri-La?

*Interestingly, Gautama Buddha's original name for Buddhism was *The Aryan Path*.

Archer went on to explain about the Ahnenerbe being a Nazi study society for Ancient History, whose goal was to research the anthropological and cultural history of the Aryan race. They were responsible for countless expeditions and experiments conducted with the intent of proving that Nordic peoples once ruled the world. The Nordic's were apparently a race of long skulled, very tall, fair skinned people with blonde or light brown hair and light coloured eyes that inhabited the countries around the North and Baltic Seas. They are believed by some to be a direct descendant of the Aryan's and hence were used as the physical template for the Nazi's Master Race.

He also explained how the Thule Society was an occultist group in Munich, named after a mythical northern country from Greek legend, and had drawn a sketch of their emblem; a German dagger overlaying a Nazi swastika with curved legs. The Society was most notable for sponsoring the Deutsche Arbeiterpartei; the party later transformed by Hitler into the Nazi Party. The occultists believed Hitler to be the prophesied "Redeemer of Germany" and were crucial to his meteoric rise. Archer wrote of how the societies meetings continued until 1923 when all mention of them seemed to disappear. Interestingly, in a diary discovered that recorded all their meetings, the attendance of many Nazi leaders were mentioned...but never Hitler?

A primary focus of the Society was a claim concerning the origins of the Aryan race. Thule was a land located by Greco-Roman geographers in the furthest north, thought possibly to be Iceland. The term "Ultima Thule", which Archer translated from the Latin to mean *'most distant Thule'*, was mentioned by the Roman poet Virgil in his works called the "Georgics".

The Society identified Ultima Thule, said by Nazi mystics to be the capital of ancient Hyperborea, as a lost ancient landmass in the extreme north, near Greenland or Iceland, and was the home of the Aryan race; a place that has been identified as a possible location for Plato's Atlantis! I have to admit that I couldn't quite fathom out whether he was suggesting these places were one and the same, or just two separate lost ancient landmasses. Perhaps Atlantis was the city located on the island of Ultima Thule in the region of Hyperborea? Or perhaps that is just wild speculation from someone who cannot get his head around how all this Ancient Greek and Roman stuff fits together? I'll leave you to decide for yourself which seems more feasible[xii].

As I read on, I found that Archer wrote of findings which suggested that, as he speculated, the Nazi expeditions sent to Tibet did actually have the primary goal of searching for Shangri-La. Apparently he'd come across some old transcript between Himmler and his head researcher. In it Himmler instructed that the expedition team should find ways to warm themselves towards the locals in order to learn more about their legends and gain their trust. Though no mention of Shangri-La was made, Archer believed strongly that the order obviously spoke of more than just research in to the origins of the Aryan race.

He also found stories of a secret Vril Society, linked to the larger Thule Society, which believed in the tales of an ancient advanced civilisation called the Vril-ya who lived in networks of subterranean caverns linked by great tunnels. A utopia under the surface of the world that harnessed a powerful energy source called Vril which granted them the power to heal all illness and change objects at will. It also granted then a terrible destructive force that could wipe out entire cities with ease. Even as I read this I couldn't help but draw conclusions with what I knew of the people of Shambhala, so it was easy to see why Archer found it such an important connection. He found this Vril energy to be described as a kind of electricity that can destroy like lighting yet has the ability to restore life, heal and cure. It could apparently also be used as a light source that burns steadier, softer and healthier than that of any flammable material. In illustrations he found, the energy was characterised by having an eerie green glow.

I began to wonder, if so many cultures all throughout human history have all had such similar beliefs, could there really exist an advanced race beneath the earth? Or were the tales just flights of fancy to bring magic into an otherwise dull existence? I truly hoped for the former in the same way that I had always held out hope for there actually being a Loch Ness Monster. There had to be something more to this world.

The final entry in the journal, before he talked of his journey onwards from Germany, was a very enlightening look into the man behind Himmler's decision to set up home in Wewelsburg.

Himmler's Rasputin

Karl Maria Wiligut was an Ariosophist and Nazi occultist. His influence in the third Reich gained him the nickname 'Himmler's Rasputin'. Born and raised in Vienna, he was conscripted into King Milan I of Serbia's army at the age of 17 in 1883.

In 1889 he joined the quasi-Masonic 'Schlaraffia Loge'. In 1906 he married a woman who bore him three children; two daughters and one son. The boy however, died in infancy which devastated Wiligut who had so desperately desired a male heir to whom he could pass on his 'Secret Knowledge'.

After almost forty years of military service he retired in 1919 and dedicated his time to studying the occult. A claim of being the bearer of a secret line of German Kingship and belief in a Judaic/Masonic/Christian world conspiracy theory saw him committed to a mental institute in 1924, at the bequest of his wife, and he remained there until 1927. In '32 he abandoned his family and emigrated to Germany where he is known to have corresponded with many admirers including Ernst Rudiger and members of the Order of the New Templar's. Shortly after being introduced to Himmler at a conference in 1933, he was inducted into the SS and given his own department for the study of Pre and Early history...... for research into the occult!

Eventually he rose to serve as one of Himmler's personal staff. It was Wiligut who allegedly called Himmler's attention to Castle Wewelsburg. Inspired by the old Westphalian legend of the 'Battle at the birch tree', Wiligut allegedly predicted to Himmler that Wewelsburg would be the bastion for a future world conflict. The Birch Tree saga tells about a future *last battle at the birch tree* in which a *huge army from the East is beaten decisively by the West*. A conflict between Asia and Europe perhaps? Very similar to the Tibetan prophesy of the rise of Shambhala!

Wiligut developed plans for the rebuilding of Wewelsburg Castle into a symbolic "centre of the world" and contributed significantly to its development. He officiated in the role of priest for the SS pseudo-religious practices. He is also credited with being the designer of the prestigious Totenkopfring (Deaths Head Ring) which was an honour award originally bestowed personally by Himmler only to senior SS officers.

He created his own runic alphabet and used it in the design of these rings which goes as follows:

The Totenkopfring (Deaths Head Ring)

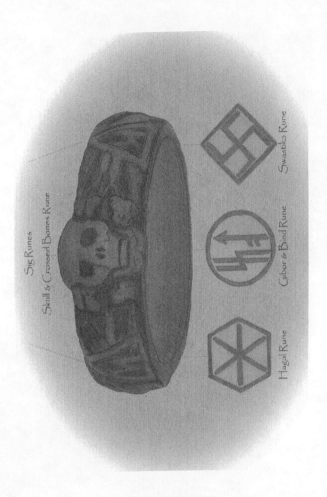

The Skull and Crossed Bones – presented on the top of the ring, it is the traditional symbol of the SS.

Two Sig Runes framed in triangles – these sit either side of the Skull and represent the lightning flash runes of the Schutztaffel.

The Hagal Rune framed in a hexagon – this comes next on the right side of the ring and represents the faith and camaraderie of the SS.

The Swastika standing on edge and framed by a quadrate – this symbolises the power of the Aryan Race.

And finally on the bottom of the ring sits the Heilszeichen – this symbolises salvation and was created purely for the purpose of the ring with no historical origin.

When a ring bearer was killed in battle his comrades were ordered to make every effort to retrieve the ring so as to prevent their enemies from taking them. Why??

He advised Himmler in the purchase of Wewelsburg Castle! He planned its rebuild! And he designed the Deaths Head Rings that couldn't be allowed to fall into enemy hands...I can't help feel that this is somehow important.

If there is a secret room in the castle kept aside for the finding of the Holy Grail, as Mr Reinhardt suspects, then this man would have undoubtedly been its architect. I also think that there may be some, as yet undiscovered, importance to his involvement with the Schlaraffia. When he left this quasi-Masonic lodge in 1909, he held the rank of Knight and the office of chancellor. Could his time within this order have been an influence upon his decision to suggest the use of Wewelsburg to Himmler? An aerial shot of the castle I recently happened upon revealed to me that its shape is more than just triangular; it is a veritable compass with the grand North Tower acting as its pivot point!

The compass is a prominent Masonic symbol so it would be easy to suggest some connection?

The axis of the North Tower was to be the centre of the new world according to Himmler. In alignment with this there are three important objects within:

∴ A sun wheel mosaic, now referred to as the Black Sun symbol, which resided upon the floor of the tower's Obergruppenfuhrersaal (the SS Generals' Hall).

∴ A stylised golden Swastika embedded into the ceiling directly below the Black Sun symbol in the Gruft or Crypt.

∴ Finally there is the planned location for an eternal flame that would burn forever in memory of the fallen, situated in a circular depression that sits at the heart of a bowl in the floor of the Crypt.

The Crypt resides in the basement of the tower and was meant to be a resting place for the ashes of SS officers. Indeed pictures of this room put me in mind of the Mycenaen tholos tombs of Bronze Age Greece; large burial chambers with high domed roofs hewn from the rock.

As mentioned, it was at the heart of this room where an eternal flame was intended. We can ascertain that preparations for such a device were at least partly realised, due to the presence of a gas pipe protruding from the side of the circular depression. What is not so clear however is whether or not it was ever completed and put in to use?

Circling this fire place, up against the wall of the room, are placed twelve pedestals that appear to be in line with the columns of the Generals' Hall above. While their meaning has never been confirmed, Mr Reinhardt has a theory about them being linked to Himmler's plans for turning the SS into a Knightly Order akin to that of the Templar's. At first I was not so sure of this, but then he showed me an account of one General Heydrich of the SS. It spoke of how Himmler imagined a rebirth of the Knights of the Round Table and of how he even appointed twelve Generals to be his followers.

When one of these men died, it was planned that their ashes would be interned within the Castle. Mr Reinhardt has speculated that perhaps the twelve pedestals were meant to eventually hold the urns of Himmler's twelve followers? Perhaps this would have then been where the eternal flame came to be of importance; a fire through which the later generations of the order could feel the souls of their forefathers.

Leaving the lower level of the tower and travelling up to the first floor takes you to the Generals' Hall; the meeting place of Himmler's most trusted. The Obergruppenfuhrersaal (literally translated to mean the 'Upper Group Leaders Hall) is a circular room on the first floor of the North Tower and consists of twelve columns, twelve niches and eight long windows all in surround of the sun wheel mosaic. The intended purpose of this room I feel requires no explanation. It is what lies embedded in the floor of the room that is of interest here. Though the origin of this sun wheel mosaic has been much debated, we do know that the term 'Black Sun' was coined by a member of the SS; in relation to this symbol at least. It has been suggested that this was due to the way the lighting within the Generals' Hall causes the symbol to appear black in colour, when in fact it is actually a dark green. However, it seems as though there is another more intriguing possibility regarding this matter; one that takes us back to Himmler's Rasputin.

Karl Wiligut claimed to have spiritual powers that allowed him direct access to the genetic memories of his ancestors form thousands of years ago. Sometime during the 1920's he wrote down 38 verses (out of over a thousand he purportedly knew) in his own runic alphabet. They apparently told the history of Santur, the invisible or burnt out Black Sun!

Emil Rudiger, a follower of Wiligut's teachings, speculated that this Sun was once the centre of the solar system, hundreds of millennia ago, and claimed that it had been the source of power for the Hyperborean's. Could this be the origin of the Wewelsburg mosaic?

Allegedly, the design was adapted from an old Aryan emblem by Wiligut for Himmler, and was meant to mimic the Round table of King Arthur. It was seen as a substitute swastika that represented a mystical source of energy capable of regenerating the Aryan race. Each spoke of the sun wheel is said to represent one Officer (Knight) of Himmler's secret order. The Wewelsburg symbol can be deconstructed into three swastikas, one rising, one at vertex, and one setting. It can also be seen as incorporating twelve reversed Sig runes and has been said to unite the three most important symbols of Nazi Ideology: the sun wheel, the swastika and the stylized victory rune. What is perhaps more interesting than the symbol itself however, is the piece that is missing. At the core of the mosaic lies a depression that was apparently meant to hold a circular plate of pure gold. Alas, what depictions may have been imprinted upon it, and even indeed its intended purpose, seems lost along with the item itself. An elaborate part of the decoration to symbolise Himmler's wealth and power perhaps, but the question that burns within my mind is.....why was it designed to be removed?

Twelve spokes of the Black Sun, twelve departments of the SS, twelve pillars in the Generals' Hall and twelve pedestals in the Crypt. As a whole, Castle Wewelsburg holds the ideal, the home and the planned resting place of Himmler's Knights of the round table; his Order of the Death's Head!

Though it seemed an aside from our main inquiry, Mr Reinhardt asked me a question regarding the subject of the Nazi symbols that I found quite intriguing. He asked if I had ever heard of the Thule Society symbol being placed over that of the Black Sun? To his disappointment I had not, but the idea of it has recently got me thinking...what if this was the symbol of Himmler's Order?

The Black Sun symbol was never directly linked to having symbolised the Order, nor was the Order ever fully acknowledged as having come to be. But we do know Himmler had planned it all out; perhaps this hybrid symbol of Sebastian's was their proposed emblem? Himmler had been a member of the Thule Society as well as the Nazi Party but had believed in his rise above them both, hence the plan to create his own Knightly Order. Perhaps the joining of the Thule Society emblem (which also contains a swastika) with that of the Wewelsburg Black Sun, was to represent the knowledge and power of Himmler's past combining with the plans for his future; a new emblem for his new world?

Alas, I never got to share this theory with Mr Reinhardt for it came to me after I'd left his company. I had asked him where he had seen this symbol but sadly he could not remember. I wonder now if it will hold any bearing upon his quest?

What became of them after Himmler's death? What became of the treasures they amassed? What knowledge of Shambhala did they glean from their time in Tibet? Did they actually manage to find the Holy Grail?

These are the questions I am left now to ponder for I no long have the time to research them. It is with much regret that I must relinquish my interest in the subject and entrust Mr Reinhardt to continue on in search of the Grail in my stead. I have been distracted from my own quest for too long and I can ill afford to lose any more time here.

Though I do not know what, if anything, young Sebastian may eventually find, I am certain that knowledge of the Grail's fate rests somehow in the secrets of Wewelsburg's North Tower.

It was a relief to now have answers to many of my earlier questions, but in many ways they had simply been replaced with all the new ones that Archer had raised. What his words gave freely however was an excitement and eagerness to explore the castle we were now speeding towards. Where Seb's thoughts and theories had left me concerned and wary, Archer's had captivated my imagination and piqued my curiosity to such a degree that, for the first time since all this began, I finally felt like I'd made the right decision in joining this quest.

If we could but find one clue to substantiate any of Archer's suspicions regarding this castle...well, my whole body tingled at the mere prospect.

As I read on to the last page before the calculated tear I found that, after leaving Seb to pursue the Germany links, Archer had abandoned his search for St. Oswald's relic and continued on to his original destination of St. Petersburg in

Russia; to a meeting with a historian who was an expert on Nicholas Roerich, just like Seb had told me. What did this man know, I had to wonder? What was so important about Roerich? What was the truth behind these stones...and where was this all going to end?

When eventually we arrived in at Paderborn, I was more than a little relived to be leaving the train part of our journey behind us. It had been in equal parts enlightening and deeply troubling, yet it was now excitement more than caution that went with me.

This final station was a stark contrast to the size and grandeur of the one we had left in Berlin. In fact, it was actually more akin to the station I had left back home in Penrith; having only a couple of tracks running through it and the same sort of open air promenade feel to it. Making such a comparison, then much as now, did briefly stir up feelings of being home sick. In light of my new found enthusiasm for our present situation, those feeling failed to find the doubt and fear they might otherwise have clung to.

Outside the station we stood at the designated bus stop and waited patiently for the next service to Wewelsburg. It was a painfully long wait, made all the worse as we watched the late evening sky above fill with ever darkening clouds and felt the gentle wind quickly become strong aggressive gusts; we weren't going to be in for a dry night.

I sat on the bus in quiet contemplation as the last light of the day slowly disappeared below the horizon. Pondering the revelations of the journal, my concentration was suddenly broken by a deep rumble of thunder that was quickly followed by the patter of heavy rain drops upon the thin metal roof of the bus that soon became a deafening down pour.

As lightening began to split the sky and the howling wind beat us from the side, Seb pointed out that ours was the next stop and it became painfully apparent that this was going to be a truly horrid night to be without shelter or a car.

'Now what?' I shouted to Seb over the roar of the now torrential rain, as we alighted from the bus and stood beneath the hazy light of a street lamp getting very wet very quickly.

'Now we go to the castle,' he replied, as if it was such an obvious answer.

'What?' I yelled back in disbelief, 'You mean right Now?'

'Yes now, unless you would rather stay out here in the rain?' he replied, hiking his jacket up over his head in a futile attempt to protect himself from rain that was almost falling horizontally.

'But how do you expect us to get in at this time of night?' I asked, feeling as though I was missing something, greatly appreciating my wide brimmed hat despite having to keep a hand firmly planted upon it against the wind, *'Are we just gonna walk up to the front door pretending to be Scottish Lords come to view their tapestries before knocking the butler unconscious so we can have a snoop around?'* I said in a tone dripping with sarcasm.

'What a stupid idea!' he said humourlessly, apparently having taken what I said seriously, *'There are no tapestries in Wewelsburg Castle that I am aware of, and I am quite sure that they do not have a butler.'*

You could have been forgiven for not realising he was German from his faint accent, but then you only had to observe his sense of humour, or rather lack of, to figure it out.

'Ookay then,' I said in a drawn out manner, finding it difficult to adapt to conversing with someone who didn't get sarcasm, *'how* Are *we going to get in?'*

'Simple!' he answered without even a fleck of emotion on his face, *'They are expecting us.'*

Day 7 - Wewelsburg, Germany
In the Presence of Evil

What I hadn't known at the time was that this castle wasn't a lived in one, at least not in the sense of someone calling it their home. Instead it had been split into part museum and part youth hostel sometime after the Second World War. Hence what Seb had meant when he said *"They are expecting us"*, was that earlier that day he'd phoned up and booked us a room in the hostel for the night.

His plan was for us rest up whilst waiting for any other guests to fall asleep. Almost like a Trojan horse, we would then be inside the walls with a golden opportunity to go sneaking about unhindered.

I had to give it to him, it was a pretty good idea. In my mind I'd been imagining us having to hide out somewhere during a visit through the day (knowing that, lived in or not, most castles are at least partly open to tourists) or perhaps even have a repeat of what happened back at Bamburgh whereby Seb would have known someone inside who could have secretly let us in after hours. But actually staying in the castle legally, with the promise of a cosy bed for a few hours, was a much more appealing concept.

My enthusiasm for this plan quickly wore off though when I realised it included having to first walk to the castle in the dark and the miserable bloody rain. My only consolation being that, with head down and turned into the wind, my hat did at least keep the rain from running down my face and neck. Unfortunately, it just wasn't quite big enough to save the rest of me and within a matter of minutes I found myself soaked wet through.

We didn't speak much along the way. Partly because I was miffed about having to be so wet, but mostly because the wind was so strong that any attempt to lift your head and say something simply became a good way to get a mouth full of rain water.

Isolated in both sound and sight by this ever worsening storm, I drudgingly followed Seb's lead closely in silent misery. I took solace only in the fact that he at least seemed to know where he was going, for I had not a clue. No road signs or markings did I see to suggest that we were even going the right way, just an endless curtain of rain wrapped in a shroud of darkness. That was a problem soon to be remedied however.

Upon nearing our destination, a brilliant flash of lightening split the sky in two and briefly cast an eerie illumination over a tree covered hill that lay before us. In that moment, like something out of the opening scene of a classic horror movie, I saw the looming towers of Wewelsburg Castle rising up above the roof of the forest. Instantly I felt the hair on the back of my neck stand on end and a sense of foreboding that ate away at my enthusiasm for the place and didn't make me feel any better about having to walk there at all.

Finally, after what had seemed like hours of trekking in waterlogged clothes, we reached a road that ran right on up to the entrance.

The Entrance to Wewelsburg Castle

An arched gateway welcomed us menacingly into an inner courtyard; the towering walls either side stained in such a way as to make it appear that the very stone was crying in horror of the evils committed within. Reluctantly following Seb across the bridge that led under the arch, I couldn't shake the feeling that we were walking into the mouth of a monster.

That feeling soon subsided however upon stepping out of the horrid night and into the warmth and dry of the Youth Hostel. As we dripped off, in what I guessed served as the reception area, I was pleasantly surprised to see that the creepy old look of the exterior had given way to quite a modern looking interior. Very light, very spacious and very clean, it was a complete contrast to what stood outside.

With all my attention focused on a nearby radiator I'd spotted, as I tried to shake the water from my hat and coat, I failed to notice the young woman coming to meet us.

'Willkommen! Ze mussen zien Herrn Reinhardt und Herrn Keeldan,' she said in a noticeably well practiced accent.

Turning round upon hearing my name, my mouth near hit the floor as my eyes ran over a tall, slim figure, moving towards us with an effortless grace. Even speaking the guttural words of the German language her voice seemed soft and welcoming, wrapped in a smile that warmed me more completely than the radiator I had been clung to.

'Yes, that is correct,' Seb replied to her, indicating that he wished to converse in English, *'I apologise for the lateness of our arrival and would like to thank you for being so accommodating.'*

'Oh, you are English?' she said with pleasant surprise, as a gentle ringlet of silky chestnut hair fell out of place to drape softly against her cheek.

'No, but my friend Mr Keeldan is,' Seb explained, with a gesture that drew her eyes to me.

'Hi there,' I said quite lamely; all manner of coolness having abandoned me as I became lost in deep oval pools of breath taking turquoise.

Her face radiated a kindness and beauty that turned my legs to jelly, yet there was an ever so slight shyness about her that suggested she perhaps did not see in herself what was so apparent to me.

'It's so nice to see someone from home all the way out here,' she said, looking at me with a shy smile, brushing her hair back behind her ear with slender fingers as a faint blush coloured her

pale skin, *'it has been a while since I last got to speak any English to someone face to face.'*

I realised then that I'd been, probably gormlessly, staring at her since her arrival and quickly shook myself out of it whilst hoping I hadn't made her feel uncomfortable.

'You are English too then?' I asked, rather awkwardly stating the obvious.

'What a stupid question to ask,' Seb chimed in, predictably voicing that which I'd hoped would go unnoticed. *'Do you ever think before you speak?'*

'It's okay really,' said the young woman coming to my rescue, *'I've been here so long that I do sometimes forget I am English, so it is nice to be reminded.'*

As she spoke, with cutest hint of a classical English accent, she gave me a little smile of understanding that I returned with gratitude. She then went on to explain how she had been there for just under a year on a sort of work experience/training thing to do with tourism and hospitality. As the trainee, she had automatically drawn the short straw of having to wait up to welcome us in. For this I felt it necessary to apologise profusely, only for her to insist that it was no trouble.

She said that it had been well worth it just for the break from having to speak German; plus, as part of her course, she was accommodated within the hostel and so it hadn't been all that much of an imposition for her anyway.

I then became acutely aware of the mess we'd made on the floor with our muddy shoes and dripping wet clothes and felt it even more necessary to apologise for that. Again she simply smiled and insisted that we were not to worry about it given the terrible state of the weather outside.

After proper introductions were made, through which I learnt her name to be Kate, she had us sign in and then follow her to our room.

Walking a few paces behind, wincing ever so slightly with every squelch of my wet shoes on the clean floor, I couldn't help but steal quick glances over the curvature of her hips down to her long slender legs, hidden teasingly beneath the understatedly form fitting cargo pants she wore.

Lingering a little over her lower back, where I could just see the tip of a delicate tattoo exposed between the bottom of her t-shirt and the top of her pants, my eyes moved up and became mesmerised by the swaying of her beautiful hair. Loosely it cascaded down her back in a shimmering dance of twists and curls. It was like seeing poetry in motion.

Thankfully, while I was watching her, Seb must have been watching me and was able to give me a quick nudge just before she turned round and would otherwise have caught me out.

Saved from embarrassment, and feeling a little ashamed, I re-focused my efforts to listening intently as she explained how the accommodation within the hostel was split into six closed wings. Each had a row of rooms, containing their own wash facilities and 6 to 10 beds, with communal showers and toilets. Fortunately for us though, whilst it was in essence a Youth hostel, they did cater for other guests with smaller rooms like ours set aside for adults and families who wanted a bit more privacy.

The room she presented to us was simple in features but had a very cosy appeal. Containing two reasonably sized beds, a small table, a wash basin and a wardrobe, it was more than enough for what we needed.

A window, slightly sunken into the sloping far wall and fronted by double door shutters, opened out to overlook the forest on the opposite side of the castle to where we had entered. A rather chilling view it was on that night if I'm honest, one that made me immediately close the shutters in order to hide us from whatever might be lurking out in the shadow of the trees.

Turning to thank Kate for her assistance, I was unable to prevent the audible rumble that came from my stomach indicating its unhappy state of emptiness. The snacks I bought for the train had taken the edge off but, in the absence of a proper meal at all that day, had done little to fill us up.

'My gosh, it sounds like someone's a bit hungry?' she said with a cute laugh.

'Both of us are actually, we have hardly eaten all day,' answered Seb, seizing the opening she had left, *'I do not suppose there is any chance of some food tonight is there?'*

I closed my eyes in embarrassment as Kate apologised that we had arrived too late for a cooked meal. There followed an awkward moment in which nobody spoke and Seb just stood looking at her with an expectant expression.

'Is there nothing you can do to help us?' he asked insistently.

'Seb, don't you think we are asking a bit much to be fed at this time of night?' I scolded him after seeing how uncomfortable he'd made the young woman feel.

'I am sorry Kate, was it rude of me to ask this of you?' he addressed to her in such a way as to still put her on the spot.

'For God's sake Seb, will you just leave her be?' I groaned at him.

'No no, its fine,' she jumped in, *'I'm sure my boss wouldn't mind me nipping into the kitchen to put together some sandwiches for you if that's alright?'*

'That would be wonderful,' Seb said with a slimy smile, accepting her offer before I had chance to object, *'We would be most appreciative for it.'*

'Only if you are sure you won't get into trouble for it though,' I added as she asked us to follow her back toward the kitchens.

I wish I could say that I went under protest but, sadly, the prospect of food was too good to turn down.

The sandwiches may have only contained slices of plain ham but, to my starving belly, it could have easily been a juicy piece of steak. As we ate, Kate told us about the hostels leisure facilities available through the day and recommended local places to visit should we be interested in doing so in the morning. She also recommended, more towards me than Seb, that should we be staying another night, the sauna was a nice place to relax in the evenings. It was at this point I started to get the feeling that she might have been flirting with me a bit. However, having been spectacularly wrong about such things in the past I decided to ignore it as being wishful thinking.

Despite her initial shyness, she seemed much more confident and self-assured now. I got the feeling that she was definitely no shrinking violet and would easily wear the trousers in any relationship. To be honest, this just made her seem even more attractive to me.

We talked for a while longer as she asked about where I was from and what had brought me to Germany. Breezing over the latter, I quickly asked her the same series of questions and was pleasantly surprised to find that, back in the UK, she'd grown up in a place called Warrington.

Though I hadn't grown up there myself, I had been born there and a lot of my family, including my nan, still lived there. I'd spend many a holiday, especially in recent years, down there visiting and had often gone on nights out with my cousin and his mates. This revelation sparked many a memory of familiar places and stories that had us both laughing and reminiscing; much to the ever increasing sighs of Seb's boredom.

Only now has it dawned on me how this wasn't the first time such a coincidence had occurred on this trip. I wonder what odds a bookie would have given me on meeting two different strangers in a foreign country that both turned out to be from places in England I knew well? Had I thought about it at the time though, I doubt I would have cared less about the probability of such things for I was too busy enjoying the feeling of having found little bits of home despite being so very far away.

I guess eventually Seb must have grown bored of being a side-line act in our production of memory lane, causing him to interrupt and suggest that we should be heading off to bed.

'We have a very busy day ahead of us tomorrow, as I am sure this young lady does too,' he said with a nod towards Kate. *'We have already taken up too much of your time and it would be impolite of us to keep you up any longer.'*

'I wish I could disagree,' she said with a sigh, turning back to me with a genuine look of regret, *'but I do have to be up at six to get the dining halls ready for breakfast. I suppose I should get on off to bed before I lose all chance of it being worthwhile.'*

She left us on route back to our room, but not before asking if she would see us again at breakfast. My tongue became a huge sponge that filled my mouth, ready to soak up the lies I would have to tell her. Thankfully, unbeknown on his part I'm sure, Seb came to my aid. He informed her politely that, whilst we would have liked too, we unfortunately had to be up and away very early and so it was unlikely that we would meet again.

Her eyes seemed to dim ever so slightly at this and her shoulders droop just a little. It was a sight that made me really wish I could tell her the truth. Some crazy part of me wished I could tell her what we were up to and invite her to come away with us; thinking that she could have been useful to our quest...even if only to provide a buffer between Seb and I.

Fortunately, there was still a greater ratio of rational maturity to teenage fancy controlling my brain and I managed instead to bid her a sad goodbye but not without offering a rather awkward handshake. Pressing her lips tight to hide the smile of coy amusement that her eyes could not, she accepted my gesture, thanked us for our company that night and, with a lingering touch of her hand against mine, wished us safe on our onwards journey.

I watched her leave as the warm touch of her skin lingered, thinking to myself that it had to have just been my imagination. I could never have been that lucky.

Back in our room, Seb suggested that we get an hour or two's sleep to recharge whilst waiting for the castle to fall silent; having noticed lights still on in a few of our neighbouring rooms. As the full weight of the last few days finally fell upon my eyelids at the sight of a waiting bed, it was a suggestion I did not need giving twice.

****

A crow circled high above me in the night. I could hear its cries as I walked a long, misty road to nowhere. A head of me stood Archer, holding an envelope in his hand, waiting for me to come.

I called out to him, but he did not respond. It was as if he couldn't even see me. I walked with an ever quickening pace desperate to reach him, but I did not seem to get any nearer.

I saw him seal the envelope and leave it on the table behind him as he turned to walk away. Again I called out to him, asking him to wait, and again he did not respond.

The world around me grew darker still. It was not a road I was running down but rather a long corridor to an open door where the table lay beyond.

Closer now, I was gaining ground at last. Feeling I was fighting against an invisible current, it was a relief to reach the doorway and stop to catch my breath.

I heard the cry of the crow once more, only this time it was much closer. This time it was right in front of me and it had Archer's envelope in its beak.

'NO!' I cried out, *'Give it Back!'*

I tried to dash forward and make a grab for it, but the retched thing was long gone before I even got close.

Reaching the window it had flown out of, I stared into the darkness and watched it fly away. But it did not go far. Just far enough to be almost out of sight, but not quite, then it stopped. Landed in the darkness and looked back at me, mockingly waiting for me.

I had to get to it. I was going to jump from the window, but then I heard a voice. A strange yet familiar voice calling to me, yet it was not calling my name. It was calling me back, calling me away from the bird and the envelope that I knew was important.

It grew louder and louder as the room began to shake.

'Tom, Tom, Wake up Tom...TOM!'

****

I suddenly found myself forced out of my dream and brought crashing back into reality as Seb shook me awake; a little more roughly than was necessary to my mind.

Feeling like I had shut my eyes only moments ago, my head was groggy and struggled to comprehend what was happening; my eye lids crying out in pain at being cheated of their rest.

Coming too just enough to realise why I had been woken, without losing the ability to easily fall back into sleep, I groaned at Seb to leave me just a little longer...I needed to find that envelope.

'No Tom, you have slept too long already,' he said mercilessly, whilst continuing to shake me. *'We need to get moving before we lose the cover of night.'*

'Sod off will ya!' I snapped, throwing a shoulder up aggressively as I tried to roll away from him.

At first I thought this had worked as the shaking stopped and I sensed him walk away from my bed. Unfortunately, I was very much mistaken.

'JESUS CHRIST!' I practically screamed as a cup full of freezing cold water was emptied over my head, leaving me questioning who I was, where I was and what the hell was going on, *'Are you out of your fucking mind?'* I added with a vicious snarl towards the German idiot stood holding the cup.

'No, I am quite within my mind thank you and I would prefer that you kept you voice down before you wake up the whole bloody castle,' replied Seb with an air of indifference towards my angry gestures, *'though I suppose if your snoring has not already done so, your screaming stands little chance,'* he added with a hard smile and challenging tone.

'Keep my voice down?' I snapped, as the world began to slowly shuffle itself back into a logical order in my head, *'You just chucked a load of cold bloody water over me, how did you expect I was gonna react you prat! I'm soaking wet now thanks to you.'*

'Stop being a child, I only poured it over your head,' he replied without sympathy or remorse, *'there is towel at the bottom of your bed if you want to dry off.'*

'IF? If I want to dry off?' I chewed over his words and spat them back, *'What possible reason could I have for wanting to stay wet?'*

'Well to me it would seem a waste of time, when five minutes from now you are going to be wet all over again anyway when we go outside. But it is your choice.'

Somewhere between the disturbing dream and the rude awakening, I'd managed to forget what it was I was being woken up for. It was of course time to begin our search for the Grail.

'Look,' he began to speak again, as I rubbed the towel over my head and fixed him with an unimpressed scowl, *'you have been asleep for nearly three hours, if we do not get going now we will have the sun chasing us down as we search. I tried to wake you gently but you would not move, therefore you left me with no choice. Now please, get up, get dressed, and let us get on with what we have come here to do.'*

Moodily stumbling out of bed, I gathered my things together and grudgingly followed him out of the room, heading cautiously back towards the entrance. He walked through the castle like it were his own home, without so much as a hesitation towards which direction we needed to go, as I just stumbled on wearily behind him.

Walking out of the hostels door was like walking into the first ring of hell; the storm having worsened if anything over the last few hours. The wind whipped around the triangular courtyard with the vicious intent of devouring anything that wasn't secured to the floor as it sent torrents of rain lashing towards us with stinging force.

'Little point in drying off indeed,' I thought to myself as my clothes began to soak up the water again.

Standing up on the exposed ramp-way that lead to the hostel door, Seb quickly instructed that we were to head into the North Tower that lay to our left; an order I gladly followed just to get out of the rain.

Reaching the tower door I asked, over the howl of the wind, how we were meant to get in. A sly smile from him and twist of the door handle provided me with my answer. The air of cockiness that surrounded him as he closed the door behind me, blocking out the wailing elements once more, suggested that he

309

had always known the door would be unlocked; quite how this was though, I never did get round to asking him. Happily for me though, that grin was soon to be wiped from his face.

As we approached the inner room of the tower's first floor, both reaching for our respective torches to light the way, Seb was taken aback to discover that there was a locked metal gate standing in our way. Obviously his plan, and his research, hadn't gone as far as to account for this obstruction.

'This gate is not meant to be here, at least it was not the last time I came,' he said in a tone of irritation, *'There is nothing in the room to steal so what logic is there in locking it, unless....?'*

'Unless what?' I asked after his pause had gone on for few seconds.

'Nothing, never mind, I was simply thinking out loud,' he said, shrugging off whatever the train of thought had been as he turned back to face me, half blinding me by forgetting what he had held in his hand. *'Okay, there must be someone around here that has a key to this gate.'*

It had been intensely dark inside the tower at first, with the only illumination coming from the occasion flash of lightening through the tall windows of the room beyond the gate. Fortunately however, we had both brought L.E.D torches which, in such a confined space, managed to bathe us in enough artificial light as to allow us to see one another quite clearly.

'So what, are we to just go around all the rooms asking if anyone has it?' I said sarcastically.

'No, that would be foolish as it would give away our intent,' I never did learn that sarcasm went straight over his head, *'But maybe your new friend has one?'* he added with a not so subtle barb.

'What if she doesn't?' I asked, rising above it.

'Well then we will just have to wait until the morning, book a guided tour and then either steal the key or think of some way to ensure the door stays open,' he replied, somewhat less than convincingly.

'That sounds like a lot of effort to get into a room you still haven't explained the significance of,' I pointed out quite sharply as I directed the light from my torch through the gate.

He shot me a rather blasé look before saying, *'Come here,'* whilst motioning for me to look through the gate, *'see there, in the centre of the room,'* he indicated with his own torch.

310

The Generals Hall in the Upper North Tower

The Black Sun Symbol

'What, that black ring on the floor,' I said, struggling to see it through the gate, 'what about it?'

'That "Ring" is what is known as "The Black Sun". A symbol of great importance to the Nazi's, second only to the swastika. It is believed to be linked to their Sun worship and the 12 rays surrounding it symbolise –'

'– the twelve knights of Himmler's Order,' I interrupted, taking great pleasure in seeing his mouth hang open still in mid-sentence. 'Yeah, Archer spoke of it in his journal, this must be the General's Hall then?'

'The Obergruppenführersaal yes,' he confirmed, with a sly look of surprise. 'It is in this room that Himmler and his Knights would meet; sat around a circular table in likeness of King Arthur and his Knights of Camelot.'

'Well, I'll admit that, from what I read of Archer's notes, the history surrounding this room is all very interesting,' I freely acknowledged, 'but it still doesn't explain why we need to get in there so badly?'

'Look,' he almost snarled, 'my research has led me to believe that Himmler had a secret vault hidden somewhere within this Castle where he planned to store any and all sacred artefacts he managed to acquire; a room whose access was known only to himself and his knights. If they did find the Holy Grail then I would bet my life on it being that room where he would have kept it,' his face was stern and resolute in belief of this, his arm left hanging behind him to point through the gate.

'I devoted a year towards learning how to access this vault. A task that took a great amount of effort but which finally led me to this,' he paused for a moment as he un-shouldered his backpack and passed me a large golden disk, engraved with a stylised swastika on one side. 'This holds the key to finding the entrance to that Vault...and, if my findings prove to be accurate, it belongs right there in the middle of that Sun Wheel.'

At this moment I did experience a shiver of excitement as I strained my eyes trying to get a clearer view of the "Black Sun" symbol.

'Where did you get this?' I asked in awe as my attention came back to the disk and I turned the thing over and over in my hands, enticed by the mystery of it all.

'That is not important,' he said levelly, holding out his hand for it to be returned, 'but now you can see why it is imperative that we get inside this room.'

313

Though curious as to why its origin wasn't important, I let the subject drop; far too intrigued by what the thing might unlock to really care about where he got it from.

As he re-shouldered his pack and slowly began to head back to the tower door, talking of the revised plan as he went, a little light bulb turned on in my head that had me to reach a hand into my satchel.

'Now, since it would be very unwise to go searching through pockets in the dead of night, I think it would be best for us to go back to the room, get some more rest and take the guided tour approach in the morning. Perhaps between now and then I can come up with a way of making it work,' he said, so wrapped up in his own thoughts that my retrieval of a small black leather pouch had gone unnoticed, as did the gentle "clicks" and "pings" that followed. *'Come on Tom, we can do no more here tonight. I guess you will get your wish of a longer sleep now after all.'*

"Click", "Click", "Ping"..."Creak"

'Tom, are you coming or n...Ich glaube es nicht! How..did.. you do that?' he stammered, eyes wide and mouth agape, after turning back toward me and seeing a now open gate.

The look of incomprehension and amazement on his face as I stood leaning against the wall, in the most nonchalant manner I could manage, was pleasing to say the least.

'Trade secrets my friend,' I answered, whilst cockily throwing the little leather case up into the air and catching it again without looking, *'Trade secrets.'*

'You picked the lock?' he surmised correctly, *'My, my, perhaps you are not entirely useless after all.'*

I let that jibe go, far too pleased with myself at still having the skill to do something I hadn't done in years, to really care what he said.

Despite what you may think, there is a perfectly honest reason for why I carried around a lock picking set. Honestly.

Following Seb into the room, I watched as he became increasingly excited about the symbol on the floor, sizing up the slight indentation at its centre with his golden disk.

Eager though I was to find out if the thing would work, I was at that moment more transfixed by the room itself. Somehow, standing inside it, I saw what I hadn't from behind the gate; it was just as Archer had described.

I know this doesn't sound like such a big thing but then, as far as I know, Archer had only seen pictures of the place, not been there himself. Yet, because of how he'd described it, I somehow felt like I'd been there before; the pillars, elongated windows and the Black Sun symbol all appearing exactly how I'd imagined them to be.

'*Right!*' Seb said as he stood up and put the disk back in his bag, '*Now we must open up the Crypt.*'

'*Crypt? What Crypt?*' I asked with unsettling concern as tiredness still prevented my brain form using its full range of memory.

'*The one that sits beneath our feet and is meant to be the place where the ashes of deceased SS officers would be brought,*' he answered, before regarding me with a tilting of his head, '*I expected you would know of this as you did the Generals Hall?*'

'*Err, yeah, no I do,*' I stumbled, trying to reshuffle my thoughts, '*I mean Archer wrote of it of course, I must have just momentarily forgotten.*'

Truthfully, I don't think I had forgotten. I think it was more that hearing the word "crypt" spoken aloud had simply invoked images of a place much different than the one Archer had written of; images of dusty coffins, piles of bones, evil looking rats, creepy noises and strange gusts of wind that came out of nowhere.

Despite knowing that this wasn't the case, I still couldn't think of anything I'd like to do less than *"Open up the Crypt"* in the dead of night during a terrible storm. This however, was something that I did not wish to admit to Seb and so just went along with it.

I followed him back out into the inner courtyard and then through the main gate; which I noted was strangely still open. It must have been to allow the coming and going of the hostels guests I concluded without giving it too much thought.

Passing under the large archway, we headed towards a set of steps to the right of a very large tree that sat facing the castle gate. The flashes of lightening and loud claps of thunder, along with the ever persistent rain, did nothing to make the place seem any less sinister.

Carefully navigating the steep slippery steps that led down into a lower courtyard, Seb brought us to the base of the North Tower. Twice more my lock picking skills where needed, once to get us into the tower, since that lower door was locked, and then again to get through another gate at the bottom of a short stairwell obstructing our entrance into the Crypt. As I worked my magic on the last of the locks, I was able to see into the room on the other side as Seb shone his torch around and was relieved to find it nothing like what I had imagined.

The Crypt in the Lower North Tower

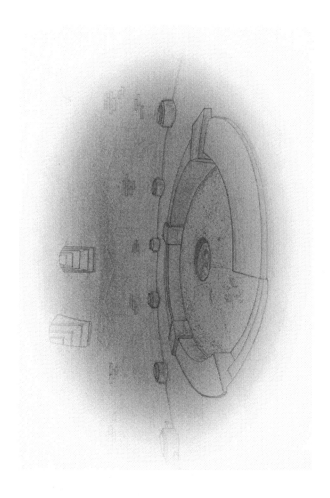

The Swastika in the Roof of the Crypt

Again it looked just as Archer had described, though it wasn't all together un-creepy. Where our torches had provided ample illumination in the room above, down in the Crypt, what light they cast now seemed to get eaten up by a much stronger darkness.

With a final "click" the last lock yielded to me and the gate opened. Holding it ajar for him to step through, I watched as Seb passed on into the room with respectful excitement and stood in the pit at its centre.

'Come and look at this Tom,' he said, looking straight up to the ceiling, *'impressive is it not?'*

'Wow!' I replied having followed his gaze up to where a large stylised swastika was carved into the centre stone; the end of each arm stretching out in a chaotic pattern.

Impressive would have been the way to describe it had it not been the symbol of an evil regime; quite what you are meant to call an interestingly designed Swastika I do not know.

'This really was a Nazi stronghold then wasn't it?' I said, as if the sight of the symbol had just made the fact seem more real.

Two feelings came over me in that moment; both of which I didn't like. The first was a realisation that I was currently standing in the very space once occupied by some of the vilest men in history, which in itself left me feeling quite uncomfortable. The second was the sensation that, as I spoke, my voice seemed to be getting sucked up out of the room. It sounds strange I know, and it is hard to really explain but it felt almost like my words were being stolen from me; a feeling that I found rather unsettling.

'Okay, so, now what?' I asked eventually.

'Well, this is going to be the difficult part,' answered Seb, finally dragging himself away from looking at the Swastika as he dropped the beam of his torch down to help illuminate more of the room. *'This is where we will have to split up.'*

An unfortunately timed crash of thunder, echoing down the window shafts sat high around the room, emphasised the feeling I had of that not being a very good idea.

'Why the hell *would we want to go and do that for?'* I said in a voice raised above the ringing in my ears.

'Well one of us must go back up and place the golden disk into the Sun Wheel, whilst the other stays down here to see what happens. That is why there needed to be two of us. If we had not needed to split up, I could have come here and done this myself

could I not?' he did have a point there I suppose, it was just that I didn't like the way this was heading.

'I thought you knew what the disk would do?' I queried.

'I do know,' he began with an exasperated sigh, *'I know that the disk being returned to its place at the heart of the Sun Wheel will reveal the entrance to the Vault, and I am certain that it will happen in this very room. What I do not know however, is how it will happen or how long it will stay open for. That is where you come in.'*

'Here it comes,' I thought to myself.

'I need you to stay down here and tell me what happens,' he added, confirming my fears.

'Why do I need to stay down here?' I protested, almost giving away my discomfort at being in the room, *'Why can't I go and place the disk?'*

'That is simple, you have to stay here because you do not know how to align the disk within the Wheel, that is why,' he answered resolutely.

'Fine!' I petulantly accepted, *'but tell me this then smart arse, how do you propose that we keep in touch? I don't know about you but my phone's not picking up any reception down in here.'*

I know it was a bit childish to lash out when I couldn't have my own way, but there was a power play constantly in motion between us, and I was determined not to lose.

'Schizer!' he cursed as he checked his own, *'No, mine neither. Well I guess I will just have to come back down once I have placed the disk then?'* he said as he began walking back to the entrance.

'Hang about!' I called after him, *'that's just gonna be too much messing around and we don't have the time for it. Here, take this instead,'* I added before throwing him one of the two-way radios I had brought from home, *'It's a good job one of us came prepared, hey?'*

'You impress me again Mr Keeldan. Archer might have been right to send you after all,' he said with a wicked smile that negated any illusion of sincerity.

'Yeah Yeah! Just switch it to channel two and let's get this over with.'

Being alone in that room made the unpleasant feelings I'd been having ten times worse, especially whenever there was a clap of thunder outside as the sound seemed to roar violently into the room from all sides before echoing up to the ceiling.

So uncomfortable was I in fact that I began to get the feeling I was being watched. There was a presence there I could neither describe nor ignore, like ghostly eyes staring at me from the shadows. Restless spirits of long dead SS members, held there in purgatory for the crimes they committed; evil guardians of the secrets we were trying to unlock.

Now, I feel I should explain that I am not normally a believer in ghosts to be fair; many an argument I have even had over the sheer improbability of such things. But there in that room my conviction of that disbelief was definitely tested. I could almost feel a build-up of hate and anger pushing against me; like there was some force down there that wanted me to leave.

My heart rate began to quicken, my nerves to tingle and an icy chill shot through my bones. I did not like this room!

After all, just because something is improbable doesn't necessarily mean it is impossible.

'There's something in here with me,' I told myself with rising panic, as the shadows seemed to draw in closer and the light from my torch grew dimmer, *'I've got to get out, I've got to leave. I can't stay any longer, the silence is deafening –'*

'OKAY TOM, I AM IN PLACE!' came the sudden crackle of Seb's voice over the radio, whose volume was oh so unfortunately loud.

'JEASUS CHRIST!!' I cried in a whisper strained to its limits as I jumped out of my skin.

In that briefest moment of pure terror, I'd instinctively wanted to run and hide in a corner away from the noise that had erupted into the void around me. In such a situation, the feeling of abject cruelty when you realise you are stood in a round room is damn near indescribable.

'TOM! ARE YOU THERE?' this second transmission brought me back to my senses and I quickly reached for the radio I'd clipped on to my belt.

'Yes, I'm here! Just dropped the radio is all!' I said by way of an excuse for my delayed response.

'Fine, I am ready to place the disk now,' he said at a much more agreeable volume after I'd adjusted my receiver, *'Remember, I am relying on you to tell me what happens so make sure you pay attention down there. The signs of this working could be very subtle.'*

'I know, I know, just get on with it will you. It's not like I'm down here playing bloody tidily-winks with the ghosts!' I

snapped back as the sound of my racing heartbeat still pounded in my ears.

Taking a moment to calm myself down, whilst waiting for whatever was to happen, I realised that the build-up of pressure I had felt before was no longer there. The shadows had retreated to their normal state and the beam from my torch was as strong as ever; it had all just been in my head.

I chastised myself for having acted like a big girl, and mentally reinforced my disbelief in ghosts as I did. Still, it did little to alleviate my dislike of that room.

Day 8 - Wewelsburg, Germany
The Secret of Wewelsburg

'Here we go!' warned Seb, moments before I heard the sound of stone grinding against stone in the ceiling above.

Moving to the centre of the room I strained to watch the carved Swastika at the faded out edge of my torch light, expecting it to move in some way. But then the sound stopped abruptly and all fell silent again...for about two seconds.

Suddenly, a blast of air rose from the circular pit beneath me and sent a cloud of dust into my eyes forcing me to stumble backwards. In that moment I felt like I couldn't breathe, as if the blast of air had stolen the very oxygen from my lungs. My head rang with a muffled sound that pounded my ear drums and caused me to become greatly disorientated.

For a length of time I was senseless to measure, I was left blindly stumbling away from the pit in the dark, gasping for air and holding my ears. Then, just as suddenly as it had begun, everything went back to normal. The air returned, the dust settled and, with a faint grinding of stone in the ceiling again, all was calm and quiet once more.

'What happened?' asked Seb with palpable suspense, as I limped to the doorway and tried to catch my breath.

'Tom! What happened?' he came again when I didn't immediately reply.

'You blasted a shit load of dust into my face that's what happened!' I coughed out irritably; trying to clear out the sharp little particles I had inhaled from the dust whilst simultaneously trying to rid them from my eyes through a process of rapid blinking.

'What?'

'Just give me a minute will you?' I said putting the radio down and placing my torch in my mouth as I searched for a bottle of water from my bag.

Using the cap of the bottle, I managed to rinse my eyes and wash out all the dust; a trick I had learned well after years of suffering from hay fever as a child. As successful as the process was, my eyes still felt red raw and blurry for a good while afterwards. Gargling a mouthful of water had about the same effect on my throat too.

Sitting with my back to the wall, I allowed myself a moment to re-compose and calm my breathing.

'Okay, I'm back,' I called in gruffly.

'What is going on Tom, what just happened?' he asked anxiously.

'You mean apart from me getting a face full of dust? Nothing, that's what happened!' I answered testily, deciding not to mention about being unable to breathe, in case it had just been the result of a panic attack or something.

Picking myself heavily up off the floor, I carefully walked back over towards the pit, curious to see if anything might have changed after the dust had been disturbed.

'Well, something must have happened, the disk has returned to its original position,' he said in a tone of mild irritation, *'you must have missed it, so that means we will just have to try again.'*

'WAIT!' I shouted, *'Let me get out of this bloody dust bowl first. I don't fancy having my face sandblasted off if it kicks up all this crap again thank you very much.'*

Retreating all the way back to the room entrance before giving him the go ahead, I heard the sound of grinding stone once more, signalling he'd activated the mechanism. As I suspected though, not much happened. Another blast of air did pick up the dust again and lifted it swirling into an, admittedly impressive, mini tornado for which I was very glad this time to be stood well back from. But other than that...nothing!

I did get the feeling of the air being sucked out of the room again however. It was not as severe as the first time mind, probably due to having been stood out in the doorway, but I could definitely feel it and this time I knew it had nothing to do with having a panic attack.

With a grinding of stone, about a minute or so later, the room once more returned to normal.

'Well, what happened? Did you pay attention this time?' his ever more annoying voice came crackling over the radio.

'I did and, just like before, other than a load of dust getting flung about, nothing happened. No doors were revealed and no

secret chambers unlocked. All we've done is discover, what was possibly, the world's first industrial sized vacuum...,' I paused suddenly.

Something about what I had just said sparked an idea in the back recesses of my mind.

'I do not understand?' began Seb in a tone of disbelief, *'This was supposed to be the k...'*

'Shut up a sec!' I interrupted him, *'Just, give me a minute,'* I added, heading once more back towards the pit.

After a few moments of quiet contemplation, the gears in my head painfully grinding into action as they tried to grasp a thought floating at the edge of my reach, I suddenly recalled something I'd read.

'Seb, in Archer's journal he said something about the SS having planned for there to be an eternal flame in the room, does that ring any bells?' I queried.

'Yes, that is correct. It was supposed to be –'

'Yeah, yeah, I know what it was for Seb, Archer explained all that,' I interrupted brashly, knowing that we didn't have time for a history lesson, *'I just need to know how they planned to achieve it.'*

'Very simply,' he spoke with a level tone after a moment of disgruntled silence, *'if you open your eyes you should see that there is a gas pipe sticking out down in the depression at the centre of the pit which they had fitted for that purpose. Am I allowed to ask why you want to know this?'*

'Well, this may be a complete shot in the dark,' I began in answer, *'but when you activate the mechanism it seems to create a sort of vacuum that sucks the air out of the room up towards the ceiling, maybe through those four holes in the swastika. If it truly is the key to unlocking the Grail room, then perhaps for it to work the eternal flame has to be lit?'*

'Perhaps,' he admitted reluctantly, *'but you are assuming that there is still, if even there ever was, a supply of gas for the pipe to draw on. It was only known to have been a proposed idea. I have not come across any accounts of the fire having actually been made in to a reality. But even if it had, I doubt it would still be working after all this time.'*

As he rambled on, I'd taken the opportunity to have a closer look at the floor of the pit. At first I couldn't really see anything, but then I crouched down in the inner circle and swept my hand through the thick layer of dust on the floor. What I should have done was just look at the very centre of the circle where I would have seen a little valve sticking up slightly from under the dust; but then it was rather dark down there and it is easy to miss small objects under the light of a torch.

As it was, I found it eventually after discovering a thin copper pipe, slightly sunk into the stone, with my fingers and following it to the centre.

By this time, the radio had fallen silent and all was peaceful for a moment as I brushed more of the dust away to reveal a small handle at the side of the valve. I can't be sure whether it was simply curiosity or a desire to prove Seb wrong, but something inside made me turn that little handle. My reward for this action was a satisfying hiss and a strong smell of gas.

'Okay,' I announced over the radio, *'do you want the good news or the bad news?'*

'What? What do you mean?'

'Well, the good news is that, despite your pessimistic attitude, there is a flow of gas down here.'

'Are you sure?' he asked with doubt in his voice.

'Oh yes,' I answered as I closed the little valve again; the smell of gas having begun to give me a headache.

'So what is the bad news then?'

'The bad news is that there is a flow of gas down here.'

'I do not understand Tom, you are not making any sense,' he scolded. *'You just said that was the good news. It cannot be both.'*

'It can if you spare a moment to wonder why there is one!' the concern I felt toward this was clear in my words. *'You said it yourself, after all this time there should not have still been a gas supply to this old pipe.'*

'Perhaps it was just never turned off after the castle fell during the end of the war? Maybe the gas supply runs off what the hostel uses and nobody has realised?' Seb offered weakly, as if trying to provide an innocent solution he didn't really believe himself.

'Okay, I suppose that is a possibility,' I tentatively admitted, *'but then it doesn't explain the valve.'*

'What do you mean?'

'Well the pipe I could believe is a relic of the war, as it's as rusty as hell, but the valve.... that's practically brand new!'

'Impossible!' he barked dismissively, *'How could you possibly know that?'*

'Well, just forgetting for the moment that I used to labour for my uncle who is a gas engineer and so I do know a thing or two

about such things, I can tell it's relatively new because it's still shiny.'

'Shiny?' he doubted me.

'Yes, as in I-can-almost-see-my-own-reflection-in-it shiny,' I stressed to him. *'Believe me it is a stark contrast in appearance to that of the aging pipe it is connected to.'*

'So what, are you suggesting that someone else must know the secrets of this tower?'

'Bingo. As far as I'm aware, a working eternal flame was not one of the listed attractions on the castle tour. They may not know about the vault, but somebody has definitely, in the last few years, finished what Himmler started; and if not for public viewing, why else would it have been done?'

The other end of the radio went silent for a moment as I could almost hear the wheels in Seb's head turning.

'Seb? You still there?' I asked, growing impatient.

'We need to move fast!'

'What?'

'Do not ask questions, just listen to me,' he snapped. *'If you are right about the flame and someone else does know about the vault, then we need to figure out how to open it before we are discovered.'*

'But that was just as true five minutes ago, why the hurry all of a sudden?' I pushed, feeling sure that there was something he wasn't telling me...again.

'Because...,' he stumbled in response, as if trying to quickly think of an excuse to fob me off with, *'because all of the noise we have been making could have alerted someone to our presence.'*

'What? Are you serious?' I half laughed at him, *'Have you heard the thunder outside? We could march a brass band around down here and no one would know! What's the real reason Seb? I know your hiding something, now spit it out.'*

'The real reason?' he repeated viciously, suggesting the power play was about to change ends, *'The real reason is that you took so long figuring out we needed the flame to be lit, that we are quickly running out of night time to do this in.'*

'Well if I'd had more than a couple of hours sleep before being rudely dragged out of bed, I might have remembered about it sooner!' I answered peevishly, foolishly rising to the bait.

'It is my own fault,' he sighed, ignoring what I'd said, *'I knew I should have stayed down there myself.'*

'I...you...What?!' I stammered in complete disbelief at the way he'd ignored his own contradiction.

He'd effectively turned the conversation on its head and left me unable to regain a foothold.

'There is no point in arguing now, we do not have time for it. Just get that flame lit and let us get this done,' he commanded, *'do have any matches?'* he then asked as an afterthought.

'Well Yes, ACTUALLY, I do,' I replied in a theatrically haughty manner, *'and it's a bloody good job one of us came prepared isn't it?'*

'That is the job of the assistant Tom and, after all, you had to be useful for something,' he said, brazenly shooting down my vain attempt to get back on top. *'Now, can we stop talking and get on with it please?'*

I was left speechless and dumbfounded by how, once again, he'd managed to turn the blame on me; insulting me in a way that left no chance of defending myself without wasting time like he had already accused me of doing. In the end all I could do was shake my head, let out a disgruntled sigh and say;

'Fine!'

The sooner we got in, the sooner we could get out and the sooner I could be rid of this irritating bastard.

If it hadn't been for the fact that he was technically holding my money to ransom, I seriously doubted I'd have still been putting up with him...I would soon be thankful that was not the case though.

'Tell me when you are ready and I will operate the sun disk again,' Seb informed me. *'Whatever mechanism this disk activates, it only lasts for a few minutes before resetting itself. This leaves me stuck up here until you get it right down there, so remember to pay attention; if this does not work, we will be out of options.'*

The radio clicked as he let go of the transmit button, but I sensed there was more he wanted to say. After a short pause it clicked again, just as I'd expected it to.

'The worth of my last two years rests in us finding this vault. If we fail, then all my efforts will have been for nothing,' he added quite morosely.

'Jesus man, lighten up will you!' I said with an irritable shake of my head, having stopped what I'd been doing to pick up the radio and verbally slap him for the unhelpful pessimism, *'I haven't even lit the damn thing yet and you're already talking about giving up for god's sake. Let's just stay optimistic for now*

ay...before you go throwing yourself from the bloody castle walls.'

'Ha, I should be so lucky?' I vindictively thought to myself.

'Well what is taking you so long then, get on with it?'

'Dick! One night in a bloody castle and he thinks he's a sodding king,' I grumbled aloud to myself, forgetting that I'd left the channel open on my end to free up both hands to search for my matches.

'What was that?' he challenged me.

'Err what?' I played for time after realising what I'd done, *'Oh, I said it's dark as night in this bloody castle and I can't see a sodding thing.'*

Not the best save in the world I'll admit, but it seemed to do the job...kind of.

'Well then use your torch Tom, that is what it is there for,' he patronisingly replied.

'I should have just repeated the insult,' I thought to myself.

One lit match later, a twist of the valve and we had ourselves a fire.

'Et Voila!' I said over the radio, *'Someone's still paying the gas bill and we have one eternal flame as ordered!'*

'As you say Tom... good news and bad,' Seb responded with a tone of worry in his voice, *'I guess we should give this one last try then.'*

As Seb once again activated the mechanism, and I heard the tell-tale grinding of stone, anticipation of what would happen made me forgot to step back away from the pit; something I soon regretted.

Instead of just picking up the dust from the floor this time though, the vacuum effect turned the small flame into a spiralling funnel of green fire and launched it up towards the swastika above.

The Strange Fire that Erupted in the Crypt

Shielding my eyes and quickly backing up to the doorway, after the blast had just about singed off my eyebrows, I caught a glimpse of something shinning on one of the pillar stumps around the edge of the room. It was some kind of runic symbol.....one I was sure I had seen before!

Quickly I reached for Archer's journal and flicked to the page were he'd described how he felt the Deaths Head Rings held some importance he had been unable to figure out. In one brilliant moment of euphoric excitement I knew, just by looking at his sketch of the ring, what that importance was.

A quick scan around the room further cemented my conviction as I could see that each of the column stumps had their own runes.

'It can't just be a coincidence,' I told myself, *'this has to be the key to opening the Vault.'*

Before I could figure out just how they were key though, the fire went out and the runes became practically invisible again as the room fell back into darkness.

'Did it work?' asked Seb, trying to temper his excitement.

'No, not yet, the fire went out before I could make a note of the runes that appeared,' I answered, forgetting that he hadn't been down here to see them.

'Runes? What runes?' he asked irritably, the annoyance at not being able to see what was going on for himself becoming ever more noticeable.

I quickly brought him up to speed on what had happened and told him my theory based on Archer's findings.

'Once again you surprise me Tom,' he said with much more sincerity than I had expected, *'A connection between the pedestals and Wiligut's runes? Very impressive.'*

'Well..erm...thanks' I said, somewhat shaken by the compliment, *'Right then, I suppose you'd best give that disk another turn and I'll see if I can figure out what they mean.'*

'Just be quick about it, we don't have all night!'

'And we're back,' I thought to myself.

As the flame erupted again I stood for a moment to acclimatise to the slight pressure on my lungs and in my ears, whilst at the same time being mesmerised by the sight before me.

It was strange in that there was hardly any sound; just a dense throbbing in my ears as I watched the magic of a green fire that seemed to be stretched far beyond itself.

Realising I was on a time limit, I quickly scribbled down a rough plan of the room, making careful note of each rune and its location.

At first I thought the ring runes were appearing in a random order amidst others that I did not recognise. I figured they were put in to test ones knowledge of the rings, seeing as how back then only a member of the SS would know of them. However, after completing my sketch and checking the runes against Archer's ring drawing, I realised that they were actually appearing as they would around the rings themselves.

Standing at the steps that dropped down into the pit, I was looking through the flames at the image of a skull and cross bones; the head of the ring runes. Scanning clockwise around from that point revealed the other five ring runes appearing upon every other pedestal. With that in mind, and little other clue as to if there would be a correct order to activate the runes in, I figured that clockwise from the skull was as good a place as any to start. Quickly approaching the pedestal, knowing that time was running away from me, I tentatively reached out a hand to see if it would react at all to my touch. Nothing happened! Then I tried pushing it, thinking that perhaps the rune would work like a button cleverly crafted to appear part of the stone. I was wrong!

'For Fucks sake!' I said with growing frustration, *'What's the bloody point of the stupid thing lighting up if doesn't bloody do anything? Oww! Fuck! Shit! Bastard, Shit, Bastard!'*

An ill-conceived physical outburst in protest of the pedestals inactivity saw my foot bounce painfully back off the cold hard stone.

With my toes throbbing worse than my temper, I sat down on the offending stump and took of my boot to nurse the injury. All of a sudden, the stump began to sink into the floor under my weight; stopping after about two inches with a grind and a click. After a moment of delayed shock, I jumped up with a yelp, surprised by the unexpected movement under my bum, and spun round to find the pedestal holding in its depressed position. As I stood there staring with blank expression at the scene, waiting for my brain to catch up with the situation, the green glow died down behind me as the mechanism reset; only then did the pedestal return to its original height.

'Have you made any progress?' Seb's voice crackled over the radio, as the air around me fell back into place and I could once again breathe easy.

'Hello? Tom? Are you still there?' he added in a voice mixed with boredom and impatience after I didn't answer.

'Yeah yeah, I'm here, I'm here, just.....give me a minute,' I said almost absentmindedly.

Though it wasn't rocket science to figure out what this new development meant, I was still feeling very tired and the cobwebs in my mind seemed to slow the pace of thought. The realisation was perhaps a little delayed in coming, but when it did I couldn't help a little smile creeping over my face.

'Seb, I think I've just figured it out!'

After explaining what had happened, I asked Seb to activate the mechanism one more time and prepared myself for what was to come. As the green fire leaped again into life, I wasted no time in racing around the room, sitting on each of the ring rune pedestals.

If anyone had seen me right then, it would have appeared as though I were playing a music-less game of musical chairs all by myself. In truth, it was actually quite exhausting and tense to boot.

The vacuum effect made it harder to breath, so running around the room felt like running a marathon to my lungs; all the while I could practically hear the time ticking away until the next reset.

Each consecutive stump seemed to depress ever more slowly, leaving my heart to pound audibly as I reached the last one and waited for the click; desperate to not go through it all over again. When at last that final pedestal sank into place, I stood anxiously waiting to see what would happen.

The excitement and adrenaline that coursed through my veins was almost palpable; I knew it would work, it had to work. But then...the silent roar of the fire ended with a piercing whine that reduced the flame back to its normal size and colour.

'So? What happened?' Seb inquired anxiously, *'the mechanism has reset Tom, please tell me something has happened.'*

For a moment I just stood there in total disbelief that, after all that, nothing did happen.

'How can this be?' I asked into the dark, *'I was sure the runes were the key to it all.'*

I was about to radio my disappointment to Seb, when the sound of grinding stone stopped me in my tracks and the floor of the pit began to move. I watched in amazement as the large stones that had encircled the flame basin slowly fell away into a

333

steep spiral stairway disappearing down beneath the crypt; it was like something out of a movie.

The Hidden Stairwell

As a chill of excitement shot through me, I had to give my head a quick shake to check I was really awake; struggling to believe what my eyes had just seen.

'What was that?' asked Seb, 'I heard something opening! Tell me it was the Vault, please say we have found the entrance to the Vault?'

'Well,' I began to answer, still suffering some degree of shock, 'there is a great stone stairwell in the centre of the floor leading down beneath my feet, so I would certainly hope so.'

'Excellent! Do not move! I am on my way down to you!'

'No Wait!' I shouted with a delayed urgency, 'What if the entrance closes up before you get here? Maybe you should stay up there and I'll go down. That way, if it does close, you can reactivate the system or something.'

The radio went quiet, as he considered what I had said.

'Fine!' he eventually replied, dejectedly, 'I guess I should stay up here then! Even though it was my research and my ideas that brought us here, I guess you will get the privilege of making the final discovery,' he added sulkily.

'Well we can swap places if you want but we'll have to be quick coz this thing could close at any minute and you'll have to explain to me how the golden disk works,' I offered, not quite sure I really wanted to venture down into the vault by myself anyway.

Flashbacks of being stuck under Bamburgh Castle accentuated this doubt as the memory of being hit by the falling rock caused me to reach up and rub where the bump had been.

'No! We have wasted too much time here already and cannot afford to start this all over again if it closes. The night is quickly fading so best you get going, but keep in constant contact. I want to know everything you see down there!'

Watching the little flame flicker, not feeling as though I could trust it, I slowly and cautiously approached the first step down; my hand readily gripping my torch as an even gloomier darkness approached my feet. The stairwell seemed to spiral away endlessly, leaving me with plenty of time to reconsider the sanity of this effort.

Only then did it dawn on me that, should the stairway close up behind me, Seb wouldn't be able to re-open it without someone to activate the rune pedestals. Before I had chance to dwell on this however, my foot hit level ground and stretching out before me lay an empty darkness. The steps had spiralled round many times, taking me god only knows how deep below the crypt, until the flickering light of the fire was just a memory and the light from my torch was all I had to see by.

I turned it off at one point, just to see if my eyes would adjust to the dark. After standing at the bottom of the stairs for a good minute, I realised that it wasn't going to happen.

There was no light down there at all; just a suffocating blackness that even a powerful beam of LED light struggled to penetrate.

It was colder down there too, though not the kind of cold you felt outside that could chill you to your bones. Down there it was a cold that could chill to your soul. An eerie feeling of forgotten years clung thick and stale in the air. Every movement I made seemed a disturbance and every breath I drew an unwelcome intrusion.

Acknowledging the persistent, yet slightly distant and static rich, calls from Seb on the radio, I finally responded and explained what I knew so far; which, to be fair, was hardly anything at all.

'Well perhaps you might want to think about looking for some kind of switch that can operate the stairwell from down there, instead of just standing around admiring the darkness!' he said in a peevish tone.

As much as his tone annoyed me, it was a good suggestion and I began to scour the walls in the immediate area for such a device.

It wasn't long before my torch light stumbled upon what looked like a wheel valve. I stared at it for a while, unsure what to do at first.

'Surely such a little wheel couldn't activate the stairs?' I thought to myself. But then, I guess I never would have thought a golden disk placed in the floor could have either!

Convinced it had to do something, I nervously gave it a twist. Looking quite old and rusty, I thought it would be a bit stiff, but to my surprise it moved very easily in my hand. After giving it a few twists I listened carefully expecting to hear the sound of grinding stone again, but all I could hear was a faint hissing.

I noticed a gentle glow appearing over my shoulder and quickly turned around to see what it was; the hairs on the back of my neck standing right on end.

To my relief, what I saw were a series of gas lamps illuminating a stone corridor that stretched out from the stairway.

'I guess I was right about the valve,' I said to myself.

Oddly enough, this new light source actually made the place look even creepier, as each lamp seemed to sit above a doorway and only gave off enough light to illuminate the area directly below it.

What this effectively did was create a long shadowy corridor broken up by just a few small patches of light. It reminded me of a computer game I once played were you had to navigate the character through the dark, running quickly between patches of light to avoid being killed by monsters that lurked in the shadows.

I fought the urge to run back up the stairs and send Seb down to do the discovering and chose instead to radio in my finding. With Seb in agreement that I shouldn't waste any more time looking for a switch to operate the stairs, I forced myself to push onwards toward the first illuminated doorway.

Standing under the dim glow of the gas lamp, I noticed a rectangular plaque on the wall beside an archway that lead into a poorly lit side room. The letters engraved upon it were best part worn away, and looked to be in German anyway, so I quickly gave up trying to decipher it.

Shining my torch into the small room beyond revealed what I can only describe as a shrine.....and an empty one at that.

It looked similar to the one I'd seen underneath Bamburgh Castle, only here the stone alter was covered in a cloth displaying the Nazi swastika and was bare apart from a few half melted candles that looked like they hadn't been lit in decades.

Moving on from room to room down the corridor, lingering less and less inside each one, I grew disheartened by the repetitiveness of what I'd seen in the first being constantly repeated. They were all empty; all of them missing the key item they had been built to house.

Some had markings on their walls, which probably would have made sense to a historian, explaining what treasure had been kept in the room. Unfortunately, to me they were just pretty, and sometimes gruesome, scribbles. Scribbles on empty walls in empty rooms! The predictability of what I would find began to get very wearisome.

There was a strange feeling down there though, one of a stored latent energy left behind by whatever use to sit in those rooms. Just as in the room above, I also felt that uncomfortable feeling of being watched again. The further I went down the corridor, the stronger that feeling became and the greater my desire to get out of there.

A brief moment of reward did arise however, as I approached one of the final rooms. More grand in design and more lavishly decorated than any of the others it was; with beautiful draped wall hangings and soft cushions, that must once have been vibrantly colourful, placed on and around the alter.

I instantly knew what this room had to have been for. A glance at the plaque outside confirmed it.

"Holy Gral"

That was a name I would have understood in any language. It was proof that Seb had been right.... proof that Himmler really did have a room set aside for the Holy Grail!

Day 8 - Wewelsburg, Germany
A Symbol in the Dark

It's hard to describe the feeling of finding evidence that brings myth into reality. A sort of bubbling excitement that makes your heart pound and your skin tingle, mixed with a strange fear that I can't really explain.

Though I am normally a considerably sceptical man, there has always been a part of me which longed to believe in mystical times and legendary treasures that may still exist today. I suppose it was the same part of me that loved reading adventure books that put new slants on old history; often revealing some doomsday prophecy that the heroes had to prevent or an ancient item of power that they had to reach before an evil enemy.

How I longed for such stories to hold some truth, for there to be something more to this world than the boring "beigeness" that scientists have left to us.

As technology advances, our planet seems to grow ever smaller. What places exist now where a camera cannot go? What mystery and magic can we believe in without there being someone who can show how the trick is done? These were the questions that would plague my mind when the end of a good story forced me back to reality. I guess when the answers finally came, they were a little more than I had bargained for.

Who would have ever believed that I would one day find myself caught up in such a story? Not I that's for sure. But the discovery of that Grail room, the fact that it just existed, left little to be cynical of anymore. Whatever form it came in, the Holy Grail had to be real.

I stood transfixed on the name plaque, almost afraid to pass into the room in case it would all somehow dissolve away. This was no dream though, it was a Grail quest to rival any work of fiction...and I was there living it.

Whilst the discovery of the room had at first filled me with a great excitement, it quickly dawned on me that the chances of this one still holding its contents when all the others had been emptied was slim to none.

Regrettably though, that was soon confirmed upon venturing beyond the archway. All that was left was a dusty old alter and faded decorations; just like the rest.

The Grail, along with all the other treasures that would have at one time filled those now hollow rooms, was gone. Where to and whom had taken it were questions with answers probably long ago forgotten.

It was an incredibly deflating moment to then realise that all the research, all the time and effort put in to arriving at that point, had been for nothing. True, Archer had warned Seb that it was unlikely the Grail would still be at the castle, had it even been there at all. But the closer we'd gotten to finding it, the more I'd begun believing that it just might be. I was not looking forward to telling Seb the truth.

It was then I realised that I hadn't been in touch with my companion since leaving the foot of the stairwell. Normally I believe I'd have been thankful for not having heard his incessant badgering chirping away at me every five minutes. However, ironically enough, the simple fact that he hadn't being hailing me to find out what was happening, cast a shadow of concern over my thoughts.

As I was about to radio in and check on him, a whisper on the wind froze the blood in my veins; a strange sound resonating through the honeycombed hallway that stole a breath from me.

Instantly I turned off my torch, in case its light gave me away to an approaching enemy, and closed my eyes in order to listen more intently.

I heard it again. Like a memory of dead words leaking out of haunted walls. This time though I could tell the direction it came from.

With great trepidation, and tingling nerves, I followed the fading echoes of the noise back out into the corridor, finding myself increasingly suspicious of every flickering shadow that caught my eye.

Poking my head around the edge of the archway, unwilling to fully expose myself to whatever might have lain in wait, I looked down towards the end of the passageway and then quickly back towards the stairwell. But there was nothing!

341

Then the noise came again, only this time it was louder and definitely coming from the end of the passage; the dark foreboding void that I had not yet explored. Where the gas lamps had provided sufficient light to see by thus far, their number and effect ended with the one above the Grail room. To see what lay beyond I knew I would have to risk providing my own.

With a slight, yet noticeable, tremble to my hand, I raised up my torch to the level of my eye line and reluctantly clicked the button with my thumb. An explosion of blue light burst forth in a thin beam from which the shadows seemed to physically recoil. For its size my torch was quite powerful, yet it struggled to penetrate the dark as it should have; its effect becoming quickly dissipated by an almost tangible dust that hung in the air.

Despite this however, it did manage to penetrate far enough to catch a reflection off of a sizable metal surface ahead of me. Using this, I was able to trace out the shape of what appeared to be a large door.

For a moment I simply stared at the thing motionlessly as I strained my ears and eyes, hoping to neither hear the ghostly sound again nor see what had made it. My heart near stopped when it did resonate once more. This time I could detect it had actually come from the door itself and, against all reason and sanity, I found myself nervously sliding from cover and leaving the comfort of the lamp light to investigate.

The way back towards the stairway behind me began to feel much longer now. A sub-conscience fear of the situation reached such levels that, upon one paranoid glance back, I could have sworn I saw the corridor stretching out away from me.

When cautiously I reached the strange door, I shone my torch over it whilst running my free hand along its cold steely surface. The first thing that came to mind being how incredibly out of place it seemed down there. It looked, for want of a better description, like a modern, square bank-vault door, with no possible way of getting through it other than by use of a small electronic keypad moulded into its centre. Above this device, something else caught my eye. It was a large emblem embossed into the metal displaying a dagger overlaying a swastika on top of a black sun. It was an image I immediately recognised from Archer's journal...it was the symbol of the Order of the Deaths Head!

Order of the Deaths Head Symbol

A lump formed in my throat that was painful to swallow as my mouth ran as dry as a desert. I didn't know why the symbol of an Order who, by all rights, should have disappeared after the end of Second World War, was present upon a modern looking door, or even why such a door was present in a secret vault beneath an ancient castle. But I had a disturbing idea, and it didn't point to anything good.

As worrying as this discovery had been though, it was nothing compared to what I saw next. Upon slowly starting to back away from the door, the edge of my torch light caught a reflection off something hanging down from the ceiling above. It was a security camera....and it was looking right at me!

'Shit!' I swore as I dropped my torch, the shock of the moment having loosened my gip around it.

Quickly crouching down, I fumbled around the floor in search of it; a task made difficult by the impact having caused it to switch off.

A black tube on a dark floor is a very hard thing to find, especially when you can feel your pulse beating through your eyes. Eventually my fingers danced over it and I snatched it up, quickly re-establishing my light source whilst backing away from both door and camera.

Right on cue the air tensed with the vibration of the ghostly sound, now seeming even more like muffled voices agitated in the distance. My stomach tied itself up in knots.

The more I heard it, the more the walls seemed to close in on me, turning the musty air into a suffocating gas. My body began to tremble and my hair stand on end. I knew I had to leave, knew I had to get out. The sound was getting louder and came at me now with the echo of footsteps. Someone or something knew I was here, and they didn't like it.

In a snap of panic I turned on my heels and ran...straight into a dark apparition that had been sneaking up behind me!

'JEASUS CHRIST!!!' I cried out as my fight or flight instinct malfunctioned and sent me falling backwards to the floor.

All communication between my head and body had ceased. My head had said run but my legs appeared to not get the message and so instead decided to simply crumple and land me flat on my backside, desperately trying to scramble away from my attacker.

'Shhh! Keep it down!' whispered the dark figure in a voice sounding incredibly similar to Seb's.

As it turned out that was mostly due to the fact that it actually was Seb stood in front of me.

'Son of a Bitch! What the hell possessed you to sneak up on me like that?' I demanded as the world started to slowly make sense again, *'You just about gave me a bloody heart attack.'*

'You stopped answering the radio,' he replied quite sternly, *'I told you to stay in touch, so when you did not answer my calls I had no option other to come and find you.'*

'I haven't heard any calls from you since I turned on the gas lamps,' I fired back defensively.

'And that did not concern you at all?' he scolded.

'Honestly,' I breathed out heavily, *'I was too busy enjoying the peace and quiet to be concerned,'* I lied just to be spiteful.

'Yes well, it seems then that our signal must have been disrupted this far underground which left me with the thankless task of coming to save you.'

'Ay? What are you talking about?'

'Something is happening upstairs,' he began to explain whilst offering a hand to help me back onto my feet. *'After my hails to you went unanswered for too long, I made to leave for the Crypt to re-establish contact and almost walked into four rather agitated men who were stood out in the courtyard. Fortunately they did not see me open the tower door, the wail of the storm covering any noise I made, and I quickly closed it over again to watch them through the thinnest of gaps. I heard only odd words spoken hurriedly between them before they split up and went off in different directions. Somehow our intrusion has been discovered!'*

'Oh Shit!' I wheezed, my mind darting almost guiltily to the memory of the security camera.

'I do not know who alerted them, but I cannot help wonder if your little friend has betrayed us,' he said accusingly, *'After all, she is the only person who knew of our arrival.'*

'I don't think it was Kate that gave us away Seb,' I offered up almost apologetically.

'Why, what do you mean?'

'It doesn't matter. Where did the men go?' I asked after brushing off his question.

'One of them came my way, another went into the hostel and the last two headed out of the main gate,' he informed, staring at me through narrowed eyes beneath a wrinkled brow, *'I managed to slip past the first man, as he went to search the General's Hall, and quickly made my way down here. Just in time I was*

345

too, as I came upon one of the men who had left through the main gate discovering that the vault was open and about to blow the whistle. I am surprised you, or anyone else for that matter, did not hear us as we fought.'

It dawned on me then that I had likely just found the origin of the ghostly noises, subconsciously refusing to acknowledge the direction they had been coming from. Sound can travel in strange ways sometimes after all?

'He was a bigger man, than I' Seb continued, attempting to give off an air of false modesty, *'and would easily have beaten me had he not lost his footing around the edge of the fire pit in the scuffle. He fell quite heavily, hitting his head on the stone steps, and thankfully knocked himself unconscious. That is when I came down here looking for you.'*

'What about the other one that came out this way?' I pressed him, beginning to feel somewhat claustrophobic down there.

'I never saw him,' he replied ominously, *'Perhaps he went to watch the road in case we should try to leave the way we came?'*

He turned and shone his torch nervously back down the corridor, as if talking about the man might have caused him to appear.

'This isn't good Seb,' I said, trying to process all that was happening whilst momentarily forgetting the urgency I'd had to leave only moments before. *'We're in way over our heads here. Those men, I..I think they might be...'*

'What were you backing away from?' he cut me off as though he hadn't been listening to a word I'd said, blinding me once again with his torch as he turned back around.

'What?' I asked irritably whilst trying to shield my eyes behind my hand.

'Before you turned and ran into me, you were backing away from something?'

'That's what I was about to tell you,' I explained peevishly as he looked around the passageway,*' I think I've found...'*

'Mine Gott! Is that the room?' he interrupted again as his eyes fell upon the grail plaque.

'Is what the room?' I said with growing irritation; knowing well what he referred to but feeling the need to be difficult about it.

'It is,' he said as if in a daze, *'the room set aside by Himmler for the Holy Grail. It truly does exist. Have you been inside?'*

'What, you mean the one over there with the plaque that says "Holy Gral"? Na, I never bothered checking that one!'

346

'*Tom?*' he replied reproachfully, seeming to detect my sarcasm for once.

'*Of course I bloody well went inside and it's empty just like all the others,*' I snapped, the strong desire to get out of there finally catching back up to me, only to be frustrated by his apparent calmness. '*Look, I'm trying to tell you what I did find and I think it's pretty damn important.*'

'*Please, just allow me one minute,*' he said peacefully as he headed toward the room.

'*Oh fine, yeah you just take your time,*' I said in flippant disbelief, '*I'll just stand out here and wait for your man upstairs to wake up and find us.*'

'*I feel like I have been searching for this most of my life,*' he explained as if having not heard what I'd said, '*To be so close is not enough, I have to see within.*'

'*But there's nothing in there,*' I protested, '*it's empty, they're all empty! Archer was right!*'

'*That may be so,*' he said from inside the room, '*but it does prove that Himmler acquired the Grail! No room would be this lavishly enshrined without having an object to display within it. It proves the Himmler stories are true, the Grail was here....we just arrived too late. About sixty years too late by the look of things.*'

I stood there for half a minute, nervously tapping my foot on the floor as time laboured on with all the speed of a snail trying to avoid the path of a hungry bird.

When my patience could stand the wait no longer (about 50 seconds after Seb had entered the room) I strode over to the archway and found him just stood there lost in thought. Though I could empathise that it must have been a huge moment for him, to be stood inside a room he'd put so much time and effort into finding, I was still annoyed that he thought it appropriate to just stand there when we had bigger things to be concerned about. All of which involved us leaving that place with every ounce of speed possible.

'*What would a symbol with a dagger overlaying a swastika on top of a black sun mean to you?*' I asked him whilst leaning against the archway and staring at my fingernails in a mockingly calm attitude.

'*What?*' he gasped without moving; his whole body seeming to go ridged on the spot, '*Why do you ask?*'

'Oh, no reason really, it's just that it seems to be imbedded on a large metal door down the end of the corridor out here. I'm sure it's nothing to worry about though.'

In a flash he turned to me, eyes wide and pale as a ghost, grabbed my shoulders and said;

'Show me!'

Having at last got his attention, I shone my light over the door once more and highlighted the symbol before slowly panning up to reveal the security camera.

'Shizer! That is how they knew we were here. We need to go Tom. Now, we have to run!'

'Oh.Okay.If.You.Say.So!'

We didn't hang around there long after that. Knowing people were looking for us, and having an idea of who they might be, provided a powerful incentive to disappear fast.

Quickly but cautiously we headed back up into the crypt and out of the castle; the sight of the unconscious man Seb had fought with brought an uncomfortable weight to the reality of our situation.

Fortunately, the full temper of the storm still raged above, lashing us with hard stinging rain that once again had me drenched in seconds. This time however, I was grateful for it. The howling of the wind, clashes of thunder and the incessant hiss of the torrential down pour served well to mask any and all sound we made as we darted for the cover of the castle bridge.

Hiding under its shadowy arch gifted us a moment to breathe and plan our next move.

'What now?' I whispered to Seb.

'We head for my father's house!' he replied without any hesitation, *'It is little more than two kilometres from here, over that way to our left. With a bit of luck we can disappear into the forest before anyone see us, get the information our secretive financer requires and be on our way back to Berlin before the little birds strike up the dawn chorus!'*

Putting it like that he made it all sound so simple, as though we could be back in Berlin by lunchtime that day, leaving little trace of us ever having been in Wewelsburg at all. Too bad it didn't quite work out that way!

As I was about to move from cover, Seb quickly pulled me back and motioned for us to be silent as he pressed himself against my side of the bridge arch. Seconds later, three men came running down the steps to our right and headed into the crypt; a sure sign that the unconscious man within must have woken up.

'Now is our chance!' he commanded, half dragging me back out into the rain.

Dashing across the lower courtyard, we jumped over a low wall and disappeared into the sinister forest that awaited us on the other side.

We ran none stop for a good few minutes; blindly navigating our way through a maze of trees and rocks made treacherously slippery by the unrelenting rain.

By the time we stopped to catch our breath, I felt like I'd been launched through a pinball machine. Caked in mud from falling over repeatedly, full of cuts and bruises from the inhospitable shrubbery and, worst of all, I somehow felt even wetter than before, if that was at all possible.

'I do not think we were followed,' said Seb through deep intakes of air.

'Do you think those guys are members of the Order then?' I asked him.

'Members of what Order?' he asked with genuine query.

'The Order of the Death's Head of course,' I replied with confounded irritation.

'What, Himmler's knights?' he near choked in disbelief, *'What could possibly have led you to such an outlandish assumption?'*

'Oh I don't know, how about the fact that we were being watched by a security camera and then they just happened to appear,' I patronisingly explained, feeling as if Seb had just forgotten the last half hour of the night.

To this he simply gave me a look of pitying amusement and laughed, slapping a hand down exhaustedly upon my shoulder.

'My dear Mr Keeldan, I do believe that lack of sleep has allowed your imagination to run wild. Order of the Death's Head indeed,' he chuckled to himself. *'No, I think it is safe to say that they were mostly likely just the castle security guards, after us for trespassing where we should not have been.'*

'Seb, what are you talking about, did you not see what was on that door down there?' I asked in pure bewilderment, *'If they were simply security guards and the camera belonged to them, how do you explain the emblem of the Death's Head Order being on the metal door?'*

Now it was his turn to look confused.

'I am afraid I do not understand. Why do you think that emblem belongs to them?' he asked with a scowl of concern.

'Because Archer bloody well said so in his journal that's why,' I snapped at him.

In the moment of silence that passed between us, it appeared as if we both had suddenly realised something, as I saw my expression mirrored upon Seb's face.

For me it was the realisation that Seb hadn't known about Archer's opinion of the symbol, the old man having arrived at it only after the two had parted ways; something that provided an explanation for the confusion of our conversation. What his revelation was I could not tell, for all he said to me was;

'Show me the journal!'

Seeking some shelter beneath a rocky outcrop in the hillside, I passed back to him the piece he had not long ago given to me and guided him to the relevant pages. Then I just watched as the colour drained from his face.

'What's wrong Seb, what's this all about,' I pushed him eventually. *'Archer wrote that you once asked him if he knew of this symbol. How did you know of it but not what it represented?'*

'I...I think in my heart I did know, I just did not want to believe it was true,' his shoulders sank as he slumped heavily against the cold rock, rolling his head back to look sightlessly at the sky, *'So obvious really,'* he exhaled with a weary laugh, *'I am a fool for dismissing the evidence seen even with my own eyes. Perhaps I just never thought about it the way Archer did? You see –'*

'Shhh!' I cut him off, positive I had just heard a distant voice on the wind.

'What is it?' he asked stubbornly.

'I thought...I thought I heard voices approaching,' I whispered in response, my ears still straining to confirm if I was right.

'Impossible, you couldn't possibly have heard anything over this wind,' was what I expected him to say, so used to people being sceptical about how good my hearing actually was. *"Ears like a shit house rat"* is what my mum used to say, and she wasn't far off. So keen was my hearing that I could hear a whisper through a brick wall without even trying.

To my surprise however, Seb said nothing of the sort. In fact, for a while, he actually said nothing at all; affording me the silence I needed to hear more clearly over the storm.

'Anything?' he asked eventually.

'No, I think we are okay.'

'Perhaps we should move on just the same,' he said insistently, shaken from whatever melancholy state he'd relaxed into before, *'we are still in the shadow of the castle and, whoever those men are, I do not relish the thought of being caught.'*

Very much in agreement with him, we were soon back on the move, though thankfully at a much more cautious pace.

As we picked our way silently through the trees, a shadow of concern crept into my mind sparked by something Archer had mentioned in his journal. What if these people were somehow connected to the Masons?

He'd written of how the shape of the castle was indicative of the Masonic compass symbol, and I recalled a mention of the architect being linked with a Masonic lodge. What if the men weren't members of the Death's Head Order at all but were instead a branch of the Masons? Worse still, what if they were both? It would then have made sense that they were after us if someone had recognised me on the security camera.

Thinking back, it seemed like such a long time ago since I ran from them across the sea that I'd almost forgotten they might still be in pursuit. But that was now no longer the case! The thought played on my mind so much that I was half expecting the men in black suits to appear at any minute.

Then another thought came screaming into mind. What would happen to Kate if I was right about all of this? She had been the one who let us in and left us to roam about. What would they do once they realised this?

Suddenly I found myself weighed down by guilt as I recalled vividly her warm smile. The woman I had spent the night, possibly, flirting with could be about to take the fall for our actions.

Fearing what might happen, I was torn by indecision as to whether I should go back for her or not. I almost stopped at one point to voice my concern to Seb, but sense told me what he would say;

'Calm down and pull yourself together,' and he'd have been right.

There was no point in getting myself all worked up by jumping to conclusions without any proof. After all, she had done nothing wrong. If they'd known enough to be aware of who I was, then perhaps they had wanted us to find the vault so that they could trap us there? It had almost worked too.

I felt the rain begin to ease and the thunder roll further and further away with each rumble. As visibility started to clear, so too did my head. I knew we had a job to do and my overactive paranoia wasn't going to help get it done.

Approaching the edge of the forest, one lingering thought echoed in my mind. A hope that I would one day get the chance to see Kate again; even if it was only to apologise for what we had done.

Day 8 - Wewelsburg, Germany
The Sins of the Father

It had sounded like a nice easy task initially - go to Seb's family home, dig through the archives and find whatever the tattooed man was looking for. In my head I'd pictured us being welcomed into a nice warm house by Seb's family who would offer us tea and biscuits while we searched.

Quite why I thought this though, having heard talk of his family, I cannot honestly say. Perhaps it was just wishful thinking after the night I'd had. Of course, as was becoming an all too regular theme of my life, it wasn't to be so easy.

'So, do any other members of your family speak English?' I asked as we edged our way around the tree line, hoping that there would be at least one to avoid any awkwardness on my part.

That is when I discovered that there was something Seb had decided to withhold from me until then.

'They do, but only my father lives here now,' there was a short pause before he spoke again. A pause that suggested he was debating the wisdom of revealing what he was about to reveal.

'I fear that, before we go any further, there is something you should know,' he began, instantly filling me with a feeling of dread. *'My great grandfather was a member of the SS, a Nazi extremist.'*

'Yes, you told me that before,' I replied, trying to hold back the disdain from my voice.

'Well, he was not the only member of my family that was! In fact it is probably easiest to say that my brother and I are the first Reinhardt's in four generations that have not been Nazi supporters.'

It surprised me that I was actually surprised by this. From the confrontation between him and his brother back in the apartment, I'd figured that Seb was the Nazi supporter and that

353

was why there seemed to be so much animosity between him and his family.

'Hold on,' I said, grabbing his arm and bringing us to a halt, 'I'm confused, if you and Anton are not Nazi followers, but the rest of your family are, then what was all that stuff about you letting your father down? And why did your brother call you an ungrateful bastard? Also, for that matter, why the hell was Anton riding your back over being the leader of an extremist political group when his own father is a Nazi?'

'Anton does not know about father!' he explained somewhat defensively, sharply pulling free of my grasp, 'I only recently found out myself, through linking memories from our childhood to the research I was conducting into the Third Reich. I confronted my father about it one day and it blew up into a great argument when he did not deny my accusations. Instead he actually made things worse by telling me of the plans he had for my party,' I'd obviously touched on a nerve here as his jaw began to clench and his lips quiver into a sneer with growing intensity. 'HE would have turned us toward Neo-Nazism if he had got his way. He said Germany was larger than the present day Federal Republic and needs a revision of the post-war border concessions. "We need a unified state," he said, "Held under one banner, one political party and one police force". What compelled him to believe he had any sway over ME I cannot even imagine.'

His neck strained to contain the seething anger rising to form in his words. His face had gotten so flushed that I half expected to see steam start to rise from him.

He paced short strides back and forth, his previously animated hands shoved sullenly into his pockets, as he tried to regain some composure.

'That was the first time we had spoken in many years,' he then continued a little more calmly. 'When I refused to make such ideals into the political goals for my party, he flew into a rage and we have not spoken since; apart from the call I made to him yesterday of course. Anton simply got a twisted version of this conversation from father, one in which the old bastard omitted to clarify just whom it was who had been arguing in favour of returning the country to fascism. I did not have the heart to tell my brother the truth, especially when I myself wish I had never discovered it,' a haunted look of sorrow draped across his face as he stared off into space. 'The few good memories I

354

had of our childhood were expunged once I began to realise why so many things had been the way they were.'

My head began to pound as I tried to comprehend all he had just said. I'd only asked if his family spoke any English...safe to say that I got a lot more than I'd bargained for in the answer. One thing was for sure though, the poor sod had a really messed up family!

Unable to think of anything worthwhile to say, I simply gave an understanding nod and let the conversation drop. This prompted him to suggest we push on.

'I know I am probably asking the obvious here, but tell me again just why exactly we are sneaking into a house that belongs to your family?' I half whispered to Seb as the pair of us stood hiding in the shadows of a neighbouring garden to the building in question. *'It's bloody cold out here, and I could really do with a piss!'* I added with a degree of pressing discomfort.

Somewhere between entering and exiting the forest, the storm had at last blown itself out, leaving a very damp but very clear night air that was rapidly dropping in temperature.

'Go in the bushes!' was his reply along with a quick turn of his head gesturing towards the shrubbery behind us, *'I never did like the neighbours on this side of us anyway. He always got us into trouble with my father and She used to let her dog piss on my bike if I left it outside our garden gate. If you go in their garden it will be justified payback.'*

'Sod Off!' I said in disgust, *'I'm not a bloody dog, and besides it feels like minus five out here or something. I could end up with frost bite,'* I physically shivered at the thought, *'Not my idea of a good time pal, I can tell you that for nothing!'*

Minus five was probably a bit of an exaggeration for that time of year, but it was still getting bloody cold and the thought of exposing myself to the elements was not one I chose to dwell on. Being stood in soaking wet clothes did not help my situation at all though.

'Well then you will just have to hold it or go in your trousers then because the house is off limits,' the faintest of smirks crossing his lips just caught my eye as he spoke.

'So much for being different from the rest of your family,' I said with a disgruntled tone of mock accusation, *'The apple really doesn't fall far from the tree does it, you bloody toilet Nazi!'*

It was an attempt to make light of an awkward subject, but it also hid the reservations I still had about it.

'What are we waiting for anyway?' I queried, trying to take my mind off of my bulging bladder.

'That!' he said, pointing towards one of the upper windows where a light had just gone on, *'Regular as clockwork. Every night he gets up at 2am to relieve himself.'*

'Agh, you had to go and say it didn't you?' I groaned as my bladder passed the point of no return.

'Aim for the roses, the old hag smells them every morning,' he said over his shoulder as I scrambled past.

A moment of sweeter relief I doubt I have ever had as the discomfort I'd been suffering just poured away. When I returned to my companion's side, with a calculated pat on his back to wipe my hand, I practically felt lighter than air.

'Feeling better?' he asked through gritted teeth as he tried to work out whether I was left or right handed.

'More than you could possibly imagine,' I replied with a satisfied grin. *'I'm guessing that was your father getting up then?'*

'It was.'

'And that's what we've been waiting for?'

'Right again. Had we gone in before this, our chances of being caught would have been much greater. Once he goes back to bed he will be out until the morning,' Seb then scoffed almost to himself as he added. *'His predictability is almost painful; you could set your watch by his regimented habits. What is the saying,* "You can take the man out of the military, but cannot take the military out of the man"*?'*

I could be wrong but, as far as I was aware, 2am pissing was not part of any military training I'd ever heard of. But I got the gist of what he meant.

'So what now then?' I asked restlessly.

'Now we wait for him to return to sleep.'

Twenty minutes later, when all had fallen quiet once more, Seb at last gave the nod for us to move on the house. Approaching the back door he stood to one side and said;

'Let us see if you can make it four for four.'

His automatic assumption that my skills could get us past the lock did annoy me a little, and I wondered how he had planned to get in had I not been so fortunately gifted. Thankfully I was and did manage to make short work of that much weaker lock.

It was due to having been locked out of my house one too many times due to a lost or forgotten key by the way. The reason I learnt how to pick locks that is. I just thought I ought to clarify this as people always think the worst otherwise, especially of someone brought up in Liverpool.

Anyway, as the last tumbler clicked in to place and the door gently swung open, I was greeted by the sound of warning bleeps, telling of an intruder alarm about to go off. Before I could react to this though, Seb dashed silently past me and disappeared into the house. Seconds later the bleeping stopped and he re-appeared with a self-satisfied grin on his face.

'The sentimental old fool still uses the birth date of my mother!'

I don't know what bothered me more, the thought of what would have happened if his father had decided to change the code, or the fact that Seb had known there would be an alarm but hadn't decided to warn me about it.

'Well, okay then,' I said softly, stepping through the doorway and quietly closing it behind me, *'At the risk of sounding like a stuck record, what now?'*

I followed Seb through the house at his request; both of us making every effort to stay as silent as humanly possible. At one point, I even caught myself doing the over the top sneaky walk that you'd expect to see in an Inspector Clouseau movie; wincing at even the faintest of noises as I tried to extinguish the sound of my own breathing.

As we moved through to the front of the house, I marvelled at how the place looked like a small mansion. Expensive artworks hung up on the walls, polished walnut furniture filled every room and the kitchen was the size of the whole ground floor of my house.

'Talk about how the other half live,' I muttered to myself.

Eventually we came to a grand double stair case that dominated the entrance hall area and, standing in awe of it all, I had to ask.

'Why would you ever want to leave a place like this?'

'My father is a retired army general, he treated us as if we were recruits. This was not a home for us, it was a military base,' he answered in pained whispers. *'Come on, it is this way!'*

'What is?' I queried.

'My father's secret study,'

He crossed over towards a door under one side of the staircase and quietly disappeared through it. Following him

357

closely, into what I was half expecting to be a small cupboard, I looked over his shoulder as he turned on his torch and illuminated a narrow stone staircase that dropped steeply beneath the floor of the house.

I really was starting to get the feeling that I was destined to spend half of my journey under the damn ground.

'He spent all of his free time down here when we were growing up,' he said as we began to descend down the steps, *'It was always off limits to the rest of us though, even to my mother.'*

'But the door wasn't locked,' I commented in confusion, *'how the hell did he keep it off limits?'*

'With fear!' he replied levelly, *'The door never had to be locked because his word was law. If he said "Do Not Go In There", we did not go in.'*

'You mean to say that you never once took a peek at what was down here?'

'No, I did look once,' he said in a far off tone. *'It is a memory I repressed a long time ago; one I could never fully recall until tonight. The memory that has made me realise just who my father really is.'*

'Why, what did you see?'

'This!'

As we reached the bottom of the stone steps, we were confronted by a large metal door that bore a symbol embossed into its surface; one that I had seen before!

'That...it's....the symbol from the vault? But that was....that means....,' I stammered as my brain tried to play catch up with my own words.

'That my father is a member of The Order of the Deaths Head,' Seb finished off for me, his voice void of all emotion. *'Yes, it would seem Himmler's Knights of the Round Table still exists to this very day. Now you understand my shock when I learnt tonight of the connection Archer had made to the symbol. It triggered the memory I had of having seen it before, a long time ago as a boy here on this very door.'*

'Jesus Seb, I know you said your family were Nazi supporters and that your great grandfather was in the SS, but this is something else. This means that your father is in league with the people who are after us.'

'That is why we must now, more than ever, be swift and silent about our business,' he cautioned.

358

'I don't believe this, it's like we've just ran out of the frying pan and sneaked into the fire, and now we are walking into a dead end,' I protested, beginning to feel rather uncomfortable with the whole situation.

'Believe me Tom, no one could be more surprised by all this than I am.'

'Yeah well...' I paused suddenly as something clicked in my mind. *'Hang on a sec. If you only just remembered about seeing this symbol down here, what made you ask Archer if he knew what it stood for?'*

'Because that symbol has plagued my nightmares ever since the night I saw it, but the trauma that followed must have caused me to block the rest of it out,' he sounded a little unsure of this, but not in a way that made me think he was lying about it. *'By the time I met Archer, I knew of the symbol from a recurring dream I had been having. I felt I had seen it somewhere before, but could not remember where. It was only upon seeing it again tonight on a similar door down in the vault that my memories began to fall back into place...worst of all is knowing now what the symbol means too.'*

'What happened that made you forget it?' I asked out of a morbid sense of curiosity.

'My father happened!' his tone was as stern as the shadows on his face. *'He found me down here looking at the door and flew into a violent rage. Dragging me back up those steps, without even a chance to say goodbye to my mother and brother, he threw me into his car and drove me away from my home,'* this was a painful story for him to tell, one that showed me a side of him I had not expected. *'For hour upon hour I sat in silence, not even allowed to cry for fear of being struck again, until eventually we reached a military boarding school. In the dead of night I was taken to this place and accepted without question. All he said to me was that I had to learn some discipline and that it was for my own good...then he left me there. I was eight when it happened and I lived there until I was sixteen.'*

As I listened to his words, and shared a part of his grief in imagining how traumatic the experience must have been for him as a child. I started to feel a growing acceptance toward him, an insight into why he was the way he was. I began to see him less as an impossible prick and more as a man who was the result of a cruel upbringing.

I'm not sure it made me like him any better, but it gave me an understanding of him; an extra degree of tolerance towards his abrasive personality. And boy was I going to need it in the times to come.

'For the first year I was not allowed home,' he continued with a faint catch in his voice, *'and I later discovered that he had forbidden my mother to come to visit me. At the time however, I was left to believe that she too had abandoned me. Two weeks I cried myself to sleep at night, for which I received regular beatings from both the other students and the teachers who said I had to toughen up. When eventually I was let home for a visit I was changed; cold and emotionless like a robot. I actually found myself longing to go back to the school as I could not stand being around the man who had done this to me. This was no longer my home and they were not my family,'* he said with a nod back up the stairs. *'One thing was for sure though...I never even looked at the door under the stairs again until this night.'*

I stood looking at him, trying to comprehend how such an event must have affected him.

'And I thought I'd had a rough childhood!' I said to myself.

It's a funny moment between men, when one learns a sad story about the others life. You want to empathise and offer support but don't really know how without coming across as being a bit gay. Not that being sensitive, or gay, is necessarily a bad thing, it's just awkward for a lot of men to show a softer side to other men; at least it always has been for me anyway.

A male Lion never shows any weakness to another male outside his own pride, because there is always the chance that it will then be used against him.

The best I could offer him was an understanding pat on the shoulder, something I actually believe he appreciated more than any words I could have spoken.

'Well, now at least I see why you are so happy to screw over your old man, and I can't say as I blame you for it either,' I said with a friendly smile. *'So, how are we going to get through this door then?'* I then offered as a way back into the present, *'It looks like it has an electronic key pad, the same kind as the one in the vault did, which means that my lock picks are useless here!'*

'This is not a problem,' he said with a grin that just barely managed to mask his sadness, *'I believe I know the code.'*

'You Believe you know?' I asked sceptically, *'It's not your mother's birthday again is it, surely your father can't be that daft?'*

'No, unfortunately he is not. But, as I have said, he is very predictable.'

'What do you mean?'

'Well, you see, two numbers were claimed by Emil Rudiger to be connected with the Black Sun; 27 and 1818. Himmler died on the 23rd May 1945 and in numerical form that is 230345. That gives us 271818230345. Twelve numbers, twelve spokes on the Black Sun and a lock that requires a twelve digit pass code!'

'And you know that they are the numbers he would pick?' I queried.

'No, not for certain at least,' he admitted quite calmly, *'but again, he is very predictable.'*

'Hang On, what kind of logic is that?' I wheezed in total disbelief, *'You can't just go picking random numbers out of the air simply because they fit a pattern you believe makes some kind of sense. I mean, what if you are wrong?'*

'Well if I am then entering these numbers will likely trigger an alarm and we will be caught!'

'This isn't funny Seb!' I snapped, angered by the weakness of his reasoning, *'What makes you think that his pass code would have anything to do with the Black Sun when you claim that you didn't know he was a member of the Death's Head before tonight? What if the last part should be Himmler's birthday, or Hitler's birthday? Christ sake, it could even be my birthday for all you know!'*

I couldn't believe that after all we had been through that night the whole operation was now dependant on the success of 12 numbers he'd practically pulled out of thin air. I mean, how did he even know that the key pad required 12 digits? It was ludicrous!

'Well do you have any better ideas?' he asked with a patronising shrug, to which I had no answer, *'No? Then I guess we shall just have to try my code and hope for the best!'*

I couldn't watch as he began to enter the numbers; closing my eyes and plugged my ears in anticipation of the inevitable alarm that was sure to follow. I could almost feel every digit he hit in sequence as a dull thud in my mind that got stronger each time and left my whole body wrought with tension.

It was like witnessing the countdown to the explosion of a bomb; a countdown to a moment of pure suspense...2!..3!...0!....3!.....4!......5!.......ENTER!

Anxiously I held my breath as I heard the soft beep of the final button. The entering of the code had taken him seconds in reality, but it had felt more like minutes and the silence afterwards seemed to last even longer.

A little green bulb lighting up on the keypad, followed by the sound of unseen locks retracting, left me in stunned disbelief as it revealed the success of Seb's code. When no alarm sounded and no angry voices came running our way, I allowed myself to breathe again; quietly thankful that, on this occasion, I had been wrong.

'You see! What did I tell you?' he said smugly.

'Yeah, Yeah, whatever! Let's just get this over with shall we,' I replied, pushing past him and adding under my breath, *'I don't think I take much more of this shit!'*

The surprisingly light door gave way with ease against my hand, swinging open gently to reveal the room beyond. It was not what I had been expecting!

In my mind I'd envisaged us walking into a shrine of Nazism with swastika bearing flags hanging from the walls, old World War 2 weapons and military uniforms displayed on mannequins and maps of the world showing the planned spread of Nazi power; like a blood red virus radiating out from Germany and infecting all other countries.

But to my utter surprise there was none of that. In fact apart from a computer terminal in the centre of the room and a couple of filling cabinets, there was barely anything in there at all.

The walls were white, the floor was white and the ceiling was, well, concrete grey actually, but it all made for a singularly depressing room.

'What kind of "study" is this?' I scoffed, strangely disappointed, *'It looks more like solitary confinement in a psycho ward!'*

'This is my father all over,' Seb insisted as he appeared at my side, *'plain and simple. The decoration of the house above was at the hand of my mother. Father always believed that, especially in the work place, "things" only served as a distraction to a productive work ethic. "A white room with a desk offers the best environment for keeping your focus", is what he used to say.'*

When imitating his father, Seb pressed his chin into his neck to elicit a deep tone from his voice, adding a degree of emotionless pomposity to it as he did. I wondered to myself if it was at all what the man sounded like or was simply a vengeful mockery of him.

'All it offers me is the desire to slit my wrists, just to spray a bit of damn colour round the place!' I responded with a deadpan sarcasm.

Apparently ignoring my statement, Seb headed for the computer terminal and sat himself down.

'Okay, here we go,' he said producing a data stick from his pocket.

'Where did you get that?' I queried, *'And hang on, how did you even know there would be a computer terminal down here? I thought you'd never been beyond the door before?'*

'It was a gift from our mysterious benefactor,' he answered without taking his attention away from the monitor screen, *'I guess he knew more than he let on!'*

I didn't like what he wasn't telling me about this guy. Seb seemed to enjoy keeping me in the dark, but for what purpose?

'How do you plan to get into that thing anyway? Surely it requires a password or something, or are you just going to magic it out of your arse like the last one?'

'It requires a fingerprint scan actually,' he stated with cool disinterest, pointing to a little device sat to one side, *'a practically unbreakable security system!'*

'Then how the hell *do you plan to get in if it's unbreakable?'* I demanded irritably, *'Did the guy give you one of your father's fingers too?'*

'Nothing so gruesome I assure you, and I only said "practically" unbreakable!' he replied with a sly grin.

'You're a hacker then?' I said as the penny dropped.

'Well, let us just say that I know a thing or two about a thing or two when it comes to computers,' he said as playfully as a cat toying with a mouse.

'Ha! And they try to say that politician's aren't all crooked bastards!'

Deciding to just leave him to it, I started rummaging through the, thankfully unlocked, filing cabinets. Sadly, most of the stuff in them was written, not surprisingly, in German and therefore could have been anything from plans for world domination to recipes for chicken noodle soup for all I could tell.

I did come across some old architectural plans that depicted, what I assumed was, Himmler's vision of Wewelsburg as his bastion at the "centre of the world". It showed the castle's triangular shape as a spear pointing northwards with a long straight road behind it acting as the shaft. At the tip of the spear, the North Tower stood central to a semi-circular estate of other buildings radiating out from its point.

'The guy was defiantly a whack-job!' I mused to myself.

'This is incredible!' cried Seb in excitement, calling my attention back to him and the computer.

'What's incredible?' I asked eagerly.

'The database held on this computer. There are hundreds and hundreds of files here that detail everything Himmler did or had planned to do. Every secret expedition the SS conducted is in here; their search for Shangri-La in Tibet, their plans for the castle and even their research into something called Vril energy.'

'Hey, Archer mentioned that in his journal,' I interrupted, moving closer to the screen while reaching for the book. *'Yeah, see here, look.'*

'Hmm, a green energy source? How strange,' he said ponderously as he read the page I presented to him, before going on to open the computer file linked to the research, *'it only talks here about the theory behind its malevolent power. I guess they never actually found it!'*

'Yes! I mean no! I mean, well they must have,' I said insistently, tripping over my own words as a sudden realisation burst into my head. *'Look at the fire back in the crypt.'*

'What about it?' he said with sceptical intrigue.

'Well it erupted into a green noiseless flame that illuminated the otherwise bare stone on the pedestals. That must have been the result of this Vril energy!' I said excitedly.

He looked at me as one would a talking grapefruit; that is with a combination of surprise and disbelief.

'Somehow Tom,' he began in a patronising tone, *'I think if the Nazi's had harnessed a power as strong as this Vril Energy is supposed to be, I doubt they would have used it just to make a quiet green flame!'*

'Well, how else do you explain what I saw then smart arse?' I fired back, suddenly realising the absurdity of what I had just said, but feeling reluctant to admit it.

'I do not know,' he replied with an impatient waving of his arms. *'Aside from the possibility that you were taking hallucinogenic drugs at the time, perhaps the vacuum you described created a negative pressure in the room which could cause the lack of noise, and the green flame may have been produced by copper particles in the dust getting kicked up into the fire which would burn green.'*

'So, what you're saying then is that someone must have been constantly topping up the pit with tonnes of copper particles then?' I challenged in a slow drawn out tone, *'because otherwise the trick would eventually wear itself out and opening the vault would no longer work.'*

'Oh look Tom, I do not know how it worked because I was not there to see it myself,' he snapped at me with a dismissive wave of his hand, *'I can only speculate an answer based on the information you have given me. There are too many factors for our limited knowledge about the place to fully comprehend. But, however it works, I very much doubt it has anything to do with this Vril energy!'*

'Fine, whatever,' I replied childishly. *'Just...just get on with finding the stuff we came for will you, so we can get the hell out of here!'*

With that I turned back towards the filing cabinets in a sulk; annoyed that I'd just allowed myself to be humiliated in such a way.

A little while later he piped up again.

'Tom! Tom, come quick, you must see this.'

'See what?' I groaned peevishly, still licking my wounded pride.

'Look here, at this file. It is about St. Oswald's Stone. Archer was not on a wild goose chase looking for it in Europe, he was just looking for it in the wrong place.'

'What, seriously?' I asked excitedly.

Snapped out of my mood by the thought of such a discovery, I found myself vacantly staring at a screen full of foreign words.

'Christ sake, I can't read sodding German Seb, what the hell does it say?'

'Yes of course, my apologies. This here is purportedly a lost page from one of Hitler's diaries. In it the Fuhrer talks of when he was imprisoned at Landsburg Prison in Munich, after the failed Beer Hall Putsch coup. It reads;

'Landsburg was a relaxed prison, barely even a prison at all. More like a secluded break away from the pressures of political life. The guards were appropriately respectful of my position and many a supporter to the cause. I was given free roam of the grounds and granted a steady flow of visitors. One was a young man from Schaffhausen in Switzerland, come to join with us. He came to me to pledge his allegiance and offer a gift of respect in the form of a precious jewel hanging from a chain. Of brilliant blue it was and alluring to the eye. A family heirloom he said

365

and I accepted it as an acceptable offering of his loyalty. It was brought into his family by his great grandfather who had brought it from England, a relic of a great healing king.'

The writing style was terrible yet I could have listened to it over and over, for it contained the answer to a mystery Archer had been unable to solve.

'So Oswald's piece DID come to Germany like Archer believed, just not in the way he believed,' I said with a burst of excitement.

'Indeed, it seems both Archer and Himmler looked to Hildesheim mistakenly. Incredible then that it should have come via Switzerland instead. I wonder the identity of this man who brought it from Schaffhausen?'

'Schaffhausen...Schaffhausen?' I repeated again and again to myself, trying to grasp why the name sounded so familiar, *'Hang about! Archer mentioned that place back in the first piece of his journal.'*

Quickly I rooted out the piece in question and scanned through to the section where he'd explained how he came to believe Hildesheim was the most likely resting place of the relics.

'Yeah look, here we go. He says here, "I have discovered that no fewer than four other claims for the possession of St. Oswald's head have been made throughout history in continental Europe; Schaffhausen in Switzerland, Utrecht in the Netherlands, Echternach in Luxembourg and Hildesheim in Germany". *He discarded Schaffhausen as a likely location because it was the only place not connected in some way to St. Willibrord, who he believed may have taken the relics from England. Talk about being unlucky,'* I said with a sympathetic wince. *'The one place he dropped from interest turns out to be the one place he should have chosen.'*

'I am afraid I cannot agree with you there Tom,' he said with a look of pity toward me. *'You see if he had gone there instead, he would have no more found the Stone than he did in Hildesheim. Nor would he have then made the connection to Himmler that led him to me. Therefore, I would say that it was in fact quite lucky that he made this mistake, otherwise we would not be here right now making the discoveries we have.'*

'And wouldn't that be a shame?' I thought to myself wickedly.

'What did Hitler do with the piece?' I asked, in an attempt to change the subject.

'Well, it says here that he kept it on him at all times, as he felt he could draw energy from it. He even goes on to credit it with being a lost piece of the Aryan legacy that found its way to him; the vessel of their return to power meant to grant him the strength to do what he must. This proves what I have been saying all along to be true!' he said, seeming quite full of himself as he slapped his hand, quietly, against the table, *'Hitler did change in prison. He became the evil man that history remembers because of having this Stone! It affected him, made him more impressionable to Himmler and the Thule Society, but at the same time it boosted his natural leadership qualities over those with weaker minds. I knew it, I knew I was right!'*

'Yes, yes okay, but what happened to that piece? Where is it now?' I asked, trying to avoid getting into THAT argument again, *'That's what we need to know Seb!'*

'Yes of course, you are right,' he admitted, shaking himself free from whatever award ceremony daydream he'd been having, before scanning through the rest of the file. *'I am afraid it does not say here anything about that, only that Himmler requested to borrow it on the grounds of aiding his research into the Holy Grail and its ability to turn the tide of the war. Apparently Hitler agreed to this, desperate for a way to destroy the unrelenting allied forces. It seems that this would likely be the cause of his eventual downfall. Without the Stone, the powers it had granted would have no longer been with him. This could explain why an otherwise brilliant tactician fell so completely through a series of idiotic mistakes; ones that culminated in him stranding himself in the bunker where he died, surrounded by his enemies who overwhelmed a scattered and unstructured defence in Berlin.'*

I gave up. He seemed more interested in vindicating his own theories than finding out the information that could be of use to us. He seemed as giddy as a school boy.

'Fascinating,' I drolly replied. *'Give me a shout if you find anything useful.'*

With that, I turned back to my cabinets once more.

'There are literally hundreds of files in here, it would take a week to sort through them all!' he said aloud a short while later.

'Yeah that's great,' I replied distractedly. *'Just hurry up and get what your man wanted so we can get the hell out of here will*

you. Something just doesn't feel right about all this...It's been too easy!'

Having become bored of reading through files that I couldn't actually read, my mind had begun to over think our situation and let the fingernails of paranoia dig in.

'Fine! I am downloading it all now alri...,' he paused mid speech, *'Tom! Quick, look at this!'*

'What now?' I grumbled with exasperation, expecting another self-serving discovery to be explained.

'I think I have just found out what happened to the Holy Grail!'

'Seriously?' I asked with shocked excitement, *'Well, what does it say, what happened to it? Does it say where it is now?'*

'Okay, give me a moment,' he replied testily, his eyes squinting to focus back on the screen.

He then began to read through the file quietly to himself; keeping me on tender hooks, desperate to know what answers were held within.

'Right, here we go!' he sounded aloud, *'Well, as we thought, the Grail was found by Otto Rahn in the ruins of Monsteguer. How and why it came to be there the report does not say. What it does say however, is that Rahn at first tried to hide its discovery from Himmler and the Nazis, but was betrayed by a man he had confided in as a friend. A man who does not seem to be named here but is revealed as having been an aspiring officer in the SS. As reward for his loyalty, the officer was promoted up into the echelons of Himmler's "Holy Knights" and entrusted with the study and safe keeping of the Grail. It seems here that he was also tasked with the retrieval of the Stone and with the silencing of Rahn as well.'*

'So wait, not only did this guy betray his friend's secret, but he then went on to orchestrate his death too? What a complete bastard!' I interrupted in disgust.

'Agreed,' said Seb in response, *'One would not need enemies with friends such as this man.'*

'What happened next then? I mean, I guess we can safely say that it was brought to the castle, but what happened after that?'

'I am about to get to that if you will let me,' he rebuked. *'It goes on to say how the Stone WAS brought back to the castle and given over to scientific study. It seems they believed it was an object of power from a place called "Agartha" where an advanced race of beings dwelled. Their study was primarily*

368

aimed at discovering a way to harness the Stones secrets to aid in the war effort.'

'Agartha? Why do I recognise that name?' I asked myself aloud.

'Could it be yet another thing Archer wrote of which you only partially remember?' Seb seemed to sigh, as if he grew tired of the glacial speed at which my memory appeared to be working that night.

'Yes of course,' I said, disregarding his tone, *'but it wasn't in his journal.'*

As the realisation came to me, I quickly dove into my satchel to retrieve the research book Archer had given me on the night of our meeting and feverishly began flicking through the pages.

'Ah, here we go. Agartha! Archer's research had led him to believe it could be one of two things. Either it was just another name for Shambhala (like Shangri-La) or it was the moralistic opposite of that place; sort of a hell to Shambhala's heaven.'

'Hmm, now you mention it,' he offered, eyes widely staring in to a faraway memory, *'I think I recall reading some Nazi conspiracy theory that talked of this. There is a legend surrounding Hitler's desire to request aid from the King of Shambhala in his fight against the Allies. When he was turned down, as the story goes, he then tried to find Agartha instead; believing that its inhabitants would be more inclined to help him. The validity of this tale is of course highly debatable,'* he added with an educated dismissal. *'However, having seen it mentioned here and in Archer's research, I find myself inclined to believe there must be at least some truth to it.'*

'Come on Seb, you can't be serious?' I looked imploringly at him, *'We're talking in the realms of a Jules Verne novel here, with lost worlds and hidden civilisations. Don't you think it's more likely that, being based as it is on Buddhist mythology, these stories speak more of the spiritual rather than the physical?'*

'Tom, if you truly believed that for one second, why on earth would have come all this way?'

This singular, surprisingly accurate, insight swiftly cut me down and shut me up. I had no answer to his question.

'Anyway, regardless of what we believe,' he continued, *'the Nazis believed in it enough to warrant a comprehensive study of the Stone being performed. What follows here is a lot of scientific results that basically show their tests to be inconclusive. They knew the Stone had power, they just did not*

know what kind or how to unlock it. It does mention here about Himmler acquiring Hitler's smaller Stone for comparative studies though. Their conclusion was that, whilst they were both of the same material, they were somehow very different,' he considered this last part quite ponderously to himself for a while.

'Look, this is all really fascinating Seb, but what does it say about the fate of the Stones?' I insisted eventually.

'Nothing,' he revealed quite blankly after scanning down to the end of the document. *'It ends with something about the unfortunate realisation that they could have done with Rahn not being dead, as he was likely one of the few people who could have made sense of it all.'*

'Well isn't hindsight a bitch!'

'Indeed!'

'Is there not more information in another file maybe? What about in these filing cabinets? All the stuff's in German so I don't know what I'm looking at.'

'I would imagine those files are just redundant hard copies of what is contained within this computer,' he said, turning back to the screen and resuming his search. *'Perhaps though, there is more in one of these other folders.'*

I watched as every folder he opened seemed to spawn a dozen more sub-folders; each containing more files than any sane person would ever have the patience to trawl through.

'Vas De?' he exclaimed all of a sudden.

'What is it?' I asked, futilely trying to see what he had seen.

'There is a file here with Archers name on it!' he replied in a slow dream like state of disbelief.

'What!! How is that possible?' I cried out.

'I do not know but... schizer! There is one on me too!' he stared with slack jaw at the screen, a look of total incomprehension haunting his face.

'Jesus Seb, what the hell is going on here? How do they know about Archer and why the hell is there one about you? What do they know?'

'Everything! They know all about Archer's research, about his quest...Mine Got, it is true then.'

'What is?' I asked tensely.

'The Order of the Death's Head, it really does exist and still operates to this day....and that means my father really is one of them,' he said with a genuine sadness. *'These files talk of how the Order came to be, more so in the wake of the war than before it. They tell of how the descendants of Himmler's original*

370

knights continued the research their fathers began and now believe that all the Stones are pieces of the Holy Grail. One main artefact whose power cannot be truly awakened until it is made whole again.'

His eyes darted quickly from side to side as he read the text faster and faster. He looked like someone witnessing a horrific accident that is unable to look away. Then he looked like was about to be sick.

'There are emails here from someone who has been providing them with information about Archer.'

'Who?'

'The person never identifies them self, saying only that they are the product of an old alliance re-made. Whoever they are it must be someone who was close to Archer, someone who knows him well enough to give such detailed reports,' he turned to me with a sullen look of dread, *'I fear this means that our friend has a traitor in his camp.'*

'Perhaps that's why Archer tore up his journal and sent it away?' I offered, trying to stay positive, which was difficult given the circumstances, *'Maybe he found out that he'd been betrayed and that's why he vanished?'*

'Your words are more accurate than you realise,' he said upon, somewhat reluctantly, turning back to the screen, *'The final piece of correspondence with this person talks of their belief that their cover has been blown and that Archer has gone to ground. It is dated two months ago.'*

'Shit! That's right about the time I received Archer's letter,' I stated, trying to piece together the timeline.

'They have been hoping he might show up back in Berlin and so...,' Seb's voice suddenly fell away.

'What's wrong?' I prompted upon seeing the colour drain from his face, *'What does it say?'*

'They have been watching me!'

'Yes my son, we have!'

Day 8 - Wewelsburg, Germany
An Enemy Revealed

The startling sound of a third voice in the room came as a shock to both of us as our heads snapped towards the door where stood a mountainous figure with a very stern expression.

'Vater?' Seb addressed him in a disbelieving tone.

I knew enough pigeon German to instantly realise that the man was Seb's father. Aside from that I could have guessed it anyway from the striking resemblance between the two.

The older man looked more like Anton than his younger son, but there was no mistaking their relation to one another. Though he was slightly taller and had more powerful frame, despite the growing paunch that suggested he had been an active man who was now less so, it was in his face that you couldn't miss the similarities. He had the same sharp, statuesque features that seemed to be a Reinhardt family trait; though his seemed somewhat blunted now by the tells of time.

'You are surprised?' he stated more than asked without a flicker of emotion, *'Your arrogance betrays you Sebastian.'*

In response to this, my companion launched into an angry tirade of heated words, the meaning of which was lost on me spoken as they were in German. As I stood watching this unexpected family reunion though, with morbid fascination, it didn't take a genius to guess that most of them were expletives. Had his father known we were there all along?

'In English boy!' the older man suddenly barked, not in a tone of anger but rather one of command, *'I did not pay for you to study in England only for you to forget your manners. Your friend here has the right to know the trouble you have dragged him into,'*

He stood with military regiment, proud and strong with an authoritative presence...one that practically filled the doorway, blocking any and all chance of a quick escape.

372

'What are you talking about? Tell me you are not part of this madness,' Seb pleaded with a gesture towards the computer screen, effortlessly switching from one language to the other with enviable ease. 'Tell me I am wrong about you.'

It was a challenge more than a request. The curling of Seb's lips as he spoke, the fury that cracked in his voice - he knew what his father was, he just wanted to hear the bastard say it.

'If you wish for me to tell you I am not one of Himmler's Holy Knights and that this computer was put here against my knowledge, I am afraid you shall be very disappointed,' the man's granite like features were nothing short of brutal, without even a single trace of parental warmth cast upon his youngest son.

'It would not be the first time Father,' Seb said venomously.

'You have allowed yourself to be used Sebastian. Blinded by misguided beliefs, you have walked freely into a trap,' that wasn't a word I'd wanted to hear, though I had rather been expecting it.

'What have you done?' my companion sneered, his face twitching either to hold back his rage or his tears...or perhaps both.

'I tried to help you Sebastian. When you called me I knew why you asked for money. I thought that refusing to give it would keep you from coming here. But you simply found another financer, and then you came to take that which was not yours to give away.'

Though easily dismissed it as a mere trick of the light, I'd have sworn there was a slight drooping of his eyes and pursing of his lips that suggested the old man truly did feel some sort of regret towards this.

'Oh, I see, so I guess I should feel grateful to you then for being a bastard all my life,' Seb's voice had a raw edge to it now as he paced from side to side, stopping only to wave and point in aggressive gestures at his father. 'I suppose you were just trying to help me then too?'

'I'm sorry,' I gingerly interrupted, reluctant to draw attention to myself but unable to ignore a question that burned in me, 'just so I know we're all on the same page here, how exactly did you know why Seb asked you for money?'

'Tom, were you not listening before,' Seb snapped at me, almost foaming at the mouth, 'the bastards have been watching me, they know everything we have been doing, right Father?'

He spat the last word out with pure disdain, as if it had left a terrible taste in his mouth.

His father just stared at him with cold eyes, watching him with the same unimpressed look he might have given a child having a tantrum.

'*Did you not wonder why it had been so easy up until now?*' his folded arms rose as he sucked in more ammunition for the cannon that fired his words, '*Did you really think that such secrets would be left so unguarded, that I would not suspect it was you Sebastian who stole my sun disk? You were allowed to get this far, and now you shall go no further.*'

Seb should have felt a pair of eyes burning into the back of his head after this revelation; my eyes, glaring at him with a look that called him a liar. True, he had never told me exactly how he'd come to possess the sun disk, but he had told me that he hadn't been back home till this night.

'*Why father? All of this for what?*' he demanded, completely ignoring my reaction.

'*We are the Holy Knights of the Order of the Deaths Head. Long have we sought to fulfil the dreams of Heinrich Himmler, Grandmaster of the order, who foretold of a time when we would once again walk in the grace of our ancestors. A new age of mankind, purified of all degenerate species until only the true Aryans remained. That was his dream and so became our task; to prepare for the final cleansing in the great battle for humanity.*'

With the horror of seeing a gargoyle come to life, I watched the giant man properly move for the first time. His feet broke free of the ground to mechanically propel him further into the room as his arms unfurled to let his hands grasp at a distant victory.

'*The key to our victory lies within the secrets of that which was stolen from us at the end of the war; that which we now must find again,*' he continued before reaching out a thick set arm to point at the computer, never once taking his eyes of his son. '*That is why you and your friend, Mr Archer, have been under surveillance. His knowledge is vital to us, but he would not give it willingly. Since his disappearance, we have searched for a way to find him and force his cooperation. That, my son, is where you were to come in. It was decided that you would be used as bait to flush him out of hiding and lure him back to Germany. I had hoped you would not come, but it seems you have failed me once again!*'

'What do you mean it was decided? Decided by who?' demanded Seb, his voice cracking into higher pitches.

'By the new head of the Order,' his father seemed to reluctantly confess. *'He seeks to capture Archer and punish me in the process.'*

'Punish You...what for?' I asked, realising too late that I had actually spoken the words aloud.

'For the failure of my plans, and for the weakness of my resolve,' the man admitted at pains, turning his soulless eyes towards me, *'I would not give everything for the Order as he believed I should and now he seeks to prove his claim as a more suited leader than I.'*

'What are you talking about? You are not making any sense Father!'

I was grateful to Seb for pulling back his father's attention. It had been an uncomfortable few seconds having him stare at me. I had been a fly on the wall to this Greek tragedy, and happily so until then. Attracting his attention had been like standing before the penetrating eye of Sauron; my ring of invisibility rendered useless. Needless to say I was happy to slink back out of sight.

The leadership of our Order was mine by right,' his father stated with proud raise of his chiselled chin, *'ever since your great grandfather stepped down and nominated my father his successor and then in turn he too me. He was the founder of the new Order that formed out of the ashes of the war and Himmler's demise. He was the man who brought the Grail to Castle Wewelsburg and through his efforts was deemed a worthy leader in place of the Grandmaster. He was a great man, as was my father who followed in the tradition of strong leaders. I am only glad that they are not here to see the madness I have let in through my failures.'*

There was a moment, just a brief one mind, were I saw him shrink just a little under the weight of this remorse and I found myself feeling a little sorry for him. How many people have ruined their lives trying to live up to the expectations of their parents?

'HE was the one who betrayed Otto Rahn?' Seb asked disparagingly, as if the realisation had sickened him, *'A man he had called a friend before planning his murder! Our definitions of a "great man" are obviously very different Father.'*

'I would not expect you to understand,' the man sneered, returning to his full imposing stature, *'you have always been blinded towards the achievements of this family by some*

misguided sense of moral integrity. Your great grandfather was a hero of the Reich, a true Aryan patriot. You would be lucky to be half the man he was.'

'But of course, how silly of me,' Seb replied mockingly, displaying an uncharacteristic level of sarcasm. *'Obviously I should be proud to be descendant from a murderous bastard whose name our family was too ashamed to even keep!'*

'Insolent boy!' bellowed his father in voice so deep I could feel it in my boots, his arms dropping down to his sides with clenched fists like jackhammers ready to punch through a wall, *'How dare you speak of such things as though they were trivial matters! It was not out of shame that my grandmother changed our family name, it was necessity.'*

A quick temper seemed to be a Reinhardt family trait, as did overly animate arms when riled. The tension in his father's rage had been contagious though, not a muscle moved during the short "David & Goliath" staring match that passed between father and son. I think even the filing cabinets had clenched their drawers in fearful anticipation. Yet Seb, to his credit, had managed to stay resolutely defiant, like a mountain against the howling wind.

It was now his father's turn to pace back and forth with flippant gestures of his arms, as he relaxed enough to regain some control.

'After the war,' he began, turning dismissively from his son, *'our kind was hunted down and persecuted simply for our ties to the SS. Changing our name was the only way to save us from this and she was not alone in doing so. Most of the families of SS officers who lived in this area acted in kind. Those that did not were forced to leave their homes and flee the country like refugees. Our family was spared such an ordeal, and it was those of us that remained who then had the strength and ability to reform Himmler's Order. We may have given up your great grandfather's family name, but out of respect and in honour of him, we took his given name in its place. We are a proud family with a proud history; at least we were until the day you defied me.'*

'Say what you like Father,' Seb responded, seeming a little more cocksure of himself after having been able to stare his old man down, *'but we are spawned from the loins of a coward and a traitor of humanity. He rose to power on the blood of his friend and took the glory for himself.'*

'*NEIN!*' the monster erupted again, standing toe to toe now trying to cower his son with sheer dominating presence, '*It was Otto Rahn who was the traitor! He sought to keep the secrets of the Grail to himself, claiming that it had been lost along with the Templar's. He was too short sighted to see past his dislike of the Nazis and would have rather see us come to ruin than help in our cause. Just as your dislike of me blinded you to the benefits our plans for the country would have brought.*'

'*What benefits?*' Seb spat the words distastefully from his mouth, trying to match his father's aggression, '*Your plans for the return of Nazi power would have only brought ruin!*'

'*Impossible Child!*' the man cried in frustration, throwing his arms up in the air and turning his back to Seb.

The air fell silent for a while and the tension eased a little. Then his father shook his head and made for the door.

'*Father!*' Seb called out, insulted by his attempt to walk away.

He stopped, half in and half out of the room with one massive paw gripping the door frame.

'*I dreamt that one day you would stand beside me as we lead humanity into a glorious new age,*' his said in a calmer voice full of regret before looking back over his shoulder, '*but here you stand now, ready to betray me instead.*'

Seb seemed a little taken back by this and stumbled to find a reply.

'*None of this is making any sense father,*' he eventually managed with a pleading frustration, '*I demand that you explain yourself.*'

'*Twenty seven years I waited. Twenty seven long years of planning undone the day you refused to accept my proposals for your political party,*' the man slowly turned to face us, once again filling the doorway and cutting off our escape. '*We were cheated out of power when the fool Hitler brought our country to its knees; his mind weakened by separation from the stone he had been given. Ever since, we have plotted and schemed and waited; waiting for the day when Himmler's Knights could rise again to succeed were the Nazis failed. You and your brother were kept from our world as part of a long term plan to regain control of this country. You were to be the tools by which we would infiltrate Nazi ideals back into modern society,*' there was a look of longing in him now that bordered on tearful. '*My command of the Army, your brother commanding the police, and you...you were the last piece of the puzzle to fall into place.*

Through our combined connections and positions of power, we would have ensured your place as head of the next government come the election. Such a slow but steady positioning of pieces would have presented us with little resistance in a takeover that none could ever have seen coming. With all aspects of the country's control headed by members of the Order, we would have been able to begin making the necessary changes need to prepare for the prophesied war. But, when you rebelled against me, that one weak link brought my plan to ruin,' his head dropped and shoulders sank, emphasising the sense of wounding in his voice. *'By denying you the knowledge of your ancestry, I allowed the poisons of a diseased world to corrupt your mind. For this show of failure and weakness, unable to even control my own son, I was conspired against and eventually deposed from leadership by a near unanimous vote.'*

Seb stood motionless, frozen with a look of anguish and disbelief on his face at having just learned the full truth of his family secret. Sadly, it was about to get much worse for him.

'Do you expect me to feel sorry for you?' he hissed in words of loathing. *'You planned to use Anton and I like puppets in your sick little show. From the beginning you have forced us down a path chosen by you, to benefit You! Do you not see what you have done? You robbed us of any kind of life we may have chosen for ourselves,'* his voice quivered as he tried to hold back the tears that filled his eyes, *'You...*(the word caught in his throat)...*You have stolen the last twenty eight years of my life and left me questioning everything I have ever known.'*

'Grow up Sebastian!' his father suddenly chastised him, regaining his air of cold, uncaring detachment, *'I gave you and your brother everything you needed to become great men. Your lives were privileged and any regrets you have are of your own making. I knew I should have been harder on you as a boy, I let your mother coddle you too much as I toughened up your brother. Her nature was gentle and acceptable in a woman, but she passed it on to you and in a man it is only a weakness.'*

Seb erratically shook his head, his chin trembling and eyes shut as he retreated slowly back from his father.

'I fear if I had not sent you away when I did,' the man continued with a cruel determination, *'she would have had you walking around in dresses before long. I just wish I had acted sooner.'*

'You Bastard,' Seb sneered through gritted teeth, trying to hold back his hatred. *'You treated us like animals; like puppies*

you could take from a mother's love and train to do as you wished,' his voice was cracking and his breath quickening. *'You are the reason she took her own life. It was You drove us apart!'* his whole body was shaking with rage as he purposefully strode towards his father now. *'She Died Because Of YOU!!'*

With that last furious cry, he launched at his father and attacked him with an anger fuelled blow to the face as his tongue lashed out with vicious words I could once again only imagine the meaning of.

But the bear-like man made no attempt to evade or stop this blow. He accepted it willingly, almost as if he felt he owed this one outburst to his son.

The second blow that came however, was not afforded such success. It was stopped firmly and suddenly by his father's hand catching it in mid-flight.

'I loved your mother, second only to you and Anton,' he said through held back tears as he threw Seb's arm away from him with a resolute force that pushed the smaller man back a few steps. *'Her death was not of my doing, or yours or anyone else's. She had an inoperable brain tumour Sebastian. She feared dying in slow agony, bound to hospitals for her remaining days, and chose instead to end things on her own terms. She knew exactly who I was, what I was, and she stood by my side all the way.'*

'LIES!' Seb cried out, *'She would Not have supported your madness, she hated you for the way you treated us, for the way you drove me away. You made up her illness to save face. If she had cancer she would have told me!'*

'You never gave her a chance to tell you son!' his father's voice softened for the first time and I saw pity in his eyes, *'After the row we had over which university you would go to and what you would study, you left and barely spoke to anyone. You took out your anger and hatred of me on her and Anton by staying away, by never even wanting to be in the same room as me.'*

As Seb stood trying to swallow his tears and shaking his head, refusing to except what he was hearing, his father slowly approached him and put his hands down upon his son's shoulders.

'Your mother was torn between her love for you and her devotion to me,' he continued in the same level tone. *'You forced her to make a choice between us by refusing to have anything to do with me. It was a choice that haunted her to her grave.'*

'*NO! It Was You! Your fault! You Drove us apart!!*' Seb cried again, the pain in his voice heart-breaking as he tried to launch himself feebly towards his father once more.

'*No Son. You did that yourself!*' was the man's regretful reply as he simply held his son and let the flailing blows break against his wall of grief.

Seb continued to rant tearfully, pleadingly at his father, but in his grief his words had fallen back into German. I was glad to be honest, not knowing what he said did make it a little easier to watch...but only a little.

With his hands still grasping his son's shoulders in restrain, Seb's father pushed him back to arm's length and looked him dead in the eye.

'*What happened the last time the two of you spoke? What Happened?*' he repeated aggressively as he shook Seb to stop his flailing. '*You slammed the phone down on her after she asked you to come home and make things right between us. It was her dying wish to see us make amends, to know that she was not leaving behind a broken family. Through your anger you denied her that wish.*'

'*NO!*' cried Seb as he struggled against his father's grip, '*Let go of me!*'

'*THROUGH YOUR ANGER SHE DIED OF A BROKEN HEART!*' his father then yelled, his voice full of pain and anguish.

Those words struck like a knife through Seb's chest causing him to slump to the floor, gasping for air through grief stricken tears.

'*I am truly sorry my son,*' said his father eventually in a calmer, almost kinder, tone, '*but while you can blame me for many things, your mother's death and the guilt you feel for it, is not amongst them.*'

It had been an uncomfortable situation to bear witness to, seeing a man falling apart before my eyes, and even hard to follow at some points. As I stood there on the side-line to it all though, a morbid fascination had bound me to watch.

I truly felt sorry for Seb, seeing him so upset was upsetting in itself. I could only imagine how his father's words had made him feel.

Out of respect, I didn't intrude on the moment for as long as I could. When the sound of his sobbing eventually faded away into remorseful silence though, I turned to his father with a burning question I could no longer contain.

'So, what happens now?'

'Now?' he repeated, looking at me as if I were a minor character who was not meant to have a speaking part in this play, *'Now I keep a promise; one I made to his mother before she died. A promise that I would do all in my power to keep our sons safe from harm,'* he added whilst turning back to look at Seb. *'Right know there is a room full of men upstairs waiting for my signal to capture the two of you and drag you back to our base under the castle.'*

'Wait, hold on a minute,' I piped up again, realising now the significance of the metal door in the Vault. *'If the plan all along was to capture and hold us under the castle, why the* Hell *didn't you make more of an effort to get us whilst we were there? Why let us even come here at all?'*

Without out looking away from his son, he answered my question as if it was Seb who'd asked it.

'You were allowed to come this far for one reason. The man you met in the cafe, the one who sent you here to discover certain "secrets", we wanted to know who he was, who he was working for and why they wanted to know about my grandfather,' his face was like granite once more, and his tone just as cold and hard. *'We thought that by letting you get the information, we could discover their intent; and now we have. You see, we have been monitoring this computer remotely and it seems as though the data stick given to you contained a program designed to search for information on one specific topic. It appears that we are not alone in the search for the Holy Grail!'*

My mouth hung open as I turned to Seb with a furrowed brow.

'Seb, did you know of this?' I asked accusingly. *'You said the man wanted secrets about your family not the Grail. We've been helping the competition for Fucks sake!'*

'Of course I did not know, do you think me a fool?' he snapped, his voice reaching a higher pitch as it caught the misery in his throat. *'Had I known my family was connected to the Grail, I would never have come,'* he added dismissively toward me.

Somehow I doubted the sincerity of his words.

'But if the goal was finding out about this man,' I queried, turning back to my conversation with his father, in an effort to understand a logic here that so far eluded me, *'then why not just*

allow us to think we had been successful and follow us back to our rendezvous with him?'

'I in fact suggested such a course of action myself but, perhaps because of that, the idea was overruled and it was decided our need to find Archer was more important. The Order could therefore not risk letting you slip through our fingers. The man you met also managed to, rather cleverly, lose the agents we had following him. It would suggest he knew he was being watched and so would be unlikely to fall into any trap we tried to set.'

'So what, are we now to be taken away father, is that it?' Seb asked scornfully, lifting his gaze but avoiding his father's eyes.

'That is the desire of our new leader, yes. However, I fear that he would see you dead once your usefulness has been outlived. This I could not bear!'

'Oh I see, so you are going to help us escape then is that it?' Seb replied with bitter scepticism, finally managing to pick himself up off the floor with tears all dried up.

'As I have said, I made your mother a promise Sebastian, and I intend to keep it! Right about now the sedatives I slipped into the keg of beer I served to the men upstairs should be taking effect. I will go and check on them and you two will leave. By the time they wake up and realise what I have done you should have made good use of the head start.'

'Oh yes, I am sure we will have gotten very far indeed,' Seb said in another rare moment of difficult sarcasm. *'I imagine we will have made it all the way back to the bus stop.'*

'Sarcasm is for the weak-minded Sebastian, speak your mind or not at all,' his father scolded him, to which I also took some offence.

'We came by train and bus Father, what good is a head start going to do us when we have to wait until morning for the services to start running again.'

'Well I would have thought that one who breaks into a house as you have done may also be inclined to check the garage for a car to provide a speedy get away,' he said with contained smirk. *'Perhaps you may even be lucky enough to find the keys foolishly left in the ignition.'*

Seb looked completely bemused by this, as if he was struggling to comprehend what his father was up to.

'Why are you doing this? Why now are you trying to help me?' he protested.

382

'You are my son Sebastian!' the man replied with a long pained look, *'Regardless of the bad blood between us and of what you think of me, I have always sought to do my best by you. The way I treated you as a child may have seemed hard, but it served to form the man you are today. A man of strong will and fortitude who stands by his convictions no matter the cost,'* there was, incredibly, a look of genuine pride as he said this. *'You would have now, and always did, make your mother proud. Though I do not agree with where you stand, and it may seem somewhat of a paradox to admit, I too am proud of you. And for what it is worth, I believe you would have made a fine Prime Minister.'*

Both men's eyes were red with the pressure of held back tears. So charged with emotion was the atmosphere that even I began to get a little misty eyed.

'What will happen to you when they find out you let us go?' I asked him, struggling to know how grateful I should be toward the man.

'Oh, I will undoubtedly be cast from the Order and, knowing Dietrich's hatred for me, they will probably arrange an unfortunate suicide for me,' he replied with feigned indifference. *'It does not make much difference now.'*

'Then...,' Seb began with difficulty, as if unsure of the words he was about to speak, *'come away with us,'* he eventually said with a conflicted resolve.

There was a long silence as the pair stared at one another, less like father and son but rather two men struggling to trust that the other isn't about to pull a pistol on him.

'Do you truly mean that Sebastian?' his father asked with a cautious optimism. *'Can there finally be reconciliation between us?'*

Seb recoiled ever so slightly as his father took a step forward, a slight smile cancelled out by the faint shaking of his head. It was painfully obvious that he was struggling with his own conscious, yet less so as to where his decision would land.

'I do not know if I can ever forgive you for all you have done Father,' he rebuked, unable at first to meet his eye, *'but you are all the family Anton and I have left. I may have lost my mother through my hatred, but it is not a mistake I wish to make twice.'*

'Thank you Sebastian,' a hard swallow preceded pursed lips and a stifled cough as the military man tried to keep his emotions in check. *'I regret that we stand too far apart in our beliefs for me to accept your offer, but I can now face the*

coming storm knowing that we have at least made peace enough to stand here as father and son.'

He looked like a man just freed from the shackles of a lifelong regret. His body seemed to relax in such a way as to suggest this meeting had come to a conclusion he could hardly have hoped for.

It was, for want of a better word, rather surreal; like I was watching a dream of how such a meeting with my own father might have one day gone. I say a dream because, for me, Seb's reluctant forgiveness had come far too easily.

Perhaps he simply had not born the same degree of hatred for his father as I had for mine, though quite how I could not imagine. Then, forgiveness never was a concept I was all that familiar with.

'I will ask one thing though,' his father continued, breaking my train of thought, *'what do you plan to do with that data stick?'*

'Well, I do not think we can in good mind hand it back now to its owner,' Seb replied, looking at me for approval. *'Knowing what he seeks, we cannot afford to help someone else on the trail of the Stones. But why do you ask?'*

'I do so because I would request that you consider giving it to me.'

Surprisingly, this did sound like a genuine request rather than a thinly veiled command. One we could have refused.

'Why? What use is it to you?' Seb asked him, still retaining a level of suspicion.

'Not a lot I fear,' his father admitted with a deep sigh, *'but then it might just arm me with a way to save my own life. If I can say that I at least stopped you from stealing the information you came for, and in the process retrieved the data stick, with which we might be able to gain some kind of knowledge of its owner, it might just keep me alive and give me the chance to stall them for you a while longer.'*

'Then it is yours,' Seb said whilst handing it over as I let out a quickly stifled groan of protest. *'WE have learnt more than enough of what it holds tonight,'* he added, shooting me a sideways glance that suggested I had no say in the matter. *'I only hope it brings you better luck than it did us.'*

I understand why he did it and I might possibly have done the same in his shoes. It didn't make it feel any less like a bad idea though. Who knows what other information we may have been able to glean from the data it held?

'*Thank you,*' his father replied, with both surprise and gratitude. '*Now I believe it is time you left. The more distance you can put between us before sunrise, the safer you will be.*'

'*One more thing though,*' I said stepping away from the wall I had tried to blend into for much of this episode, '*there is still something on that stick we need to know about.*'

'*And that would be?*' the older man asked tolerantly.

'*After your grandfather brought the Grail back to the castle, what happened to it?*'

'*It was stolen from us,*' he admitted with a sigh, standing now with guarded regiment.

'*Who by?*' Seb chimed in.

'*In truth we are not completely sure. It happened around the time that Berlin fell to the Allied forces. Himmler had lost focus and ran off to try and bargain with the enemy for his freedom, at the expense of gifting them Hitler and the country. When the Fuhrer learnt of this he became enraged at the prospect of betrayal from one of his closest friends and ordered the return of his stone and the delivery of all other items procured by the SS to his command bunker,*' at least I could find some common ground with this man over his obvious distain for the one time leader of his country. '*He probably hoped that there would be something in amongst those items that could help turn the tide of his imminent defeat.*'

He shifted his weight, looking down to the floor and then back up to where Seb and I now stood closer together, avidly awaiting the answer we sought.

'*My grandfather tried to stop the taking of the Grail but, with the castle forces weakened by the call to defend Berlin, his defence was cast aside by the contingent of troops that came to collect. That was the last he saw of it. It never reached Hitler's bunker; disappeared along with everything else the troops had taken. One report from a surviving solider, who claimed to be a part of that contingent, told of how the transport vehicle was attacked by monks upon their return to Berlin.*'

'*Monks! You mean like as in Buddhist Monks?*' I questioned, unable to keep the surprise from my voice.

'*Indeed.*'

'*Surly that can't be true? A group of monks just appearing out of the blue in the middle of a war, it's ridiculous.*' I scoffed.

'*Not as much as you might imagine,*' said Seb ponderously, having looked to be considering this information more intently than I. '*It is known, after all, that there were such men in Berlin during that time; their bodies were found amongst the dead in the aftermath of the city's fall. They were brought back from Tibet during the SS expeditions to secure relations between the two nations, am I not right Father?'*

'That is correct. Herr Himmler believed that they were also of Aryan decent. However, the likelihood of them attacking an armed transport unit is something I personally find hard to believe. It is much more probable that it was attacked by the advancing Allied troops and looted of it precious treasures,' he looked at me almost as if this had been my fault. *'The Grail could be anywhere now, hidden in America, England, Russia or any of the other Allied countries; probably sitting on a mantel piece in the home of its thief who is ignorant to its identity.'*

'Archer was headed to Russia on leaving Berlin. Maybe that was the reason!' I said absent-mindedly out loud before realising my mistake.

Seb shot me a look of wide-eyed chastisement as his father bore one of thanks that made me feel very stupid.

'I must warn you Sebastian, though my duty towards you is strong, as is my distaste for Dietrich's more "forceful" approach to amassing power, I do still believe in the Order and what it stands for. Therefore I will not be able to stand in the way of our hunt for the Grail.'

As he spoke, the big man resumed his wall-like stance between us and the doorway that momentarily caused me to fear he'd reconsidered letting us go.

'I would ask that you give up your search but know it would fall on deaf ears,' he continued remorsefully. *'Know this though Sebastian, should members of the Death's Head ever catch up to you, they will not respect that you are my son, nor will I be able to help you again. They will hunt you now as a threat to our plans. Wherever you go, you should at all cost avoid any check points where you identities could be discovered, and be mindful of those who you choose to trust,'* his words were spoken as both caution and threat and I struggled to decide which he meant more. *'As much as it now pains me to say, you can never return to this country in safety, for there is no place you can hide where they will not find you.'*

'I know Father,' Seb admitted with a heavy heart, *'I wish I too could turn you from your path, but I respect what you are doing for us in spite of your beliefs.'*

'I only wish those beliefs were not so contradictory to your own as to yet again force our parting,' his father said with a

386

pained smile as he reached out a hand toward his son. *'At least this time though, it shall not be in anger.'*

Seb mirrored the gesture, and they clasped each other, hand and arm, in what would likely be their last meeting.

They had both entered the room as enemies but they left now as merely two men on opposing sides. A father and son divided by a parallel search for the same item. So strange the twists and turns that fate should cast upon us.

On leaving the basement, we quickly headed for the garage and into a very expensive looking BMW that sat in wait.

'Where to now?' I asked with a nervous excitement as Seb started up the engine.

'To Russia!' he said in answer. *'As you said, it is where Archer was headed and so is where we must now follow. We cannot let my father's Order find the Grail. Wherever it is, we must get there first.'*

He paused as he was about to shift the car in to gear and, without turning to look at me, said;

'I never expected it to be like this you know. I am truly sorry for getting you involved.'

'Are you kidding, I got myself involved Seb!' I said with a nudge from my elbow, *'A race against time to find the Holy Grail, Nazi forces biting at our heels, following only the clues left to us in a tattered old journal. This is turning into more of an adventure than I could ever have dreamed of.'*

I think at this point I had become a little drunk on the adrenaline pumping through my body and was a bit over excited.

'Besides,' I added as I fastened my seat belt, *'I told you before, we're in this thing together; to the very end. Now let's go get our Stone.'*

He looked at me now with a respectful gratitude and I felt that, for the first time since our meeting, he actually started to see me as a friend.

I guess that room under his house had changed things for all of us?

And so we left behind the village of Wewelsburg. Dawn was still hours away but the sky had begun to light just enough for me to watch the foreboding castle shrink away in the side mirror.

We were heading to a destination we had yet to discover, pursued by enemies now both old and new, on the adventure of a life time that was only just beginning.

How did I end up here in this prison then, you ask? Well, that is down to the tricks of one enemy who was yet to be revealed!

Taking Stock

I risked revealing my Amulet today. It was hidden within a secret lining in my satchel. It's been there ever since I realised that my capture was imminent as I could not risk them getting hold of it.

I needed to see it today though. You see, sometimes I find myself wondering if any of this is really real. Parts of my tale seem so outlandish, even to me, that I begin to question whether any of it actually happened. Is all this just in my head? Have I gone mad? Lately, those doubts have become strong enough to warrant the necessity of seeing the Amulet. It is the one shred of proof I have left to show myself it hasn't all just been some crazy dream.

As beautiful as ever it sat in my hand weightless yet strong, cold and yet warming to the heart. Running my fingers over its engravings and starring deeply into the stone at its core, I found the faith in my own words restored and renewed. I feel it no exaggeration to say that I must have stared at the thing for nigh on an hour. At least that's what it felt like.

It's difficult to judge time in here. After a while you just start to forget what time even is; a construct of human making so that man can measure the length of his life. But without a watch and without a window to see the rise and fall of the sun, keeping time becomes a pointless practice. For me, time now is endless. Days are measured only by the arrival of my food and the number of sleeps I take. What good is time to me now?

Having since put the Amulet back into its safe place, an idea struck me that I should make a catalogue of my other things; a list of every item that makes up my restricted world. I don't know why I decided to do this really, it just seems like a good idea.

Perhaps it will serve to keep my mind sane a while longer. If I have on record all the things I can see when my mind is stable,

389

I can then know that anything else that appears isn't real. The way things have been going lately, this could be a vital practice.

So here's what I have:

- My first aid kit, now minus a few plasters and bandages.
- My journal and pencils (obviously).
- My pocket book Atlas of the world; a maddeningly useless possession in here.
- A collection of left over currency that serves as a road map of my travels.
- And two mobile phones, one Paddy's and the other my own.

Of all the items I have here with me, these last two are the ones I wish they'd taken from me. What kind of sick bastard leaves a captive with a phone? I remember the first time I saw they were still in my bag, the joy and hope I felt.

'Perhaps they didn't see them,' I thought, *'perhaps I can get a call out for help, or at least use the GPS to find out where I am.'*

That excitement rose as I turned them on and found life in them still. Alas, with a bitter and crushing disappointment that excitement fell when neither could acquire a signal. I should have known it would be the case. After all, it wasn't the first time I'd tried to use a phone underground.

Though they have long since ran out of charge, mine being the first to go from endlessly staring at pictures of home, I still look at them from time to time. I can't help but imagine that my captors left them with me on purpose, knowing what I would try and hoping it would break my spirit. I wish I could say they'd been wrong.

I think now of the things they did take from me;

- My rope.
- My spare clothes.
- Archer's research book.
- My Terry Pratchett book.
- And my torch.

These are things that could have in no way helped me escape, but would have made my imprisonment here just a little more bearable.

The clothes especially would have been a god-send. As fortunate as it was that they left me wearing the warm clothes I was wearing when they took me, the comfort of them has almost completely worn out. My coat was turned quickly into a cushion to sit on and ground mat to sleep on in a desperate attempt to keep the cold of the stone floor away from my body. That left only a jumper and a T-shirt to keep me warm against the chill of the air.

The coat is now flat and offers only the barest of comforts. The jumper is damp from leaning back against the wall and starting to look thin from the amount of times bits have become stuck to it. My hair is lank, I smell like a horse, and I truly cannot recall what it feels like to be warm anymore.

But despite all this, my spirits are buoyed by the knowledge that they at least did not find my Amulet. It somehow comforts me with memories of better days. A blessing that they did not find it for I think its loss would have pained me the most. There is just something about it, something about the colour of the___

My bulb just flickered! I thought I was over my fears but I was wrong. Why does it torment me, allowing the dark to briefly creep closer? What could be out there in the dark areas of my room? Why can I not find the courage to explore past the influence of the light bulb?

I fear for my sanity, the dark hasn't scared me since my childhood when my older cousin would tell me that there was a giant wolf outside my window waiting to get me in the night. Yet here and now, looking into the void surrounding me, I can feel the same crippling terror well up inside. I must focus my mind. I need to keep myself occupied, need to keep writing, I have to finish my tale!

Yes, that is what I must do. My Story has to be told. The secrets contained in my mind cannot be lost should I fall to madness. It's just...I cannot seem to steady my hand. My thoughts are becoming chaotic, I don't know if I can do it. I just want to go home, just want to be free of this nightmare.

Weak! I feel so weak! I want to finish my tale. The thought of the consequences should I not is more than I can bear.

But I am tired, so so tired! I must sleep. I must rest. The story can wait a while. I have time. Time to rest, time to sleep.

May my dreams be of happier times!

Author's Note

This journal sat forgotten on my desk for three months. Though the accompanying letter piqued my curiosity, its tome-like size put me off starting to read it until I had the time to really concentrate. That time just never seemed to arrive.

I used it as a coaster, an elbow rest and a prop for a landscape I'd painted. Then my young niece uncovered it on Sunday and I showed her how to take a rubbing of the etching on the cover.

After her and her mother left I sat with it in my hands for a long time, finger mindlessly tracing the symbol. I can't remember the exact moment I opened it and began to read, nor why I decided to. I only know that soon it was dark and I was still reading, taking notes, researching. It was only when I started typing it up that I knew I'd publish it.

I promised myself I'd edit it, refine it, make it more than it was. In reality I edited nothing, except to include some of the notes I made as I read.

"Journals don't have endings", he said.
Well, this one does, and I promise to share it with you soon.

D.A.

Acknowledgments

Writing this book has been a labour of love, one that has taken up nearly four years of my life. Four years of single minded determination for which I have to thank my family and friends for their support and patience.

Thank you to everyone who read early copies of my work, supported and encouraged me despite my reclusiveness and stood as pillars of strength during the biggest undertaking of my life. I couldn't have gotten here without you.

Special thanks must however go to Karen and Amy Fox for their tireless efforts in helping me edit the book and for their creative input. Though I may not have always liked it at the time, their advice has helped shape the story for the better. Also I'd like to thank Jackie Keeling for her last minute proof read that helped iron out the last few kinks.

Finally I have to say an extra big thank you to Lena Keeling. Not just for being my biggest fan and her unyielding support throughout this whole experience, but also for helping to discover a link in the story that saved me from a very early period of writers block.

This book is for all of you.

Read on for an excerpt from the concluding part of Tom's journal.

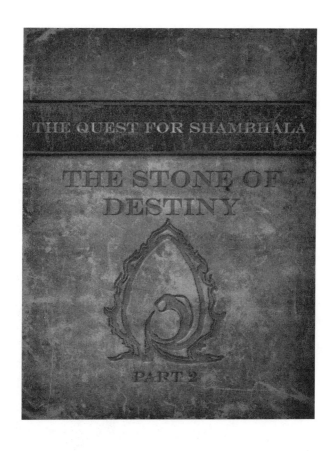

THE QUEST FOR SHAMBHALA

THE STONE OF
DESTINY

PART 2

Into the Valley of Death

The ride was long and we were not allowed to talk without receiving a blow to the face for it. Not that we could have said much to each other anyway. Without Seb to translate, Mr Saraff's English was reduced to a few phrase book words awkwardly strung together, which I found rather annoying to listen to. Quite ironic really come to think of it, I couldn't have even said "Hello" in his language. I guess what I should have felt was shame.

Though disorientating, the weave of the sack on my head wasn't quite tight enough to fully obstruct mv vision. Whilst this actually made little difference to mv situation, whenever the wind blew open a gap in the canopy, I at least got to see that we were heading up into the mountains. This however, also allowed me to occasionally see just how narrow a road we now travelled upon

The black clouds that had been threatening us earlier finally released there payload, as if triggered by my own sorrow. The furious cry of the rain, dropping like liquid bullets against the canvas, droned into my skull until I couldn't even think clearly.

When the vehicle eventually came to a stop, we were roughly removed from it and immediately lead away on a long trek up into the higher region of the mountain. Thankfully by this point the rain had stopped, like someone had just turned off the tap. That at least was one less misery to contend with.

Many things went through my mind during that time, chief of which was whether my companions would realise what had happened. How long had they waited for our return before growing concerned? Would Lee come after us? Would Seb even care? Was I to end up just another skeleton found in a sleeping bag?

From the slow movement of fading light filtering through the sack on my head, I estimated there were only a few hours of light left before we would be climbing in the dark. There had been no rest and very little variation to the determined pace our captors set, yet we'd been trekking for longer than we'd driven and still not reached their destination.

Unable to see where I was placing my feet on the slippery, and often muddy, ground I soon lost count of the amount of times I fell over and smashed my knees against the loose rocky path below. It was a horribly steep climb in some parts, were I was dragged up more than I walked, leaving my arms aching so badly that I felt the next hard pull would dislocate them from my shoulders.

It was a chilling surprise, yet also somewhat of a relief, when we reached ground that was covered by snow - the falling began to hurt a little less. It did slow us down a lot though, as the higher we got the thicker the snow became and the less of a path we had to follow. God we must have been high.

Eventually the relentless incline levelled off and we were brought to a stop. At that point, my legs simply gave way to exhaustion and I collapsed to my knees, straining to suck enough oxygen out of the cold thin air. Roughly pulled back onto my feet, I heard the voice of our lead captor talking to someone in front of us. Uncomfortably aware that I was being approached I stood up tall and tried to see through the weaves in the sack. I felt something gently grasp at the Amulet around my neck and looked down past my nose to a sight that froze my blood.

Brushing against my chest was four jagged, bone like, claws that held the Amulet in the palm of a deformed hand. I closed my eyes, fear pulsing, heart rate quickening, daring to imagine what kind of beast might be looking at me from the other end of the inhuman appendage. In a sickeningly raspy voice, the creature hissed an order at our captors and quickly withdrew its claws, lightly scratching my chest as it did so as if just to prove how sharp they were.

A violent tug of the rope around my wrists forced me to walk once more, only this time we seemed to be heading

397

into some kind of cave as the light disappeared and the fresh air became replaced by a close dusty atmosphere. After a considerable amount of time, we were brought to a halt once more and forced to our knees before having the sacks roughly removed from or heads. My eyes, adjusting to the unpleasantly low light, looked up into the empty face of a wraith. A tall figure dressed in dark robes, its face hidden in a draping hood with only those nightmarish claws visible to us. It began to talk. I couldn't understand the words but I could tell from its tone and body language that it was angry.

Mr Saraff did his best to try and translate for me, but his own terror flowed from him in frightened tears as he listened to the devils voice. In three wept words I understood just what kind of hell I had found myself in.

'Treasure ...! Stolen...! Sacrifice...!'

Endnotes

[i] Authors Note: One of the most striking things about the journal is the sketches that break up the text. Possibly included simply to aid his memory of events or places, their lack of colour somehow echoes the cell in which he seems to have found himself. I did not feel it prudent to include all of them here but I have picked a selection that should give a glimpse into their effect. Due to the condition of the journal itself, some of the sketches were quite faint and smudged. As such, I have attempted to digitally enhance and repair them prior to publication.

[ii] Authors Note: I believe it worth pointing out that this is a scan of the writers attempt to recreate the letter sent to him by Archer and not of the original letter itself. It is obvious that he has tried hard to imitate the writing style of Archer, though without the original for comparison I cannot comment on his success. I have included this scan as well as the text to show the format that may otherwise be difficult to see.

[iii] Authors Note: This sketch was digitally enhanced

[iv] Authors Note: According to Wikipedia, the Picts were a tribal confederation of Celtic peoples during the Late Iron Age and Early Medieval periods living in ancient eastern and northern Scotland.

[v] Authors Note: I discovered that the table top of an altar is called the "mensa", therefore "mensa space" literally means the space in the altar where the altar stone would sit.

[vi] Authors Note: The Sword of Light or Shining Sword – in this reference it would be the sword of Nuada Airgetlám, the first king of the Tuatha Dé Danann. Described as a sword that none could escape from nor resist, it is a legend that became quite popular though one that is often dismissed as having little evidence to support it outside of mythological circles.

[vii] Authors Note: A spear wielded by Lugh, the legendary warrior of the Tuatha Dé Danann, that no battle could be maintained against

[viii] Authors Note: A cauldron said to be bottomless that no man would walk from feeling unsatisfied that belonged to Dagda, the High King of the Tuatha Dé Danann in succession of the first king who was injured in battle.

[ix] Authors Note: This sketch has been digitally enhanced.

[x] Authors Note: The Bamburgh Castle Website states that this symbol was first discovered upon a small gold plaque during an archaeological excavation at the castle in 1971. Thought to be based on Celtic zoomorphological artwork, what it is meant to represent is still a subject of much debate.

[xi] Authors Note: Reichsführer was a special title given to the commander, the highest rank, of the German Schutzstaffel (SS).

399

Heinrich Himmler held the position longer than all the other commanders combined.

[xii] Authors Note: In medieval geography, the term ultima Thule could describe any distant place located beyond the borders of the known world. In some instances though, I found Ultima Thule given as the Latin name for Greenland and Thule given for Iceland. One of the Nazi party's founding members apparently wrote that Thule was a Nordic equivalent of Atlantis giving credence to Tom's theory. Interestingly an account of Thule from a Roman author and philosopher, Gaius Plinius Secundus, described it as a place in which there were no nights during mid-summer and no days in mid-winter. This is a description echoed in tales of Hyperborea which has been described as a place where the sun shone for twenty four hours a day. This suggests that both places lie above the Arctic Circle, a theory that could be backed up by followers of the Gothicisim ideology (a cultural movement in Sweden during the 17th Century). They declared the Scandinavian Peninsula to be both the location of the lost Atlantis and the land of Hyperborea. The top of this peninsula is crossed by the Arctic Circle to the north of which there are days of endless sun in the summer and endless nights in the winter. In Summary then, they could in fact all point to the same place. Perhaps a good place to look might be to the Norwegian archipelago of Svalbard. Sitting north of mainland Europe in the Arctic Ocean, this group of islands seems to match the description of all three places.

Made in the USA
Charleston, SC
28 June 2014